It was the kind of stalking Brody hated most. . . .

He moved silently, carefully scoping out the jungle ahead of him before creeping forward to the next position. It was slow, but safe. In the dense foliage, each man was on his own.

Suddenly, Brody caught movement behind a clump of bushes a hundred meters ahead. He dove for cover behind the trunk of a large tree. Cautiously he eased his head around the side to take another look. Through the leaves he could see the light gray and brown colors of a Russian camouflage uniform, a quick glimpse of lighter color where only the green of the jungle should have been.

Easing the barrel of his rifle around the tree trunk, he ranged the scope in on the bushes and triggered off three quick shots. He waited a few seconds.

There was no movement or return fire.

Brody stepped out and worked his way through the brush. When he got up to the clump of bushes he parted the leaves to see his kill.

His heart jolted in his chest. A Russian camouflage jacket was draped over a bush, with Brody's three 7.62mm bullet holes through it.

A decoy. He'd been had.

He was straightening up fast when a noise came from the jungle behind him. Brody spun around, frantically trying to aim his long-barreled sniper rifle.

Too late!

The Russian sonofabitch had him cold!

Other Books in the **Chopper 1** series:

#1 Blood Trails
#2 Tunnel Warriors
#3 Jungle Sweep
#4 Red River
#5 Renegade MIAs
#6 Suicide Mission
#7 Kill Zone
#8 Death Brigade
#9 Payback
#10 Monsoon Massacre
#11 Sky Strike

Jack Hawkins

IVY BOOKS • NEW YORK

Special thanks to Michael W. Kasner

To the men of the Sniper Platoon, Echo Company, 3d Battalion, 22d Infantry, 1970, and to Chris. Thanks for all your help.
And, as always, to Claudia.

Ivy Books
Published by Ballantine Books

Produced by Butterfield Press, Inc.
133 Fifth Avenue
New York, New York 10003

Library of Congress Catalog Card Number: 88-91251

ISBN: 0-8041-0316-X

Manufactured in the United States of America

First Edition: January 1989

AUTHOR'S NOTE

In August 1967, the First Air Cavalry Division took their clearing operation, Operation Pershing, north of the An Lao into the Song Re Valley in Quang Ngai Province. A long-suspected VC/NVA stronghold, the Song Re soon proved to be as heavily defended as the Kim Son and An Lao valleys had been in earlier battles.

While the men of the Air Cav battled the 3d NVA Division in the Song Re and wrote additional chapters in the book of heroism in places like LZ Pat, smaller engagements throughout Binh Dinh Province kept the pressure on the enemy forces.

Though it was not widely known during the war, the Soviet Union kept a very close eye on combat in Vietnam and aided the North in every way that they could. Not only did they send military advisors to the North Vietnamese and Viet Cong forces, they also sent countless tons of weapons and military supplies. Some of these weapons were standard equipment of the Soviet armed forces, items such as the MiG-21 jet fighter, the AK-47 assault rifle, and the RPG rocket launchers. The troops in the field were well aware of this level of Soviet aid to the NVA. They had to face it every day.

Less well known was that Russian weapons were sent to the war zone specifically for testing under combat conditions. Most of those neither the grunts nor the American public were ever told about.

Like any other machine, a weapon will not always operate in the precise way that its designer intends. The only way to learn its strengths and weaknesses is to test it in the live fire conditions of war. Also, in a combat environment, the enemy's efforts to counter a weapon must always be taken into consideration.

For instance, the Russian SA-2 antiaircraft guided missile, known to us as the Sam, was the standard Soviet air-defense missile. It had never been tested in combat, so dozens of them were sent to North Vietnam and fired at American aircraft. After the initial surprise wore off, they proved not to live up to expectations. The U.S. Air Force was soon able to come up with effective countermeasures, weapons that rendered the Sams almost useless.

One new Russian weapon, however, that proved to be very effective in Vietnam, and is in wide use today throughout the Soviet Bloc world is the sniper rifle known as the SVD or the Dragunov. This potent, long-range killer was first tested by Russian military personnel, members of their secret Spetsnaz, Special Forces, units.

While the exact details of Russian Spetsnaz involvement in Vietnam still remain classified, this is a work of fiction about the Dragunov rifle and its use during the battles in the Song Re Valley.

Other than public or historic figures, all characters in this book are fictional. Any resemblance to actual persons, living or dead, is unintended and purely coincidental.

Jack Hawkins
Portland, Oregon
July 1988

CHAPTER 1

The Song Re Valley, Quang Ngai Province

"Warlokk!" Sergeant Treat Brody yelled over the intercom. He leaned into his M-60 doorgun, the 7.62mm tracers a stream of red fire reaching down into the jungle below. "Machine gun on the left!"

"Got it," the pilot, Warrant Officer Lance Lawless Warlokk snapped back. He racked his UH-1C Huey Hog gunship around sharply to line up for another run. Brody leaned out against his lifeline into the slipstream and continued to pour fire into the enemy position. He had to keep their heads down until they were out of range. The overused barrel of his doorgun smoked in the cool mountain air. The floor of the door gunner's pocket was littered with empty 7.62mm brass and machine-gun belt links.

The last of the ammo belt ran through the breech, and the gun fell silent. Brody reached down to the rack of ammo cans at his feet and ripped open the lid on another can of 7.62mm linked belts. Flipping up the feed tray cover on the hot sixty, he laid the ammo belt in place and snapped the cover back down. He reached down to the right side of the gun and hauled back on the charging handle, pulling the bolt to the rear. He was ready to go again.

Warlokk completed his low-level turn and brought the gunship screaming down again, lined up on the glowing green tracer fire coming up out of the trees at him. In the left-hand seat, his copilot-gunner peered through the gunsight at the source of the fire. He triggered the rocketpods hanging off the pylons on the sides of the ship. Two-point-seven-five-inch HE rockets shot out of the pods in pairs, trailing dirty white smoke as they raced down toward their target. The jungle exploded in front of them.

The gunship swept down closer, and the gunner switched to the automatic 40mm grenade launcher mounted in the turret under the Huey's nose. With its characteristic chunking sound, the short-barreled thumper spat its small, deadly rounds down into the trees. The green tracer fire abruptly stopped.

As the gunship swept over the smoking hole in the jungle, Brody leaned out of the open door gunner's pocket on his lifeline and gave it another long burst just in case.

"Yahoo!" he yelled. Just like the motto painted on the front of his flight helmet, Treat Brody was in "Hog Heaven" again. With his gloved fingers wrapped around the twin spade grips of his M-60D doorgun, he was doing a job on the gooks the way he knew best.

Warlokk, Brody, and the other men of Python Flight, Echo Company, First of the 7th Cav, were flying in support of the men and machines of the 3rd Brigade of the First Air Cav, the Pony Soldiers, in the Song Re Valley north of the deadly An Lao.

Located high in the mountains, this nearly treeless valley had long been under VC control, a staging area for North Vietnamese infiltration into the An Lao Valley and the coastal plains of Binh Dinh Province. As they had done in the Kim Son and An Lao valleys, the Air Cav intended to clear the Song Re of the North Vietnamese Army. In the process they would also destroy its rice crops and hidden jungle fortresses in addition to killing as many NVA as they could find.

To accomplish this mission, the Air Cav Division's commander, Major General Tolson, was conducting cavalry raids. But in the modern airmobile mode—with helicopters, not horses. The theory was, however, the same. Use light forces, strike quick, strike hard, and keep moving.

At first, the tactic had worked well. The North Vietnamese were caught off balance. The enemy camps brazenly built out in the open valley floor were obliterated by strafing jets and gunships. Hundreds of NVA and VC were killed. When the floor of the valley was clear, the Air Cav stormed into the jungle-covered mountains surrounding the Song Re Valley in hot pursuit of the fleeing remnants of the enemy forces.

On August 9, the 2d Battalion of the 8th Cav hit Landing Zone Pat.

Early in the morning, the first company of infantry was scheduled to make an air assault into a small ridgeline overlooking the abandoned airstrip at Ta Ma. They were to secure their LZ, sweep down the ridge, and link up with the rest of the battalion later that afternoon.

The artillery preparation of LZ Pat was followed by the first lift ships bringing in the troops. The first platoons got on the ground without meeting any resistance and secured a small perimeter. But when the last of the company lift arrived, bringing the Weapons Platoon, they ran into a shit storm.

Enemy antiaircraft guns on the hilltops surrounding the ridgeline opened up on the choppers orbiting the LZ. An OH-13 bubble-top scout ship was quickly blown out of the sky, and even the brigade command-and-control ship was hit. Choppers were going down everywhere, and the call went out to the Air Cav An Khe basecamp for everyone to get into the air to recover the crewmen from the crashed birds.

That was when the men and machines of Echo Company's Python Flight went to work in the Song Re.

While the A-1E Skyraider and F4C Phantom fighter bombers circled above the trapped company of the 8th Cav, pounding the antiaircraft guns on the hilltops with napalm and bombs, Brody and Warlokk flew escort for the rescue slicks as they looked for the wreckage of downed choppers.

"Python Niner Two," one of the slick pilots called to Warlokk. "This is Three Seven. I've got a crash spotted. I can see at least three of the crew. How 'bout giving me a little cover so I can pick 'em up. Over."

"This is Niner Two," the gunship pilot radioed back. "Roger, I'm on the way."

"Brody, we're going in." Warlokk warned the door gunner.

"Get some, Lawless!" Brody ripped off a short burst into the trees.

"You just keep a cool tool back there, dude," the pilot cautioned. "What you been drinking anyway?"

"I'm just high on love," Brody laughed.

"You're one crazy motherfucker today." Warlokk shook his head.

"You got that shit right, man. Let's waste some gooks."

"Roger that. There they are."

Brody looked through the canopy in front of the copilot and spotted the wreckage of a Huey. The pilot had tried to put down in a small clearing in the jungle, but had not quite made it. The damaged chopper had lost power and had fallen short of its landing site. The crumpled fuselage was halfway in the clearing, but the tail boom was hung up in the trees. Three men huddled behind the wreckage, waving at the approaching choppers. A third figure lay on the ground beside them, not moving.

The slick made a cautious approach. It was only fifty feet off the ground when the tree line erupted with fire.

"Three Seven!" Warlokk shouted over the radio. "Get your ass outta there!"

The slick staggered back up into the air, followed by lines of green tracer fire. Warlokk kicked down on his rudder pedals, and the gunship's nose skidded to the left, lining up on the enemy fire.

Brody leaned out into the slipstream, his sixty hammering out long bursts. With a whoosh, rockets leaped from the side pods in front of him and streaked for the jungle. The smoke from their launch obscured his target for a second, and he backed off his trigger.

The Huey swept past the tree line, the thumper spitting rounds, and Brody saw dark, uniformed figures in the tree line, raising their rifles. He swung the gun and gave them a long, sustained burst. He was right on target. The gooks went down.

He held the doorgun on them as long as he could. By this time, the slick had climbed out and was orbiting safely out of range until the LZ was clear.

Warlokk kicked the Huey around again in a sharply banked turn. The airframe shuddered as the rotors unloaded and lost lift. He was very close to stalling out and crashing in the jungle himself. At the last moment, the pilot rolled out, dropped the nose to regain his airspeed, and swept back down on the target.

This time he came in directly at them. It was dangerous to overfly the target after the gun run, but coming dead on to it gave him a better shot. Brody and the gunner on the other side saw what he was doing and braced themselves. When the gunship flew over the tree line, it would be up to them to keep the gooks' heads down until they were clear.

Warlokk kicked the Huey from side to side as the gunner fired the rockets, spreading them in a shotgun pattern. The wood line came apart with the explosions. Dirt, broken tree limbs, and pieces of smashed men flew into the air.

Brody started firing even before they were past, laying down on the trigger. A solid stream of red tracers reached into the smoke-filled jungle. The speeding ship whooshed over the tree line, and Brody swung out on his lifeline, keeping the gun on target as they passed overhead.

"Yahoo," he yelled into the slipstream.

This time Warlokk pulled up into the sky and circled the small clearing, waiting for the smoke to clear. No one fired at them. He dropped down again, trolling for fire. Nothing moved in the tree line. This time it appeared to be empty.

The three men at the wrecked chopper picked themselves up off the ground and started waving their arms frantically in the air.

"Three Seven, this is Niner Two," Warlokk called up to the orbiting slick. "It seems clear. Try it again. Over."

"This is Three Seven, rolling in now."

The slick came down again, much more cautiously this time, his door gunners in the back blasting the tree line. The pilot flared out as close to the downed bird as the could. The skids weren't even on the ground when the three men grabbed the fourth man by the arms and dragged him to the slick. They threw him inside and scrambled in themselves. The last man was still on the skids when the pilot pulled pitch and got out of there.

When he was back in the air, the slick pilot waved to Warlokk. "Niner Two, this is Three Seven, thanks. I've got a casualty in the back so I'm going to split for An Khe. Over."

"This is Niner Two, glad to help. Out."

High on a hill overlooking a small clearing in a neighboring valley to the Song Re, five men patiently waited. The clearing was just large enough to be a platoon landing zone. Four Huey slicks could make it in with no difficulties. To make the clearing even more inviting, the LZ had been littered with the bodies of several dead NVA, and a wrecked 12.7mm heavy antiaircraft machine gun had been set up. Supplies and ammunition had been set on fire, sending a pall of thick, black smoke up into the clear mountain air.

One of the American scout choppers would be sure to see the smoke and come to investigate. Infantry would be sent in to retrieve the gun and recon the area just in case more NVA were lurking nearby in the jungle.

The waiting men, all Caucasians, wore camouflage uniforms in a jagged print of gray, brown, and light green. These were unusual camouflage colors to wear in the jungles of southeast Asia, much too light for the surrounding foliage. They were, however, the standard-issue camouflage uniforms for the Soviet army.

Four of the men were soldiers in the Russian army, the fifth man was a major in the Russian secret police, the KGB. The soldiers were not just regular Russian troops, but members of the elite Spetsnaz, the Russian special forces. The KGB man, Major Gregor Zerinski, was an old Asia hand. He had served in North Vietnam, Cambodia, and Laos for over two years now. This was his first mission in South Vietnam.

The major and two of the troops were armed with AK-47s, the standard assault rifle of the Communist forces worldwide. But the other men carried weapons no one in the Western world had ever seen. They were long rifles, with cutaway stocks, extended barrels, and high-powered scopes mounted on top of the receivers. Short box magazines were fitted to the bottom of the receivers. These rifles did not fire the intermediate-range 7.62 × 39mm cartridge that the AKs used. Instead, they fired the old, full-sized 7.62 × 54mm round that dated back to before the days of the Russian Revolution.

This was a long-range rifle cartridge, a little more powerful than the similar American .30-caliber Springfield cartridge, and they were loaded with steel-core bullets. The Russians called these semi-armor-piercing rounds "Heavy Ball" ammunition. Unlike standard military ball bullets which had a lead core, with a steel core these bullets would not deform when they penetrated Plexiglass or the aluminum skin of a helicopter. They would go right through and hit where they had been aimed.

The rounds they fired were old, but the rifle was the newest design from a Russian weaponsmaker named Dragunov. In the Soviet army, the rifle was known as the SVD for Samozaryadnaya Vintovka Dragunova—a Dragunov semi-automatic rifle. They would reach out well over a thousand meters and kill with pinpoint accuracy.

A heavily laden Huey C gunship roared in over the clearing for a quick look at the landing zone. No one shot at him, so the pilot reported the LZ green. Except for the bodies, there was no enemy in sight. The lone gunship was quickly joined by another one, forming a light fire team. They circled the smoke column high in the air.

A few minutes later, a gaggle of four slicks appeared. As the two gunships flew a protective orbit over the LZ, the slicks came down for a landing. Two ships, side by side, followed by the other two.

On the hilltop, a thousand meters away, the two Spetsnaz troops with the Dragunovs focused their PSO-1 scopes on the descending Hueys, aiming for the pilots in the right-hand seats.

When the lead pair of Hueys were only five hundred feet off the ground, the snipers fired, two rounds each. They shifted their aim to the pilots in the second two choppers and fired again.

The first pair of slicks staggered in the sky, their dead pilots' hands frozen on the controls. They collided in midair. Whirling rotor blades chopped into the fuselages and split the fuel tanks. Both ships exploded and slammed to the ground.

The third Huey nosed over and dove with a rending crash, scattering pieces of men and helicopter in the tree line. The fourth machine impacted on top of the burning wreckage of the first two slicks and burst into flames.

In seconds, over forty men were dead or wounded, and four Hueys had been destroyed. The Russian snipers had fired only eight rounds.

On the hilltop position, Zerinski smiled. The first combat test of the new sniper rifle had been an outstanding success. Moscow would be pleased. Maybe now they would let him get out of southeast Asia and return to Europe where he belonged. But, he had to admit, things were certainly not dull here.

Above the LZ, the two gunships circled the rising pall of greasy black smoke and frantically fired into the tree line around the small clearing. They did not see the five camouflaged Russians, a klick away, slip down off of the hilltop and back into the jungle.

CHAPTER 2

Firebase Rhonda

Warlokk flared his gunship out next to the fuel bladder and shut the turbine down. Before the rotor blades had even stopped turning, Brody jumped out and started refueling the chopper.

"Brody!" a voice came from behind him. He turned and saw Lieutenant Michael Alexander, the new platoon leader of Echo Company's Aero Rifle Platoon, the Blues.

"We've got a mission, we'll be moving out in ten minutes. I want you to get someone else to handle the gun on Warlokk's bird and get back with Gabe."

"Yes, sir, I'll be there."

Brody was the squad leader of Second Squad of the Blues and usually flew with them. But today, the Blues had been just sitting around the firebase waiting for a mission, and Brody had gotten tired of lying dead in the heat. He has asked to go out on one of the doorguns in Warlokk's gunbird more to cool down than anything else.

He finished refueling the gunship, told Warlokk that he had to get back to work, and walked over to *Pegasus*, Cliff Gabriel's slick.

" 'Bout time you showed up," Master Sergeant Leo Zack growled when Brody sauntered up, his flight helmet tucked up under his arm.

"Hey, Sarge, give me a break. I've been working."

"You've been sight-seeing, you mean. Get your people ready to move out."

"What're we going to do?"

"You're going to go in with a platoon of Alpha Company to secure an LZ."

"Why us, Leo? Why not give it to First Squad?"

Zack grinned. The combination of his grin and his shaved head gave him a distinctly sinister look. " 'Cause I like your young ass, boy, that's why. Now move it!" the NCO bellowed.

"Okay, okay." Brody stuck his hands up in a gesture of mock surrender. "I'm going!"

The men of Brody's squad were all standing in the shade of the commo bunker, waiting for Gabe to crank up.

"What's Zack on the rag about today?" Brody asked as he walked up.

"Beats the shit outta me," Spec-4 Juan "Corky" Cordova answered. The Chicano machine gunner was leaning on his M-60, using it as a crutch. "But I do know that he's been looking for you all morning."

"The ell tee knew where I was."

"I don't know, *amigo*, all I know is that the Black Buddha was hot on your ass."

"Well, fuck it. He says that we got to go secure some LZ, so let's saddle up."

"But, Sarge. . . ," one of the men spoke up. It was a freckle-faced, gangly redheaded kid who looked like he should have been in high school, not Vietnam. PFC Ralph Burns was enjoying his nap in the shade.

"Goddamnit, Farmer," Brody said, "for the last fucking time, stop calling me 'Sarge' and get your ass in gear."

Burns, better known as Farmer from the fact that he came from a potato farm in Idaho, slowly stood up and reached for his rifle. He had wanted to protest the fact that they had not had lunch yet. He sighed and tried to remember what C-rations he had packed in his ruck. Farmer enjoyed eating even more than he did his naps.

Brody looked around and noticed that one of the men was missing. "Where's Bunny?" he asked.

A tall, dark-skinned grunt with longish black hair wearing a tiger-stripe camouflage uniform shouldered his ruck. "Last I saw of him, he was heading over to shoot the shit with the cannon cockers," Spec-4 Chance Broken Arrow answered.

"Can you go get him?"

"Sure thing." A modern-day Comanche Indian warrior, Broken Arrow was known to his friends as "Two-Step" or "the Indian." Two-Step wasn't an Indian name, however, it was the nickname of the deadliest snake in all of southeast Asia, the krait. The moniker was derived from the observation that when a man was bitten by a krait, he took two more steps and fell over, stone cold dead. Broken Arrow was one of the very few men who had ever survived a krait bite.

There had been a Dustoff close by that day, and he had been rushed back to the hospital at Camp Radcliff, where the medics had purged the venom from his body. While he was recovering in the hospital, Sergeant Zack had pinned the nickname on him, and it had stuck. Most people thought it was some kind of Indian name.

The Comanche slung his sawed-off pump gun over his shoulder and headed over to the artillery battery's gun pits to find Bunny, their artillery forward observer.

Spec-4 Bernie Rabdo was the newest member of Brody's squad. Somehow he had gained the nickname of "Bunny Rabbit," but it was nothing to laugh about when he was laying his high-explosive Easter eggs on a target. Bunny was one of the best FOs in the business, and the grunts were very happy to have him around. When they had their asses in a crack, it was nice to know that he was there to call upon the artillery for a helping hand.

Two-Step found Rabdo in one of the gun pits, sitting

on a pile of 105mm howitzer ammunition boxes. "Bunny!" he yelled. "Got to go."

"Be right with you."

"Zack says now!"

"Okay, okay!"

The small, dark-haired FO bid his artillery crewmen friends good-bye and vaulted over the sandbagged parapet around the gun. "Where we going?"

"Fucked if I know. We got to hit some LZ with Alpha Company."

The six-slick lift flared out over the LZ in pairs. As soon as the skids of the first two ships touched the ground, the grunts jumped out and ran through the rippling elephant grass to secure a small perimeter for the other choppers.

When the slicks had all landed and off-loaded their infantry, the men got to their feet and started for the wood line. They were about fifty meters away when a machine gun opened up on them from a bunker hidden back deep in the trees.

At the first burst of fire, they all dove for the dirt. There was no cover at all on the LZ, just the elephant grass, and it wouldn't stop bullets.

The gun had them cold. They were dead meat.

"Bunny!" Brody shouted back to the FO. "Get some artillery on those fuckers!"

From his prone position, Bunny pointed the Prick-25 antenna straight up in the air and pressed the push-to-talk switch on the hand set. "Reg Leg Bravo, Red Leg Bravo. This is Blue Two Tango, Two Tango. Fire mission. Over."

"This is Red Leg Bravo, send it."

"This is Two Tango. From eight-seven-three seven-four-eight, azmuth one eighty-seven, two hundred meters, machine-gun bunker, battery two, H.E., will adjust, over."

"This is Red Leg Bravo, Roger, wait one."

"Two Tango, this is Bravo, shot over."

"Tango, shot out."

Bunny heard the rushing express-train sound of the 105mm marking round pass overhead. It exploded in the air with a puff of white smoke off to the right and a little behind the target.

"Red Leg, this is Tango. Left one hundred, drop five zero, over."

"Red Leg, Roger, shot over."

The round hit right next to the bunker.

"This is Tango," Bunny shouted. "Right on target, fire for effect."

"Red Leg, Roger."

This time the rumbling express-train sound was louder as all six guns in the battery fired. One round sounded lower, closer. Bunny froze. He knew what it was—a short round.

"Hit it!" he screamed. He buried his head in his arms.

The 105 round detonated not ten feet away from the point element of Alpha Company.

"Check fire! Check fire!" Bunny screamed into the radio. "Oh, my God, check fire!"

The distant rumble of the guns abruptly cut off. "Check fire" meant to stop shooting. Instantly. Now Bunny heard the screams of the wounded and the cries for medics.

Bunny frantically changed the frequency on the Prick-25 radio. "Dull Thunder, this is Blue Two Tango," he called up to the C-and-C bird. "We need a priority Dustoff quick, over."

"Two Tango, this is Thunder. Send location, over."

"This is Two Tango, Roger. Eight-seven-three seven-four-eight. How copy? Over."

"This is Dull Thunder, Roger, copy eight-seven-three seven-four-eight. Priority Dustoff on the way, Echo Tango Alpha three zero mikes. Out."

Bunny sat up and looked around. Bodies were scattered all around the smoking crater. The platoon medic ran from one man to the next, trying to find someone to help, but the first three men he came to were dead. He finally found someone who was still alive.

The FO held his head in his hands. He was stunned. He knew that it had been a short round, a defective shell that did not travel far enough. He had never had a short round before, never, not even when they had been firing training ammunition in FO school back at Fort Bliss.

Brody walked up and laid a hand on Rabdo's shoulder. "Not your fault, man," he said grimly.

"I was right on target," Bunny answered. "I know I was."

"I know, the cannon cockers got a bad round. It's not your fault."

By this time, the medic had done all he could for the three wounded by carrying them out into the middle of the LZ to await the Dustoff. The four dead had been wrapped in ponchos and taken out as well.

"Here it comes!"

Bunny got to his feet and snatched a smoke grenade from his harness. Pulling the pin, he tossed it out to the side. As the red smoke billowed up into the air, he stood holding his rifle above his head in both hands as the pilot made a slow and easy approach. "Come on, come on," he growled. "Get your ass down here."

As the Huey flared out for a landing, Bunny noticed that the chopper was very, very shiny. It looked like it had been waxed. Then he noticed it didn't have a red cross on the nose.

As the grunts ran forward with the wounded, several men stepped out of the passenger compartment of the chopper. Most of them were in civilian clothes and had cameras around their necks. A first lieutenant in a clean, starched uniform and a baseball cap followed them off. He looked around for a moment, turned, and walked toward Bunny.

"Hi," he said sticking his hand out. "I'm Lieutenant Henderson from the PIO office. Who's in charge here?"

Bunny was shocked. "Uh, Sergeant Brody is, sir," he stammered. "Where's the Dustoff?"

"Dustoff? I don't know anything about a Dustoff. I

brought these reporters out here to see how well you men are doing. Where do I find Sergeant Brody?"

"Right here, sir."

"Sergeant, I am Lieutenant . . ."

Brody turned abruptly and ran over to the chopper. One of the reporters had pulled back the poncho covering one of the dead men and was taking a picture of his bloody face. A piece of shrapnel had cut off the side of his skull, exposing his brain. The concussion had bulged the man's sightless eyes from their sockets.

"What in the fuck are you doing!" he yelled. He slapped the camera away.

The reporter just looked at him. "The people back home need to see this soldier."

Brody swung his sixteen up and centered it on the man's chest. "The fuck they do, mister. You get your sorry ass out of here."

"Wait just a minute, Sergeant," the PIO said, running between the two men.

Brody stared him down. "Nobody takes fucking pictures of dead grunts as long as I'm around." He paused long enough to look the spit-shined officer up and down. "Sir," he ended with a sneer.

The PIO backed away slightly.

A slim man in a khaki safari suit stepped up. "I'm David Janson with the Independent News Service. How did these men die, Sergeant?" he asked, his pen poised over a notebook.

"Artillery."

"The enemy has artillery here?" another of the reporters squeaked.

"No." Brody was disgusted. "Ours. It was a short round."

"Whose fault was that?" the man with the notebook asked.

"It wasn't nobody's 'fault,' mister. It just fucking happens."

"Who was controlling the artillery fire?"

"My FO."

"And who is that?"

"Sergeant," the medic yelled out before Brody had a chance to answer. "We got to get these people out of here ASAP!"

"Lieutenant, how 'bout taking our wounded back to An Khe."

"I'm sorry, Sergeant. I can't do that. I've got several more stops to make with these gentlemen."

"Look, sir, we've got men here who're going to die if they don't get help real soon."

"I'm sorry, Sergeant, that's not my problem." The lieutenant turned back to the reporters. "If you gentlemen are through here, we'll . . .

One of the grunts with a bloody bandage tied around his head stepped up to the officer and stuck the muzzle of his sixteen in his face. "It just became your problem, fuckface."

The PIO officer froze. "You can't talk to me that way." His voice was shrill.

The grunt smiled tightly. "I just did, motherfucker. Now what're you going to do about it? Send me to Vietnam?"

The officer looked around in panic.

"You'd better do what he says, sir," Brody suggested softly. "He's been shot in the head and there's no telling what he might do."

"Get 'em on board!" the grunt shouted to the medic.

The wounded man turned back to the PIO. "Now, Ell Tee, you and me are going to take a little trip to An Khe. Move it!"

"You're going to go to jail for this."

"Send me to jail, man." The grunt grinned. "It'll beat the fuck outta humping this fucking brush. Do it to me."

Brody had a hard time keeping a smile off of his face when the PIO climbed on board with the casualties. The pilot pulled pitch and lifted off as soon as he was inside.

"It looks like you reporters are just going to have to

stay here until the ell tee gets back with your chopper," Brody told the astonished civilians. "You just make yourselves right at home."

"Sergeant." The reporter with the notebook raised a pen. "I'd like to get back to this incident, if you don't mind."

"What incident?"

"This so-called short round. How did it happen? Who was responsible?"

Brody was starting to lose his temper. "It ain't no one's fault, goddamnit, it just happens."

"Who was directing the artillery fire?"

"I was," Bunny spoke up for the first time.

"How did you make the mistake?"

"I didn't make a mistake," Bunny was almost crying. "I was right on target."

"Wait just a fucking minute," Brody broke in. "Bunny's my FO, and he's the best there is. If he says that he was on target, then he was on target. Just leave it alone."

"I understand your sticking up for your men, Sergeant, but . . ."

"The name's Brody, mister." Brody's voice was cold. "And you'd better shut your fucking face while you still can."

The reporter smoothly shut his notebook and put it back into his pocket, but he held his ground. "My name is Janson, Sergeant, David Janson. You'll be hearing from me again."

Brody slowly looked the man up and down, a smile playing at the corners of his mouth. "I'm looking forward to it."

CHAPTER 3

Camp Radcliff, An Khe

Back at the sprawling Air Cav base outside the dusty little village of An Khe, the last member of Brody's squad, PFC Jungle Jim Gardner, was sitting on his bunk in the deserted tent, getting his gear together.

Gardner had just been released from the hospital that morning. He had been recuperating from a belly wound received on the Blues' last big mission, a raid into Cambodia to destroy an enemy gunship.

He was fit for duty, but the big man had lost his grunt's tan, and he was still looking a little tired. He had just started to break his M-16 rifle down for cleaning when the mail clerk walked in the tent, dragging his yellow U.S. Mail bag behind him.

"Hey, where the hell is everybody?" he asked.

"They're out on a mission."

"Well, shit, why didn't anybody tell me?" The mail clerk dug into the bag. "I drag this fucking sack all over the fucking place and can't find anybody to give this fucking mail to." He came out with a letter. "At least you're here. This is yours."

Gardner took the letter. It was from his wife. It was a thin letter, and he was almost afraid to open it. During the last three weeks he had been in the hospital recovering from his wound, he hadn't heard a word from Sandra. He checked the date on the postmark. It was a week old. He felt the letter again. It was very, very thin.

He opened it and started reading.

"Dear Jim, I really don't know how to say this to you, but . . ."

He let the single sheet of paper fall down onto his bunk. He didn't want to read the rest. He already knew what it said. His wife, the smiling cheerleader that he had married as soon as they had both graduated from Gray's Harbor High School on the coast of Washington, was telling him good-bye.

He had felt it coming for weeks, but he just hadn't wanted to believe that it was really happening. Over the last couple of months, Sandra's letters had become shorter and shorter. Where once she had written him at least every other day, it had gotten to the point that he rarely got one letter a week. He had tried to reach out to her in his letters, to tell her that he loved her and that when he returned, everything would be as good as it had been. But obviously she was not willing to wait and see.

He put the letter, unread, back in the envelope and stuck it in the top pocket of his fatigue jacket. He put on his jungle boots and buttoned up his jacket. Grabbing his brush hat, he headed out the door of the big tent. He glanced down at his watch. The EM club was open, and he needed a drink. Badly.

He had always thought that this was something that happened to other people, not to couples like him and Sandra. They had dated all through high school and had both been virgins when they finally made love for the first time. They had been the perfect couple—everybody in town had said so. He simply could not understand what had happened.

Part of it, he knew, was his being in the army. And

part of is was their baby. She had been too young to become a mother.

He stopped, got the letter out again, and started scanning it, looking for what she had to say about their boy. What was she going to do about him?

". . . and, I'm sure that he will be a good father to little . . ."

A cry of anguish burst from his throat. Savagely, he slammed his fist into the sandbags of the mortar bunker next to the walkway. The pain felt good. He hammered his fist against the rock-hard bags again and felt the skin on his knuckles tear. That felt even better.

He threw the crumpled letter down and ground it into the dirt under his boot.

He walked away, blood dripping from his right hand. After a few steps, he turned back and retrieved the letter. Jamming it into his pocket, he turned around again and walked on. Maybe he'd go see the captain about getting an emergency leave to go home. But right now, he wanted that drink and time alone to think.

The enlisted men's club was dark and cool as he walked inside, and it was almost deserted. For once, no one was playing the juke box. He didn't think that he could deal with rock and roll, or the Beach Boys, either, for that matter. The lone Vietnamese waitress came over to his table.

"What you want, GI?"

He looked up at her dark eyes. Sandra's eyes were blue. "Jim. My name is Jim."

"*Xin loi,* Jim." She looked down for a moment. "Sorry 'bout that. What you want?"

"Beer," he paused. "No. Make that bourbon and beer."

"Okay, Jim."

He watched her walk off. She was new. He didn't recognize her at all. But that wasn't surprising. He didn't come in the club that often, and the turnover among the waitresses was pretty high. She was slim and delicate. Sandra was tall and full breasted.

Ruthlessly he smashed that thought. He was not going to think about Sandra now. He was going to get drunk. He would think about her later when his mind stopped spinning around like a top.

The waitress brought his drinks and put them on the table. "Fifty cents," she said.

He dug into his wallet, pulled out a dollar MPC note, and handed it to her. "Bring me another one."

She looked down at him and smiled. "Okay, Jim."

The bourbon went down like water. He followed it with half of the beer. The cool liquid felt good. He wet the corner of his handkerchief in the beer and was washing the blood from his hand when the girl returned with his second round of drinks.

"Oh, Jim, you no do that. Beer bookoo bad. I get water."

"No, it's okay."

"No, I go get water and wash so you no have to go to *bac si.*"

Gardner smiled thinly. "Okay, go ahead."

"You drink your beer. I come back *tee tee.*"

The girl came back with a bowl of warm water and a clean towel. Taking his big hand in hers, she gently washed the blood and sand from his torn knuckles.

"What's your name?" Gardner asked.

"My name is Mai." She smiled up at him, her dark eyes glowing.

"You're a very pretty girl."

"I don't think so," she said modestly. "How you hurt your hand?"

"I had an accident," he said bitterly.

"I'm so sorry."

"So am I. Believe me, so am I."

The girl was confused by his tone of voice. "I don't understand, Jim."

"I don't, either."

"It better now. I go get bandage for you."

Gardner laughed. It was a harsh sardonic laugh. "No," he said. "I don't need that. Thank you." He raised the glass of bourbon. "This is enough bandage for me right now."

"Please? I do not understand."

He looked at her more closely. She was beautiful. Her small, heart-shaped face, her glowing almond eyes, and her long, glossy black hair were Oriental perfection. Her slim body under the silk ao-dai was lithe, but softly rounded. Her small, high breasts were firm. He felt the heat of the bourbon in his belly spread out to his groin. He grew hard. He gulped his beer.

"No, I guess you wouldn't. It's not your fault. You didn't do anything."

The girl sensed Gardner's inner pain. "You want to talk to Mai? I no have to work bookoo now." She waved a slim arm around at the almost empty club. "You can tell me what is wrong." She stood up. "First, I go get you 'nother drink."

Gardner watched her walk away, her high-heeled shoes clicking on the concrete floor as her hips swayed slightly from side to side. Now he was really confused. He drained the last of his beer.

She returned to his table with two beers. "You drink beer. Bourbon make you bookoo drunk. Then you no want to talk to me."

"No," he protested, "I want to talk to you. I want to talk to you very much."

She cocked her head to one side. "You want me play music?"

"No, please," he said, reaching out and touching her hand. "I want to talk to you."

She smiled at him, her dark cat's eyes warm and inviting. She squeezed his hand and then pulled hers away. "Be careful, Jim, I no want bartender to see you. He make trouble for me, bookoo trouble."

Gardner looked over at the bartender, a skinny, rat-faced E-5. He was leering at Mai.

"You wait here." He pushed his chair back abruptly from the table and stood up.

"No, Jim, please! He make bookoo trouble for me!"

He stopped and turned back to her. "Don't worry, Mai. This guy is never going to give you any trouble. Ever again." He smiled.

"Mai says that you've been giving her a hard time," Gardner leaned across the bar and glared at the tiny Asian. The bartender looked up at the solid block of muscle towering over him.

"Ah . . . no . . . not me," he gulped. "She be talking about the other guy. Yeah, I think the night man has been hassling her, trying to get into her pants."

Gardner was really disappointed.

Obviously, the jerk wasn't going to get smart with him, so he looked around for something else to vent his building anger on. He grabbed up the heavy stainless-steel water pitcher from behind the bar and held it in his hand like a beer can. Locking eyes with the bartender, he squeezed his hand shut.

"You'd better tell the other guy that if I ever hear of anyone trying to hit on Mai, I'm going to take it real personal."

The sturdy steel pitcher crumpled like tin foil.

The bartender gulped and backed away even farther until his skinny ass was jammed up against the counter behind him.

"Yes, sir," he squeaked.

Gardner dropped the ruined pitcher on the bar. "Don't make me have to remind you of this again."

"Yes, sir. Er . . . I mean, no, sir."

Gardner sat back down at his table and took a drink of his beer. Now his hand really hurt.

"I don't think he'll bother you anymore," he told Mai. "But if he does, you just let me know."

"Thank you, Jim."

"No sweat," he grinned. "Now, where were we?"

* * *

When the small LZ had finally been secured, Brody and his people were extracted and flown back to Camp Radcliff. After a quick stop at the refueling point, Gabe taxied *Pegasus* over to her parking spot on the ramp and shut the turbine down. "End of the line," he called back. "Everybody off."

Brody stepped down to the ground and pulled his helmet off. Reaching up to his doorgun, he pulled the lock pin securing the M-60 to the flexible mount and lifted it up onto his shoulder. He was turning away when Bunny came up behind him.

"Sergeant Brody?"

He turned around. The short, dark-haired FO looked miserable. "What am I going to do if that reporter writes that I killed those guys 'cause I fucked up?"

Brody grounded his heave gun. "Bunny, you and I both know what really happened out there today, man. Even those Alpha Company grunts know shit like that happens sometimes."

"Yeah, but what if he says that I did something wrong?" Bunny sounded panicked.

"I don't know," Brody replied honestly. "I just don't know what to tell you. Maybe you'd better go talk to the Old Man about it, see what he has to say."

"Yeah, I think I'll do that."

"But remember," Brody said, putting his hand on the man's shoulder, "no matter what that asshole says or even writes about you, we all know that it wasn't your fault. You're good, man, you're one of the best I've ever seen. So don't let this shit get to you. Fuck that guy."

"Sure."

Brody watched the New Yorker walk off. This was a real bitch, and he was worried about Bunny. He hoped that the FO got it resolved real quick, because he didn't want it affecting the man's work.

A good artillery FO needed to be sure of himself, almost to the point of being cocky. Directing long-range artillery fire was tricky. There was a lot at stake, and it required a great deal of self-confidence on the part of the man calling the shots. The FO had to be able to make quick and accurate decisions while under the worst possible conditions. If he was not sure of himself and took his time to double-check everything, the artillery support might come too late to help them. And if he made a mistake, it might land right on top of them.

The forward observer's job carried a hell of a lot of responsibilities. Not everyone could do a good job of it—the pressure was just too great. Not only did an FO have to be good, he had to *know* that he was good. Bunny was not only good, he was the best FO Brody had ever worked with. That little trick he had pulled off, using a single 105 howitzer to snipe at an RPG launcher from miles away was the best artillery shooting that Brody had ever seen.

No matter how good he was, though, Bunny had had his props kicked out from under him by that short round. Brody prayed for another fire mission, soon. Like a surfer who had wiped out badly, Bunny needed to get back on the horn and shoot the big guns again. If he brooded about it too long, he might loose his touch. That could mean a disaster.

Brody headed over to the arms room to turn in his door-gun. He'd talk to Zack about it as soon as he got back to the company area. Maybe the master sergeant would have a little chat with the wise-ass reporter. The man needed a lesson on the realities of Nam.

CHAPTER 4

Camp Radcliff, An Khe

Lieutenant Colonel Maxwell T. Jordan, battalion commander of the First of the 7th Cav, was in his office, going over his property books. As usual, everything was all fucked up. Running a line battalion in the Air Cav was not all it was cracked up to be. He'd had much more fun back when he'd been running an advisory team down in the Delta. At least then, when he got pissed off, he could go out in the woods and kill somebody.

He butted his Marlboro in the overflowing ashtray and lit another one. "Muller!" he called out.

A nondescript face appeared around the corner of the open door. "Yes, sir?"

Jordan looked up at his adjutant, First Lieutenant Muller. As usual, Muller looked scared to death. Jordan sighed. "Muller," he said quietly so as not to frighten him more than he already was, "where's the report of the survey I wanted to see?"

"It's still down in S-four, sir."

"Call down there and tell them that I need it up here ASAP."

"Yes, sir."

Jordan had a mental image of Muller clicking his heels. The adjutant hesitated.

"Sir, there's an officer here from the MACV PIO Office who says that he has to talk to you right now, sir."

Jordan sighed again.

A tall lieutenant in starched fatigues marched into the office. Halting the regulation three feet in front of his desk, he rendered a snappy salute. "Lieutenant Henderson, sir, MACV PIO Office."

"Have a seat, Henderson. What can I do for MACV Public Information today?"

The PIO sat uneasily on the forward half of the folding metal chair. "Well, sir, it's about one of your men. I'd like to press charges against him."

Jordan leaned across his desk. Now that he looked more closely, he saw that the Saigon warrior's starched jungle fatigues were spotted with blood. "And why is that, Lieutenant?"

"He hijacked me, sir. He held a gun on me and made me order my chopper to make an unauthorized flight."

Jordan's ears perked up. He needed something to brighten up his otherwise dull morning. "Why don't you tell me exactly what happened?"

"Well, sir, I was taking a group of reporters on a tour when I heard about your Alpha Company contact on the radio." He went on to tell Jordan the story of the confrontation in the LZ and of being forced to make the dust-off run.

Jordan couldn't believe what he was hearing. "And you want me to press charges against this man?"

"Well, of course, sir." The PIO was indignant. "He threatened me! And he made me get off my schedule."

Jordan was really pissed. Back in the Delta he had been known as Mack the Knife, not only for the Randall fighting knife he wore strapped to the top of his boot, but also for the fact that when he got pissed, he lashed out at anything that happened to be standing in front of him.

Jordan inhaled deeply on the last of his cigarette and stabbed the butt into the ashtray. "Lieutenant, I don't know what you think is going on around here. But in case you haven't heard, there's a fucking war going on out there. Men are being killed and wounded every day."

"Of course I know that there's a war going on, sir. My job is to see that it is reported."

Jordan stood up behind his desk. He had heard enough bullshit. "Your job, Lieutenant, is to be a company-grade gopher for a bunch of fucking vultures. You don't have the slightest idea what this war's all about. You think that Vietnam's an air-conditioned office in Saigon and cold beer every afternoon. You live like you were back in the States, and you have the balls to come into my office and tell me that you were not willing to disrupt your precious schedule to help some of my wounded men get to a hospital. And on top of that, you want me to court-martial the man who saved the lives of my men?"

Jordan's voice grew cuttingly cold. "Mister, you had better pray to God that I don't press charges against you instead. Or, better than that, I ought to pull some strings and get your worthless ass transferred down into this battalion, and then send you out into the woods. Then when you get hit, you can tell me how important it is that a bunch of fucking reporters make their next scheduled stop when you're fucking bleeding to death."

Henderson blanched.

"If I were you, Lieutenant," Jordan leaned across his desk, "I would get the fuck out of Camp Radcliff while I still could. There are some people around here who would be glad to waste your sorry ass for that little performance out there today. In case you don't know, it's open season on REMFs around here. And as for that grunt, I'm going to put him in for a medal."

"Yes, sir," Henderson gulped.

"Now move it!" Jordan screamed.

Henderson jumped to his feet and beat a hasty retreat.

"Fucking REMFs!" Jordan snarled. Speaking of REMFs, "Muller!" he shouted. "Get your ass in here!"

Captain Roger "Rat" Gaines, the Echo Company commander of the First of the 7th, was just stepping out of the cockpit of his Cobra gunship when his friend Walt, the aircraft-maintenance officer from the division G-4, drove up in his Jeep.

"Hey, Rat, got a minute?"

"Sure, what's up?" Gaines pulled his gloves off and stuffed them in the pocket of his nomex flight suit.

Walt stepped out of his Jeep. "We had a little incident out there today. I don't know if you heard about it yet."

Gaines laughed. "This whole fucking AO was full of 'little incidents' today. Which one in particular are you talking about?"

"I lost all four slicks on a platoon lift today."

"Shit! Where'd that happen, LZ Pat?"

"No, this was a routine search of a cold LZ."

"Jesus! What happened? What do the pilots have to say about it?"

"All four pilots are dead along with three of the copilots. The only survivor is in critical condition in the hospital."

"You're shitting me!"

"I've got the CG on my ass thinking that it was maintenance failure. The escorts said that it looked like they had control failure on the final approach."

"You can't have four ships just go tits up all at the same time." Rat looked incredulous. "That's impossible!"

"Yeah, that's what I tried to tell him." Walt looked down the flight line at the dozens of choppers parked there. "They were making a side-by-side approach, and it looked like one ship had a tail-rotor failure and crashed into the one beside it. Then, for no reason, the next two crashed right on top of them."

"And no one saw or heard any gunfire?"

"Nope." He shook his head. "I talked to the surviving grunt in the hospital, and no one heard anything. But you know how hard it is to hear anything in the back of a Huey."

"Jesus. What do you think happened?"

"I don't know, I just fucking don't know. I was hoping that you could help me figure it out. I've got to recover what's left of the choppers tomorrow and go over them for mechanical failure, but I figured that since you're a pilot with an engineering background, you might be able to help me."

Gaines had an idea. "Tell you what, let's stop over at my place. Let me drop this gear, and we'll talk about it over a drink."

"Yeah, I could sure use one right now myself."

The tall, slim Russian KGB major, Gregor Zerinski, raised his bottle of warm Vietnamese *ba-muoi-ba* beer. "It went very well today, comrades."

The nine other Russians seated around the wooden table in the small room answered his toast. They were in a bamboo building in a North Vietnamese Army basecamp hidden deep in the jungle-covered mountains north of the Song Re Valley.

The other officer in the room, Soviet army major Mikhail Yuravitch, was a heavyset man in his mid-forties. He had been a sniper back in the Great Patriotic War and had many long-range kills to his credit. Most of them had been German officers and tank commanders.

In World War II, the Red Army had made great use of snipers in their front lines, probably greater use of the marksmen than in any other army except for the Germans. The Allies, America and England, had never quite gotten used to the idea of killing a man with no warning. There was something just a little too personal about it, and it smacked of assassination. What few snipers they had employed had been primarily used in an anti-sniper role. The

Russians and Germans, however, used their snipers to kill anyone who came into the cross hairs of a scope.

Armed with his long-barreled M-1891/30 Mosin-Nagant bolt-action rifle and a 3.5-power PU telescopic sight, the young Yuravitch had gained a great reputation in the Soviet army for taking out enemy commanders from great distances. The Reds had awarded him numerous medals for his feats of marksmanship.

In the early 1960s, the Russian army high command decided that they needed to update their sniper rifle, and called Yuravitch back into uniform to take over the development program for the new SVD.

It had been his idea that a small team of Spetsnaz marksmen take the rifle into South Vietnam and try it out under actual combat conditions. Yuravitch knew that endless firing at targets on ranges was no substitute for field testing. And since the Russians were engaged in advisory duties in several Asian and African countries where the weapon might be employed, it seemed to be a good idea to run the test in the jungle.

He, too, was pleased with the results that day. Eight shots to take out four helicopters. At that rate, his small team could end the war in just a few weeks.

He was not pleased, however, with the KGB watchdog that had been sent to keep an eye on him. Like almost every Russian who was not in the KGB, and certainly every army officer, Yuravitch had absolutely no use for the gray-eyed State Security policeman who always seemed to have a smile on his face. The Red Army and the KGB had long been at loggerheads. The Soviet system of government demanded that the two most powerful forces in the Soviet Union always remain enemies.

This animosity was fostered for a very good reason. It ensured that the two factions would remain separated and would never join together to plan the overthrow of the Central Committee and take over the country.

Yuravitch would have much rather been allowed to run his team without the KGB major looking over his shoulder. But all Russian clandestine operations in southeast Asia were under the authority of the KGB, not the GRU, the army's military-intelligence service. That system dated back to the days of the Russian Revolution when the KGB had been targeted against the anti-Communist White Armies in Asia, and it had remained that way ever since.

The old sniper knew that there was nothing he could do about Zerinski, but it set his teeth on edge to even be in the same room with a KGB man. During one of Stalin's postwar purges, his father's brother had been put up against the wall by the KGB and shot, and he had never forgotten that. The man had been a war hero. It had not mattered to the KGB.

"Well, Zerinski, what do you have planned for us to do next?" Yuravitch addressed the younger man.

The KGB officer knew that Yuravitch was uneasy around him, and he was pleased. It made his job easier, and he wanted it to stay that way. "Well, Comrade Major, I think that we should see what else that rifle of yours will do. Maybe see how effective it is against the machines themselves."

"It's not a fucking antiaircraft gun!" the old sniper exploded.

"That is true, comrade. The American Bell helicopter is not a *Shturmovik,*" Zerinski countered, referring to the heavily armored Russian Il-2 attack plane of World War II. "They are fragile machines. One of your bullets in the right place can bring it down from the sky."

"We did that today."

"Yes, but sometimes you might not be able to get a clear shot at the pilot and might only be able to shoot at the machine itself."

He reached into a battered leather briefcase and pulled out a thick file of papers. "These are drawings of the mechanical systems of the Bell Huey. I want your men to study them and pay particular attention to the fuel tanks and the hydraulic systems. Our analysts have determined that these are the two weakest points on these machines."

Yuravitch took the papers from him. "In a few days we will go out and try it again," Zerinski added.

The army officer admitted to himself that the plan made sense. He handed the files to the four marksmen sitting around the small wooden table.

"In the meantime," Zerinski continued, "I have convinced the Vietnamese commander that it would be a comradely thing to see that we are supplied with entertainment. He promised me that the girls will be here tonight and that there will be enough of them to go around."

The young Spetsnaz troopers grinned broadly. They had all heard tales about the sexual prowess of the women in Vietnam and they were more than ready to see if the stories were true.

Yuravitch scowled. He didn't want any part in whoring around. He had been sent to do a job and he wanted to get on with it so he could get out of the stinking jungle.

Reactionary old bastard, Zerinski thought as he watched the look of distaste pass over the older man's face. But that was just as well. There would be all the more for him.

A North Vietnamese orderly knocked on the doorframe. "*Chao ong, thieu ta,* I am to tell you that the evening meal is ready."

"*Cam on,* thank you," Zerinski replied. "We will eat in here tonight.'

"At once, Comrade Major."

Yuravitch looked with disgust as the meal was brought in. "Rice and pork again. Is there no way that a man can get a decent meal around here?" he muttered as he pushed his plate away.

Zerinski reached down with his chopsticks, expertly picked a piece of delicately roasted pork from the dish in the middle of the table, dipped it in a vinegar sauce, and carried it to his mouth.

"Yuravitch," he said with a grin, "if you think this is bad, you should be glad that you're not working with the mountain tribesmen in northern Laos. The food there is really shit.''

The army major snorted and got to his feet. ''Do we have any of the canned rations left?''

''I think there are some in the radio room, sir,'' one of the Spetsnaz replied.

Zerinski laughed.

CHAPTER 5

Camp Radcliff, An Khe

Throughout the rest of the afternoon, Gardner continued to drink by himself. No one even tried to approach his table. He was just a little too big and a little too drunk for anyone to want to mess with him.

When one of the few other customers in the EM club needed to be waited on, Mai would quickly leave the table, get the man his drink, and return. She was concerned about Gardner, and her concern grew with every additional beer that went down. She tried to get him to slow down, but he wasn't having any of it. He was too far gone for that now. When she got off work at six o'clock, she finally decided that she would take him home with her and look after him for the night.

For once, the bartender didn't even sneer when she led him out of the club. He was too afraid that Gardner would see him, come back, and crush his head like he had crushed the water pitcher. He didn't know that Gardner couldn't see two feet in front of him, much less all the way back to the bar.

Mai had her work pass, so she had no trouble going out

the main gate to the camp. Even though Gardner was drunk, he was in uniform, so the MPs let him go.

Once they passed through the gate, Mai hurriedly led him down the dusty, noisy strip of bars, souvenir shops, and whorehouses of Sin City to the corner of the street where she lived.

"Hey, soldier!"

Gardner slowly turned around. He was able to make out the figure of an MP coming down the main street. The man came to a halt in front of them.

"Let's see your ID."

Gardner fumbled at his wallet while the MP looked Mai up and down. "Going in there for a little boom-boom, troop?"

Mai clutched Gardner's arm and looked down at the ground.

"Maybe you like to souvenir me a little, too?" the MP said, leering at her.

"Leave her 'lone," Gardner mumbled, holding out his ID card.

"Okay, let's see your pass, buddy," the MP ordered, all business now.

"No pass," Gardner slurred.

The MP inspected his ID card. "Well, it looks like you got a little problem here, buddy. But maybe we can work something out. Like, if she gives me a little blow job back in the alley, maybe I can just let you go this time."

Suddenly, Gardner unleashed the fury that had been building in him all day. For a drunk, the big man could still move fast. Coming up from his right side, his fist connected with the MP's jaw and knocked him flat on his back. The man sprawled on the ground, not moving.

"Jim!" Mai said urgently, looking up and down the street. "We have to go now! Hurry! Please!"

Gardner stood there for a moment, hoping that the MP would get up so he could knock him down again. He didn't feel the pain in his battered right hand this time. Mai had the presence of mind to snatch Gardner's ID card up from the street, where the MP had dropped it, and put it in her pocket.

"Come, Jim, we go now." She tugged at his arm.

Gardner let her lead him around the corner and down the side street to her small two-room house.

He sat at a wooden table in the main room while Mai hurried to boil water for tea. When he slumped down over the table, she decided that he probably needed to sleep it off. Tea was not going to help him right now. She got him up on his feet and led him into the back room where she slept. He sat down on the edge of the narrow bed and watched as she took his boots off.

"Good idea," he mumbled. "I'm tired."

He flopped back down on the bed, his long legs hanging over the edge. She took his legs and pulled him around straight.

Trying to make him more comfortable, she unbuttoned his fatigue jacket and eased it down over his shoulders. She was fascinated with the mat of dark hair on his chest and his broadly muscled shoulders. Vietnamese men were slender and had no chest hair.

Almost absentmindedly, she ran her hand through the thatch of soft, curly hair. Lon Le Mai was older than she looked—Gardner had no idea that she was almost thirty. She had been married for a short time to an ARVN soldier, but he had been killed in the fighting years ago. Because she was a war widow, when the Americans first came to An Khe in 1966 she had gotten a job in the new Air Cav Division basecamp.

Over the last two years Mai had not been exactly celibate, but she had not made a practice of taking GIs home with her every night, either. She still didn't know exactly why she had been attracted to this big, young American. He was good looking in a Western sort of way and she sensed a softness about him, even under the pain that had caused him to get so drunk today. Also, his skin was soft to her touch. She slid her small hand down past his rib cage.

When he felt her hand on his belly, Gardner moaned softly. Smiling to herself, Mai reached down, unbuckled his belt, and slipped her hand down inside the front of his pants.

"Choi oi!" she said suddenly. She had never felt a man that big. Carefully, she unbuttoned his fatigue pants and slipped them down over his hips; she had to see this for herself.

"Oh, Jim," she said with a secret smile on her face. "You bookoo man."

His penis grew hard in her hand. Quickly she slipped out of her silk *ao-dai* and lay down beside him. He muttered something in his sleep and reached for her. She rolled over on top of him and guided his hardness into her. She was wet and ready for him.

Moving slowly so as not to wake him, she thrust herself down and felt the full length of him drive deep inside her. It had been a long time since she had had a man inside her and never had she had a man like this. She felt her climax come almost instantly. Biting her lips to keep from crying aloud, she held herself motionless above him and let the waves of pleasure sweep over her. When the first spasms had subsided, she started moving again, driving him even deeper inside her, moving faster. Without warning, a second orgasm hit her, and she cried out with pleasure.

Something in her cry awoke a primal instinct in Gardner. Unconsciously he reached up, pulled her hips down tighter against him and thrust himself deeply inside her. He repeatedly thrust up into her wet softness, driving hard and fast as she kneeled above him, her head thrown back and her eyes closed.

A third shattering climax coincided with his and she cried out again. When he stopped moving inside her, she collapsed limply on top of him, his strong arms holding her tightly as he quickly fell back to sleep.

She gently disengaged his arms and pulled herself off him. Lying down beside him again, she cuddled up against his broad chest and drew his arms around her once more. He was a Western barbarian, but for now he was her man and she was going to do everything that she could to protect him, even from himself. Later she would try to learn what pain had caused him to get so drunk. Right now though, she didn't care. She was glad that it had happened that way.

Lulled by the security of his warm body, Mai quickly fell asleep, more content than she had been in months.

David Janson sat at the bar in the air-conditioned Division officer's club, nursing a gin and tonic as he listened with half an ear to the young artillery captain seated beside him. The man had been going on and on about the vagaries of artillery ammunition for almost fifteen minutes now. One thing about asking a question of an expert, the reporter knew, was that you always heard more than you ever wanted to know about the subject.

He interrupted the captain in midsentence. "But how often does a short round occur?" he asked for the third or fourth time.

The officer started into a long discourse about lot numbers on ammunition propellant charges. Janson started to really get annoyed. It wasn't what he wanted to know. He wanted to know how often someone got killed because of faulty ammunition, and who was responsible. He suddenly realized that he was being sandbagged. His informant was not about to commit himself and be quoted on a concrete answer.

"That's very interesting, Captain," he broke in again. "Thank you for enlightening me."

"Oh, no problem," the Red Leg officer replied. "Look, maybe you'd like to go out to one of the firebases and interview some of our artillerymen?"

Janson thought for a moment. "No thanks, not right now. I think I'm going to stay with the infantry for a while. Maybe later."

The artilleryman was disappointed. Grunts always got the best press coverage, particularly in the Air Cav. "Well, I've got to get back to work." He laid his empty glass on the bar. "No rest for the wicked. I'll see you later."

Janson raised his glass in salute. *Although I sincerely doubt it,* he thought to himself.

The reporter ordered another drink. He decided that he was going talk to the Air Cav PIO first thing in the morning. He wanted to go out on a couple of missions with the same Aero Rifle platoon he had dropped in on unexpectedly that morning. He wanted to get a closer look at that one blond sergeant, Brody, the one who had kept him from talking to the artillery forward observer who had fucked up on the fire mission.

To Janson's eye, Brody looked like a California beach bum with his wild shock of long blond hair and bushy mustache, not a professional non-commissioned officer in the army. All of his reporter's instincts told him that Brody was hiding something, and he wanted to find out exactly what it was. He smelled a story in it, a big story—like an incompetent sergeant who let his men kill other Americans.

Janson smiled to himself. He vowed that when he got done, that smart-mouthed punk would wish that he had kept his fucking mouth shut.

He finished his drink, left the club, and headed back to the room that had been assigned to him in the VIP quarters next to the Division headquarters. It was comfortably air-conditioned, and a courtesy bar had been set up. He had to admit that the Air Cav really knew how to treat their reporters. It was almost too bad that he was going to expose them as a bunch of bumbling clowns who made a habit of killing other American soldiers. He smiled again. The folks at home were going to love this one.

He quickly mixed himself another drink from the bar in the room, telling himself that just one more wouldn't hurt. He carried the glass over to the bed and sat down to go over the notes he had taken.

David Janson badly needed a good story that would be picked up on all the wire services and get him a job with one of the big news agencies again. He had gotten the drinking that had cost him his last steady job under control, but working as a free-lance reporter was frustrating. Even when he wrote good stories, he had trouble selling them to the wire services. His only salvation was to dig up something that would catch the public's eye in a big way. He had to get out where the action was instead of staying at the Caravel Hotel in Saigon, drinking imported Lowenbrau beer with the rest of the press corps and their high-priced French whores, and writing his combat stories at the polished mahogany bar.

The Air Cav division had gotten real good press since they had first arrived in Vietnam. They were the glory boys, the Pony Soldiers, the First Team, all of that carefully planned PR shit. Just because they rode around in helicopters instead of stumbling around in the hot sun like line infantry, reporters liked to go along with them and cover their operations. It was a hell of a lot easier to do it that way, to say nothing of being much more comfortable. And the Air Cav made a point of treating the press the way they felt they should be treated—like visiting royalty. The well-stocked bar in his room was a good example.

But the Air Cav didn't walk on water. They had their problems just like any other organization in the military, and Janson was determined to stick around until he found out what was really going on. Then he'd write his exposé, make his fortune, and get the fuck out.

CHAPTER 6

Camp Radcliff, An Khe

When Brody learned that Jim Gardner had been released from the hospital earlier that morning, he went looking for him. He had to put a mission together for the next day and he wanted to know how JJ was feeling. He could use him if he was ready to go out again.

In the Blues' tent, Gardner's field gear was scattered all over his bunk. His M-16 was lying on his footlocker half-broken down, but the man was nowhere in sight. It wasn't like him at all.

"Hey, has anybody seen JJ?" he shouted to the other men in the tent.

"Gardner? I ain't seen him around here, but he was in the club earlier this afternoon," one of the guys in First Squad offered.

"When?"

"Couple of hours ago."

Brody thought that he had better try to track him down and find out what was going on. If Gardner was hitting the club that early, he had to be in pretty bad shape.

"Thanks." Brody headed out the door of the tent.

He walked into the EM club and looked around, but didn't see the big man at any of the tables. He went up to the bar and took a seat on one of the stools.

"What ya need?" the rat-faced, skinny guy behind the counter asked him.

"I'm looking for a buddy who was in here earlier today. A big guy, name of Gardner. Brown hair, looks like he played football."

The bartender glanced down at the bent steel water pitcher under the counter. "Bad tempered?"

"Not usually, why?"

"Oh, nothing."

Brody's ears pricked up. "What happened? Give it to me!"

"Well, there was a guy in here all afternoon, see, a big guy, and he was knocking back boilermakers like they were water."

That didn't sound like JJ, but Brody was interested. "Go on."

"Anyway, a couple of hours ago, he left here with one of the girls."

"You know where she lives?"

The bartender hesitated. He didn't want Gardner coming after him again.

"Look, goddammit!" Brody leaned over the bar. "I'm his squad leader and I'm just trying to keep him from getting his ass in trouble."

"Okay, okay, just as long as he don't come looking for me."

Brody laughed. "Don't worry, man. I won't tell him how I found him."

The rat-faced bartender quickly told Brody who Mai was and where she lived.

"Thank, man." Brody left the club and headed down into Sin City. Mai's house wasn't hard to find. It was a little place on a side street just off the main strip. He walked up and knocked on the door.

A girl answered his knock. She had obviously been in bed and had just thrown a robe on to cover herself. Brody quickly checked her out from top to bottom. He nodded approvingly. He was glad to see that Jungle Jim has finally broken his straight arrow. Brody had begun to worry about the boy.

"Are you Mai?"

"Yes," she answered hesitantly .

"I'm looking for Gardner, Jim Gardner?"

Mai clutched the robe at her throat, and her eyes darted up and down the street. "He not here!"

"Look . . ." Brody glanced down the street himself. "I'm not an MP, I'm one of his buddies. I've got to get him back to the camp before he gets in trouble."

"What your name?" she asked suspiciously.

"Brody, Treat Brody. Listen, Mai, he's in my squad. I just want to help him. Please just let me come in and talk to him."

The girl studied his face. "Okay," she finally said. "You come inside."

Mai led him through the small house into the back room. Gardner was passed out on the tangled sheets wearing only his boot socks.

"Hey, JJ!" Brody shook him. "Gardner! Wake up!"

He didn't even moan.

"JJ!" Brody shouted in his ear. "Goddammit, wake up!"

"Go 'way." He groaned and turned his face away.

Brody tried to pull the bigger man into a sitting position but he was dead weight. "Come on, man, come on. You've got to wake up."

He turned to Mai. "How much did he have to drink?"

"He drink bookoo too much."

"Shit! Can you make some coffee?"

"No have coffee, but I make tea."

"Make it strong, real strong."

The girl quickly came back with steaming tea in a delicate porcelain pot. She helped Brody maneuver Gardner into a sitting position.

"Come on, JJ, wake up, man."

"What you want?" Gardner slurred, pulling away. "Leave me 'lone."

"Here, drink this." Brody put the steaming cup under his nose.

"Don't want to."

Brody looked up at the girl. "Mai, do you have any water?"

She came back with an aluminum cooking pot full of water. Brody took it from her, threw it in Gardner's face, and stepped back quickly.

The big man exploded.

"Sonofabitch!" he cried flailing his arms. "Go 'way an' leave me 'lone!"

"JJ, you've got to go back to camp. Come on, get your shit together. You're going back with me."

"No! I'm gonna stay right here."

"Gardner, you'd better get your fucking ass up out of that sack, man, or you're going to be AWOL."

That got a response from him. The big man sat up and swung his legs over the side of the bed. He held his head in his hands.

"Here," Brody handed him the cup again. "Drink some of this."

Gardner sipped at thc tea. His eyes slowly came into focus. "What're you doing here?"

"I came to get you, man. We got a mission tomorrow."

"Jesus." Gardner stood up.

Brody handed him his pants. "Get dressed," he ordered.

" 'Kay." Gardner sat back down on the edge of the bed and tried to put them on.

"I'll wait for you in the other room." Brody turned to go.

Mai followed him out. She held out Gardner's ID card. "Brody, you take this."

"Where'd you get that?" he asked, slipping the card into his jacket pocket.

"Jim hit MP, and MP drop card."

"For Christ's sakes, why'd he hit an MP?"

Mai looked down. "I don't know," she said softly. Brody knew without asking that the MP had given Gardner a hard time about the girl, probably trying to get a piece of the action himself.

Now he had to find a way to get Gardner back into the camp without running into the MPs. They'd be on the alert and just waiting for him to come back in the main gate. And if they identified him, they'd put his ass up on assault charges.

"Thanks," he said to Mai. "I'll take care of it."

He started thinking, trying to remember what company had guard duty tonight on his battalion's section of the berm line. If it was Charlie Company, he'd be in fat city. They owed the Blues a favor and would help him over the fence, no sweat. Maybe even Bravo Company would help, but Alpha Company was pissed off about that short round. Whoever it was, Brody had to take the chance that he could talk their way in over the perimeter fence. It was still early in the evening. That would help a little.

Half dressed, Gardner stumbled out into the main room. "You ready?" Brody asked.

Gardner nodded.

"Button your jacket up." He looked around the room. "Where's your hat?"

Mai handed him a battered brush hat. Brody put it on Gardner's head, and then slung his arm over his shoulder. "Let's go."

The alley outside Mai's door was clear, so he headed out, keeping well in the shadows, helping JJ along. As they walked, Gardner launched into a long-winded story about his wife, his baby boy, and the "Dear John" letter he had gotten in the mail.

Brody tried to keep him quiet, but he finally gave up. *That poor son of a bitch,* he thought. The last fucking thing a grunt needed was a wife fucking around back home. Gardner needed to talk to someone about it.

Brody took the long way around, skirting the main strip of Sin City until he got to the section of the perimeter that was guarded by their battalion, the First of the 7th Cav.

He stopped well outside the area lighted by the perimeter lights. The grass was cut short, and there was no cover. "Stay down and keep your fucking mouth shut till I get back," he cautioned Gardner.

"Okay." Gardner lay flat on the ground.

Brody slowly made his way closer to the barbed-wire perimeter. "Hey!" he called out. "Don't shoot, I'm coming in."

He walked out into the lights with his hands held high up over his head.

"Who is it?" someone called from the bunker in front of him.

"Treat Brody," he answered, squinting against the glare of the perimeter lights. "Echo Company Blues."

"Come closer, slowly."

Brody obeyed, making certain not to make any sudden movements.

"What the fuck are you doing out here, man?" The second voice also came from inside the bunker.

"I've got a buddy back there who has to come in over the fence. The MPs are looking for him."

"What'd he do?"

"Not much, really. An MP was trying to hit on his girl, so he knocked him flat on his ass."

The bunker guard laughed. Every grunt in An Khe had had that kind of problem with the MPs now and then. "Okay, bring him in."

Brody put his arms down and ran back to get Gardner. This time when he approached the wire, three men were standing in the shadows thrown by the perimeter lights, holding their M-16s on them. He helped JJ make his way through the barbed-wire tanglefoot. One of the guards came through from his side to help him up over three rows of concertina wire.

"Come on, man, come on! Get a move on it!" the

grunt hissed as he helped Gardner over the second coil of wire. "The guard officer's about due to come through here any minute now."

They had just gotten Gardner over the fence when they saw Jeep headlights coming down the road inside the perimeter. "Quick! Inside the bunker."

Brody helped JJ inside the sandbag-and-timber guard post and hid in the darkness at the far end. Outside, he heard the Jeep screech to a stop and the officer talking to the guards. When he was satisfied that they were doing their job of adequately protecting Camp Radcliff from enemy infiltration, he drove off.

"Fucking butter-bar," one of the guards growled. "You can come out now, he's gone."

"Thanks, guys," Brody said when he led Gardner back outside. "I really appreciate it."

"No sweat, man."

"Hey," another one of the guards spoke up. "Next time that your buddy wants to punch out an MP, tell him to hit one of the motherfuckers for me."

"And me!" someone else added.

Brody laughed. "As soon as he sobers up, I'll tell him."

Walking the rest of the way to the company area was relatively easy. Brody only had to hide in the shadows once when an MP Jeep drove by. Leading Gardner into the Blues' tent, Brody deposited him on his bunk. He didn't bother undressing him.

CHAPTER 7

Camp Radcliff, An Khe

The next morning, Brody came back from chow and saw that Gardner was awake. He walked up to his bunk. "How you feeling this morning, dude?"

Gardner groaned and rolled over to face him. "Jesus, Brody. How the hell did I get back here?"

"I went down to Mai's house and brought you back."

Painfully, Gardner sat up. The knuckles of his right hand were bruised and swollen. He winced when he clenched his fist. "What the fuck did I do, anyway?"

Brody sat down on the footlocker at the end of the bunk. "Well, as near as I can figure out, you got drunk in the club, terrorized that skinny REMF behind the bar, and then Mai got you outta there. Somewhere along the line, you apparently knocked some MP on his ass. At least that's what she told me."

"Oh, shit." Gardner swung his legs over the side of the bunk. "Are they looking for me?"

"Not yet."

"How'd you get me back?"

"I brought you back in over the fence."

"Oh, Jesus. I gotta get me some coffee." Gardner took a deep breath and caught a whiff of himself. "And a shower."

Brody glanced down at his watch. "The mess hall's still open if you haul ass. Why don't you get some chow, get cleaned up, and report back here. We've got a mission to fly this morning, if you feel up to it."

"Sure." He looked around with blurry eyes. "I'll go, just give me a few minutes."

Brody stood up to leave.

"Treat?"

"Yeah."

"Thanks a lot."

"No sweat, man," he laughed. "Maybe you can do the same for me someday."

A couple of hours later, Brody and his people were down at the Python alert pad waiting for the mission to get underway. For some reason, Gabe was late. The men were sitting on their rucks in the shade of *Pegasus*'s fuselage, smoking and joking, when Bunny saw three men come out of the Python operations shack on the other side of the pad.

"Fuck," he exploded. "Look who's coming."

Walking up to the chopper with Zack and Gabe was one of the reporters who had flown into the LZ the day before. The one who had gotten into the argument with Brody and the FO.

Brody watched them approach. The reporter had a wise-ass smile on his face when he recognized him. Brody didn't like this at all. He stood up and ground the butt of his cigarette under his jungle boot.

"Listen up, guys," Sergeant Zack said, stepping up to them. "This is Mr. David Janson. He's a reporter and he's going out with you today to get a firsthand look at how the Air Cav operates."

The platoon sergeant started making the introductions. "This is Sergeant Brody, the squad leader."

"We've met," Janson said dryly, locking eyes with Brody. He did not extend his hand.

Brody didn't bother to answer. He just smiled tightly.

"And this is Specialist Chance Broken Arrow," Zack continued.

Two-Step shook the offered hand, but didn't say anything.

"PFC Ralph Burns."

Farmer shook, too. "They call me Farmer," he said with a big grin, " 'cause I'm from Idaho. 'Home of Famous Potatoes.' "

Janson made no comment.

"PFC Jim Gardner."

JJ still looked rough. He shook the reporter's hand and winced inwardly.

"Spec-four Cordova."

Corky leaned on his sixty and grinned like a Mexican bandit in a grade-B western. The Pancho Villa mustache and machine-gun ammo belts crossed over his chest helped to bolster the image.

"Que pasa, hombre?"

Brody snapped his head around at the sound of the machine gunner's Spanish. Cordova was very sensitive about being from the Mexican barrios of Los Angeles and he tried hard not to act like a typical Chicano. He usually didn't speak Spanish unless he was really pissed off about something.

"And our FO, Specialist Bernie Rabdo."

Bunny stared at the reporter for a second and turned his head away. Janson smiled.

Zack frowned, wondering why the hell the boys were on the rag. Usually they were all over any reporter who came around, trying to get their names in the newspapers. He had heard about the short round on the LZ the day before. But no one had told him about the reporter and his run-in with Brody and Bunny, so he hadn't made the connection. Zack shrugged and turned to the pilot.

"Okay, Mr. Gabriel, I guess you'd better get going now."

The grunts silently climbed on board the chopper. For once they were not laughing and joking. Brody went back into his door gunner's pocket behind the troop compartment and put his helmet on. The words "Hog Heaven" were painted in red and yellow on the front of the fiberglass helmet shell. Brody was proud of his membership in the Hog Heaven fraternity. To join that exclusive club, a door gunner had to have scored at least a hundred confirmed kills with his Hog, his M-60D doorgun. He had racked up that score in less than six months.

Janson sat down in the canvas troop seat closest to the doorgun on the same side. Zack handed the reporter a spare flight helmet, and he quickly put it on.

"Well, Mr. Janson, I'll meet you here when you get back," the master sergeant concluded.

Janson buckled his seat belt and watched the men go through their pre-flight routines. Brody was very much aware of the man's eyes on him as he got the ammunition cans ready to load his doorgun sixty.

"We're ready back here," he called up to Gabe.

"Roger. Cranking now."

With the reporter sitting in the back listening in over the intercom, Gabe was very careful to do a full pre-takeoff check rather than making a hot start like he usually did. He called off each item on the entire checklist, and the copilot rogered it, just like they were back in flight school at Fort Wolters, Texas.

Gabe's hands moved swiftly over the switches and controls of his bird, beginning with the start-up.

"Battery, on. Inverter switch, off. RPM warning light, on. Fuel, both main and start, on. RPM governor, decrease." He looked over his shoulder to both sides of the ship. "Rotor, clear. Light it!"

Reaching down with his right hand, Gabe twisted the

throttle open to flight idle and pulled the starting trigger on the collective.

In the rear of the bird, *Pegasus*'s big Lycoming T-53 turbine burst into life with a screech and the smell of burning kerosene. Over their heads, the forty-eight-foot main rotor slowly began to turn. As the turbine RPMs built and the blades came up to speed, the pilot released the start trigger and held the throttle to idle as he checked his instruments.

Everything was in the green. Gabe twisted the throttle all the way up against the stop.

The whine built to a bone-shaking scream as the turbine ran all the way up to 6,000 RPMs. Everything was still in the green. He flipped the RPM switch to increase. The turbine screamed higher at 6,700 RPMs. They were ready to go.

Gabe radioed the control tower for takeoff clearance. "Golf Course Control, this is Python Five Eight. Request permission to take off. Over."

"Python Five Eight, this is Control, Roger, you're cleared for takeoff. Keep an eye out for bubble-top traffic. Over."

"Five Eight, wilco."

Gabe eased up on the collective, pulling pitch on the rotor blades, and came to a hover three feet off the ground. Easing down on the rudder pedal, he swung the tail of the chopper around. Nudging forward on the cyclic, the tail came up, and they started down the PSP runway in a gentle gunship takeoff. Gabe let his airspeed build before he pulled up on the collective, changing pitch on the rotor blades.

Pegasus rose smoothly into the air and headed over the perimeter of Camp Radcliff. In the clear blue sky, the sun caught the painted mural of a mythical winged horse on the underside of her nose.

"Golf Course Control, this is Python Five Eight," the pilot radioed. "I am airborne and heading out, over."

"Control, Roger."

This time, Brody didn't have the sense of exhilaration that he usually experienced when his chopper cleared the berm line and headed out into enemy territory. Usually when he was standing behind his doorgun, he felt a surge of adrenaline shooting through his body at the start of a mission, a rush of heat that almost made him feel light-headed. He had become addicted to the feeling, but today it didn't come. Having the reporter on board was too much like an invasion of privacy, an intrusion into his thoughts.

He had no illusions about what the reporter was doing with them today. He was looking for a story, probably something to make them look bad. Brody had seen it in Janson's eyes.

He went about getting himself ready for war. Flipping up the latch on the feed tray cover to the M-60, he opened it and laid the linked 7.62mm ammunition belt into place in the feed tray. Then he snapped the cover back down.

The ammo in the linked belts was loaded with a mix of ball and tracer ammunition, one round of tracer for every four rounds of ball. That way, when his sixty was talking, he could see where his fire was going and bring it accurately into the target.

Reaching down to the right side of the gun's breech, he pulled back on the charging handle to jack a round into the chamber. Sliding the handle back forward again into the latched position, he flipped the safety on. Now he was ready. His gloved hands were wrapped around the spade grips of the gun, and his thumbs rested on the triggers.

He looked over at the reporter and grinned. Fuck Janson and the horse he rode in on.

Major Zerinski and a four-man team of Spetsnaz snipers were in a camouflaged position on a hilltop overlooking one of the smaller valleys leading into the Song Re. Today, he had an additional security team of North Vietnamese Red Guards along with them, courtesy of his counterpart in the North Vietnamese Dac Cong, their own version of the KGB.

With all of the increased American activity in the area, the Russian officer felt that they needed the additional security rather than relying on the two Spetsnaz on the team. He could not allow one of the new SVD rifles to fall into American hands.

Major Yuravitch and the other sniper team were at another site also being secured by Red Guard troops.

Today, they were going to test Zerinski's theory about killing choppers by damaging their systems with sniper fire. They had not set any bait out like they had done before. There was no need to. There was so much chopper traffic in the area that he was sure they would find a suitable target before too long.

Gabe flew down low into the small valley right over the top of the triple-canopy jungle. "Brody," he called back, "keep a sharp eye out, this is the area where those choppers went down."

"Roger," Brody answered curtly. With the reporter listening in on the intercom, he did not want to get into his usual grab-ass session over the radio with Gabe.

He peered down into the thick jungle below. In the triple-canopied jungle he couldn't see a thing. There could be an entire company of NVA marching through the woods below them and he'd never spot them.

Brody leaned out further on the lifeline, trying to look straight down. His hands were around the spade grips of his gun, his fingers resting on the triggers, waiting. Any sign of movement below and he'd blast it.

Suddenly, a camouflage-painted A-1E Skyraider flashed past overhead. Gabe slammed the cyclic over to the side and kicked down on the rudder pedal to skid *Pegasus* out of the way of the diving attack plane.

The violent maneuver threw Brody against the end of his lifeline. "What the fuck you doing, Gabe!" he called up on the intercom.

"We're in an airstrike zone!"

The pilot quickly changed frequency on his radio to the TAC AIR net.

". . . army chopper, you are in an air-strike zone. I say again, get the hell out of the area, we have napalm coming in. Do you roger? Over."

"This is Python Five Eight, what in the hell are you doing here? There's no air strike scheduled for today, over."

"This is the strike commander, there is now, buddy. You'd better get your ass out of the area. Vector to the east."

"This is Python Five Eight, Roger. Turning left now." Gabe banked off to the west, leaving the Skyraiders behind him. He popped up over the ridgeline and dropped into the next valley.

On the hilltop, the Russians heard the chopper approaching. The two snipers snapped the safeties on their SVD rifles down into the off position, focused the four-power PSO-1 scopes, and began tracking the Huey as it started down into the valley. It was only about a thousand meters away, well within range, and flying about level with them. They had a good, clear shot at it.

"Now!" Zerinski commanded.

The two rifles fired as one. The weapons cycled, kicking out the empty brass and feeding new rounds into the chambers. They fired again.

Back in the door gunner's pocket, Brody heard a noise over his head in the engine compartment. It sounded like they had taken a hit, but he had heard no gunfire. Nor had he seen any muzzle flashes.

He heard it again.

They were under fire!

"Gabe!" he called up on the intercom. "We're taking fire!"

The pilot instantly banked *Pegasus* over onto her side and kicked down on the rudder pedals. The chopper skidded in the air.

When he tried to pull back, the controls felt stiff in his hand. The hydraulics were out!

His gloved hand stabbed for the hydraulic control circuit breaker on the electrical panel. He punched it out and then back in. Nothing happened.

He flipped the hydraulic control switch to off. Still nothing. He flipped it back on.

Something had knocked out their entire hydraulic system—and it controlled the rotor head.

The chopper started bucking from collective bounce. Gabe increased the friction adjustment on the collective pitch control, trying to stop the oscillations. It only got worse. *Pegasus* was bucking badly.

"Help me!" he yelled to the copilot.

The copilot got on the controls with him, but there was nothing they could do. They had to put the machine down while it was still possible.

The problem was that there was nothing below them but the thick triple-canopy jungle. And they were headed back into the strike zone. Gabe had no choice but to try for a straight-in landing on the treetops in front of him.

"Hang on!" he called back. "We're going down!"

CHAPTER 8

North of the Song Re Valley

Gabe chopped his throttle, trying to cut his airspeed. It helped some, but the collective wasn't responding properly, and they were still going in too fast. He pulled the nose of the ship up sharply, and at the last possible moment, hauled up on the collective as hard as he could. The chopper shuddered as it tried to go into a stall.

Nose high, *Pegasus* slammed into the treetops, burying herself in the branches all the way up to the rotor hub.

Pieces of shattered rotor blades showered down all around them, and the ends of broken branches stabbed into the troop compartment as the pilot killed the electrical system. The scream of the turbine died.

"Everybody okay?" Gabe asked, looking back over his shoulder. The chopper swayed precariously and settled a few inches further down in the treetop. The limbs creaked ominously from the weight of the machine. All that was keeping them from crashing down to the ground were the giant trees of the rain forest.

The impact had thrown Brody back into the corner of his gunner's pocket. He painfully picked himself up and looked down over the side of the chopper. They seemed to be caught firmly. He parted the branches and looked down, but all he could see were more limbs below him. They had to be at least thirty feet up in the air.

He unsnapped his lifeline and staggered forward into the troop compartment. The chopper shivered again as the weight shifted. He looked through the canopy and saw a diving Skyraider deliver napalm at the end of the valley. A nasty orange-and-black ball of flame boiled into the sky.

"Gabe!" he shouted. "We'd better get out of this fucking thing!"

Gardner was extricating himself from under the troop seats against the back bulkhead. He massaged his bruised hand. Now it hurt badly, and he had a headache as well. Everyone else had managed to hang on tight, and no one was injured.

Janson, however, looked like he was having a heart attack. His face was pasty white, and his eyes looked like sewer lids. Brody would have laughed at the expression on the reporter's face except for the fact that he was frantically trying to figure out how they were going to get down from their perch.

In the pilot's seat, Gabe tried to make a radio call back to An Khe to report the crash. He wasn't getting a response.

"Fuck!" he hammered the radio panel. He looked up through the Plexiglass panels in the top of the canopy and saw that the UHF blade antenna on the top of the chopper's fuselage had snapped off. The FM radio's whip antenna on the tail boom was probably gone as well.

"Bunny," he called back.

"Yeah."

"Your Prick-twenty-five working?"

"I think so."

Bunny turned the small tactical on, keyed the mike, and listened. "It's okay," he reported.

"Try calling An Khe," the pilot said.

"Just a sec." Bunny took out his SOI to look up the

radio frequency and call sign for the An Khe control tower. He keyed the hand set.

"Golf Course Control, Golf Course Control, this is Python Five Eight, Python Five Eight, come in, please."

Nothing came in over the handset except static. He tried again. Still nothing.

"We're going to have to get out of this valley," he told the pilot. "I can't get through to them."

"Shit." Gabe was tired of getting shot down and having to stumble around in the woods for a week until they were picked up.

"Okay, Brody," the pilot asked. "Just how in hell are we going to get down outta here?"

"Beats the fuck outta me." Brody shrugged. "Anybody got a rope?"

"Just a second," Gardner said, opening the top of his rucksack. "I think I do."

He reached into the bottom of the pack and came up with a coil of nylon rope that was intended for rappeling to the ground from hovering choppers.

Brody secured the loose end of the rope around the pillar between the pilot's door and the troop compartment and let the rest of it down over the side. "Okay," he asked. "Who's going to be first?"

Two-Step slipped into his ruck and checked the load in his sawed-off shotgun. "I'll go."

"Careful now."

"You got that shit right."

Brody kept a watch as the Indian went down the rope hand over hand, kicking away from the branches as he went down. Soon, he was lost from sight in the thick foliage. When he reached the ground he shook the rope, signaling to Brody that he had made it.

"Who's next?"

Gardner went. He didn't want Two-Step to be on the ground all by himself. Since he had a bad hand, he slung his M-79 thumper over his back to have both completely free. About halfway down, he realized how dark it was.

Even the blazing tropical sun couldn't penetrate the dense cover of the triple-canopy jungle. When he reached the ground, it was twilight. Except for the hollow crumps of the napalm air strike in the distance, it was eerily quiet.

Two-Step crouched at the base of a huge tree trunk. He waved Gardner to go to the other side. JJ tugged on the rope to signal Brody that he was down, and took up his position.

Corky was the next man to make it down. Although the underbrush was so thick that it was hard to see more than fifteen or twenty feet in front of them, he quickly set up his machine gun.

Farmer came down with his eyes closed, relieved when his feet finally touched the damp ground. Two-Step had him take over his position while he went out a little farther to extend their perimeter.

When Bunny reached the ground, he joined Corky as the loader for the machine gun. Borg, the copilot, was next, followed closely by Gabe. Then Janson came down slowly. Lastly, Brody slid down the rope and landed heavily on his feet at the base of the tree.

The reporter looked around the dense jungle. It was so dark and thick that he could hardly see ten feet in front of him. The Viet Cong could be hiding anywhere, and he wouldn't know it until he ran right into them. Half of his mind told him that it was better to stay with the downed chopper. But he could smell napalm and the burning jungle in the air. They had to get moving in case the fire spread.

Janson had never really liked Vietnam, but for the first time since he had been in-country, he started to get nervous. He walked over to where Brody and Two-Step were taking a compass reading.

"Uh, Sergeant," the reporter said anxiously, trying to smile, "you don't happen to have an extra gun I could use, do you?"

Brody smiled broadly. He enjoyed seeing the older man sweat like this. Now he would see just how much this loudmouthed bastard liked playing soldier. It was one thing for the reporter to fly into a safe LZ and harass people, but it was something else to be stuck out in the woods and have to depend on a grunt to save his life.

"If you want a fucking gun, Mr. Janson, I guess that you're just going to have to join the fucking army. I don't carry extra weapons around for straphanging civilians."

Janson reacted like he had been slapped in the face. He wasn't used to being talked to that way. Wisely, he didn't reply. Instead, he turned abruptly and walked back to where Gabe was looking over his map with the copilot.

"Excuse me," the reporter said.

Gabe looked up.

"I asked the sergeant if he had an extra weapon I could use to defend myself, but he doesn't seem to think that I should have one."

"Well, that's his decision," the pilot answered. "On the ground, he's in command."

"I see." Janson clenched his teeth.

"It's totally up to him if he wants you to have a piece, but I'll talk to him about it if you want," Gabe offered helpfully.

"No, don't bother."

Janson decided that he would try to stay with the pilots. They were the only ones who weren't pissed off at him. From the looks he was getting from the grunts, he figured that he'd be lucky to get out alive.

"You guys mind if I walk with you?"

"Not at all," Gabe replied.

Brody came back and announced that they had better get on the move.

"I don't want to stay here too long," he explained to Gabe. "I know the wind's blowing the fire away from us, but I don't want to stick around here. Two-Step and I think there's a hill to our east. We'd be safe there and we should be able to use our radio up there, too. It's going to be a long hump, but it's better than trying to stay here."

"That's okay with me," Gabe agreed. "They couldn't extract us from here anyway."

"Not without a jungle penetrator, they sure as hell couldn't."

Back at Camp Radcliff, Python Operations noted that Cliff Gabriel's ship was overdue and tried to contact him on the radio. After several tries, the Ops sergeant went into Rat Gaines's small office. "Sir," he began. "I hate to be the one to have to tell you this, but Gabe's down again."

"Fuck me dead!" Gaines exploded. "I swear to Christ that I'm going to ground his ass. Permanently. What the fuck happened this time?"

"We don't know, sir. When he didn't make his scheduled return, we tried to contact him, but no joy."

Gaines stood up and walked over to the big topo map hanging on his wall. "Where was he going today?"

"He was scheduled for a search mission over here." The sergeant pointed to a spot north of the Song Re Valley. "Looking for more of those downed choppers from that Eighth Cav contact."

"Who can you get up to look for them?"

"Well, I've got two bubble-tops on hand that I can use, sir," the sergeant said, referring to the small OH-47 scout ships of the White Team.

"Good, get 'em going, 'rat' now."

"Will do, sir." The Ops sergeant turned to go. Like all of the men in Echo Company, he had learned that when the Georgia-born Rat Gaines said he wanted something done now, he meant "rat" now. He stopped at the door and turned around. "Oh, and one more thing, sir. He had that reporter on board with him."

Gaines stared at the map. "What reporter?"

"Division sent a guy down here this morning and wanted me to send him out on the flight. I don't think you were around at the time, sir."

Rat slowly shook his head. No, he hadn't been around.

He'd been having breakfast with Lisa Maddox over at the hospital mess hall. A nice, long, leisurely breakfast with extra cups of decent coffee for a change.

"Didn't anyone think to inform me that I had a fucking civilian on one of my choppers?"

The sergeant shrugged his shoulders. "Well, sir, I guess that's my fault. I got busy and it kinda slipped my mind."

Gaines sighed. "Okay, fuck it, that happens. New policy, effective today. No fucking body rides in my ships unless they're wearing a green suit or they have my personal permission to do so. Clear?"

"Yes, sir."

"And I don't give a shit what the Division PIO says. You tell him to talk to me first."

"Yes, sir.'

"Now get those scout ships in the air and find Gabe. I don't want to have to spend another fucking week looking for him again like we did last time. Christ, why can't someone else get shot down for a fucking change."

The sergeant left in a hurry.

Gaines sat back down at his desk. Suddenly this wasn't such a good day after all. He had been doing just fine until this came up. Lisa wasn't mad at him anymore, and he was planning to take the blond nurse to dinner at the club that night.

"Oh, well," he sighed. "Some days you get the bear, some days he gets you, and some fucking days it just doesn't pay to go into the fucking woods."

He turned back to his paper work. Suddenly a thought struck him. He picked up the phone and dialed his orderly room on the other side of the camp.

"Echo Company, First Sergeant Richardson speaking, sir!"

"Top, this is Gaines. Get hold of Alexander and have him stand by with a squad of the Blues. Gabe's down again, and we may have to go in and bail him out of God only knows where."

"Yes, sir. Lieutenant Alexander is right here."

"Good. Tell him to get 'em on down to the alert pad, and I'll send a slick for him."

"Right, sir."

Gaines put the phone back down. At least with the Blues standing by, as soon as Gabe and his crew were found, he could get somebody in there to pick them up. Of all the days to have a reporter flying with them!

Gaines looked down at the flight suit he was wearing. It was stained with dirt and grease. He had to change into a clean uniform. As soon as Division headquarters learned that a member of the press was down, they'd call him over there and ask him a bunch of dumb-ass questions.

He sighed and slowly got up from his desk. Walking into the radio room, he told the operator on duty, "If anyone calls, I'm going to my hooch for a minute, and then I'll be over in the orderly room."

CHAPTER 9

North of the Song Re Valley

Major Zerinski watched intently through his high-powered, East German binoculars as Gabe brought *Pegasus* in for a crash landing in the treetops. He had to admit that it was a spectacular feat of airmanship. He almost regretted he could not let the Yankee pilot go free. He needed to learn more about the American helicopter battle tactics and even more about the machines themselves.

When he saw the crew leaving the chopper, going down the rope one by one, he turned to the North Vietnamese captain standing beside him.

"Send your men after them now, *dai uy,*" he ordered in Vietnamese.

The NVA Red Guard officer smiled. "Right away, Comrade Major."

Zerinski went back to scanning the skies for another target. The SVD rifles were proving to be a very valuable asset on the battlefield.

* * *

When Brody gave the order to move out, Two-Step went up on the point position as he always did. The Indian didn't walk point because anyone made him do it, he did it because he liked it. It was his personal form of playing cowboys and Indians, but with real guns and the NVA playing the part of the cowboys.

Instead of carrying an M-16 rifle on that dangerous assignment, however, he armed himself with a sawed-off, twelve-gauge pump shotgun. He also reloaded his own ammunition for the piece, replacing the lead balls in the standard double-aught buckshot shells with steel ball bearings. Not only could he fit more of the steel balls into the shells, but they were lighter than the lead shot, so they traveled farther and hit harder. Also, they didn't deform when they hit a human body. They just tore on through and kept going.

When Two-Step got serious with that gun of his, he worked the slide so fast that it sounded like it was firing on full automatic. He could clear an area half the size of a football field in no time at all.

Following behind the point in the slack position came Corky and his M-60. Usually Brody didn't have the machine gun walk that close behind the point man, but with the jungle as thick as it was, he wanted to have as much firepower up front as he could get. Farmer covered Corky as he always did with his M-16, ready to load for him when the pig went into action.

Brody and Bunny where in the middle of the formation with the reporter and the two flyers, while Gardner took the drag with his M-79 grenade launcher.

In the dim light, the green and black colors of Two-Step's tiger-stripe camouflage uniform made him blend into the jungle, and he was almost lost from sight before he had gone ten meters. Corky had to keep a sharp eye out so as not to run into him in the brush.

Back in the middle of the formation, Janson became even more nervous. At least back at the base of the tree, he had known where he was. Now he didn't.

"Where are we going . . . ," he started to ask Gabe.

Brody clamped his hand over the man's mouth and leaned his face in real close.

"One more word out of you, fuckhead," he whispered hoarsely in the reporter's ear, "and I'm going to cut your fucking throat. You got that?"

Janson gulped and nodded his head.

Brody took his hand away and moved up closer to the point. He had meant exactly what he had said to Janson. They were in enough trouble already without some fucking civilian running his mouth off in the woods. If he had to kill him and leave the body, it was no sweat off his nuts. He could always say that Janson had wandered off during a firefight.

Brody heard a hiss from the man in front of him and saw Farmer drop to the ground. He went down and crawled up beside him. Farmer pointed toward the front of their little patrol. Brody looked and saw Corky behind a tree, motioning for him to come forward.

He got to the tree at the same time that Two-Step crawled out of the brush in front of him. The Indian had a grim look on his face. He pointed off to their left and opened and closed his hand three times. There were at least fifteen NVA on that side. They were in some real deep shit!

Brody shrugged his shoulders, silently asking what were they going to do.

Two-Step made a curving motion with his hand off to the right. He wanted to try to swing way out on that side and get around them. Brody nodded. They didn't have any other choice. They sure as hell didn't want to get into a fight where they were. Their best chance was to make it to the mountaintop. If they could get up there, they might have a fighting chance.

He went back down their path and whispered in each man's ear as he passed, telling them what they were going to try. He didn't bother telling Janson a thing.

After two hours of very slow travel, the men had made it to the base of the mountain, and Brody called a rest halt. The NVA were still out there searching the jungle for them. Every so often they could hear them. So far, they had been lucky.

He went up to where Two-Step was lying under a big clump of brush. "How long till we get to the top?" he whispered.

The Indian shrugged. "An hour, maybe."

Brody looked down at his watch. Under the triple canopy, it was hard to tell how much daylight they had left, but it was only two o'clock. They still had time to be picked up today.

"You go ahead," the Indian said. "Take Bunny, Farmer, and the pilots with you. I'll keep Corky and JJ here with me to cover your rear."

Brody nodded. It was a good plan. He didn't like splitting their small group, but when he reached the top, he could set up and cover them on their way up. Silently, he made his way back and told the others.

When the break was over, Brody took his group and started up the steep side of the mountain. Not only did they have to fight the dense jungle, they had to do it while moving uphill.

About halfway up, Janson collapsed. He wasn't as young as the grunts, nor hardened by months of humping the brush. Brody had been keeping an eye on him all day and knew that Janson was having trouble keeping up. He halted and went back to the man. The reporter looked like he was about to die, and Brody suspected he was suffering from heat exhaustion.

"Come on, on your feet." Quietly he reached down to the exhausted man.

"Leave me here," Janson panted. "I can't make it any further."

"Yes, you can." Brody took his canteen from his field belt. "Here, have a little water and a couple salt tabs."

The reporter drank deeply.

"Hey, not too much at once," Brody cautioned.

"Thanks."

"No sweat," Brody said dryly. "Now let's get going."

Janson painfully got to his feet. "You're trying to kill me, aren't you?"

Brody met his eyes. "I really don't give a shit if you die, mister. But I'm not leaving you behind unless you're dead, so let's move it."

They hadn't gone another ten steps before Brody heard the characteristic roar of Two-Step's sawed-off shotgun, followed by ripping bursts of AK fire.

The slopes had caught up with them!

"Di-di!" he yelled up to the others. It was no time to be cautious. They had to reach the top of the hill before the gooks did.

Janson put on a burst of speed, suddenly not tired anymore. Brody smiled when he saw the reporter scrambling through the tangled underbrush. All it had taken was a little AK fire to motivate him.

Behind him, he heard Corky's sixty working out, snapping out short bursts. And over the chatter of the machine gun came the sharp crumps of Gardner's thumper grenades exploding in the jungle.

Just then Farmer broke through to the top of the mountain.

"Brody!" he yelled back down. "We made it!"

Brody was panting when he dashed the last few meters up the side of the hill and broke out into the open. The top of the mountain was almost bare, spotted only by a few trees and scattered underbrush. It was almost perfect for a small perimeter as well as being a good pickup zone for the extraction.

He got his people into their positions and started back down the hill to bring the rest of them up. The firing had gotten more intense. He could count at least a dozen AKs. He checked the hand grenades on his ammo pouches. He only had four, and he had a feeling that he was going to need every last one of them.

Halfway down the hill, he ran into Gardner crouched down behind a boulder.

"Two-Step and Cork are coming," the big man panted. He slapped another short, stubby 40mm round into the breech of his thumper and snapped it shut with a flick of his wrist. Throwing it to his shoulder, he triggered it off. They could see the slow-moving grenade as it sailed through the air and disappeared into the jungle with a puff of dirty black smoke.

Corky came crashing out of the brush, the barrel of his sixty smoking. He dove behind the rock and quickly loaded another ammo belt into the receiver. *"Tu madre!"* he muttered.

"Where's the Indian?" Brody asked.

"He's 'bout fifty meters out, over on the left, getting ready to spring a 'bush on 'em."

Brody checked the magazine in his sixteen. "I'll go give him a hand."

He slithered down the hill, keeping a sharp eye out for the Indian's camouflage uniform. He found him lying behind a tree. Two-Step whirled around, bringing his sawed-off to bear on him.

"Jesus!" he whispered. "You scared the shit outta me!"

"Didn't want you to have all the fun by yourself," Brody grinned. Pulling two grenades from his ammo pouch, he tossed one to the Indian and slid in beside him. In front of them, they heard men crawling through the brush. They waited till the NVA were almost on top of them.

In one motion, they lobbed the grenades in front of them, followed up with long bursts of fire, and took off up the hill to where Corky and Gardner were waiting. Behind them, they heard high-pitched screams when the frags went off.

From the big boulder, Corky and Gardner kept up a steady stream of fire until Brody and Two-Step got under cover with them. Suddenly, the jungle was quiet. After a few minutes, Brody whispered, "Let's go."

The four grunts cautiously started back up the hill,

moving as fast as they could but still keeping a careful watch on their rear. They made it all the way up without anyone taking another shot at them.

"How many of them you think are out there?" Brody asked once they had rejoined the others.

"At least a platoon," Two-Step answered, stuffing shotgun shells into the magazine underneath the barrel of his piece. "But I think we got them thinned out quite a bit."

Brody got to his knees and looked around. It was high time that they tried to get out of there. "Bunny!" he called out. "Radio!"

The FO crawled over to him and handed him the handset. Brody took a quick reading on his compass and aimed the Prick-25 antenna in the direction of Camp Radcliff. This far away, they needed all the help they could get to reach their basecamp. He keyed the handset. "Python, Python, this is Blue Two, Blue Two, over."

Nothing came back but the hiss of the carrier wave. They should have been high up enough to get through. He switched frequencies and tried for the Battalion Tactical Operations Center. They had bigger antennas and might be able to pick him up. "Crazy Bull, Crazy Bull, this is Blue Two, Blue Two. Come in, over."

"This is Crazy Bull," came the voice in the handset. "Go ahead."

"This is Blue Two. I need you to relay a message to Python Operations. Python Five Eight is down, and we need an extract ASAP. We are at nine-five-four eight-three-eight. How copy, over?"

"This is Crazy Bull. Roger, copy Five Eight down, need extract at nine-five-four eight-three-eight. Over."

"That's an emergency extract, tell 'em to haul ass. We got gooks crawling all over us. Over."

"Roger, copy. I have flight time to your location of three zero mikes, over."

"This is Two. Roger, out."

Brody gave the handset back to Bunny. Thirty minutes

was going to be cutting it a little too close for his taste. He had just started crawling back to his position when a burst of AK fire came ripping over his head.

"Fuck!" Brody exploded. The gooks had circled around and were coming in on their right flank. He ripped off a long burst at the wood line and saw an olive-uniformed body fall out of the tree.

"Bunny," he asked, dropping the empty magazine from the bottom of his M-16 and slapping a fresh one into place. "Can you get us some artillery? I don't think that Python's going to get here in time."

The FO looked confused. He glanced over to the reporter. "I don't know, Brody. I'm not sure where we're at."

Brody whipped the map back out of his side pants pocket and stabbed his finger down on it. "Here. Can you do it?"

"I don't know. We're a long ways off."

"Bunny!" Brody said sharply. "You're the best fucking FO I've ever seen. And if you've ever needed to shoot in your whole life, man, this is the time. If we don't get some help here real quick, we're all going to be dead. You can do it, Bunny, you can do it."

The FO took the map, rapidly counted the grid squares, and did a quick calculation in his head. "Hey, I think I can get the long toms from Rhonda!"

"Good man," Brody clapped him on the shoulder. "Now get those fucking cannon cockers working. I don't think we can hold out till those choppers get here."

The long toms, the M-107 175mm, self-propelled, long-range guns could fire their 174-pound shells a distance of over twenty miles with extreme accuracy. There was a battery of the long-barreled weapons stationed at Firebase Rhonda, only eighteen miles away. It would be a long shoot, and their accuracy wasn't as good at the longer ranges, but Bunny would give it a try.

He had almost forgotten the short round at the LZ the

other day until he looked over and saw Janson watching him closely.

"Hey, Mr. Reporter," Bunny called out. "If I fuck up this time, you're going to die right along with us. How'd ya like that?"

The FO laughed and keyed the handset to the radio.

CHAPTER 10

The Song Re Valley

"Red Leg Bravo, Red Leg Bravo," Bunny urgently radioed from the mountaintop. "This is Blue Two Tango, Blue Two Tango. Fire mission, over."

"Two Tango, this is Bravo," came the return call from Fire Base Rhonda. "I hear you weak, but steady. Send your mission, over."

"This is Two Tango. I'm at nine-five-four eight-three-eight and I need one-seven-five, VT, danger close. Pop one overhead and I'll adjust, over."

"This is Bravo, Roger, copy nine-five-four eight-three-eight, one-seven-five, VT, danger close, will adjust. Tango, are you sure on the danger close? Over."

"This is Tango, Roger, good copy. I say again danger close. Get it coming," he shouted. "We're up to our ass in dinks."

"This is Bravo, wait one, out."

It took a long time to get a battery of 175's in action. The big guns simply did not respond as fast as a battery of the lighter 105mm guns. Not only were they bigger and heavier, but their ammunition was separately loaded. First the projectile was rammed into the breech, and then the powder bags followed, unlike the 105's which were loaded with one big cartridge.

Also, Bunny was calling for the most dangerous artillery shoot of all, the artillery's version of a bayonet charge, done only in extreme circumstances. He was calling for air-burst rounds to come in "danger close," less than one hundred meters from their position. The calculations from the fire direction center had to be spot-on. If someone in the FDC misplaced a decimal point, and one of the big shells burst over their heads, they would all be dead before they even had time to realize that someone had fucked up.

Usually, 175's did not fire danger close. That mission was given to the shorter-range 155mm howitzers because the bigger guns were not all that accurate at their greatest range. But this time Bunny had no choice. He crossed his fingers that the cannon cockers back at the firebase were not hungover.

It seemed like an eternity before the thin voice on the radio said, "Tango, this is Bravo, shot over."

"This is Tango, shot out," Bunny acknowledged.

The first round was on the way. The sound of a speeding train filled the air.

"This is Bravo. Splash, over."

"Roger. Splash out."

The 175mm round exploded in the air at least a thousand meters away from them to the north. Brody had given him the wrong location, one grid square off! Bunny leapt for the radio.

"Red Leg, this is Tango. Major correction. My correct location is one thousand, I say again, one thousand meters to the Sierra. Over."

"Bravo, Roger copy, wait one."

The calculations for artillery fire were based on the FO's reported position. Since he had given them the wrong location, the FDC had to do them all over again. Again the FO waited.

"Blue Tango, this is Red Leg Bravo, shot, over."

"Tango, shot out."

This time, the burst coincided with Bravo's warning of "splash," and it was almost on target, just a little behind them and off to the right.

"Bravo, this is Blue Tango. From registration, drop one hundred, left one hundred, fire a three-sided box. Over."

"Bravo, Roger, copy." There was a long pause before Bravo came back on the air. "Tango, this is Bravo, shot over."

"Hit it!" Bunny screamed, burying his head in his hands. The sound of a dozen speeding trains coming one right after the other filled the air. A hundred feet above the tops of the trees, the air blossomed with puffs of dirty black smoke as the rounds exploded on all three sides of them.

"Bravo, this is Tango," Bunny screamed over the thundering detonations. "You're right on target, keep it coming!"

"This is Bravo, Roger."

The concussion of the big rounds slapped at the grunts' ears and deadly, red-hot shards of shrapnel whizzed through the air. A foot-long, jagged piece of steel slammed into the ground a few inches from Bunny's head. It sizzled and steamed in the damp earth.

This was a little too close for comfort, but Bunny did not call for check fire. He had asked for danger close and he was getting it.

With a vengeance.

Five klicks away from the beleaguered grunts on the mountaintop, the two gunships piloted by Rat Gaines and Lance Warlokk were escorting a speeding slick to make the pickup.

"Captain," Warrant Officer Joe Schmuchatelli, Rat's copilot-gunner, called back from the front cockpit in the sleek Cobra. "It looks like Brody's got himself a little artillery support going."

"That's a rodg," Gaines called back.

From high in the sky, they could see smoke and the flashes

of detonating artillery shells around the bare mountaintop off to their right. It looked like hell had come to visit that part of Vietnam.

"It's probably coming in from Rhonda," Gaines said when he checked his map. "We'd better stay clear of that until he gets done shooting."

He keyed his throat mike. "Python, Python, this is Lead. I want to get out of the artillery flight path. Vector to the north and orbit, over."

Quick rogers followed from both of the other choppers as Gaines banked away. Getting hit by an artillery shell in mid-flight was a real good way to ruin your whole day. When that happened, there usually wasn't enough left of the chopper and its crew to even bury, much less identify.

Gaines switched over to the FM tactical radio to talk to Brody. "Blue Two, Blue Two, this is Python Lead on your push, over."

"Python, this is Two Tango," came the voice in his helmet headphones. "Go ahead."

Gaines realized that he was talking to Brody's artillery FO, the guy who was controlling that artillery fire mission. "Two Tango, this is Lead. If you'll call off that arty, we'll come in and finish them off for you. Over."

"This is Tango, Roger, wait one."

"Brody!" the FO yelled over the thundering crash of the 175's. "The choppers are here!"

Brody couldn't hear a word he was saying so Bunny pointed up to the sky. In the distance, three black specks flew in a circle. He made a slashing motion across his throat.

"Bravo, this is Tango," Bunny shouted into the microphone. "Cease fire, cease fire. Over."

"Bravo, Roger."

The last round was a Willie Peter, a blossoming white cloud of white phosphorus that grew in the air above them, the signal that the long-range fire mission was over.

The sudden silence was deafening.

The grunts cautiously picked themselves up off of the ground and looked around. The tree line was shredded, and the air was sharp with smoke and the harsh smell of the explosives. No one was shooting at them.

Bunny slowly got to his feet, a big grin on his face. He looked over to where Janson still lay huddled on the ground with his arms up over his head. "How'd you like that shit, Mr. Reporter Man?"

Janson had no comment. His ears were ringing, and he was dazed. He would have dearly loved to have driven his fist into the jeering grunt's face, but he couldn't move. He was having a difficult time realizing that he was still alive.

Bunny walked over and stood next to him, his hands on his hips. "You know, dude, you really lucked out this time. No short rounds." The FO laughed.

Janson continued to hug the ground and didn't say a word.

A single shot rang out. Bunny heard the round pass right by his head.

"Sniper!" he cried out, dropping to the ground.

Brody low-crawled over to Bunny and took the radio handset from him. "Python, this is Blue Two. We've still got some bad guys hiding in the woods to the south of us, can you take care of 'em for us, over?"

"Two, this is Lead, Roger. Keep your heads down, we're rolling in now."

Brody looked up and saw the tan-and-green camouflaged Cobra, with the bloody red shark's mouth painted on its nose, sweep down over the tree line. The rocketpods under the stub wings spouted flame, and 2.75-inch rockets lanced to the ground, leaving a trail of white smoke. Over the hissing *whoosh* of the rockets, Brody heard the ripping sound of the turret-mounted minigun spitting 4,000 rounds a minute into the jungle.

The explosions of the rocket warheads weren't as loud as the thundering artillery had been, but they went off with a sharp crack that sent shrapnel tearing into the underbrush. The solid stream of 7.62mm fire from the minigun shredded what little was left of the already broken foliage.

What the artillery barrage had not torn up, Rat Gaines was taking care of, and he was doing a great job of it.

Just as Gaines banked his Cobra away, Warlokk opened up with his UH-1C Huey Hog, coming in from the other direction. Warlokk's gunship was a real Hog in the air. It mounted the XM-21 weapons system, two 7.62mm miniguns on the side pylons along with rocketpods and a XM-5 thumper system in the nose turret. It wasn't as fast or as maneuverable as Rat's AH-1 Cobra, but when Warlokk talked, the gooks listened.

Warlokk bore in on the target, his nose turret and side guns blazing. Suddenly, from down the mountainside, a machine gun opened up on the diving Huey. Lines of green tracer fire reached for him.

Warlokk kicked down on the rudder pedal and slammed the cyclic control stick to the side. His speeding gunship skidding in the air, throwing off the enemy gunner's aim. The tracer fire fell behind him.

Rat's Cobra had completed its turn, and he dove for the point in the jungle where the enemy fire originated. In the front cockpit, "Alphabet" Schmuchatelli leaned forward against his shoulder harness and peered through his gunsight. His gloved fingers rested lightly on his firing controls.

When the source of the tracer fire was centered in the lighted sight, he triggered off everything he had. Two-point-seven-five HE rockets salvoed from the pods. The thumper spit forty-mike-mike grenades, and the minigun put thousands of rounds a minute into the jungle.

Now the gooks really had a problem.

As soon as Rat was clear, Warlokk came in again and kicked their asses, adding to the destruction.

It was not necessary a third time. Only a smoking hole in the jungle marked the spot where the NVA machine gunner had decided that he wanted to shoot at a chopper. It had been a bad decision for him.

When the gunships pulled away, it was quiet again on the mountain. Only the crackle of a fire that had been started by the artillery could be heard.

"Blue Two, Python Lead, over."

"Two, go."

"Lead, how's it look down there now, over?"

"This is Two. It looks good to me. But wait one. Let me sweep the area and check it out. Over."

"Roger, I'll stand by."

Motioning to Two-Step, Brody got up and headed for the tree line under the protection of the two orbiting gunships. The two men were in there only a few minutes before they came out with their arms full of AK-47 assault rifles.

"Python, this is Blue Two. It looks like they've *di-di*'ed. You got yourself a body count of seven that we could find. Over."

"This is Lead, Roger. The slick's on its way, pop smoke."

"Roger, smoke out." Brody pulled the pin on a smoke grenade and tossed it on the ground at the edge of the clearing. Billowing purple smoke rose up into the still air.

"This is Lead, I see goofy grape, over."

"Roger, purple," Brody confirmed.

"Two, this is Python Niner Three," radioed the slick pilot. "I'm coming in now."

"Roger." Brody turned to the men. "Let's go, guys."

The grunts clustered around the smoke grenade as the chopper made its approach. Brody put his back to the wind and held his rifle over his head to signal where the pilot was supposed to land.

When Janson saw the slick flare out over the small clearing, for the first time since the whole thing had started he thought that he might live through it. He slowly got to his feet and found that his legs were shaking.

As he scrambled his way on board, he vowed that he would never set foot on an actual mission again. Now he knew why the rest of the press corps either hung around the Saigon bars or went on their safe little guided tours of secure areas. A man could get killed out here.

From now on, Janson decided, he would write his war stories from the safety of the air-conditioned bar at the Caravel Hotel like most of the other war correspondents, and quit trying to go out in the field to get the big story that would put him on top again. He had had just about all the excitement that he could deal with and desperately needed a drink. As Janson climbed in past the port-side doorgun, Bunny caught the expression on the reporter's face.

"What's the matter, Mr. Janson," he asked sweetly. "You shit in your pants?"

Brody laughed.

Walt Johnson was standing at the edge of the division maintenance area when the recovery flight returned with *Pegasus* loaded in the sling under the Chinook. He had sent the big, twin-rotor CH-47 Chinook—affectionately called a "shithook"—out with a two-gunship escort to bring back what was left of Gabe's slick. From what Gabe had told him, it was intact enough for him to examine to find out why it had crashed.

Observing the chopper as it was gently lowered to the ground under the watchful eye of the recovery NCO, Walt saw that the slick wasn't badly damaged. The people in his repair shops could have her patched up and back in the air in no time at all. One skid was bent, the copilot's canopy was split, and the rotor head would have to be replaced. But that seemed to be about all the damage. Cliff Gabriel had made one hell of a landing. The tail boom didn't even seem to be bent, and that was usually the first thing to go in a hard landing.

As soon as the sling was unhooked from the rotor head, the maintenance officer clambered onto the top of the machine and started taking the access panels off the engine compartment. It was about as good a place as any to start his inspection.

CHAPTER 11

Camp Radcliff, An Khe.

It was early evening and still light outside, but things were already getting under way in the Python Club. Rat Gaines had made it a tradition in Python Flight to hold a crash party every time one of their choppers was shot down.

If no one had been killed, it was a riotous party. If someone had died, it was a wake. But no matter, the party went on.

Gaines didn't have to be a psychiatrist to know that men in combat needed a chance to let off a little steam every now and then. And right after a helicopter had gone down was the best time that he could think of to do it. Every time a chopper crashed, whether from enemy fire or mechanical failure, it forcefully brought home the fact to everyone that it could happen to them. Getting smashed was the time-honored military way of dealing with the cold, hard facts of war. When you're dead drunk, you don't worry too much about little things like falling out of the sky.

Tonight Gaines was instituting a new tradition by making a special presentation to Cliff Gabriel. He was going to award him the "Royal Order of the Broken Wing" in honor of the fact that he had been shot down or crashed ten times since he had been flying in Vietnam. As near as Gaines could tell, that was an in-country record, and he felt that Gabe deserved some recognition for a somewhat dubious achievement. Gaines had had the people in the maintenance shop cut a two-inch section from the tip of *Pegasus*'s bent tail rotor. It had been engraved with Gabe's name and the date of his tenth crash.

When the company commander was satisfied that everything was ready for the evening's festivities, Gaines grabbed his black Stetson hat adorned with his rank bars and gold crossed sabers, and headed out the door. He had a dinner date with Lisa Maddox and he didn't dare be late. As he drove over to the nurses' quarters at the 45th Surge to pick her up, he couldn't help but wonder what little surprise she had in store for him.

Usually the blond nurse was very even-tempered but last month she had gotten royally pissed at him because he had not been one hundred percent truthful about a mission he had going. Ever since then, she had been acting a little strange, friendly one minute, cold the next. One thing for sure—Rat was never bored when he was around her.

Lisa was waiting in front of the nurses' building when he pulled up into the parking lot. She had on a clean set of fatigues, but she had let her long blond mane down and was wearing makeup. The effect was dazzling.

"Can you help me, miss?" Gaines asked her. "I'm looking for a Lisa Maddox. She's rather plain looking and usually wears her beautiful hair pinned up so it doesn't get in her way."

"Watch it, Gaines. You're looking for a fat lip."

"Oops, sorry, Lisa," he said with a grin. "I almost didn't recognize you there."

She swung into the passenger seat of the Jeep. "Where are we going?"

"I thought we'd try the Headquarters Club for a change.

I'm getting tired of our cooks burning the reheated C-rats they try to pass off as food."

"That sounds good to me. I'm hungry."

Gaines liked a woman with a good appetite.

The officers' club at Division headquarters had a limited menu, but the food was good. It had to be. Sometimes the general ate there.

He ordered the ham steak with a baked potato, and she tried the fried chicken. Their meals soon arrived and, as usual, they were well-prepared.

"How's yours?" she asked.

"Not all that bad," he replied, looking at a piece of ham on his fork. "It's really hard to screw up a slice of canned ham. How's the chicken today?"

"Crisp for a change. Want some?"

"No, thanks." He knew that grease was the primary flavoring agent used by army cooks no matter what they were cooking. "I've had my quota of lard this month. I ate breakfast last week."

"Well," Gaines said, finishing his coffee. "I'd like to linger over a glass of wine, but I think it's about time that we put in an appearance at the club." He glanced at his watch. "They should be dancing on the tables by now."

Lisa laughed. "You do have the strangest collection of people down there, Rat. I'm surprised that you don't keep them in cages."

"Yes, but under their crude exteriors, they truly have hearts of gold. Most of them are just misunderstood boys, and like their fearless leader, all they need is the love of a good woman to keep them on the straight-and-narrow."

Lisa looked closely at him, trying to figure out if he had just made a serious comment about himself. Too often she couldn't tell when Gaines was joking, particularly when it had anything to do with committing himself to her. Ever since their first attempt to make love had been so rudely interrupted, he had been real skitterish around her, like he was afraid that taking her to bed would turn their relationship into a lifetime commitment.

She still wasn't sure where she stood on that issue herself, but she had decided that she wanted to finish what they had started. If nothing else, she wanted to try it again just so she could finally see what lay behind Rat's smiling eyes and smooth southern charm.

She smiled. "Let's go feed the animals."

Lisa was quiet on the drive over to the club, busily planning how she was going to get Rat Gaines into bed. Unlike the other officers who had taken her out, he had never come on to her, which, as she knew, was a big part of the reason why she was so curious about him.

They could hear the party going a full block away. Someone had the jury-rigged juke box turned up full blast, and it was playing the Rolling Stones. Mick Jagger's ragged voice screamed about not being able to get satisfaction, accompanied by a dozen drunken male voices singing along with him.

"Are you sure that you want to take a defenseless woman into a place like that?" she asked.

Gaines laughed. "Don't worry, I'll protect you."

"That's what I'm afraid of."

Rat glanced over at her. Had he detected a slight note of sarcasm there? The beautiful blond nurse had a cat-eating-cream smile on her face. Gaines sighed. Not for the first time he realized that he really did not understand women.

He came to a stop in the graveled parking lot and jumped out to open the nonexistent Jeep door on her side. "Your coach has arrived, Princess."

"Clown," she smiled at him.

The juke box broke down again just as they walked in the door, and the silence was deafening. It was a perfect entrance.

Cheers broke out in the smoke-filled room when the men saw their favorite nurse. They also booed when they saw that she was with the pilot. Gaines slowly took his Stetson off and, with a big grin plastered all over his face, made a sweeping, cavalier bow. *Eat your hearts out, mothers,* he thought.

When hammering on the juke box wouldn't get it going again, a bunch of bombed chopper pilots at the end of the bar started lustfully singing a traditional military ballad at the top of their voices. It was a little ditty sung to the tune of the German Christmas carol "Tannenbaum". It was called, "We Like it Here."

We like it here, we like it here,
You fucking A, we like it here.
Although we have malaria,
We still police the area.
We like it here, we like it here,
You fucking A, we like it here.

None of the singers could remember any of the other verses so they kept singing that one over and over. About the third time they sang it, people started throwing empty beer cans but they only sang louder. Someone finally turned a fire extinguisher on them. That shut them up.

Rat guided Lisa over to the bar in the middle of the room. "What're you having?"

She looked him straight in the eye. "Whatever you're drinking," she purred.

"Good girl, I like women with courage." Gaines turned to the bartender. "Two Southern Comforts on the rocks."

"Coming up, sir."

When the drinks arrived, Gaines picked his up. "Here's looking at you, kid."

Bogart couldn't have done it better.

Lisa groaned. She could already tell it was going to be one of those nights.

Back in the Blues' tent, Gardner sat on his bunk and tried to write Sandra a letter. He had the place all to himself, and he had fully recovered from the night before. There was something about crashing in the jungle and fighting your way out that cleared up a hangover like magic. He thought that it was time that he got back to trying to deal with his problem.

He started a letter, wrote half of a sentence, and wadded the paper up. He knew what he wanted to say to her, but it just wasn't coming out right. How did he say what he was feeling without it sounding like he was crying, or begging her to stay with him? He stared at the paper as if the right words would appear if he would just think hard enough.

He tried again and got a sentence and a half before throwing it on the floor beside the previous attempt. It was going to take hours at that rate.

He thought of going back to the EM club and seeing if Mai was on duty tonight, but he wasn't too sure that that was a real good idea right now. He was afraid that seeing her again so soon would confuse him to the point that he would not be able to write Sandra at all. He did want to see Mai again, that was a fact. But he really wanted to get the letter out of the way first.

He took out another sheet of paper and tried it again. He had gotten two sentences down this time when Brody strolled into the tent.

"Hey, JJ!" he called out. "What say you and me motor on down to Sin City for a couple of cold ones?"

"No, thanks, I think I'd probably better stay here. If I run into the MP again, I'm likely to find my ass in deep shit."

"Aw, fuck that guy and the horse he rode in on, man." Brody put his boot up on the foot locker at the end of the bunk. "Come on. They're reopening The Pink Butterfly tonight and throwing a big party. You don't want to miss that, the drinks are on the house."

"Well . . ."

"Goddammit, let's go." Brody took his arm. "Come on."

"Okay." Gardner stood up. "Let me change into a clean uniform first."

"Don't take all night, JJ. The beer's getting cold."

"Walt, my man," Gaines called out when he saw the maintenance officer making his way through the crowd. "Have a drink."

"What the fuck for?" Walt snapped back. He had grease ground into his face, his uniform was filthy, and he had busted the skin over most of the knuckles on both hands. "To celebrate Gabe's having wrecked another chopper?"

He shoved his way through the last couple of feet and bellied up to the bar. "Gimme a beer!" he snapped. The bartender handed him a cold Bud.

"But what the fuck, that's what they pay me for, isn't it? Piecing choppers back together so you assholes can take them out and crash them again."

Rat could tell that Walt had been having a particularly interesting day. He threw his arm around the maintenance officer's shoulder. "Why don't you tell Uncle Rat what's wrong."

"What's wrong?" Walt swallowed half of his beer in one gulp. "What's wrong?" he wiped his mouth on the back of his hand, leaving even more grease on his face. "I'll tell you what's fucking wrong, Rat Gaines!"

He took another drink.

"Someone's been shooting armor-piercing holes in your fucking choppers, that's what's wrong."

Rat's heart stopped. "That's not too fucking funny, Walt."

"This ain't, either." He dug into his pants pocket. His hand came out with a bullet, which he gave to the pilot.

Rat examined it closely. It looked to be about a 7.62mm round and it had a steel core. "Where'd you get this thing?"

"Outta Gabe's chopper. I found four holes in the skin

of the engine compartment and that round came out of the hydraulic pump.''

Rat looked around the club. ''Don't say anything about this to him right now. I want to have this checked out first.''

''Be my guest. But you gotta buy me another drink to keep me quiet.''

''Bartender,'' Gaines called out. ''Put this man's drinks on my tab. Both of them.''

''Yes, sir.''

''Gaines, you got class.''

''Well, somebody has to set the tone around here and be a good example for these men to follow.'' Rat waved his arms to indicate the two drunks passed out face first on the tables, and the few serious seductions of Red Cross girls that were going on in the dark corners.

Walt followed his gesture. ''Yep, you're right. This is really a class act.''

CHAPTER 12

Sin City, An Khe

"Be back in a flash," Brody said, getting up from their table in The Pink Butterfly Bar. "I've gotta tap a kidney."

Gardner reached down into his pants pocket and pulled out a handful of wadded-up MPC notes. "How 'bout getting us a couple more beers on your way back?"

"You got that shit right."

The Pink Butterfly was wall-to-wall people from all over Camp Radcliff, and everybody was having a good time. The bar had been shut down for a couple of weeks after the last owner, a woman they had all called Big Mama, had been killed in a shoot-out with the Military Intelligence.

In the aftermath of the shooting, it had been discovered that she had been a spy for the VC for a long time, using the girls who worked the back rooms to get information from unsuspecting GIs. The sex-for-information operation had been very effective, and the authorities had thought about keeping the place closed, but a new owner had been found who was completely clean, and the bar was allowed to re-open.

Gardner was finishing off his beer when he heard a voice

behind him. ''Well, well, what do we have here? The smart motherfucker who thinks he can get away with punching out an MP.''

Gardner turned around to see a man in civilian clothes, standing with two other men. He didn't recognize him, but he knew that this had to be the guy he had hit last night.

''Look, man.'' He stood up and tried to apologize. ''I'm really sorry about that. I was really fucked up and I didn't know what I was doing. Here, let me buy you a drink.''

''When I get done with you, motherfucker, you ain't going to be drinking nothing.''

''Hey.'' Gardner backed away from him. ''Look, man, I don't want any trouble. I told you I was drunk last night. I'm sorry.''

''You ain't drunk now, are you?'' the MP sneered, stepping up to him.

''What the fuck's going on here?'' Brody asked, walking up with two beers in his hands. He quickly set them on the table and moved in between the two men.

''Just what the fuck is it to you, asshole?'' the MP snarled.

Brody slowly looked him up and down. He looked like a typical MP, all mouth and no balls. He checked out the other two guys with him. They were the same. This was not going to be a problem.

He leaned closer to the MP and smiled. ''Well, let me just put it to you this way. You're talking to my man JJ, and he's a real good buddy of mine. Where we come from, when you talk to my buddy, you're also talking to me.'' He paused. ''Fuckhead.''

The MP bristled, but one of his friends broke in. ''Hey, man, let's cool it. We don't want a fight in here.''

Brody grinned. ''I didn't think so.''

The MP let his friends take him away. ''I'm going to be looking for you two motherfuckers,'' he warned.

''I can hardly wait,'' Brody laughed as he sat down.

''Hadn't we better get back to camp?'' Gardner asked.

''Why?'' Brody shrugged. ''They're not going to try anything tonight, they're off duty and they don't have their little clubs with them. Fuck 'em. Let's have another drink."

The two men sat back down.

"Thanks," Gardner said, raising his bottle.

"For what?"

"Lending a hand there."

"As Corky says, *'de nada.'* No fucking MP's going to mess with any of the Blues when I'm around."

"Speaking of the guys," JJ mused. "I wonder where they are tonight."

"Probably in the back, getting their asses hauled. I saw Farmer lurking in the corner when we came in. He had his hand down the pants of one of the bar girls and was talking his shit a mile a minute." Brody shook his head. "Man, is that kid ever cunt crazy. He'd save himself a lot of trouble if he'd just save his breath and pay up when they ask for the money. He ain't never going to get any pussy for free in this place."

Gardner didn't want to talk about women tonight, even bar girls, so he tried to change the subject. "When you going to go home, Treat?"

Brody ran a hand through his shock of blond hair. "Well, I don't know. I'm not sure that I am. I'm going to take a burst of six this week."

"A six-month extension?"

"Nope. I still got a little over two months to go on this one." He grinned. "I'm reenlisting for six years. I'm going to be a fucking lifer."

"Well, I'll be goddamned." Gardner stuck his hand out. "Congratulations."

"Yeah, that's what I thought. There're worse things in the world than being a professional grunt."

"That's a rodg. You could always be a fucking draft dodger."

"Yeah, that's lower than whale shit in the bottom of the ocean."

"I'll drink to that."

When the last of their beer was gone, Gardner made a run

for a couple more. He wasn't getting drunk at all. It was pissing him off, but he stuck with the beer. He knew better than to drink any of the bottled panther piss that the Vietnamese passed off as hard liquor. He wanted to get drunk, not puking, crawling blind.

The party was starting to get a little rowdy, and the new owner didn't want any trouble on his first night, so he called out the all-girl Korean band he had hired for the evening. When the four girls stepped up onto the makeshift stage in their skimpy halter tops and miniskirts, the crowd started cheering and whistling. They didn't quiet down until the girls started singing.

Watching the lead singer dancing around up on the stage in her white boots and crotch-length miniskirt trying for a Nancy Sinatra imitation wasn't doing Gardner any good—particularly since their table was so close to the stage. Each time she kicked her leg, he got an eyeful of tiger-striped bikini panties.

He gulped his beer. This was not why he had come down here this evening. He wanted to get away from women, not have some little bitch waving her pussy under his nose. When the band finished "These Boots Are Made for Walking," they broke into the "Limbo Rock," Chubby Checker style.

It brought down the house.

The way the girls did their version of the Limbo, they placed the limbo bar facing the audience. That way, as each girl hiked her already short skirt up over her hips when she wiggled her way under the bar, all that the GIs could see was pussy. Nice, plump Asian pussy. The girls in the back rooms would be working double time before too long.

Gardner groaned. "Treat," he yelled over the music and the cheers of the crowd. "Let's split this joint."

Brody laughed. "Okay, let's find someplace a little quieter."

There was almost a fight when they vacated their table. Everybody wanted to get closer to the show on stage. It was a little cooler outside in the open air. Brody looked around at the row of gaudy bars and whorehouses lining both sides of the dusty street.

"I know," he said. "How 'bout a bowl of soup?"

"Sounds good to me."

The two men had just rounded the corner of the building when four figures stepped out of the alley. All of them were carrying clubs. "Look what we got here," the MP sneered. "Howdy, assholes."

Brody burst into action, kicking out with his booted foot. "Gary Owen!" he yelled. "Gary Owen!"

His jungle boot connected with the nearest man's leg, knocking it out from under him and sending him to the ground.

A club smashed into his shoulder, numbing his arm. He saw Gardner unleash a powerful punch, catching one of the men in the gut. But his MP buddy hammered at him with his club, driving JJ to his knees.

If they didn't get some help quick, they were going to get beaten to death. Brody called out again, as loud as he could, "Gary Owen!"

Somebody grabbed his arms from behind, pinning them back. He lashed out to the rear with his foot, but the man sidestepped the blow. The first MP stepped up to him, his club drawn back.

"I told you to mind your own fucking business, motherfucker," he snarled as he swung.

Brody tried to duck and couldn't, but the blow didn't connect. When he opened his eyes, he saw Two-Step karate-kick the MP's gut. The man was down on his hands and knees, puking. The club lay unnoticed in the dirt.

The Indian's sudden appearance had startled the man holding Brody's arms, and the young sergeant was able to jerk loose. Spinning around, he caught the man in the throat with his extended forearm. As the MP clutched his throat and gagged for breath, Brody stepped up closer and kicked him in the nuts.

By this time, Two-Step had taken out Gardner's second opponent, and JJ was doing just fine with the last one on his own, hammering his man with repeated blows to the head. The last man went down just as Farmer came racing into the street.

"Where the fuck you been?" Brody panted, catching his breath. "Didn't you hear me call 'Gary Owen'?"

"What does that mean?" Farmer shrugged.

"That's the Seventh Cav battle cry, you dumb shit. It means someone's in trouble and needs help."

"Oh." Farmer walked over to one of the fallen MPs and kicked him in the side. "He was moving," he explained. "I didn't want him to get away."

"Drag 'em back into the alley," Brody ordered, glancing around to see if anyone had noticed the brief fight.

Brody personally got the ringleader to his feet. Holding his arm in a hammerlock, he walked him into the darkened alley. While the other grunts held their captives, Brody slammed his man up against the wall and grabbed his throat.

"What's your name, motherfucker?" he spat.

"Dillard," the MP said painfully.

"Okay, Dillard, here's how it is. If I hear one fucking word outta you or any of your buddies about this, I'm personally going to track your worthless ass down and cut your fucking nuts off. You got that, boy?" he shouted in the MP's face.

The man nodded his head.

"And," Brody continued, "if for some reason I'm not around to do that little job, the Indian will do it for me. Only, he'll skin your nuts before he cuts them off and feeds them to you. Furthermore, the next fucking time that you or any of your candy-ass buddies think you can fuck with the Echo Company Blues, they'd better think about something else or there's going to be a body count right here in Sin City."

Brody released the man and stepped back. "Any questions?"

The MP shook his head.

"I didn't think so. Now move out!"

The MPs quickly disappeared into the night.

"Thanks, man," Brody told Two-Step.

The Indian grinned. "I wouldn't have missed it for the world. But I fucking near didn't hear you call. The band was too loud."

"Gardner and I were just going to get a soup. Want to join us?"

"Sure."

"Farmer?"

"Ah, no thanks, Sarge. I've got to get back. I left my hat in there."

"Right," Brody laughed. "Drill her one time for me."

Farmer grinned.

The Graves Registration Facility was one of the coolest places in Camp Radcliff since it had to be air-conditioned. But even the cold carried a faint smell of death.

In the operating room, a surgeon was doing a complete autopsy on what was left of a man's burned body. He was trying to learn why the pilot had lost control of his chopper and crashed into another one in midair. Although the body was badly burned, it was the least damaged of the four pilots who had died in the spectacular crash.

After having spent all day in surgery, it was the last thing in the world that the doctor wanted to be doing. But it had to be done. Of the four choppers that went down, the fires had been so intense that little remained except puddles of melted aluminum, the turbines, and the transfer cases. Two of the tail booms had survived more or less intact, but they weren't much help in answering the question of what had caused the crash.

"The outer layers of skin in the thoracic region are burned through to the muscle tissue," he said, dictating the results of his findings into a small tape recorder.

"No superficial signs of injury."

He had placed a wet towel over the burned face so he wouldn't have the pilot's melted eyes staring at him while he worked.

Taking up a small electric saw, he cut through the cadaver's sternum from the collar bone to the bottom of the rib cage. Using a retractor, he forcefully pried the chest cavity open. After a cursory inspection, he cut the major vessels to the heart, reached in, and brought it out into the light.

There was a wound in it. A bullet hole!

He went back to the rib cage and reexamined the area right over the heart. Under the layer of burned and blackened skin and muscle, one of the ribs had a small nick in it where the round had entered the body.

The man had been shot!

He turned the body over and looked for an exit wound but there was none. He rolled the body back down, reached into the chest cavity and felt around for the bullet. He found the hole it had made in the lung and traced it down to the spine. It was lodged in the T-4 vertebrae. The doctor pulled it out.

Wiping the congealed blood from the copper-clad round, he held it up to the light and examined it.

"Subject was killed by a seven-point-six-two-millimeter bullet," he dictated. "The round entered the chest, pierced the left ventricle of the heart, and exited, lodging in the fourth thoracic vertebra."

He dropped the bullet into the stainless-steel tray by the autopsy table and started stripping off his latex gloves.

He didn't need to go any further now that he knew what had caused the crash. There could be no question about it.

It was very difficult to fly a helicopter with a bullet through the heart.

CHAPTER 13

The Song Re Valley

KGB Major Gregor Zerinski sat as his desk in the radio room of a small building at his jungle headquarters and worked on his operations report. The harsh light from the kerosene lantern glared off the paper, forcing him to squint, but he wanted to get the report finished and sent out first thing in the morning.

At the other end of the building, he could hear Spetsnaz troopers partying again, but he didn't mind. They were young men and they needed their outlets, particularly outlets as nice as the young Vietnamese girls who had been provided for their use. He made a mental note to himself to write a favorable report on the North Vietnamese commander who was looking after the details of their supply and support. So far, he had done an exemplary job.

This was the first time that Zerinski had worked with the Spetsnaz, his country's elite special-forces troops, and he was impressed with them, too. The Spetsnaz were part of the Soviet military intelligence, the GRU. As a KGB officer, Zerinski had had very little contact with the GRU—two organizations that were more often than not enemies rather than allies, competing for power in the Soviet system.

The KGB had been operating in the Far East ever since the early days of the Russian Revolution. The GRU, however, had no Far East connections, having operated traditionally in Europe and the Middle East. When they had wanted to test their new Dragunov SVD sniper rifle in Vietnam, they had been forced to deal with the KGB.

So far, the Western world was not aware of this new rifle, and Zerinski had to keep it that way. Yuravitch, his GRU counterpart, wanted to take one of the teams to do some close-in work at one of the Yankee firebases. Zerinski vetoed that idea. There was too great of a chance that, if anything went wrong, one of the rifles would be captured.

Like too many Russians, Yuravitch had a low opinion of the American army after reading too much Russian propaganda. Zerinski, however, knew what the Americans were like. He had faced them in the field and he had had drinks with them in their clubs. He knew exactly how dangerous they could be.

The courage and tenacity of the average American GI had amazed Zerinski at first. They were some of the best field troops that he had ever seen. Not only did they fight well, they fought smart. He was glad that he was not commanding Vietnamese troops against the Americans. Most of the time, it was no contest. The Americans won hands down.

The KGB man knew that plans were being made in Hanoi to invade the major cities in the south early next spring, and he couldn't believe that the North Vietnamese were going to do something so stupid. The Americans would be caught off guard at first. The rose-colored glasses that were part of the uniform of every high-ranking officer in Saigon would make sure of that. But after the initial surprise, the NVA would be slaughtered like sheep.

Zerinski was a good Communist but he was not blind. He was well aware of the shortcomings of his wartime allies as well as those of his potential enemies, and he reported those shortcomings to Moscow. It would be on the KGB section chief's desk in Hanoi within the week. Now it was time for him to relax.

He hoped that the young Spetsnaz studs had left him a little vodka and one of the girls. The KGB man smiled to himself. There were some compensations for having to live like an animal in a bug-infested, steaming jungle. He got up from his chair and turned down the lamp. Rank had its priviledges, and he was going to exercise them.

Lisa was quiet on the ride back to the nurses' quarters. The party at Camp Radcliff had finally collapsed under the sheer weight of empty beer bottles. Even Colonel Jordan had stopped by—for a quick one, so he said. But he stayed until he was staggering like the rest of them. It had been a good party.

Rat drove carefully. The last thing he needed was for an MP to catch him wandering all over the road and write him up. He shot a quick glance over at Lisa sitting beside him. In the faint glow of the lights from the instrument panel, he could see that she was looking back at him with an interesting face.

"You have a good time?" he asked.

She placed her hand on his leg. "Yes," she said after a moment. "I always have a good time with you, Rat. You know that."

Gaines smiled to himself, placed his right hand on top of hers, and gave it a squeeze. He, too, was very pleased at how the evening had gone. Without meaning to, he slipped into thinking of how nice it would be to spend every evening with Lisa. It was a pleasant thought.

All too soon, they reached the nurses' building and pulled into the parking lot.

"I don't have any of that 'Sudden Discomfort' you seem to like so much," Lisa said, "but I've got a bottle of brandy inside, if you'd like a nightcap."

Rat looked at her and smiled. "That's the nicest thing you've said to me all night."

He hurried around to her side of the Jeep and helped her step out. Gaines had been raised a southern gentleman, and Lisa liked to be treated like a lady. Sometimes, in a world of shapeless olive drab uniforms and war, it was very hard for her to remember what it was like to feel really feminine. It was the reason why Lisa had clung to her mane of long blond hair instead of whacking it off short, as most of the nurses had done.

She took Rat's arm and led him down the dim hallway to her room. As a senior nurse, Lisa didn't have to share it with one of the other girls. She quietly opened the door and went inside. Gaines followed her in, grinning when he remembered the last time that he had been in there. In spite of their having been interrupted, it had been quite an evening.

He took a seat on the edge of her bed while she got their drinks. She handed him a water glass full of brandy and sat down beside him. Since her hair was already down, she didn't have to go through her nightly ritual of combing it out.

They talked comfortably as they sipped the warm brandy, both of them aware of what was next on the agenda. Rat was from the old school and moved slowly, waiting like a gentleman for a clear sign that she wanted him in her bed. He was very much aware that any woman had the prerogative to change her mind at a moment's notice, and he didn't want to rush her.

Lisa finally got tired of waiting for Gaines to make his move. She knew he was trying to be considerate, but there are times when considerate just didn't cut it. She wanted action.

She drained the last of her brandy and put the empty glass on the floor. She stood up and started taking her clothes off. Though they were technically not lovers yet, she felt as if she had done this with him dozens of times before. There was something very right about it.

Rat took his cue, reached out, and started unlacing his jungle boots. He tried hard not to stare as she finished undressing and climbed over him to get into bed. She was beautiful—that much he remembered from their earlier ill-fated attempt to make love.

What he had not remembered was just how beautiful she was. Suddenly, he became a bit hesitant. Like a kid in a candy shop with a twenty-dollar bill, he didn't quite know where to start.

She lay back against the wall and watched him get out of his pants, smiling softly when she noticed that it made him a bit nervous. He got under the single sheet and rolled onto his side to face her.

She was soft and she was warm. Her tanned skin was a perfect, silky, golden match for her hair. He nuzzled his face into the hollow of her neck. She smelled good. He brought his hand up to the fullness of her breasts and felt her nipples harden under his touch. He became erect and pressed against the softness of her belly.

Her hand crept down between their bodies and fastened around him. Unconsciously, she parted her long legs and wrapped them around his thighs, pressing herself against the hard muscles of his leg.

They were both ready.

He rolled on top of her and she pulled her legs up. Kneeling above her, Rat paused for a second, his head turned slightly to the side.

"What's wrong?" she asked.

He grinned down at her. "Oh, nothing. I'm waiting for some asshole to knock on your door again."

"Rat, you idiot," she laughed. Reaching down, she drew him inside her.

It had been a long time for him, so he didn't last any time at all. He wasn't worried.

The second round went much more slowly and Lisa was able to participate fully. Before too long, they were both frantically clutching one another as their climaxes hit.

Gaines took a short break, exploring the curves and hollows of her lush body. Finally, she reached over and pulled him on top of her again. When it was over, Gaines flopped over on his belly, fighting to catch his breath. He was badly out of shape for bedroom athletics. He made a mental note to get into better shape. Maybe she could be his coach.

Lisa watched her new lover drift off to sleep, wondering why men always went to sleep afterward. She reached over and touched his shoulder. "Rat?" she said softly.

"Mmm."

"Gaines!"

"What!" he awoke, startled.

"Wake up, you bastard, I want to talk to you."

Rat sat up and looked at her. With her blond hair spread out around her head, she looked like a storybook angel. Why was it that women always wanted to talk about it afterward?

"Yes, dear," he said mockingly.

"Rat," she grinned, reaching out for him. "I want to do it again."

Instantly, his fatigue vanished. He lunged for her.

CHAPTER 14

Camp Radcliff, An Khe

The next morning, Treat Brody was nursing a slight hang-over and sore knuckles when he went to the arms room to see about getting a new M-60 doorgun to replace the one that had been damaged in the crash.

"Here you go," the armorer said cheerfully, handing a brand new M-60D over the counter. "Sign for it here."

Brody signed the property book, carried the new gun around to the side of the operations building, and laid it on the wooden cleaning table set up next to the cut-down fifty-five gallon oil drums full of solvent. Flipping up the barrel-locking lever, he pulled the barrel out of the re-ceiver and laid it in the solvent bath to loosen up the cos-moline in the bore. All weapons were packed with the heavy, sticky grease for shipping, and it was a bitch to clean the stuff off. He had just started to break down the receiver when he heard a voice behind him.

"Hey, man, what's happening?"

Brody spun around. Snakeman Fletcher was standing there with a silly grin on his face. He had a brand-new duffel bag in one hand and an M-16 in the other.

''Snake!'' Brody ran over and pounded his old buddy on the back, almost knocking the slighter man down to his knees.

''Easy, man, easy!'' Fletcher said, straightening his jacket. ''You'll damage the merchandise.''

''Goddamn, it's good to see you!'' Except for the brand-new, unfaded jungle fatigues and the black leather on the bottom of his jungle boots, Fletcher looked like he had never left the Nam. He hadn't even lost his deep tan.

Fletcher dropped his duffel bag and looked around. ''It sure as hell ain't good to see this place. It don't look like it's changed much, still the same old shit. Bugs and fucking red dirt. I don't know why the fuck I came back to this fucking place. I shoulda gotten myself a dick job somewhere back in Saigon. Something with an air-conditioner and a big desk.''

Brody laughed. ''You ain't changed one fucking bit, Snakeman. When did you get in?''

''I caught a ride on the early Herky Bird run from Long Binh.''

''You been down to the Company yet?''

''No, I heard that you guys were working down here today, so I thought I'd drop by and see if I could find you.''

''Tell you what. Let me put this gun back together real quick here, and we'll go have a beer. Break down the door to the club if we have to.''

''I am a mite parched,'' Snakeman admitted.

While Brody did a quick clean-up on his M-60, Snakeman Fletcher kept up a steady chatter about the REMFs in Camp Alpha, the replacement center. He bitched about them putting him on morning police call and having him pull KP in the mess hall.

''What'd they have you doing that shit for?'' Brody asked. ''You're an E-five now.''

''Well,'' Fletcher hesitated and looked down at the ground, obviously embarrassed. ''Not really, not anymore. I'm a PFC again.''

"Aw shit! What happened, man?"

"Well, there was this limp-dicked, lard-assed, E-seven REMF back at Hood who wouldn't stay off my case," Fletcher grinned. "And one day I'd decided that this ole Texas boy had enjoyed just about all of his shit that I could put up with."

"So?"

"I gave him a real good talking-to. Texas style."

"And you got busted for that?"

"Well . . ." Fletcher grinned widely now. "The colonel was standing right next to him when I punched his fucking lights out."

"Snakeman, you dumb fuck," Brody shook his head. "You know better than that. You're supposed to wait till you can get him alone."

"I know, I know. But it sure seemed like a good thing to do at the time."

Brody laughed.

"But," Fletcher continued, "it didn't turn out all bad. The colonel let me come back here instead of throwing my ass in the stockade."

"I'm glad to have you back, man. We're real shorthanded again right now, and I can sure use you on the doorgun."

"How's it been going?"

"Well, you missed out on a real gold-plated motherfucker here last month. We did this Sneaky Pete number across the fence again and got our asses in a real crack."

"Anybody get hurt?"

"Gardner got hit pretty bad with a piece of frag, but he got out of the hospital a couple of days ago. Then we had a hydraulic failure yesterday, and Gabe put us down on top of the triple canopy."

"That's candy-ass stuff."

"Your ass, too, Snakeman. There were gooks all over the fucking place, and we had to bring arty in on 'em until we could get an extract."

Fletcher wasn't impressed. He'd been through all of it

many times before. "How's ole Leo the Lionhearted," he asked, changing the subject.

"Still trucking. 'Bout the only thing that's changed is that we got ourselves a real FO now. You remember that last mission we went on when you were short, that resupply mission?"

"How the fuck could I not remember that? You guys were trying to get my young ass killed!"

Brody laughed. "Well, remember in that LZ, that little guy from New York who took out that RPG with a one oh five? The Bunny Rabbit? He's transferred in and I've got him in my squad now."

"That crazy little motherfucker?"

"Yeah," Brody laughed. "He fits right in. He's the one that got us out of that jam yesterday."

Fletcher didn't want to talk about firefights anymore. It was old hat to him. "Why don't you hurry up and turn that thing in, and let's go get that fucking beer you were talking about, man. I'm thirsty."

"You got that shit right."

Lieutenant Colonel Jordan raced into his headquarters building and headed down the hall to his office. Lieutenant Muller jumped to his feet and assumed a rigid position of attention when he saw his battalion commander. "Get Gaines on the horn," Jordan barked. "Tell him I need to see him ASAP!"

"Yes, sir!" Muller almost shouted.

Jordan winced, his head was still throbbing. Absolutely the last thing he needed right now was to have Muller bellowing in his ear. Gaines's party last night had been a little more than he had bargained for. He went into his office.

The Echo Company commander entered a few minutes later. "What's going on?" he asked Muller.

"I don't know, sir!" the adjutant bellowed, doing a bad imitation of a respectful and knowledgeable junior officer.

As he went on into the colonel's office, Gaines thought that Muller really should stop watching old war movies.

"Have a seat, Gaines." Jordan pointed to the chair at the side of his desk. "I've got something here I want to read to you."

Jordan opened a folder marked with a red TOP SECRET cover sheet and started reading.

It was the report of the division G-2's analysis of the bullet that had been found in the pilot's body. The G-2's conclusion was that the round had been fired from an as yet unknown type of weapon, probably a new heavy machine gun.

"That's not really new to me, sir," Gaines said when the colonel had finished reading. "Last night, Walt Johnson told me that Gabriel's slick went down yesterday from an armor-piercing bullet that shattered the hydraulic pump."

He fished in his pocket and brought a bullet out. "I was going to take this over to the Ordnance people today and see if they could identify it for me."

"Let's see that!"

Gaines handed the bullet over.

The colonel examined it. It looked the same as the one that had been shown at the briefing earlier this morning, a copper-clad projectile slightly longer than the NATO 7.62mm round fired from the M-14 rifle and the M-60 machine gun. The main difference was that this bullet had a hardened steel, armor-piercing core rather than one of lead like the standard military ball ammunition.

He couldn't tell if the rifling marks on the round were the same as those on the other one, but they looked similar. It was certainly the same kind of bullet.

"Grab your hat," Jordan said, getting up from his chair. "We're going over to G-two. I want him to take a look at this."

In the division intelligence officer's comfortable, wood-paneled office, the G-2 listened to Gaines tell him what

Walt had said about how Gabe's chopper had been shot down.

"He said there were four holes in it?"

"Yes, sir."

The G-2 turned the bullet over and over in his fingers. "I'd say that means that either there were four men shooting, which isn't too bloody likely, or that they were using some kind of semi-automatic rifle. Something like our M-fourteen."

He got up from his chair. "Let's go down to the Tech Intell people and have them match this round with the one that came out of that pilot's body."

In the Technical Intelligence Office, the elderly warrant officer in charge put the two bullets under a special microscope and focused it on the grooves that had been cut into the soft copper sheathing when the bullets went through the rifling of the barrel.

"Here, sir," he said to the G-2. "Take a look. They were fired from the same kind of weapon, but from two different examples of it."

Under the magnification, it was easy to see that the rifling grooves in the two bullets were the same width and spacing, but that the microscopic scratches in the grooves were different.

"What do you think we have here, Chief?" the G-2 asked.

The warrant officer leaned back in his chair. "Well, Colonel, first off, the round is the Russian seven-point-six-two by fifty-four-millimeter rimmed cartridge. That's their old rifle round, left over from the Tsarist days. Right now, it's mostly used in the Mosin-Nagant carbine, the one we call the Chi-Com Type XX. It is also fired in a couple of their machine guns, the DP and the SGM. Mostly, though, we don't see it very much anymore since they switched to the intermediate seven-point-six-two by thirty-nine-millimeter round used in the SKS, AK, and RPD. Only a few local VC units are still armed with the Chi-Com carbine or the DP."

He reached over and pulled a book off a shelf and ran through the pages. "Now, here you can see the rifling marks for those older weapons. You will notice that they do not match up with what you saw in the scope."

"Okay, then where do you think these two rounds came from?"

"Colonel, considering where these bullets were found, I think that we've got a new kind of weapon here. Probably a semi-automatic sniper rifle. For one thing, the current Russian sniper rifle is the old Mosin-Nagant M-1891/thirty rifle. As the name implies, it was designed in 1891, and it's a bolt-action rifle. It's not a bad piece and it can reach out past a thousand meters, but it's a bolt-action. Modern sniping tactics call for semi-automatic rifles, so the shooter doesn't have to take his eye away from the sniper scope when he works the bolt for his second shot. That's the primary reason why we modified the M-fourteen for our own sniper weapon. It's true that the Marine Corps is using the bolt-action Winchester Model Seventy rifle up north, but we feel that our semi-automatic XM-twenty-one is a little more effective in the sniping role."

"What do you think this new weapon looks like?"

The warrant officer shrugged his shoulders. "I really couldn't tell you that. They might have reworked an SKS action kinda like what we did with the M-fourteen. Or they might have done something completely new. There's no way that I can tell. But whatever it is, with this round it will probably reach out almost fifteen hundred meters."

"That's well over a mile!"

"I know."

The G-2 got to his feet. "Well, I guess I'd better put the word out about this ASAP and let everybody know what we're dealing with here."

On the Jeep ride back to the battalion headquarters with Colonel Jordan, Gaines was deep in thought, trying to figure out if there was anything he could do to help protect his pilots from snipers. He didn't want his men to end up as cold meat in Graves Registration if he could help it.

One answer would be to have all of them wear the armored vest that had been developed to protect chopper crews, commonly known as chickenplate. It consisted of a single plate of a tough ceramic that could stop a 7.62mm armor-piercing round cold. It left one hell of a bruise on a man, but it left him alive.

Unfortunatley, it had always been in short supply in the First Air Cav. Through some vague shortfall of what the army laughingly called a supply system, the largest helicopter combat unit in the world was basically without adequate armor protection for its aircrew.

CHAPTER 15

Camp Radcliff, An Khe

The word about the chopper-killing snipers quickly spread from one end of the Air Cav basecamp to the other. Overnight, pilot and aircrew armored vests became very valuable commodities. Chickenplate had been hard to get before, but now it was almost impossible. What few pieces of it that had filtered down to the Cav were now worth their weight in gold.

Rat Gaines sat in his office and went over the armor problem in his mind. He had dozens of valid requisitions for the armored vests filed away at S-4, the battalion supply section, but they had not been filled, and it was highly unlikely that they would be anytime in the near future.

Gaines was also aware that other chopper companies in Nam had more chickenplate than they could ever possibly use, particularly the helicopter transportation companies of the First Aviation Brigade. The question was, how could he get some of their vests up to An Khe short of armed robbery?

Suddenly, he had an idea. Reaching across his desk, he picked up the phone.

* * *

The UH-1 Huey slick settled down on the chopper pad at Quin Nhon just down the coastline from An Khe. Quin Nhon had a big supply and support base, part of the army's First Logistical Command. It was a nice, quiet place, and not too much ever happened around there.

When the rotor stopped turning, four men stepped out of the slick. All of them were wearing standard jungle fatigue uniforms devoid of identifying unit insignia, topped off with baseball caps. Even the chopper had had its unit markings, the crossed sabers and the Cavalry guidon marked E 1/7, freshly painted out.

As he stepped out onto the PSP runway, Lieutenant Mike Alexander hoped that the big, shield-shaped dark area on his right sleeve didn't give them away. It looked suspiciously like someone had just recently taken a big First Air Cav horse blanket patch off the sleeve. Which, of course, he had.

Back at An Khe, Rat Gaines had been very specific about it. "Take it all off," he had told them emphatically. "I don't want to make it easy for 'em in case anyone figures out what happened. No horse blankets, no Aero Rifles patches, no Cav shit at all. Remember, you're all supposed to be REMF."

That got a big laugh out of everyone.

Their mission in Quin Nhon was simple, and all the men had volunteered for it. They were to trade for, or steal, as many aircrew armored vests as they could get their hands on. And if they got caught, they were on their own.

Alexander walked over to the slick sitting on the pad next to them and peeked inside. There were two chickenplate vests lying on the troop seats in back. Quickly, he snatched them up and walked back over to his own bird.

"This'll do for a start," he said, handing them to the pilot and copilot. "Put 'em on."

"Okay, Wolfsmitt," he said to the Echo Company supply sergeant. "Let's get to work."

He grabbed up a couple of AK-47s and slung them over his shoulder. The sergeant had his arms full of captured enemy weapons and equipment as well.

"How far is it to your friend's place?" Alexander asked, looking around the large, well-kept supply base. There were even fences and trees planted in front of some of the painted buildings. It almost looked like they were back in the States.

" 'Bout a five-minute walk, sir."

"Let's get at it."

It was a little more than five minutes on the sunbaked laterite road before they came to a giant prefab metal building. The sign above the door had the "Leaning Shithouse" insignia of the First Log Command displayed over the words, Tech Supply.

It must have been ninety-five degrees in the sun, but it was cool when they walked into the building.

"Let me handle this," the supply sergeant said. He walked up to the counter.

"Is Sergeant Billings around?" he asked the bored clerk, who wore a pencil stuck behind his ear.

"Yeah, he's in his office." The clerk pointed to a door over to one side.

"Thanks."

The sergeant opened it. "Hey, Al! How's it hanging?"

"Hey, Smitty, come on in," answered a heavyset E-7 behind the desk. "What the hell you doing down here? I heard you were stuck up in the Cav."

"No fucking way, man. I found me a job in Pleiku with a transportation outfit."

"How 'bout a beer?" Al asked, turning around in his swivel chair and opening a small refrigerator pushed up against the wall.

"Sounds good. By the way, this is Lieutenant Alexander."

"Nice to meet you, sir. Would you care for a beer, too?"

"Please."

"Now, what can I do for you gents?"

"How's the AK market?"

"Great! I can use all I can get my hands on."

Al had a racket going. He traded captured enemy weapons to Air Force pilots for choice items that he later sold—items like Air Force steaks, survival knives, and air-conditioners.

"What do you need?" Al asked.

"Chickenplate."

"What the hell you need that stuff for?"

"I got a deal working with some pilots."

Al became all business now. "What kind of deal did you have in mind?"

"I need as much of it as I can get."

By the time the delicate negotiations were completed, Al drove them back to the helipad with three cases of armored vests in the back of the Jeep, four to a case. Alexander had left four AKs, two SKs, a couple of VC flags, and several red-star NVA belt buckles behind in the supply office.

"Remember," Al said as the pilot wound up the turbine, "I could use at least four or five RPGs and all the AKs you can get."

"I'll keep it in mind," Sergeant Wolfsmitt promised him.

The chopper took off and flew north for a few minutes as if they were heading back to Pleiku. Then they changed course and continued south down the coast to the next big supply base at Cam Ram Bay. A similar transaction took place there for another case of the vests. But this time, while the sergeant was making the deal, Lieutenant Alexander cruised the flight line looking for more vests that had been left behind in empty choppers. He snagged three more that way.

Their last stop was in Nha Trang. The deal was different there. This time Lieutenant Alexander would have to make the play.

The chopper landed at the 5th Special Forces SFOB pad, and Alexander caught a ride to Camp McDermott, the big supply base next door. He headed for the 63rd Maintenance Battalion, looking for a Captain Kasnowski, the material officer. Before he left, Sergeant Wolfsmitt had given him a detailed briefing on how to deal with Kasnowski.

The material officer's office was a whitewashed Quonset hut in front of a headquarters building that featured a flower garden in front of it. He walked up the steps and, through the open door, saw an officer with a cigarette in his mouth and his feet up on the corner of his desk reading a *Playboy* magazine.

"I'm looking for a Captain Kasnowski?" Alexander asked.

"I'm the Kaz," the officer said. "What can I do for you, Ell Tee?"

"Well, sir," Alexander began. "I'm from the Cav up in An Khe, and I've got a little problem I wonder if you could help me with. See, I'm new to all this chopper shit. I'm an old Mech man myself and . . ."

"No shit!" Kasnowski broke in. "So am I, who were you with?"

"First of the Thirteenth, in Coleman Barracks, Mannheim, Germany."

"Well, I'll be dipped in shit." Kasnowski stood up, extending his hand. "I was in the Second of the Eighty Seventh, in Sullivan. What's you name again?"

"Alexander, sir."

"Look, I don't have any Eichbaum," the captain said, referring to the local German beer in Mannheim, "but I can offer you a Budweiser." He turned around, pulled two cans out of the refrigerator behind his desk, opened them with the church key tied to the arm of his chair, and handed one to Alexander. *"Prosit!"* he said.

"Prosit!" Alexander replied to the toast in German.

The Kaz drained about half of his beer and wiped his mouth on the back of his hand. "Now, what can I do for you?"

"Well, sir, I've got these requisitions that I can't seem to get filled up in the Cav."

The Kaz got serious now. "For what?"

"Chickenplate vests."

"How many?"

"Three dozen sets."

Kasnowski thought for a moment. "Wait just a sec." He picked up the phone and dialed a number.

"Kaz here, let me talk to Sergeant Winters. . . . Sarge, this is the Kaz. What's the story on armored vests, air-crew, commonly known as chickenplate? . . . Great, I'll be right down."

"He's got a dozen or so. Where's your paperwork?" Kasnowski asked Alexander.

"Right here, sir," he answered, reaching into his pocket.

"Okay. Let's go."

On the short drive over to another big prefab metal building, Kasnowski and Alexander talked about their days in the Mechanized Infantry battalions in Germany. It was very obvious that the Captain really missed crashing around in the woods of Germany in his M-113 armored personnel carrier. Alexander wondered how a hard-charging Mech officer had ever wound up in Vietnam wearing the "Flaming Pisspot" of the Ordnance Corps, but he was afraid to ask.

Kaz screeched his Jeep to a halt in front of the supply building and jumped out.

A harried-looking second lieutenant was waiting behind the counter when Kasnowski charged into the issue point.

"Sir," the young man began before the Kaz could even open his mouth. "I can't issue you any armored vests, sir. You remember what happened last time I let you give something away without the proper requisitions."

Kasnowski looked at the young supply officer. "Son, how long have you been in the Nam?"

"A little over six months, sir."

"Right. You're short, aren't you?"

"Uh, yes, sir."

"And you want to get home safely to Suzie Sweet Shorts, don't you?"

"Yes, sir."

"And you remember our last conversation about the needs of your fighting units, the men who are protecting your young ass for Suzie?" He waved his hand to encompass the entirety of Camp McDermott. "And I mean fighting units, not this collection of no-combat, ash-and-trash REMFs."

The lieutenant winced. He was very much aware that he was not really making a fighting contribution to the war effort where he was. "But, sir, the colonel specifically said that he would put me up on charges if I filled any more of your requisitions."

Kasnowski leaned over the counter. "Fuck that lard-assed REMF and the horse he rode in on."

The supply officer's eyes darted around the room as if he were trying to find a place to hide.

"I'll tell you what," Kaz said smoothly. "It's about lunchtime. Why don't you hurry on over to the mess hall and have lunch with the colonel, rack up a few brownie points, and let me talk to Sergeant Winters. That way, you can't possibly be held responsible for anything that happens here."

The lieutenant grabbed his hat and headed out the door, almost at a run.

"He's really not a bad kid," Kasnowski said to Alexander. "He just needs to get his priorities straight. He hasn't figured out that there's a war going on here yet."

He leaned over the counter. "Winters!" he called out. "Get your ass out here."

The NCOIC of the supply point came out of the back

with his arms full of vests. "You do have some kind of paper work to cover this, don't you, sir?"

"Winters, what kind of talk is that? Of course I do." Kaz turned to Alexander. "Ell Tee, show the man your requisitions."

Winters looked the forms over. He had a frown on his face. "These are completely valid!" he said in disbelief.

"Why, of course they are, Sarge. What do you think is going on here?"

Winters didn't reply. Kasnowski was known through Nha Trang as a man who would give anything away to the first grunt who asked for it. Once he had even taken the spare tire off of the colonel's Jeep and given it to an infantry officer who had driven into the camp with a flat tire. As far as the Kaz was concerned, the rear-echelon commandos came last in the book, not first as they usually did in Vietnam. This attitude did not endear him to the REMFs he worked for, but he figured that sooner or later they would get tired of his act and transfer him to a combat unit—which was what he wanted.

Alexander watched the whole performance with his mouth halfway open. He had never seen anything like it in his whole life.

"Is there anything else you need?" Kasnowski asked him while the sergeant loaded a dozen vests into the back of his Jeep.

"I can't think of anything right now, sir."

"Well, if you do, just let me know. We Mech types have to stick together around here or the REMFs will overrun us."

"Yes, sir!" Alexander grinned.

On the Jeep ride back to his chopper, Alexander got up the nerve to ask the question that had been bothering him ever since he had met the captain. "Sir, if you don't mind my asking, how in hell did you get stuck in the Ordnance Corps?"

"Well, son, it's a long story and it has to do with the dart board that they use back in the Department of the

Army to do officer assignments. Anyway, they say that I have to wear the Flaming Pisspot for two years before I can transfer back into the infantry. But there's nothing that says I can't make life interesting for them in the meantime. Like right now. I've got my paper work in to do an in-country transfer to the Special Forces and it's driving them crazy down in Saigon." He laughed.

"I'm planning to get me a field assignment one way or the other. There's no fucking way that I'm going to do a whole year sitting on my ass here in REMF town."

Alexander could just see Kasnowski leading a CIDG unit while wearing the insignia of an Ordnance officer. Somehow, it seemed to fit.

CHAPTER 16

The Song Re Valley

Russian KGB Major Gregor Zerinski stepped out of the door of his temporary headquarters. He had had a good lunch followed by another furious ride between the sleek thighs of his favorite camp whore. Everything was going well. Even the field test of the Dragunov rifle was progressing well ahead of schedule.

He looked out from under the camouflage netting that covered the small bamboo building to the improvised rifle range that had been cut into the side of the hill. Behind the firing butts, four green-and-brown-and-gray camouflaged Spetsnaz snipers were rezeroing their rifles in the hot sun. The four security men were on the spotting scopes, telling the shooters where the rounds hit.

The SVD was not a delicate weapon, but like all sniper rifles, each time that they were taken apart for a detailed cleaning, the scope had to be rezeroed. Zeroing was a relatively simple procedure and it gave the young Russians a break from beating around in the brush. Lounging around in the sun and shooting was far preferable to hiding in the jungle.

When he went back to his office, the KGB man found Yuravitch waiting for him again. Zerinski knew what this was about already. For the hundredth time, the army major was going to try to talk him into letting him move in close to an American basecamp to kill men. Zerinski didn't have anything against killing people—as a KGB man he had done enough of that. But he didn't have the craving for it that Yuravitch seemed to have.

Looking at Yuravitch now, Zerinski had a hard time seeing a celebrated cold-eyed killer of World War II in the stocky, graying Soviet army major with glasses and a slight paunch. But as he knew full well, Yuravitch had been a terror on the battlefield back in the big war. Something about coming to Vietnam to test the Dragunovs had set Yuravitch's killer instinct off again. He wasn't satisfied with just training the new snipers. He wanted to make a personal kill.

Zerinski had had this conversation with him several times, but his orders were not going to be any different. No close-in work. It was just too dangerous.

"Yes, Major?" he addressed Yuravitch finally.

"Zerinski," the old sniper began, "I have come up with a new testing program that I want to discuss with you. If you have the time, that is." He shot a glance back to Zerinski's quarters, where the Vietnamese girl was still sleeping after their noontime bout. "I feel that we have been limited in our testing so far. Mostly we have shot at helicopters and their pilots from a great distance."

"Isn't that the purest essence of sniping?" Zerinski queried. "Killing from afar?"

"Certainly. But in the war to come, we will not only be using the Dragunovs against helicopters, we need to get more practice against ground targets. Infantrymen."

Zerinski held up his hand. "We have been over this several times before, comrade," he said wearily. "My orders are that the rifles are not to be risked. Not under any circumstances."

"Yes, comrade, that I understand. But we do not have to put them at risk if we follow my plan. What I want to do is simple. I have arranged to have a platoon of the Red Guard assigned to provide security for my shooters while we work.''

''How did you accomplish that?'' Zerinski was interested. He did not have a good relationship with the Red Guard's commander, Captain Van of the Dac Cong, the North Vietnamese counterpart of the KGB. Primarily, he felt, because Van was jealous that he was screwing the NVA officer's favorite whore.

''We think alike,'' Yuravitch answered with a smile. ''Like me, he wants to kill as many Yankees as he possibly can. And,'' the old army major smirked, ''he is not overly cautious.''

''And how do you intend to do this?''' Zerinski asked.

''I want to use part of the Red Guard to draw the American infantry into combat. Once they're on the ground and engaged, my shooters can take out their officers and sergeants and render them ineffective. I think that we can kill many of them that way.''

''What about the armed helicopters? You know that the Yankees never assault a landing zone without their gunship escorts.''

''We will still keep one of the teams positioned where they can take the helicopters under fire, but I want to put one of them in the jungle, closer to the infantry.''

''Good idea,'' Zerinski agreed. ''We'll do it tomorrow. You take the high team, and I'll take the team in the jungle.''

''But Major! . . .''

The KGB man enjoyed the look of shock on Yuravitch's face.

''No.'' Zerinski held up his hand. ''I insist. I am the one responsible for the security of the rifles, so it is only proper that I be the officer leading the team closest to the Yankees.''

Yuravitch was furious, but he knew better than to make an issue of it. Zerinski was trying to cheat him out of his rightful kill, but he also knew that there was little he could do about it—right now. Perhaps later he would have a chance to do something—like put a Dragunov bullet in the KGB agent's back.

"Of course, Comrade Major," Yuravitch said politely. "As you say, the guns are your responsibility."

Zerinski smiled to himself as he watched the stocky major walk out of the room. Zerinski was going to make Yuravitch sweat before he gave him a chance to get in close to the Americans. Yuravitch was going to have to learn proper respect for the KGB first.

Gardner finally finished the letter to his wife. It still wasn't exactly what he wanted to say, but it was going to have to do. He folded the three pages of lined notebook paper covered with closely packed sentences and put them in an envelope. He wrote the word *Free* in the place that the stamp should go. That was one of the few real benefits of being in the Nam, you got to send your mail home for free. Then he headed for the mail drop outside the orderly room.

He stuffed the letter in the slot and looked around the company area trying to figure out what he should be doing next. He needed to do something fast before the first sergeant or Zack saw him hanging around and put him to work filling sandbags or something.

Deciding to get a haircut and a shave, he moved out of the Echo Company area smartly. He had learned a long time ago not to look like he was strolling. Even when he was fucking off, he moved like a man on a mission vital to national security.

The haircut and head massage felt good. It was very relaxing the way Viet barbers went about making a grand production out of something so simple. The man even massaged his eyebrows and cut the long hairs inside of his nose before it was all done.

Throughout the half-hour production, however, he had been forced to stare at pictures of scantily clad Western women cut from men's magazines that the barber had tacked to the wall for his customers' amusement. There were also several pictures of Vietnamese women, but they were all fully dressed in silk *ao-dais*.

For some reason, Gardner's eyes kept leaving the lush figures of the Western women and going back to the slim, delicate, dark-eyed Asian beauties with their long, flowing hair. Suddenly, he knew how he was going to spend the rest of his day off.

He paid the wizened barber and, putting his brush hat back on, headed for the EM club. It was late enough in the day that they would be serving beer, and he wanted to see Mai again. Now that he had finally sent the letter to Sandra, he could put it out of his mind until he received her answer.

This did not mean that his wife was completely out of his mind, but there was not a fucking thing he could do about the problem right now. Gardner had learned one of the most important lessons of all, the Nam grunt's philosophy that was best expressed by the oft-heard phrase, "Fuck it, it don't mean nothing."

The inside of the EM club was dim but when his eyes adjusted to the dark, he saw Brody, Fletcher, and Bunny Rabdo sitting at one of the tables.

"Hi, guys," Gardner said, taking a chair.

"Howdy, JJ," Fletcher said. "How 'bout a cool one?"

"Or three," Brody added.

"Sounds about right." Gardner turned around to see if Mai was working.

"I haven't seen her yet," Brody offered, unsolicited.

"Wonder where she is . . ."

"Why don't you go ask the guy behind the bar?" Brody suggested. "He likes to talk to you."

Gardner laughed. "Yeah, I'll see if he remembers me."

The rat-faced, skinny bartender remembered him, all right. He started backing away as soon as he saw the big man approaching.

"Where's Mai today?" Gardner smiled.

"I don't know, man. She didn't show up for work today, and that ain't like her at all."

Gardner frowned and the bartender continued hurriedly. "There was an MP in here yesterday asking about her, so maybe she's in some kind of trouble."

"A guy named Dillard?"

"Yeah, that's him. Red hair."

Gardner's face was grim. "Thanks, man." He turned and went back to his table.

"I hope you find her okay," the bartender called out.

"Me, too," Gardner said under his breath.

"What's the problem?" Brody asked when he saw the look on Gardner's face.

"I think that MP's making trouble for Mai."

"What's his name? Dillard?"

"Dillard." Gardner grabbed his hat.

"Wait up," Brody said, pushing his chair back. "I'm coming with you."

"Me, too!" Fletcher added.

Gardner was halfway to the door when the two grunts caught up with him.

"You owe me a piece of ass, cunt!" Dillard spat, his hand locked around Mai's throat. "But first, you're gonna give me a little hum job first."

He forced her to her knees and unzipped his fly. "Lock your lips around that, bitch!"

Mai's small, usually well-kept little house was in a shambles. In his rage, the MP had destroyed everything that would break as well as tearing the girl's clothes from her body. There might not be anything that he could do to her GI boyfriend and his buddies, but he could sure as hell make her pay for the beating he had received at their hands.

The fact that he had started the fight that had left him badly bruised never once crossed his mind. He was used to having people back down at the sight of his MP armband.

"Get on it, bitch!" he screamed, twisting his hand in her hair. Mai's sobs only made him feel better. They also covered the quiet sound of Gardner entering the door behind him.

Suddenly, Dillard was jerked backward off his feet, spun

around, and slammed against the opposite wall. A big hand clamped around his neck, cutting off his air.

He opened his eyes to see Gardner standing in front of him and fainted.

When he came to, he was tied to a chair. The girl, who was now wearing a robe, was sobbing in the arms of the big man. In front of him were two other grunts with grim looks on their faces. One of them was one of the guys from the fight the other night. Brody noticed that the MP was awake again.

"I didn't do nothing." Dillard started running off at the mouth. "She invited me in here and . . ."

The point of the knife blade under his chin choked off anything else he might have wanted to say. The small man on the other end of the knife grinned. Dillard shivered.

"What're we going to do with this scumbag, Treat?" the little guy asked. "Back home we nut 'em for doing shit like that."

The MP tried to say something, but the knife dug deeper into his throat. The small man leaned closer to him. "Say one word, you sorry motherfucker, and it'll be your last. *Comprende*?"

The MP nodded his head. The knife did not move a millimeter from his neck.

"She's okay," Gardner said, clenching his big fists. "We got here in time."

"Well, almost," Brody replied, looking at all of the smashed things in the room. He walked over to the MP and, reaching down, took the man's wallet out of his back pocket. He took out a wad of MPC notes and quickly counted them out, almost two hundred dollars.

"Tell the lady that you want to pay for the damage you did to her house," Brody said, smiling sweetly as he ruffled the notes.

"Sure," he squeaked. "Take the money."

"Please," Snakeman prompted.

"Please take it," the MP repeated.

Gardner looked down at him. "What are we going to do about him? The minute we're gone, he'll come back."

"Oh no, he won't," Brody grinned. "When we're done with him, he ain't ever going to hurt anyone again, I promise you that."

"You can't kill me!" Dillard managed to gasp before the knife point cut him off.

"Why not?" Brody asked. "As far as I'm concerned, you're VC." He paused. "And we kill VC."

"Get him on his feet," Brody ordered Snakeman, "and take him outside."

"JJ, you stay here with Mai, help her get this mess cleaned up. We'll take care of that scumbag. Mai, believe me, he'll never bother you again, ever."

The girl nodded, wanting to believe the American, but she knew about the MPs. Some of them were worse than the Vietnamese gangsters everyone called Cowboys.

"JJ, you tell her that it'll be safe."

Gardner looked down at her tear-streaked face. "We'll protect you," he said grimly. "You can count on that."

It was two hours before an MP patrol found Dillard. He was gagged and tied belly down over the hood of his Jeep on the outskirts of the village of An Khe. His pants were gathered around his knees, and a Coke bottle had been shoved part-way up his ass. Painted on both cheeks were the Vietnamese words for "kick me," and a sign around his neck proclaimed him to be a cowardly scumbag who attacked defenseless women and children. It was signed, "The people of An Khe."

The two MPs who found him couldn't stop laughing all the way back to Camp Radcliff.

CHAPTER 17

Camp Radcliff, An Khe

"Hey, man!" Fletcher looked at the twenty-pound aircrew armored vest laying on the floor of *Pegasus*. "I ain't going to wear no fucking chickenplate. No fucking way, man. You can't move around with all that shit hanging on you."

Brody buckled his own armor on. "The old man said we all got to wear it, Snake."

"Hey, not me, man. I ain't wearing chickenplate, and that's that."

First Lieutenant Mike Alexander walked around the nose of the bird. "Where's your armor, troop?" he asked when he saw the Snakeman climbing in behind his doorgun.

"Sir, I can't wear that stuff."

"Captain Gaines ordered all of his aircrew to wear it."

"But, sir, I . . ."

"Fletcher," Alexander's voice rang out, remembering what the last platoon leader had warned him about this guy. "The man said that he wants his door gunners wearing chickenplate. So unless you want me to lighten up your sleeves a little more, the next time I see you, you had better be wearing a protective vest. You got that?"

"Yes, sir," Fletcher sighed.

"Good."

Fletcher watched the platoon leader walk off. "Man, that is one real hard-core dude. Vande didn't hard-ass us that way. He let us do what we wanted to do."

Brody laughed. "Well, Snake, my man, welcome to the new, improved Echo Company. Alexander the Great sure as hell ain't Vance. He's got his own way of doing things and he figures it's about time we all learned how to do it his way."

Suddenly, Fletcher brightened up. "I know what I'll do, Treat," he said. "I'll just go get me one of those grunt flak vests and wear it. It's a hell of a lot more comfortable than that fucking chickenplate."

Brody shook his head. "Snakeman, you never did have any fucking common sense."

"He said a protective vest right? Well, a flak vest is a protective vest."

"It's your funeral, man, but don't come bitching to me when Captain Rat takes a strip off of your lily white ass."

Snakeman grinned. "Well, he sure as hell won't be getting a virgin."

Brody laughed as Snake dashed off to the arms room. He returned shortly, wearing an M-69 flak vest. The M-69 weighed just a little over eight pounds and contained twelve layers of ballistic nylon. It would stop most shell fragments, but it had not been designed to stop small arms rounds. It would, however, slow them down and limit penetration. It was also only a third as heavy as the ceramic chickenplate Brody was wearing.

Just then, Gabe came running out of the operations shack at a dead run. "Crank it up!" he shouted. "We've got an emergency dustoff!"

In the left-hand seat, the copilot frantically started flipping switches and punching buttons for a hot start while the door gunners scrambled into the back and plugged their helmet radio cords into the intercom system. The turbine was burning and the rotor turning by the time the pilot had buckled himself in.

"We got a call to make an emergency run to the Twelfth Cav," Gabe explained. "They got hit bad, and all the other Dustoffs are busy."

"Roger," Brody called back. "Let's get it."

The copilot radioed the tower for clearance as Gabe maneuvered the hovering *Pegasus* onto the runway. In seconds, her tail came up and she lifted off.

As soon as they cleared the perimeter fence around the basecamp, Brody reached down and flipped up the feed cover on his doorgun. Laying the linked ammo belt in place in the feed tray, he snapped the cover down over it and hauled back on the charging handle, jacking a 7.62mm round into the chamber. He was ready to go.

A dustoff run on a hot LZ could get real hairy, and he was not looking forward to it. It was not going to be a quick in-and-out air assault, doorguns blazing to keep the gooks' heads down. They would be under enemy fire on the ground for far too long while the wounded were being loaded on board.

It was the kind of mission that made door gunners wish that they were cooks or MPs.

He looked around the corner at Fletcher. The Snakeman had a big grin on his face as he beat his hands against the front of his flak vest, King Kong style. Brody shook his head and shot him the finger.

Sometimes the Snakeman didn't have enough fucking sense to come in out of the rain.

On a ridgeline overlooking the small valley, Mikhail Yuravitch had his Spetsnaz sniper team well concealed. Zerinski and his team were employed down in the woods with the NVA Red Guard platoon. Between the two of them, they had had a real good morning.

The sudden ferocity of the American air assault had caught them by surprise, but they had reacted quickly, and now had the Americans pinned down. Yuravitch's two snipers were concentrating on the choppers while Zerinski's people were trying to kill the Yankee infantry officers and NCOs in the clearing. The four SVD sniper rifles were taking a fearful toll in the small LZ below.

The Americans, however, had responded quickly. Supporting gunships had appeared like magic and they were within the artillery fan, so it was not all one sided. In fact, the gunship attacks were so effective that Zerinski had already radioed for Yuravitch to provide a little covering fire from the ridgeline while his sniper team tried to break contact. He couldn't risk losing them to gunship rockets and miniguns.

While the North Vietnamese Red Guards fought a frantic delaying action from the tree line at the edge of the clearing, Zerinski managed to pull his team back almost a thousand meters. Soon, it would be Yuravitch's turn to disappear into the jungle.

Looking forward past the nose of the slick, Brody could see the LZ right in front of them. Through the smoke hanging in the valley, he saw the small perimeter that the infantry company had set up. It did not look like a very healthy place to be right then. The gunships swarmed overhead, working the edge of the tree line, but they didn't seem to be doing that much good. There was still a lot of green tracer fire coming out of the trees.

The infantry had stepped on a hornet's nest and the Air Cav had to fly into it to help them out.

Brody rechecked his lifeline and the linked ammunition belt feeding into his doorgun. He reached down to the side of the gun's receiver and flicked the M-60's safety to the rock-and-roll position.

He was going to earn his pay and then some.

Red smoke billowed up from a small group of men in the center of the clearing, most of them lying flat on the ground.

Gabe banked *Pegasus* around and started his landing approach.

From the ridgeline, Yuravitch saw the lone slick coming in hot and fast. "Take them!" he ordered.

The young Russian sergeant in front of him focused the four-power, PSO-1 telescope on *Pegasus*. The ship was at his maximum range and landing across his front, so he only had a side-on shot. He fired at the pilot's window once, then again. To his disgust, the chopper went in, flared out, and landed unharmed in the middle of the clearing.

The last two shots had emptied the ten-round magazine of the SVD sniper rifle, and the bolt locked back in the open position. The Russian dropped the empty magazine from the bottom of the receiver. Taking a new one from the ammo pouch strapped to his chest, he slapped it into position. He pulled back on the bolt handle to unlock it, and let it go forward again. The rifle was loaded.

The lone slick in the clearing had somehow survived the storm of lead and would be taking off again soon. The Russian sniper focused in on the open doors of the troop compartment. If he couldn't kill the pilots, he would try for some of the crew and passengers. A dead Yankee was a dead Yankee.

He saw a man step into the cross hairs of his scope. His finger slowly tightened on the trigger. The rifle fired.

Spotting through his high-powered binoculars, Yuravitch saw the sniper's bullet miss again. "You incompetent fool," he thundered. "Give me that rifle, they're getting away!"

The young Russian handed the Dragunov up to his commander. Now he would have an opportunity to see the master at work.

Gabe set *Pegasus* down as close as he could to the waiting group of grunts, but he kept the turbine turning at full throttle. The spinning rotors blew a storm of dust and dirt into the air as the grunts picked up their casualties and ran toward the chopper.

The clearing was ablaze with small-arms fire, both outgoing and incoming. Both pilots huddled behind the armored sides of their seats, staying low as rounds smashed into the side of the ship.

The medics threw their patients on board as fast as they could while from the back, Brody and Snakeman kept up a steady stream of fire from their doorguns over the grunts' heads.

When one of the medics shouted "Go!", Gabe hauled up on the collective and hit the overrev switch. *Pegasus* leaped into the sky, her rotor blades clawing for altitude in the thin mountain air. When they were about fifty feet off of the ground, Fletcher left his doorgun and turned to help one of the casualties who was sliding out of the open door.

Yuravitch saw the slick rising back into the air. He threw the rifle to his shoulder and took up an offhand stance. The machine was rapidly pulling out of range, so he had no time to get into a better position for the difficult shot.

Like the younger Russian who had tried before, he focused the scope on the troop compartment and saw a man come into view. It was a crewman from the looks of him, facing outward. Yuravitch took up the slack on the trigger. The sudden recoil when the rifle fired slammed the butt into his shoulder with a satisfying thud. It felt good.

In the scope, he saw the man fall over backward. Now he was happy. He had just killed his first American. He handed the rifle back to the awed sergeant.

"See," Yuravitch said with a big grin on his broad Slavic face. "It is easy. All you have to do is to remember what I taught you."

"Yes, Comrade Major."

Fletcher had gotten the man situated comfortably and had just straightened up to go back to his gun when, from a thousand meters away, the Russian sniper's round took him high in the center of the chest.

"Treat!" he screamed.

Brody looked around in time to see him fall over backward, his arms flailing to keep his balance.

"Snake!"

Brody ripped his own lifeline loose and scrambled over the other wounded men in the troop compartment to reach him.

He knelt by Fletcher's side and cradled his head in his lap. There was a hole in Fletcher's grunt flak vest, a small round hole. Dark red blood welled from it, and was whipped into a red spray by the rotor blast. Brody ripped open the vest and pressed his hand against the wound to try to stop the bleeding.

"I need a dressing!" he yelled.

Fletcher opened his eyes and looked up at him. "I guess I really fucked up, didn't I, Treat? I'm sor—"

The wounded door gunner's body was racked by spasms of coughing, and a bloody froth appeared on his lips. He opened his eyes again. "Ain't this a bitch?" he said weakly. Suddenly, his body went limp in Brody's arms.

"Fletcher!" Brody screamed over the whine of the turbine. "Fletcher!"

The Snakeman's vacant eyes stared, unseeing, out the open door of the speeding chopper. Brody leaned over and started giving him mouth-to-mouth resuscitation.

"Hang it up, man," one of the wounded grunts said, laying his hand on Brody's shoulder. "He's dead."

Brody seemed not to hear him.

"I'm a medic," the man explained. "He's dead, I tell you."

Brody slowly pulled his head back up. He could taste Fletcher's warm blood in his mouth. In a daze, he reached down and gently closed the lids over Fletcher's dull, staring eyes.

He cradled Fletcher's body in his arms all the way back to An Khe. Even when Gabe had put down on the Dustoff pad, he did not want to let him go. The medics rushing to take the wounded away had to pry his arms from around his dead friend.

* * *

Unnoticed by Brody, David Janson stood off to the side of the Dustoff pad, his 35mm camera with the zoom lens hanging around his neck. He had not left An Khe yet. By the time he had recovered from his unscheduled jaunt through the woods after the crash, he started picking up rumors about all of the choppers that had been shot down by sniper fire. His curiosity was fueled when the people refused to answer his questions about it.

He realized that there was something serious going on, something far more important than a short round on an artillery fire mission. He had delayed his flight back to Saigon so he could look into it further. It might be the big story he needed.

A stroll through the flight line of some of the chopper units had given him the distinct impression that the men were very scared. He even saw two men get into a fight over a flak vest. He made a few discreet inquiries and learned about the shortage of aircrew armor. That alone was worth a story, but the real story was why the armor was needed so desperately.

He had been talking with the alert crew of the Dustoff chopper sitting on the pad behind the 45th Mobile Surge when they monitored the radio transmission about the most recent sniper kill, so he was standing in the crowd when Snakeman's body was carried out of the chopper.

He recognized Brody and remembered that he had gotten angry when another reporter had tried to take photos of the dead on the LZ. He didn't need a pissed-off grunt smashing his camera, so he was careful to be as unobtrusive as possible when he took several photos of Fletcher laid out on the stretcher.

Shots that clearly showed the bloody hole in the front of his infantry flak vest.

Janson slid back through the crowd of onlookers and headed for the photo lab run by the PIO. They would let him develop his film there. He wanted to see if the photo had turned out. He prayed to God that it had.

CHAPTER 18

Camp Radcliff, An Khe

Brody sat down heavily on the end of Snakeman's bunk. He was totally drained. All he wanted to do was to sleep for a week and wake up to hear Fletcher bitching about something again. He wanted to sleep more than he had ever wanted to sleep before, but there was something that he had to do first.

He absentmindedly rubbed at his blood-soaked fatigue pants. Snakeman's blood wouldn't come off. It was soaked deep into the rip-stop fabric. He opened Fletcher's foot-locker. It was in its usual chaotic condition, with things stuffed everywhere. The Snakeman had never been known for neatness.

Brody pawed through Fletcher's uniforms, smelling the odor particular to new army issue. It usually took several washings to completely remove the smell, and most of the Snakeman's things had not been laundered once yet. He hadn't been back in-country long enough.

Down in the bottom of the locker, Brody found a brass plaque. The Blues had all chipped in to give it to Fletcher when he had rotated back to the States. Brody pulled it out and stared at the inscription engraved on the brass tag. *To Snakeman Fletcher,* it read. *The baddest door gunner in the Nam. Get some Snake! From the Blues, E Company, First of the 7th Cav.*

Brody had a hard time remembering how long ago it had been that they had given it to him. Two months, three? It seemed like a lifetime. Fletcher had been safe. Why hadn't he stayed home? Treat gently put the plaque on the bunk and stared at the open locker.

Brody was supposed to collect Fletcher's personal items and turn them in to the supply room so they could be sent to his folks back in Texas, but he couldn't bring himself to do it. He lit a cigarette and stared out the door of the tent. A slick was coming in. Maybe Fletcher was on it. Unnoticed tears formed in the corners of his eyes as he watched the helicopter traffic coming in and out of the Golf Course.

Fletcher would not come sauntering in the door in a few minutes bitching about something. Brody knew that he was across the camp in the Graves Registration Point with all the other GIs who had been killed that day.

He butted his smoke under his boot and went back to the task of gathering up what remained of his friend.

Under a pile of uniforms, he found a box of PX stationery, the sheets of paper imprinted with the First Air Cav patch and a drawing of a Huey at the top. He opened the box to make sure that the Snakeman had not stashed his beaver shots in it. He didn't want to send Fletcher's porno collection back to his parents.

In the bottom of the box was an envelope with Brody's name written on the front. What could that be?

He opened the envelope and took out a folded piece of paper. It was Fletcher's copy of the form he had filled out for his ten-thousand-dollar government life-insurance policy. He quickly scanned it. In the block for the designated beneficiary, he saw his name. *Sergeant Treat Brody, E Co, 1/7 Cav, First Cav Div (AM).*

Folded up with the insurance form was a letter addressed to him, dated a week ago. It had been written at Camp Alpha, the replacement center.

Treat, Brody read, *If you're reading this, it means that I must have bought the big wienie. It must be a real bitch, I hope that I died quick.*

Brody blinked his eyes. He was having trouble reading the words.

Anyway, as you probably know, I left the money to you. My folks don't need it that much, and I'd rather see you have it. Man, it sure feels strange to write this letter. Fuck it. Take the bread and throw a party for me. Take all the guys down to Sin City and get laid and drunk one last time for me. Well, I can't think of anything more to say. Take care. Your buddy, Elliot Fletcher, the Snakeman.

Now the tears were streaming down Brody's face, staining the letter. Sobbing, he put his head in his hands. He heard someone come in behind him, but he didn't bother to turn around.

"Brody." It was Zack's low voice. The sergeant laid his hand on his shoulder. "I just heard about Fletcher. I'm real sorry. We'll all miss him."

Brody looked up at him. "Oh, Leo . . ." He couldn't finish his sentence.

"I know, son, I know."

Brody cried openly, the sobs racking his body. For some reason he knew that it was safe to cry around Leo Zack. The tough black NCO understood.

"You want me to help you get his gear together?" Zack asked softly after a moment.

"No, thanks, Sarge." Brody looked down at the open locker. "I can get it."

"Are you sure?"

"Yeah, I can handle it."

"Okay," Zack turned to go. "If you need me, I'll be in my hooch."

"Thanks, Leo."

"No sweat. He was my friend, too."

"Thanks."

Brody wiped his eyes, folded the letter, and put it in his pocket. He got out Fletcher's new duffel bag and started stuffing his army-issue gear into it.

Just then, Corky ran in the door. "Brody," he shouted. "What's this about Snakeman?"

When Brody turned to face the machine gunner, he didn't have to say a word, Cordova could read it on his face. *"Madre de Dios!"* Corky stopped and buried his face in his hands.

Brody stepped up to him. He wanted to take Corky in his arms and hug him, but he didn't dare. "It was quick," he said. "I don't think he felt a thing."

Corky sat down on a footlocker, stunned. "Not the Snakeman. Please, God."

Two-Step and Gardner came in together. They had already heard. Two-Step didn't say a thing. He took Brody by the arm and looked into his eyes for a long moment.

"You okay?" he finally asked.

Brody looked away. He couldn't stand to see his pain reflected in the Indian's eyes.

"Yeah, I'm okay."

Gardner didn't quite know what to say. He didn't want to intrude, but he also didn't want to just stand around with his hands in his pockets.

"Is there anything I can do, Treat?" he asked softly. "Anything?"

"No, thanks, JJ, it's all right. I can handle it."

"Are you sure?"

"Yeah."

Gardner was beginning to understand that there were some things that just took time.

Throughout the rest of the afternoon, men drifted into the Blues' tent from all over the camp to express their condolences. Elliot Snakeman Fletcher had been known far and wide around An Khe.

Most people knew him from the snakes he had been so

fond of. He had gotten his nickname from his habit of gathering up all of the odd reptiles he found and keeping them in his helmet. And since thirty-one of the thirty-three different kinds of snakes that were found in Vietnam were poisonous, most of his little reptilian pets were deadly. But being raised in Texas, Fletcher had been around snakes all of his life and had known how to handle them.

Other people know Fletcher for his carefree, give-a-shit attitude. This had not endeared him to many of the sergeants and officers he had run into, but the troops had loved it. Farmer had been so taken with the Snakeman that he had unconsciously copied many of his mannerisms and speech patterns. To others, Fletcher had been a real friend. A guy who would always share his last beer or smoke, even though he would bitch about it later.

It was late afternoon before Brody got all of Fletcher's personal effects sorted out and turned in to the supply room. When the supply sergeant signed for them, Brody headed across the camp to the barracks of the Ranger Company. He wanted to talk to the sniper who had gone with them on their last mission into Cambodia, the Indian they all called Chief.

He found John Metcack in the Rangers' tent, sitting on his bunk cleaning his rifle.

"Hey, Brody! What's up?" the Indian greeted him enthusiastically.

"I need to talk to you."

"Sure, grab a seat."

Brody sat and looked at the sniper for a moment. "How do I go about killing a sniper?"

Metcack's face lost its smile. "Just who did you have in mind?"

Brody's gaze was level and his voice was cold. "The sorry gook motherfucker who wasted Snakeman."

"The Snakeman is dead? I hadn't heard," Chief said softly.

"Yeah," Brody tried hard to keep the emotion out of his voice. "They got him this afternoon on a hot LZ."

"I'm sorry, Brody, he was a good man. A little crazy, but a good man. Are you sure it was a sniper?"

"Yeah, the bullet checked out. They think that it was the same bunch of guys who've been shooting at the choppers lately."

"I heard about that."

"So." Brody locked eyes with the Indian. "How do I kill him?"

"It's difficult."

"Fletcher was my friend. I owe it to him."

"I see." Chief was silent for a moment. Because of the way he had been raised, vengeance was one thing that the Indian sniper understood very well. John Miluk Metcack was a Siletz Indian from a reservation along a river that ran through the coast range of Oregon. The Siletz were a peaceful people, loggers and fishermen, but Metcack's grandfather had been one of the last warriors of the feared Tututni tribe in northern California. The old man had been rounded up by the army at the turn of the century and sent into exile in Oregon for being caught on a cattle raid when he was a teenager.

Metcack's father died in a logging accident when his son was six years old, and the old man took over the young Indian's care. Along with the hunting and tracking skills needed to feed a family, the old man taught the boy the ancient warrior tradition with its strong sense of obligation and responsibility. Part of these obligations was the duty one owed to another warrior. Even though he was a white man, Brody was a true warrior, and they had shared danger on the warpath together. If Brody needed assistance with his mission of vengeance, Chief owed it to him to help in any way he could.

"It ain't going to be easy."

"I don't give a flying fuck if it's going to be easy or not, man!" Brody's anger finally broke through the surface. "How do I do it?"

"The best way is to use another sniper against him."

"How?"

"First, you spend a lot of time finding out where he's been working. Then you go out and track him down. When you find him, you kill him. Preferably, from a long distance," he added.

"What do I need to know to do that?"

"How good are you with a rifle?"

"I qualified as a marksman back in Basic."

"On what?"

"Both the M-fourteen and the sixteen."

"On the Known Distance Range or the Train Fire?"

"We did both."

The Indian was thoughtful for a moment. "You might do," he said.

"For what?"

"A sniper." He paused. "But it'll take a lot of training and a rifle."

"Will you teach me?"

"Better than that, why don't I go with you?" the Indian volunteered. "I can probably get Gambini to go, too. He's my partner and one of the best spotters in the business. If you're going to get these guys, you're going to need to have a good team."

"Okay, so all I have to do is to get my CO to let us go out there and do it."

"Maybe I can help you with that."

"How?"

"Well, we need to come up with a plan." The Indian looked thoughtful. "Something that will justify them letting us stay out there alone for a long time."

Back in the hidden NVA jungle headquarters north of the Song Re, the contingent of Russian snipers were celebrating the kill that their leader had made that day. A shot of over a thousand meters at a moving helicopter from the offhand position was quite a feat and a fine example of what a well-trained marksman could do with a Dragunov rifle in his hands.

Yuravitch was already drunk and keeping the younger men enthralled with stories from the Great Patriotic War, especially tales of his sniping prowess. He threw vodka back and stuffed his face with canned sausages.

Zerinski was disgusted with the man's behavior. The old man had finally gotten his kill, and he had done it without defying his orders, too. It had been pure, blind luck, but Zerinski still had to admire the feat for what it had been, a great shot.

His admiration did not, however, mean that he was going to let the army major have a greater say in how the operation was run. It was still a KGB show. Yuravitch was valuable, but only if he did not get in the way. He was not the only ex-sniper in the Soviet Union and he could easily be replaced.

Zerinski's problem was that he had been posted outside the Soviet Union for too long and he was beginning to think like a foreigner. He was almost ashamed to be from the same country as the red-faced, drunken Yuravitch who had now started singing patriotic songs from the Great War of the Motherland. He hammered the table, bellowing off key and pausing every few phrases to pour more vodka down his throat.

Yuravitch was a crude Russian peasant, a man only one generation away from being a barefooted, stinking farmer. Zerinski's family had been minor aristocracy who had joined with Lenin back in the days of the Revolution. He was a killer, but refined, a man who hated to see his country represented by buffoons like the old sniper.

Zerinski finished the last of his vodka and headed back to his small quarters. The girl was waiting for him again.

CHAPTER 19

Camp Radcliff, An Khe

A lone pair of spit-shined jungle boots stood next to an upside-down M-16 rifle and an empty steel helmet in front of Echo Company's orderly room. All the men were assembled in formation, gathered for an infantryman's memorial service. The boots, rifle, and helmet in front of the ranks symbolized the job of the Air Mobile Infantry—closing with and destroying the enemy.

The ceremony was something else that Rat Gaines firmly believed in—saying a proper good-bye to the dead. It was part of the job of commanding men in combat. The company commander wasn't a religious man himself and he knew that the service wouldn't help Elliot Fletcher at all. But the service wasn't being held for the Snakeman's benefit. It was for the benefit of the friends he had left behind.

"Company!" Gaines bellowed, stepping out in front of the ranks. "A-ten-hut!"

The assembled grunts and aircrew, all of them in complete uniform for a change, snapped to a rigid position of attention. Everyone who was not on duty had made a point of being at the service. It was one of the few times that the whole company had ever been together.

"Stand at ease," Gaines commanded.

In unison, the men placed their hands behind their backs and moved their left feet over to the parade rest position.

"The battalion chaplain," Gaines announced. He stepped back out of the way.

An older man wearing the robes of a Catholic priest over his jungle fatigues stepped forward and briefly looked up and down the ranks. "We are here today," he started, "to honor one of our dead, Private First Class Elliot Fletcher. I understand that he was known to most of you as the Snakeman."

A soft murmur ran through the ranks, not laughter, but approval that the priest knew at least that much about the man. All too often the chaplain referred to the deceased by the wrong name. Standing with the rest of his squad in the second rank of the Blues, Brody listened to the chaplain's words, but they brought no comfort. He knew, however, that Snakeman would have gotten a real kick out of seeing everyone in the company standing there all dressed up just because of him.

Brody wasn't so sure about the certain hope of resurrection that the priest promised was coming to Fletcher. Questions of life after death didn't mean much to him. He knew that some of the men fervently clung to the promise of heaven as a way of escaping the realities of the war, but it didn't make much sense to him. As far as Brody was concerned, if God existed He was doing a pretty piss-poor job of running His planet. Brody had seen too much in Vietnam to ever be comforted by the pious words of priests.

And if there was a Heaven, Brody knew that Fletcher wouldn't be in it. Heaven was for preachers, housewives, and young children. The Snakeman would be somewhere down in hell with all the rest of the grunts, whores, and lawyers, bitching about the booze and the broads.

Thankfully, the memorial service was short. But then

came the hardest part. A bugler from the division bank played taps. As the mournful notes rang out, Brody had to fight back tears. It suddenly came to him that taps would be the last song that would ever be played for him. He shivered.

When the company commander dismissed the formation, Brody wandered back to the Blues' tent and sat down on the end of his bunk.

He briefly thought about writing Fletcher's parents and giving them more details about their son's death. He knew that the army's standard notification to them would be painfully short of details. But telling them everything really wouldn't help them, or him. The only thing he wanted to do was to get out in the bush and track down the sniper who had wasted the Snakeman.

That's a real religious solution, he thought grimly, remembering the Sunday school classes of his childhood. As the Old Testament said, an eye for an eye, a tooth for a tooth, a life for a life.

The only problem was that Brody knew he wouldn't be satisfied with taking the life of just one gook in payment for Fletcher's death. Since he didn't know how to measure the life of a friend against the lives of his enemies, he was going to kill as many of those motherfuckers as he possibly could.

Even after he had killed, though, there would always be an empty space inside him that Fletcher had once filled. Brody shook his head angrily and got to his feet. He had to go learn how to shoot a sniper's rifle.

On his way over to the Ranger Company, Brody stopped off at the Division Finance Office and drew two hundred dollars out of his army savings account. He wasn't going to wait until the paper work for the insurance money was processed before he held Snakeman's wake. It was something that needed to be done soon, and he intended to set it up for that evening. He had once read somewhere that the Irish used to bring the deceased to the wake so he could see that everyone was enjoying the party. Brody wanted to make sure that Snakeman, wherever he was, saw that they were enjoying his.

Chief was already on the sniper's zeroing range behind the Ranger barracks.

"The first thing we need to do," he told Brody, "is to get you acquainted with this rifle and the scope."

"But I've fired a fourteen before. Hundreds of times!" Brody protested.

"Yes, but this is not an issue M-fourteen," Chief cautioned him. "It's an XM-twenty-one. Sure, it looks like a M-fourteen, but it feels differently, it handles differently, and it shoots differently."

Brody decided to shut up and let the expert teach him what he needed to know. He took the rifle from Metcack's hands. It did feel different. For one thing, the added weight of the scope and silencer added several pounds. He threw it up to his shoulder. Even with the extra weight, it balanced very well.

"We're about the same size," Chief continued, "so this piece should fit you about as well as it does me. Now, the main difference between this rifle and the ones that you shot before is that this one has a match-grade barrel and a glass-bedded stock. That, along with the match-grade ammunition, gives it the accuracy."

He pointed to the variable-power Redfield scope mounted on the top of the receiver. "This is what brings the rounds onto the target, the ranging scope. Put it up to your eye."

Brody threw the rifle to his shoulder and brought his eye up to the sight reticle. Along the vertical line of the cross hairs, he saw two short tick marks, one above and one below the horizontal line.

"See those two ranging marks in there?"

Brody nodded.

"Rotate the rear reticle a little."

Brody turned it and saw the small marks move farther apart.

"That's the ranging function of the scope. You place the top mark on a man's head, the bottom one on his boots, and he's in range. It's just that simple. Range him in, squeeze it off, and he's dead."

Brody knew that it wasn't quite as simple as the Indian made it out to be, but he was going to try to master the art of sniping one way or the other.

"Okay, let's start shooting." Chief handed him a magazine of twenty rounds of NATO 7.62mm match-grade ammunition.

As he was putting the magazine in the bottom of the receiver, Brody noticed that the rifle had the automatic-fire selector switch mounted on the side of the receiver. "Why's this thing got the rock-and-roll lever on it? You can't snipe on automatic fire."

"That's true," Metcack grinned. "But if you get your ass in a crack, you can sure as hell blast your way out with it. The only problem is that full auto blows the silencer out and scraps it. But if you need it, you got it. And if you get out alive, they can always give you a new silencer."

For the next hour, Brody fired at targets on the range, familiarizing himself with the rifle and the scope. If everything went according to their plan, he wouldn't need to shoot the XM-21 because Chief would do the killing for him. But Brody wanted to know for himself how to use the weapon. Just in case.

"You're not bad for a line grunt," Metcack said when they were finished. "Another month or so and I might make a decent sniper outta you after all."

Brody was pleased. It was always good to hear acclamation from an expert.

"But shooting is only half of it," the Indian continued. "The other half is getting the guy in the scope to take the shot. But you've spent enough time crawling around out in the brush. You should be able to handle that part of it."

Chief put lens caps on both ends of the scope. "Let's go run a brush down the bore of this thing and get us a beer or two."

Over half of the rest of the Blues, including all of the men in Brody's Second Squad, were in The Pink Butterfly Bar early that evening for the Snakeman's wake. Even Sergeant Zack and Lieutenant Alexander had shown up to pay their respects. Alexander hadn't known Fletcher well, but he had heard enough about the door gunner's legendary exploits to put in an appearance.

Everyone was rather subdued at first. They greeted one another as they came in and sat down quietly with a beer. No one quite knew how to act at a party for a dead friend. A few of the bar girls came over to try to stir up some business for the beds in the back rooms. They left quickly when Brody snarled and told them to fuck off.

Sergeant Zack sat and watched the younger men drink in silence. He knew what Brody was trying to do, but he also knew that the young grunt didn't have much experience with this kind of soldier's memorial for a fallen comrade. Leo the Lionhearted realized that it was up to him to start the necessary and cathartic process that would lead to all of them getting falling-down drunk and crying.

"Treat," he said, to begin the opening floodgates of their memories. "Do you remember the time when Fletcher went outside the perimeter to take a shit and stumbled into that bunch of gooks?"

Brody looked up from his beer and smiled. "Yeah, the Old Snake's pucker factor was a solid ten that day."

Corky broke in. "He couldn't shit for a week after he saw them standing there, watching him."

"I didn't know a guy could run that fast with his pants down around his ankles," Two-Step laughed.

"But he wasn't really running, though," Brody remembered. "Sure, he'd run a couple of steps, but then he'd stop, scream his head off, wave his arms around, and take off again.''

''We were all laughing so hard at him that the gooks got away,'' Corky smiled.

That broke the ice and they started going around the table, one by one, each man telling his favorite story about Fletcher's deeds and misdeeds. Each man added creatively, telling it as he remembered it, more than as it happened. No one minded. A ten percent-bullshit factor was allowed in the retelling of any war story.

Leo watched silently as the men went through the process of saying good-bye to their buddy. It was hard, but the platoon sergeant knew that it was healing for them to be going through this. Fletcher had been kind of a good-luck charm around the Blues, one of those guys who always seemed to come out of any scrape he got into without getting hurt.

Some men were born to die in battle. You could see it in their eyes the first time you met them. But the Snakeman wasn't like that. Everyone had expected him to live forever, and his death had been a real shock. If the legendary Snakeman could get killed, then it could happen to any of them, and no one wanted to acknowledge that possibility.

Before too long, the empty *ba-muoi-ba* beer bottles were three deep on the table, and Farmer was trying to make pyramids out of them. The bar girls had been keeping an eye on the party and decided that it was time to close in for the kill. One of them had noticed Farmer eyeing her. She sauntered up to him.

''Hello, GI.'' She smiled knowingly, one hand on her hip, and her eyes clearly focused on his crotch. ''My name is Suzie. You buy me a drink?''

Farmer blushed and looked around the table. ''Oh, no. I can't, not tonight.''

''Hey, Farmer!'' Corky laughed. ''Get some, man!''

''No, I can't do that tonight,'' he repeated, hoping that someone else would disagree with him.

Brody handed him a five-hundred P note. "Get on it, man. The Snakeman never passed up a chance to get a piece of the action, so why should you?"

Farmer got up from the table with a big grin on his face. "I'll be right back," he said.

That got howls from everybody, and they launched into outrageous tales of Fletcher's bar-girl exploits and his marathon whorehouse sessions on R and R.

Farmer came back to the table in a few minutes, a big, shit-eating grin plastered all over his face.

"How was it?" Corky asked.

"Oh, not bad, not bad at all."

For some reason, that struck everyone as hilarious, and the men howled. One of the guys from First Squad stood up and knocked back the rest of his beer with one swallow. "Well, if it was that good, I think I'll try me a little too."

That started a mass exodus to the back rooms. Everyone except Brody, Gardner, Zack, and the ell tee made a beeline for the girls at the bar. A few minutes later, they heard the squeals, shouts, and laughter coming from the girls' rooms.

"Sergeant Brody, Sergeant Zack," Alexander said, standing up. "Thanks for inviting me here tonight, but I've got to get back now."

Brody understood. The lieutenant didn't want to be around when the brawl started. It wouldn't look right, and the colonel wouldn't understand.

"Good night, Ell Tee. Thanks for coming."

"I'll make sure they all get back," Zack told the officer.

"Good," Alexander said. "I'll see you all in the morning."

Zack turned to Brody. "This is quite a party."

"Yeah," Brody answered softly. "Too bad the Snakeman had to miss it."

CHAPTER 20

Camp Radcliff, An Khe

Captain Rat Gaines was in his office at the Python Operations building going over the monthly chopper maintenance reports. Though he had been the Echo Company commander for several months now, he was still overwhelmed by the sheer volume of paper work that went with his job. He made another mental note to get on Muller's case again about getting a new company XO to handle some of it. He had signed the last report and barely dumped it in his out-box when there was a knock on his door.

"Come in!"

A grim-faced Treat Brody and a dark-haired Spec-4 marched into the small office, halted in front of his desk, snapped to attention, and saluted.

Rat returned their salutes. "At ease. What can I do for you guys?"

"Well, sir," Brody began, not quite sure where to begin. Captain Gaines had proven himself to be a man who understood the realities of Nam, but this was a real outrageous scheme they had come up with. "You remember Specialist

Metcack here, the Ranger sniper who went into Cambodia with us?''

''Yes, of course,'' Gaines nodded. ''How are you, Metcack?''

''Just fine, sir.''

''Anyway, sir,'' Brody continued, ''Chief and I have come up with an idea that we'd like to talk to you about. I think we've figured out how we can get that sniper who's been shooting down all those choppers and who killed Fletcher.''

''Have a seat.'' Gaines motioned to the folding metal chairs against the wall and took out a thin cigar. ''Let's hear it.''

''Well, sir. We want to go out there, track that sniper down, and waste him.''

Gaines looked at Brody like he had just said he was going to flap his arms and fly. ''You're going to do this all by yourselves?''

''Oh, no, sir. We plan on taking one of the other Ranger snipers with us, along with Gardner and Two-Step from the Blues.''

''The five of you are going to track this guy down and kill him?''

''Yes, sir.''

''Do you have any idea just how big Vietnam is?'' Gaines pointed to his wall. It was completely covered with a map just of their AO.

''Yes, sir,'' Brody replied, ''but we're going to make him come to us. Sir.''

''And just how are you going to do that?''

''By making ourselves good targets and drawing him out.''

''Look, guys,'' Gaines said seriously. ''I appreciate what you're trying to do here, I really do. But don't you think that your plan's a bit suicidal?''

''Not the way we plan to do it, sir,'' Chief broke in for the first time. ''It's just good countersniper tactics.''

''Okay,'' Gaines leaned back in his chair. ''Let's hear it. All of it.''

* * *

When the two grunts left Gaines's office, Brody felt a little better about their chances of getting the mission approved. After hearing them out, Gaines had agreed that it made sense after all. The only way to effectively take out a sniper was to put another sniper in the field after him. Before they left, the company commander promised to take their plan to the battalion commander and do his best to get approval for it.

When the men had gone, Gaines decided that taking their plan to Colonel Jordan was a good excuse for him to put off finishing his paper work for the day. He grabbed his Stetson and headed for the door.

Second Lieutenant Muller jumped to his feet and assumed the position of attention when he saw Gaines come down the hallway of Battalion headquarters. "Good morning, sir!" he snapped out.

"Good morning, Muller," Gaines replied pleasantly. "Oh, by the way. In case it has slipped your mind, I need a new executive officer. If you remember, my last one became the new Aero Rifle Platoon leader."

"Yes, sir!" Muller sang out. "I'll get right on it, sir!"

"Great, is the colonel in?"

"Yes, sir, he is. Shall I announce you, sir?"

"No, that's all right."

"Yes, sir!"

"Muller?"

"Yes, sir!"

"You'd better relax before you give yourself a heart attack."

"Yes, sir!"

Gaines shook his head and walked off, thanking God that the overly enthusiastic adjutant hadn't been assigned to Echo Company. He peered around the corner of Jordan's office and saw him at his desk doing paper work. "Got a minute, sir?"

Jordan looked up. "Sure, Rat, come on in." He, too, was glad to have a good excuse to put his paper work aside. "Have a seat."

Jordan lit up a Marlboro. "What's on your mind today?"

"Well, Colonel, I've got a good one this time. A couple of my men want to go out in the woods and track down that sniper in the Song Re."

"A couple of your mental cases, you mean."

"That's what I thought until I talked to them about their plan."

"Okay." Jordan leaned back. "Tell me. I could use a laugh today."

When Gaines had finished telling him Brody's plan, Jordan said, "That's a crazy enough idea that it just might work. It takes a thief to catch a thief, as they say. When do they want to do this?"

"As soon as they can get your approval."

"Considering the way that your mob usually operates, I'm surprised that they just didn't head into the bush the minute they thought of it."

"Well, sir, I've been trying to teach them how we do things in the army," Gaines smiled.

"It's about time somebody did. Anyway, let's go see what Brigade thinks of this wild idea. If they'll buy it, we'll get right on it."

Brody and Chief spent most of the rest of the day on the rifle range shooting at targets farther and farther away. By the time they finally called it quits, Brody was starting to hit the eight-hundred-meter targets with some regularity.

Brody dropped the empty magazine out of the bottom of the rifle. The last round had been a bull's eye. The rifle and the scope made it seem easier than it really was.

" 'Bout time for chow, don't you think?" Chief asked.

"Yeah, this sucker's hammered my shoulder just about enough for one day," Brody agreed, handing the rifle to the sniper.

Compared to the light-caliber M-16, the XM-21's full-power, 7.62mm round had quite a kick to it, and Brody had forgotten how sore a man could get after spending all day on the rifle range with something like that. It was one thing to shoot in combat, the adrenaline racing through his veins till he got so high that he didn't feel things like a weapon's recoil. But shooting on the range was different. There was no adrenaline, no combat high. Each time he triggered the rifle off, he felt the butt slam painfully into his shoulder. His shoulder would be black and blue when he took his jacket off.

They cleaned the rifle and made an appointment to meet on the range the next morning if nothing came up that would send them out on a mission.

Brody was standing in the chow line outside the mess hall when a spec-4 wearing glasses walked up to him. "You're from the Echo Blues, aren't you?" the man asked, eyeing the blue bandanna tied around Brody's neck.

"Yeah, why?"

"Well, I work in the photo lab over at PIO and I saw something the day before yesterday that really pissed me off. There was this reporter, see, and he came in with a roll of film to develop."

"An older guy?" Brody asked. "Always wears a smirk on his face?"

"Yeah, that's him. Guy named Janson. Anyway, he'd been down at the Dustoff pad that day and he came in with a bunch of pictures of the guy they took off the chopper, the one who'd been shot by that sniper."

Brody's heart stopped for a second. "Fletcher? He took pictures of Fletcher?"

"I guess that's what his name was," the man shrugged his shoulders. "Anyway, I just thought that you guys would like to know that your buddy's picture's going to wind up in some stateside paper."

"Oh no, it's fucking not." Brody's face was chalk white. "You can count on that." He stepped out of the chow line. "Here, take my place. And thanks, man, I really appreciate your taking the time to tell me that."

"No sweat, man, I just didn't think it was right."

"You fucking A, it ain't. I'll get that shit squared away ASAP."

Brody didn't want to take time to change into a clean uniform, so he brushed the dirt off his fatigues on his way over to the division headquarters. He didn't know where the press people stayed, but he figured that he could find out easily enough.

The first person he asked was the MP on duty outside the main door. "I wonder if you can help me?" he asked politely. "I'm looking for the press quarters?"

"That's off limits to troops."

He started thinking fast. "One of the reporters, a guy named Janson, went out with us the other day and when we got back, he said that he wanted to talk to me about the operation."

"I'm sorry, buddy, but it's off limits. You can call and he can come out and escort you in, but I can't let you go over there on your own."

"Yeah," Brody laughed. "I guess they're real VIPs and don't need to be bothered by a bunch of grunts."

"That's why they put them in the VIP quarters."

That was all Brody needed to know. "Thanks a lot, man, I guess I'd better go call him."

As soon as he was out of the MP's sight, he turned around and headed back around the side of the headquarters compound. The VIP quarters were just across the street from the officers' club. There was even a white sign on the side of the building reading Off Limits.

He waited around the corner of the building until it got dark, then he walked into the place like he owned it. The PIO had thoughtfully provided little name tags for all the doors so he was able to find Janson's room with no trouble.

He knocked on the door. There was no answer.

He tried the doorknob. It was not locked. Since it was so early, he figured that the reporter was probably over at the club. He opened the door. The darkroom was empty.

He found an easy chair next to the window and sat down to wait. Janson would have to come back sooner or later. He wished that he had brought a weapon, just in case Janson didn't see eye to eye with him about the photos. Then he realized that if he killed the reporter it would be all too easy to trace it back to him. The MP would remember that someone had asked directions to Janson's room. If the reporter wouldn't listen to reason, Brody decided he would still kill him, but later and quietly.

Brody only had to wait about a half an hour before he heard footsteps in the hallway. He got up from the chair and stood behind the door.

Janson walked into the room and snapped on the light.

"Janson, we've got to talk," Brody said from behind him.

The reporter spun around, his hands up in a defensive posture.

"Whoa, I'm not armed." Brody stepped out with his hands held out. "I need to talk to you, and the MPs wouldn't let me in."

"What do you want?"

"Mind if I sit down?" Brody said, taking a seat.

Janson looked at the young, blond grunt and remembered their little walk in the woods. He didn't know what Brody wanted with him, but whatever it was, he didn't trust him. "What do you want?" he repeated.

"I understand that you were down at the Dustoff pad the other day when we brought Fletcher in."

"And if I was?"

"I also understand that you took pictures of his body."

Janson froze. He remembered that Brody was the grunt who had gotten so disturbed when someone had tried to take pictures of the dead GI from that artillery short round.

"I took some photographs, yes."

"I want them. All of them. And the negatives."

"I don't know if I can do that, Sergeant."

Brody looked down at his hands and paused a second before going on. "Mr. Janson," he looked up and locked eyes with the older man. "I don't quite know how to put this to you, so I guess that I'll just come right out with it. If a single one of those pictures is printed anywhere in the world, I am going to kill you."

"Now wait a minute!" Janson backed up.

"No, you wait a minute, mister!" Brody jumped to his feet. "Elliot Fletcher was one of my best friends and one of the best fucking door gunners in the Cav. Like everyone else around here, he was doing his best to keep the fucking Communists from taking over this country, and they finally killed him. Now all you can think of doing for him is to take a picture of his dead body and print it to make a sensation in the papers back home." Brody shook his head. "It ain't right, mister. It just ain't fucking right at all."

Janson didn't know what to say.

"If you want a big story," Brody continued, "why don't you write about grunts like Snakeman trying to do their jobs? Why don't you write about the snipers that killed him? But that ain't news, is it? It ain't news unless you print a picture of a dead GI."

"Sergeant Brody, I am trying to do a story about those sniping incidents. That's why I took a picture of your friend. He was killed by the sniper. I took it so people could see what is happening here."

"Janson, you and your kind are fucking vultures. Most of what gets in the papers about us here in Nam is twisted. I don't know why you guys do it that way. I do know that there's not much I can do about it. But I kill people for a living. Most of the time I kill people that I am told to kill or people who are trying to kill me."

He stabbed his finger at Janson's chest. "In your case, I am going to make an exception. If you print those pictures of Fletcher, I am going to kill you. And I'm going to do it for Fletcher and for every other grunt who has died in this fucking war."

Brody headed for the door. "And if I am not able to do it, there are several other people waiting in line to take care of that little job for me. One other thing. There ain't no place you can hide that we can't get to you."

CHAPTER 21

Camp Radcliff, An Khe

Even after securing Brigade's approval for the sniper hunting mission, it took some time to get everything ready to go. For one thing, the combat reports relating to the snipers' activities had to be analyzed to see if there was a pattern to them that might reveal where they were based. As Gaines had reminded Brody, Vietnam was a big place, even the First Cav's AO was big. Also, sniping had been a VC specialty for years, going back to the days of the French in Indochina. It was necessary to cull out the reports of normal sniping activity. It soon became apparent, however, that the recent sniper attacks seemed to be centered around the Song Re Valley. Exactly where, was the big question. While this was going on, Brody was putting his team together and getting their equipment squared away.

The hardest part of choosing the team was having to tell a number of people that they couldn't go along on the trip. Even though the mission was classified, the word about it had spread quickly and everybody wanted to get in on the act. Some of them wanted to go for the adventure, and others because they wanted to be in on the payback for Fletcher's death.

Brody quickly got the team narrowed down to the five men he wanted. The only real problem he had was with the men in his own squad. Everybody wanted to go.

"Goddamnit, Farmer," Brody shouted. "For the last fucking time, no! You can't go!"

"But, Sarge," Farmer tried one more time. "That's not fair."

"Farmer," Brody said wearily, "there isn't a single fucking thing in this goddamned place that is fucking fair."

"I'm just not good enough to play with the big boys, is that it?" Farmer looked like he was about to cry.

"No, man, that's not it at all. You're a good grunt, but this requires just a little more experience than you have."

"But you're taking JJ, and we came in-country together."

"I know you did, but he's spent a lot of time hunting in the woods back where he came from."

Farmer finally gave up. "Okay, okay." He turned to go.

"Just a sec," Brody called after him. "You can be on our pickup team with Corky and Zack. They're going to be standing by in case we need a backup or an emergency extract."

"Gee, thanks, Sarge." Farmer's face brightened.

"No sweat."

Convincing Farmer to stay back had been easier than talking Corky out of going. Corky was real proud of being a grunt. He had volunteered for both the army and infantry duty in the Nam to prove that he was as good an American as any Anglo. Being the son of wetbacks, illegal immigrants, in California, he had grown up trying to prove that he was a good citizen even if he was Hispanic.

Even the slightly xenophobic Snakeman had finally come to agree with the machine gunner on that subject. All it had taken was for Corky to knock the Texan on his ass every time that he made a wisecrack about Mexicans. It hadn't taken long for Corky to get Fletcher to change his mind.

Brody found the machine gunner getting his field gear ready. "Corky," he began, "I'm going to have to ask you to stay back on this one."

"Why?"

"I'm not going to take the Pig." The M-60 machine gun was commonly referred to as the Pig because of its weight. "We can't afford to carry the ammo for it."

"Hey," Corky said hotly, getting to his feet. "What kinda shit are you talking, man? I can keep up with any fucking grunt in the Nam."

"I know you can, man." Brody put his hand on his shoulder. "But if we get into a long, drawn-out pissing contest out there, you're gonna run dry and we won't have any extra ammo for you."

Corky shrugged his hand off. "Don't give me that shit, man. I ain't no fucking FNG. I can handle myself in the brush."

"I know that, Corky, but I don't want to pack that fucking gun, man."

The Chicano was silent for a moment. "Brody, I'm going to get your ass for this," he hissed. "I swear by the Virgin."

Brody had known for a fact that this was going to happen, but there was no way to avoid it. "At least wait until we get back, okay?"

"You got it, motherfucker." The machine gunner stomped out of the tent.

As Brody watched him go, he began to see why officers did not make friends with their troops. He hated to have Corky pissed off at him. He was one of the originals along with the Snakeman, and they had been through a lot together. He'd settle it with Corky later. For now, Brody had to get back to the problem at hand. He picked up the list of the gear he wanted to take.

A lot of things that they needed were not in the regular

supply channels and had to be borrowed or requisitioned from the Ranger company. The sniper rifles and their associated equipment, the scopes and the match-grade ammunition came from the Rangers, as did a large supply of the freeze-dried LRRP rations—Lurps as the troops called them. Since they were going to be out in the jungle for an extended period of time without any resupply, they couldn't pack the weight of regular canned C-rations. He had also secured several of the new two-quart canteens. They needed water, lots of water.

Brody was also able to get his team issued oak-leaf-pattern camouflage uniforms. Where they were going, deep into Indian country, they needed every last bit of protection that they could get. The whole topic of camouflage uniforms in Vietnam was a real sore subject with grunts. At a time when almost all other armies in the world were in camouflage field uniforms, the senior officers in the U.S. Army strongly resisted the idea. It smacked too much of elitism and of foreign armies. And after all, they hadn't been worn in World War II or Korea.

Although camouflage uniforms were very effective in a jungle combat environment, they were still frowned upon by the army's high brass. Almost every airman in the U.S. Air Force wore camies around the concrete jungles of their air bases, but the line infantry troops were not allowed to wear them.

That was just one of the many things in Vietnam that defied logic, reasoning, or even common sense.

As for weapons, the two Ranger snipers came with their own sniper rifles and whatever backup pieces they wanted. Two-Step carried his sawed-off shotgun as well as an M-16. Gardner also chose to take a sixteen along with his usual thumper. Brody packed his trusty M-16 and borrowed a .45-caliber pistol as a backup piece. Everyone had their fighting knives, plenty of hand frags, and a claymore apiece.

Gardner was chosen to pack the team's Prick-25 radio because he was the biggest man in the group, but everyone carried an extra battery in their rucks. The radio batteries were only good for about a day's continuous operation, so they would use the radio only when they absolutely needed to talk to someone. The rest of the time, they would be cut off from all communication.

There would be no resupply, probably no dustoff, and no reinforcements. There was also a good chance that they would all die out there and no one would ever know what had happened to them.

Brody shrugged that thought off and went back to his list.

Gardner didn't know quite how he felt about going on the sniper hunt. He had been proud when Brody asked him to join the team, but in the back of his mind there was fear. He knew how dangerous it was going to be and how little chance any of them had of coming back. He also knew that he couldn't turn down the invitation. Some things were even more important than death. Being true to friends was one of them.

Now, more than ever, these men were all that he had. Since Sandra had given him the brush-off, the only people that he could depend on were the grunts he lived with. He could not, and would not, let them down. Fortunately, along with nagging fear, there was also the thrill of going on an important and risky mission.

Combat was always an adventure to Gardner, but going deep into enemy territory to track down and kill a sniper was more like a commando raid in World War II, like Merrill's Marauders in the jungles of Burma or the Green Beret missions along the Ho Chi Minh Trail. Rather than stumbling around in the woods or flying overhead in a slick waiting for the NVA to open up on them, they would be taking the war to the enemy in their own backyard.

He was extra-careful about putting his gear together, making sure that he had everything he would need. With no resupply, if his life depended on having something, he had to have it on his back or he was going to be SOL, "shit outta luck."

The first thing he packed was lots of ammunition. In fact, almost half the weight in his ruck was ammo, 40mm grenades for his thumper and bandoliers of magazines of 5.56mm bullets for the M-16. He had debated taking the sixteen, but had finally decided that with so few men, if they got into a close-in fight, he would need it. Usually a grenadier carried a .45-caliber pistol as a backup piece for the grenade launcher, but that was when there was a full squad of infantry around to cover him if he needed it. This time, he would have to be able to provide his own covering fire.

Next came his chow. Thankfully, the freeze-dried LRRP rations were light. He could carry a week's worth of the plastic bags for the same weight of two days' worth of canned C-rations. He could go without eating for a couple of days if he needed to, but they were planning to be out there for a couple of weeks.

He also packed a couple of extra field dressings and a bag of blood expander, called Ringer's Lactate by the medics. After their last little trip to Cambodia when he had gotten hit by a piece of rocket frag, he firmly believed in blood expander. Had it not been for that, he would have bled to death.

The balance of his ruck was packed with ass-wipe, extra socks, his poncho liner, and a claymore mine.

With three two-quart canteens clipped to the sides, the pack weighed almost eighty pounds. And on top of that, he would also be carrying the team's Prick-25 radio. The mission was going to be a real ass-kicker, but he was strong and he had reason to punish himself that way. Revenge.

Gardner finally put the loaded ruck aside and looked down at his watch. Mai would be getting off of work in just a little while. He decided to go down to the club and meet her when she came out. On his last night in camp, he didn't want to hang around the tent shooting the shit with the guys. Maybe he would go home with her instead and spend a few hours. Anything would be better than staying in the camp.

"Hello, Jim," Mai said, smiling when she saw him standing outside the EM club. "What you do here?"

"I came to walk you home."

"Oh, thank you."

They didn't say much to each other on the way to the main gate. Gardner had been too busy to see her since the afternoon when he and Brody had caught Dillard trying to rape her. He was still pissed about that, but he had heard through the grapevine that Dillard had been sent down to Saigon. He wouldn't be bothering her anymore.

Mai felt a little shy around the big American today. She felt a deep debt for his having rescued her from the MP, and she didn't quite know how to repay him. "Maybe you like to eat special Vietnamese dinner with me tonight?" she asked, looking up at him.

"Yes, that would be nice."

"Okay. First we must go to the market, maybe buy a chicken."

She led him past the Sin City strip of bars and souvenir shops into the village of An Khe. He had not been down into the Vietnamese part of the village before. Few GIs went there. It was a crowded, busy place and he felt a little uncomfortable around so many Vietnamese without his weapon. It was still daylight, but he knew full well that there were VC mingling in the crowd. There always were.

Mai quickly bought a chicken, some vegetables, rice wine, and a block of ice. He offered to help her pay for the food, but she refused to take his money. "No, Jim," she said. "I want to do this for you."

Their shopping completed, she led him on a winding path back through the maze of streets and alleys to her small house. "Make yourself comfortable, Jim." She brought a glass full of ice and a beer to the table in the main room. "I go make dinner now."

Gardner sipped his beer and watched her prepare the meal. This was a different side of her, one he had not seen before. He almost felt like he was back home waiting for Sandra to put dinner on the table. He realized that he had missed these domestic moments since he had been in the army. There was something very satisfying about watching a woman cook for him. It focused his mind on the other things she could do as a woman. He was looking forward to taking her to bed later that evening.

CHAPTER 22

Camp Radcliff, An Khe

The next morning, Brody, Gardner, Two-Step, and the two Ranger snipers waited down at the edge of the Python alert pad while the chopper crews preflighted the machines that would take them into the target area. Lieutenant Alexander, Sergeant Zack, and the rest of Brody's squad were on hand to see the team off. Most of them didn't think that the five men had a chance in hell of returning from the mission alive.

Almost everyone in the group was a little tense, and no one had much to say. Corky was still pissed about not being able to go. Even after Zack had talked to him, his pride was hurt. Brody was grim, aching inside to get on with it. Gardner was quiet, lost in his own thoughts. Two-Step was off to one side talking to Metcack and Gambini, the other Ranger sniper.

Gambini was totally unlike Chief. He was a short, dark Italian from Detroit, a fast talker and high-strung. He seemed to be a little nervous about the mission. Chief had vouched for his abilities in the field, and that was good enough for Brody, but Two-Step wondered about him.

On the flight line, the chopper pilots and crew got themselves ready as soon as the birds had been checked over. Gabe insisted on flying *Pegasus* as the bait chopper, but he was doing everything he could to even the odds against them. He and his copilot were wearing chickenplate when they climbed into the bird, and the pilot had even placed two of the armored vests under his and the copilot's feet for added protection from low-angle shots. Gabe knew that there was a good chance that they were going to be shot at again, but he was pissed and determined to do anything he possibly could to get the snipers who had shot him down before.

"Let's go, boys and girls," the slick pilot called out to the waiting grunts. "Party time!"

Brody didn't need to say a word. The men had been itching to get this show on the road all morning. They put on their chickenplate vests and picked up their heavily laden rucks.

"Good luck, men," Alexander said.

"Brody." Zack looked concerned. "Remember, if it gets too hairy out there, you can always call for an extract and go back in later."

They both knew that that was not the case. This was a one-shot mission, all or nothing. Zack was just trying to give him an out.

"Thanks, Leo. You just keep the pickup team from fucking the dog, and it'll work okay."

"Take care, Treat," Corky finally said.

"Yeah, you, too, man."

The grunts scrambled to get on board *Pegasus*. Gabe was carrying two door gunners from another crew, so the five men strapped themselves into the canvas jump seats in the crew compartment and settled down for the ride.

Sitting in the rear cockpit of his green-and-tan camouflaged AH-1 Cobra gunship at the head of the line of choppers, Rat Gaines still had severe reservations about the whole operation. Still, after talking to the Ranger Company commander and several people in the G-3 Operations

Staff Section at Division, he realized that as crazy as it sounded, this mission was probably the best chance they had of taking out the snipers who had cost them so many lives.

Gaines was flying the high bird. *Sudden Discomfort* could fly higher than the Hueys and had the added capability of being able to kick the living shit out of anyone who bothered them if the plan went wrong.

His gunner, Alphabet, would be doing the spotting from the front seat. His pockets were stuffed with maps and he had a pair of very high-powered binoculars he had borrowed from the Rangers. If the snipers shot at Gabe this time, Alphabet should be able to spot them.

Gaines also had the rest of a heavy-gun team, four Huey Hogs, on call if he needed them, but since they had to be so far away for the plan to work, he was having second thoughts about their usefulness.

He keyed the throat mike on his helmet. "Python, Python, this is Lead, crank 'em, over."

A chorus of rogers followed as the six helicopters fired up their turbines at the same time. One by one they called in that they were ready for takeoff.

"Golf Course Control," Gaines radioed the tower at the end of the airfield. "This is Python Flight Leader. Request permission to take off, over."

"Python Lead, this is Control. Roger, you are cleared for takeoff."

With Gaines's Cobra leading, the choppers taxied out onto the PSP runway. They stopped and wound up their turbines.

"Python, this is Lead. Pull pitch now!"

The six choppers rose from the giant Air Cav chopper field in formation and started down the runway as if they were tied together with a string. Rat was real particular about how his people looked when they flew. On this of all days, with so many people watching, he wanted his boys to look good, and they did.

As soon as their airspeed had built up, they rose into

the air and banked off to the north. Heading out over the perimeter of the camp, the Cobra and the other heavily laden gunships clawed for altitude while Gabe's slick stayed low to the ground.

In the back of the slick, Brody and the men looked out the open doors at the jungle that rushed by below them. It felt real strange to Brody not to be behind one of the doorguns. He never flew anywhere unless he had a loaded sixty in his hands. But this time, until they landed, he was just along for the ride. That and bait.

Thirty minutes later, they were north of the Song Re Valley, in the general area where the sniper had been active before. The Air Cav still had a mopping-up operation going on in the valley, and there was a lot of air traffic. There was a good chance that the sniper would be operating.

The heavy-gun-team broke off and headed to the side to orbit well out of sight a couple of miles away. There, they would await Gaines's call. *Pegasus* swooped down low over the jungle and started looking for a likely place to get shot at.

Rat stayed high above Gabe. From eight thousand feet in the air, Alphabet could barely make out the olive drab shape of *Pegasus* as she skimmed over the treetops, trolling for fire. The top sides of her main rotor blades had been hastily spray-painted white to make it easier for him to catch sight of the spinning rotor disk from above. Otherwise, she would have been lost from sight against the dense greens of the thick jungle foliage.

Gabe had the wick turned up all the way, and the slick was making almost a hundred and fifty miles an hour as he dodged in and out of the small valleys and ridgelines. He flew on for over half an hour, right down on the treetops.

From the top cover spot, Gaines was beginning to think that the whole operation was going to be a bust when he heard Gabe's voice in his headphones. "We're taking fire," the pilot said calmly. "The rounds are impacting on the starboard side. I'm climbing out now."

In the front cockpit of the Cobra, Alphabet trained his fieldglasses on the area to Gabe's right where the fire was coming from. He saw very little except for the densely forested hills and valleys as he swept the binoculars along the ridgelines. He started looking farther off to the side.

A thousand meters off of Gabe's flight path there was one small hilltop that was less densely covered than the rest. He could actually see the bare ground in places. It was far away, but it was good place to position a sniper. "Rat," he called back. "Go into a left-hand orbit, I may have 'em."

"Roger."

As Gaines went into a hard banked turn, Alphabet caught a glimpse of movement heading down the small hill.

"I got 'em", he called out triumphantly. "That bare hilltop at nine o'clock. See it?"

Gaines looked and didn't see it, but he trusted his gunner. "Mark it," he called up.

Alphabet circled the area on his map and plotted the coordinates. "I've got it, oh-three-four nine-eight-seven."

Gaines copied the coordinates and got on the radio to Gabe. "Python Five Eight, this is Lead. We've got movement at oh-three-four nine-eight-seven. Over."

"Lead, this is Five Eight," the slick pilot answered. "Roger, copy oh-three-four nine-eight-seven. We'll be setting down to the Echo of that about two or three klicks. Over."

This is Lead, Roger. We'll be keeping a close eye on you, out."

This was the tricky part of the operation. Gabe had to set down somewhere and off-load the men without the enemy seeing them. When the first rounds had started hitting them, Gabe had thrown his machine into violent maneuvers, trying to throw the shooter's aim off and had headed down even closer to the treetops. Jinking the chopper wildly from side to side, he ducked around a ridgeline into another small valley and spotted a small clearing in the distance. They were probably out of sight now.

"LZ coming up!" he called back to the grunts as he set up for a landing.

Before Gabe had even flared out, Brody and the rest of the men had shucked their chickenplate vests, gotten into their rucksacks, and were standing out on the skids. The pilot touched down and they leaped off, running crouched down to clear the rotor blades.

With a quick glance over his shoulder to make sure that everyone had cleared the ship, the pilot pulled pitch, and the slick rose back up into the air. They had been on the ground for such a short time that no one could have known that he had dropped the men off unless they had been watching from the edge of the small clearing.

As soon as he cleared the treetops, Gabe swung the bird around and continued in the direction he had been flying for several minutes before he climbed higher and banked away to return to An Khe.

The five men on the ground were on their own.

From the Cobra orbiting high in the sky, Alphabet watched the small, camouflaged figures disappear into the trees around the clearing. "Skipper," he called back, "they're on their way."

Gaines keyed his throat mike. "Python, Python, this is Lead. The party's over, everybody back to the barn."

Zerinski was not too angry that his snipers had missed the Huey helicopter. They couldn't get them all. It had been moving too fast and the pilot had been good. The Russian had never seen a helicopter thrown around in the sky that way. It had evaded their fire but it had been good target practice for the men.

From their vantage point on the small hill, the Russians had a good command of the valleys leading into the Song Re, and since the Yankees were still operating in the area there was a lot of air traffic going in and out. There were still a few hours of daylight left. Something else would fly by before too long and they would take a shot at it, instead.

Zerinski had finally allowed Yuravitch to take his team in closer to the Yankee ground units to try his hand at some close-in shots. He wondered how the old sniper was doing. Yuravitch had been so ecstatic about his first long-range kill with the Dragunov rifle the other day that the KGB man had relented and finally let him do what he did best.

Both teams had been in the field for three days and they were due to rendezvous back at the NVA camp tomorrow for a rest break and to pull maintenance on the rifles. He glanced down at his watch. If they didn't get something in the next two hours, Zerinski would start back before dark. Even though they had to spend one more night in the jungle on their way back, he thought fondly of a shower and a hot meal.

He was glad that this operation was winding down and that he would soon be getting back to more civilized surroundings, if you could call wartime Hanoi civilized. For his money, he would have much rather spent his time in wartime Saigon. At least in the south, they knew how to live and have fun.

CHAPTER 23

Camp Radcliff, An Khe

When Rat Gaines stepped out of the rear cockpit of his Cobra back at An Khe, he saw his operations sergeant waiting on the edge of the pad to talk to him.

"Captain," the NCO said as soon as Rat had pulled off his helmet. "We got us a small problem here. Mr. Worthington was supposed to take out one of the People Sniffer missions tonight, but he's down with a raging case of the shits."

"The shits?"

"Yes, sir, and he's got it bad, too. The doc put him in the hospital. Who do you want to use to replace him?"

Rat knew that into each life a little rain must fall, but it always seemed to be monsoon season around him.

"Come on inside," he said wearily. "I'll have a look at the mission board to see who we've got on hand."

In the operations shack, Rat scanned the blackboard listing the scheduled missions. Everyone was pretty well booked up for the next couple of days. If he pulled somebody off to take the night mission, it would bugger up the flight schedule for days.

"I'll take it myself," he told the sergeant, resigning himself to another long night. "Who's going to be my peter pilot?"

"Warrant Officer Brown, sir."

"Brownie?" Rat groaned.

"Yes, sir."

Rat sighed. Brownie was one of the most irritating assholes in the entire battalion. On top of that, he wasn't a good flyer. But it couldn't be helped. If Brown was assigned to fly the mission, Rat had to go with him. "Okay, when do we take off?"

"Twenty hundred hours for the briefing at Brigade, sir."

Gaines glanced at his watch. That just gave him enough time to shower, change, and grab a quick bite to eat. He'd have to call Lisa and tell her that he couldn't make it for dinner in the club tonight as they planned.

Rat hated People Sniffer missions with a passion and considered them to be a gigantic waste of time. Flying around in circles at night waiting for a bunch of bedbugs to get excited was not his idea of a good time. And to make it worse, Lisa was going to be pissed off again.

The People Sniffer was the brainstorm of some REMF working in the Limited War Laboratory back in the States. He thought that it would be a great way to catch the elusive Cong when they moved at night. His device was based on the fact that the common bedbug, *Cimex lectularius*, got excited when it smelled humans, and it could smell them from a couple of hundred meters away.

This unsung scientific genius made a little box and filled it with bedbugs. Attached to the box was a recording device that monitored the movement of the bugs. In theory, when a chopper carrying the device flew close enough to humans, the bugs would start jumping around all over the place. The pilot would then fly around in a circle until he pinpointed the exact spot where the VC were and would unload on them. At least in theory that's the way it was supposed to work.

In practice, however, it was a slightly different matter. Mostly the People Sniffer pilots simply flew around in the sky for a couple of hours. If the bugs detected anything, it was more often a water buffalo or a herd of wild pigs instead of a band of marauding Cong. It turned out that bedbugs seemed to like water buffalo almost as much as they did humans.

Like too many other people in Vietnam, the bedbugs were confused as to who the real enemy was.

Two-Step was on point with Brody and Metcack following close behind when he saw the small hill that Alphabet had spotted. It had taken them almost three hours to get close enough to take a look at it and they were starting to lose the light. He halted under a big tree and waited for Brody to catch up.

"What ya got?" Brody said softly, sliding into position beside the Indian.

"It's right up there ahead of us."

"Let me take a look." Brody got the powerful sniper-spotting scope out of his ruck and focused it through a break in the leaves. He couldn't see any obvious positions. If they were up there, they were well camouflaged. A sniper's life depended on no one being able to find him.

Brody caught some movement from the left crest of the hill.

"What you got?" Metcack asked.

"Put your scope on the left side of that hill 'bout two fingers from the center."

Chief put his rifle up to his shoulder. Peering through the telescopic sight, he scanned the area Brody had indicated. "Don't see a thing. Hey, wait a minute. I've got a guy taking a piss."

The sniper refocused his scope. "Treat," he said softly. "That fucker's a white man. I think he's a Russian."

"Don't shoot!" Brody hissed.

"Why?" Chief looked over at him.

"Let me have a look."

Chief slid over and Brody got behind the rifle. It was a white man, blond in an unusual brown-gray-and-green camouflage uniform. As he watched, the man finished urinating, buttoned his fly, and dropped out of sight in the brush.

"He's gone," Brody told the sniper. "Are you sure that guy was a Russian and not a Frenchman or something?"

"Well," Chief answered, "that might be, but whoever he was, he was wearing a Russian camie suit, that much I know for sure. Are you going to call it in? I'm sure the Division headquarters would love to know that we've spotted a Russian."

Brody thought for a moment. "No, I think I'll wait till we kill one of them first. Otherwise they won't believe us."

"You've got a good point there."

"Two-Step," Brody called. "You think you can get us into position so we can follow those guys if they pull out? I want to find their camp. Find out just what in the fuck is going on here."

The Indian scout checked his map and looked up at the hill again. "I think we might be able to swing around on this side," he pointed. "And pick 'em up when they cross that stream."

"Let's do it," Brody said getting to his feet. "And, Chief, don't shoot unless they spot us."

"You're the boss."

The five men were in position to observe the hill when Zerinski decided that it was time to start back.

Two-Step was on the spotting scope when the Russians pulled out. "Treat," he called out softly. "I've got at least three of them, maybe four. Two of them are carrying weapons that I've never seen before. They look like some kind of sniper rifle, long barrels and scopes."

Suddenly Brody realized what was going on. For some reason the Russians were in Vietnam testing a new kind of sniper rifle. That was the only reason Snakeman had been killed.

"Let's get going," Brody hissed. "I don't want to lose them."

At the overly long briefing in the Brigade operations room, Rat was given an area over the Song Re to check out with his People Sniffer flight. The division was still trying to get a fix on the elusive enemy in the valley, and every bit of information helped. When the briefing was finally over, he grabbed his gear and headed out to the part of the Golf Course where the Night Hawk and People Sniffer choppers were parked.

When he got to the bug-infested Huey slick, he found Brownie sitting in the open door shooting the shit with the People Sniffer operator instead of supervising the refueling operation. "Are we 'bout ready to go, mister?" Rat growled.

"Uh . . . yes, sir," the copilot answered.

"Then let's get this fucking show on the road, 'rat' now," Gaines snapped as he climbed on board. He quickly strapped himself in and started going over his preflight checks.

Brownie and the operator finished the refueling and scrambled in after him. They got very busy with their preflight checks, not willing to test Rat Gaines's famous temper.

As soon as the Huey's big Lycoming T-53 turbine had been fired up and the main rotor was spinning, Rat radioed the tower. "Control, this is Bedbug Two, request clearance, over."

"This is Control, Roger, Bedbug, you are cleared for takeoff. Remember now, nighty, night, don't let the bedbugs bite."

"Up yours, wise ass!" Gaines growled as he pushed forward on the cyclic and started down the runway. He could tell that this was going to be a fun night. Flying anywhere at night in a Huey was a bitch.

As soon as he had cleared the lighted perimeter of Camp Radcliff and banked off to the north, Gaines switched off all of the external navigation lights on the chopper, went to dim lighting on the instruments, and let his eyes adjust to the darkness. Below him, the land was a sea of velvety black darkness. Only a few, isolated pinpoints of light shone from farmers' huts in small villages. When the map told him that he was over the target area, he turned back to the People Sniffer operator.

"This is it, mister. Get your bugs working."

"Yes, sir." The man opened the duct bringing outside air in from the scoop below the chopper's nose back to his little box full of bugs. From now on Gaines would fly where the operator told him to go, based on what the bugs did. It promised to be a very boring night.

A half an hour later, Gaines was scanning his instrument panel when he noticed that his fuel gauge was reading almost empty. "Brown, did you top this thing off?" he asked the copilot.

"Yes, sir, I sure did."

It had been reading full when they took off, so Gaines attributed it to a faulty gauge. He decided to note it on the Dash Thirteen when they got back and have the maintenance people look at it in the morning.

"Sir, I've got a contact," the People Sniffer operator called up to Gaines. "I need you to circle over to the right."

"Roger."

Gaines had just started a slow right-hand turn in accordance with the operator's instructions when the turbine faltered and cut out.

The pilot instantly bottomed the collective and tried to establish an autorotation glide. "Look for a place to put her down!" he yelled over to Brownie.

While the copilot peered down into the darkness, looking for a break in the trees, Gaines chopped the throttle and flipped the engine fuel control and the governor over to emergency. He punched the start fuel control on and triggered the switch on the collective column to energize the starter.

The starter whined, and the turbine spun, but it would not light off.

He tried it again, advancing the throttle slightly to flight idle. Still nothing.

"Hang on, we're going down!"

"Over to your left, sir!" Brownie shouted excitedly. "I think I see a clearing!"

Rat eased down on the rudder pedal, slowly bringing the ship around. There had better be a clearing. They were coming down fast and if there wasn't they were going to be splattered all over the trees. He locked his shoulder harness tight and readied himself for the crash. *What a stupid way to die,* he thought, *flying a load of fucking bugs.*

At the last moment, Gaines thought he saw the clearing himself. At least it was some kind of break in the solid black. He kicked down on the rudder pedal, aimed the falling chopper for it, and hauled up on the collective as hard as he could.

The blades caught air and gave him a little precious lift. He frantically pulled the nose upright as they hit the trees with a grinding crash.

With the screech of tearing metal, the tail boom caught in a tree and was ripped off. The main rotors snapped off close to the hub and went spinning away into the night. The fuselage tore through the trees and came to a rending, shuddering halt, right side up.

For a moment, there was dead silence.

"Everybody okay?" Gaines called back, unlocking his shoulder harness and pulling his helmet off.

The other two men were shaken up but unhurt. The bedbugs had also survived intact.

Gaines kicked his cockpit door open and cautiously stepped out into the night. His boots touched bare ground, so they must have just made it to the edge of the clearing Brownie had spotted. Gaines drew the 9mm Browning Hi-Power pistol from his shoulder holster, walked out in front of the wrecked chopper, and peered into the darkness. He couldn't see his hand in front of his face, much less anything else.

"Now all we've got to do is figure out where the fuck we are," he muttered, staring into the pitch black jungle.

CHAPTER 24

The Song Re Valley

Rat Gaines crouched under the nose of his crashed bird and pulled his map from the side pocket of his nomex flight suit. He shone the small beam of light from a red-filtered penlight on it and tried to figure out where they had come down. He peered around in the night to see if he could find any identifying landmarks, but it was just too dark for him to pick out anything in the terrain.

It was just as well. The crash had shattered the antennas to the radios and he couldn't call for help anyway. He patted the pockets of his flight suit to see if he had remembered to bring his survival radio. No, of course not. He only carried it with him when he didn't crash.

It looked like they were going to have to just sit tight and wait for the morning. When they didn't return, the search planes would be up at first light, and since Flight Control knew where they had gone they would be able to find the downed Huey real soon.

He walked back toward the tail of the bird to see how bad the damage was. As he passed the aft section of fuselage, he smelled JP-4 jet fuel. He ran his hand along the side of the bird and it came back wet with kerosene.

He opened the fuel filler door and reached inside. The fuel cap was missing. That stupid son of a bitch Brownie had forgotten to put it back on.

"Mr. Brown!" Gaines called out softly. "Get your ass over here."

"Yes, sir." The voice was nearby in the darkness but Gaines couldn't even see his face.

"You topped this bird off this evening, right?"

"Uh, yes, sir," the copilot answered hesitantly.

"Then why in Christ's name didn't you put the fucking fuel cap back on?" Gaines was having trouble keeping his voice down.

"Oh shit!"

"You're going to think 'oh shit,' mister," Gaines growled. "I swear to Christ that when I get your ass back to An Khe, you're going to be burning shitters for a solid month."

Gaines was so pissed off at Brownie's stupidity that he did something very stupid himself. He walked away from the crashed ship, and the other two men to give himself time to cool off.

He was all the way to the other side of the small clearing when a crashing blow to the back of his head sent him reeling into unconsciousness.

In the jungle a few hundred meters from the downed chopper, Major Zerinski and his Spetsnaz sniper team had bedded down for the night. In fact, it had been their campsite that the bedbugs had picked up. They heard the chopper when it flew over their heads, and heard it stutter and fall from the sky.

When the Russian officer heard the chopper crash nearby, he decided to investigate the impact to see if someone had survived. It would be fortuitous to capture an American helicopter pilot. He had a lot of questions he wanted to ask.

Taking only their weapons, the five Russians left their

camp and moved silently through the brush, homing in on the faint voices of the Americans. They had stopped at the edge of the clearing and were scoping out the crash site with the sniper's infrared night scopes when suddenly Rat Gaines's shadowy shape appeared in front of them.

The Spetsnaz closest to the man slammed his rifle butt into Gaines's head, and he went down.

Zerinski knelt down beside the American and ran his hands over the body. He was wearing captain's bars on his flight suit.

"Take him with us," he hissed.

The Russians faded into the night, leaving Brownie and the bug man still at the wrecked chopper wondering where Gaines had gone.

Just as the Russians had done, Brody finally called a halt when it became too dark for even the sniper's Starlight scopes to be of any use to them. Unlike the Russian's infrared night scopes, the Starlight was a light-intensifying device and depended on light, however faint, to work. But the stars were not visible in the overcast sky and there was not enough light of any kind for the scope to work.

Also, the brush was so thick in that part of the jungle that it was an exercise in futility to move at night. Even if they could have seen their way to travel, they could not have followed the trail of the Russians they were tracking.

Brody hated to stop, but he knew that they had to. Still, they had not done too badly on their first day out. They had made contact with their prey and they were on the trail. In the morning, they would pick up the Russians' tracks again.

Since they were so deep into enemy territory, there was none of the grab-ass that usually took place at a halt, no smoking, joking around, or fires. There were too few of them and they had to be careful to avoid detection. The woods were full of wandering NVA and VC patrols.

Silently they lay down in a patrol star formation, feet toward the center, and prepared something to eat by pouring water into the plastic bags of Lurp rations. They tucked the bags up inside their shirts and lay on them. In fifteen minutes, the freeze-dried food was warm enough to eat.

For the rest of the night, they lay on the ground with their poncho liners wrapped around them, sleeping in turns and waiting for dawn.

Lisa wasn't pissed that Rat had had to break their date, but she was a little disappointed. She, too, had been looking forward to spending another night with him. She realized that she was starting to act like a hot-pants nurse out of a story in a men's magazine.

She smiled to herself. That wasn't a bad idea. She could send off for some of that outrageous underwear from Fredrick's of Hollywood and wear it the next time they went to bed. That should really convince Gaines that she had been in Vietnam too long.

When she got off of her shift, she really didn't feel like hanging around in her room by herself trying to read or write letters. Going to the club wouldn't be any fun without Rat, so she decided to go over to Division headquarters mess for a quiet meal and a couple of drinks before she turned in. At least there she wouldn't have to put up with Rat's pilot buddies asking her where he was and trying to hustle her.

She had just finished her meal and was having her gin and tonic at the bar when Janson walked up and sat on the barstool next to her.

Lisa saw an older man, wearing tan-wash pants and a safari jacket. From the length of his hair he had to be a civilian, probably a reporter. For some strange reason, the press always seemed to think that army nurses were ready to jump into bed at the drop of the hat, and they were always hitting on them.

She turned away and ignored him.

"Excuse me, Lieutenant," Janson said.

She turned to face him. At least he hadn't given her the

"Hi there, honey, what's a girl like you doing here?" routine that they all thought was so original.

"Yes?" she said coolly.

"You were at the Dustoff pad the other day when they brought in that door gunner who had been killed by a sniper, weren't you?"

"Yes, I was, why?"

The reporter stuck his hand out and said, "My name's Janson, David Janson. I'm a reporter and I'm trying to do a story on that incident."

Lisa looked at him coolly, ignoring his hand. "And, what does that have to do with me? I'm a nurse, I always meet the Dustoffs. I should think that the Division PIO should be able to help you with anything you wanted to know about that."

Janson ignored her rebuff. "Yes, they have been very helpful, but I'm trying to get a different angle on the story."

"A 'human-interest piece' for the folks back home? Or an exposé?" Lisa's voice dripped with sarcasm. Like most GIs in Nam, she had little use for the press. Even when they got the facts right, their stories were always slanted against the GIs.

Janson wasn't at all surprised that the nurse was hostile toward him. He knew he had few friends in the army except for the self-serving senior officers in Saigon who kissed his ass every chance they had, hoping to see their names in print.

"No, Lieutenant, not that." He tried his best to sound open and friendly and, at the same time, sympathetic. "I'm just trying to find out a little more about the man who was killed."

"Fletcher, the Snakeman?" Lisa was surprised. "If you want to know more about him, why don't you talk to the men in Echo Company, First of the Seventh."

"You knew him?"

"Sure I knew him. Almost everyone in An Khe knew the Snakeman. He'd been a fixture around here for a quite a long time."

"Why don't I buy you another drink while you tell me about him."

"I buy my own drinks, thank you." Lisa flared up.

Janson was not taken aback, he was starting to get used to everyone in the Air Cav thinking that he was an asshole. "Sorry, Lieutenant, no offense meant. Will you tell me about him anyway?"

Lisa looked at him for a moment. "Sure. Why not. Somebody needs to hear about the Snakeman. He was a good grunt. He saved my life once."

"I'd really like to hear about that."

"Well, I was coming back from a madcap at one of the orphanages . . . ," Lisa started, telling the story of the time she had been shot down in the Kim Son Valley and how Fletcher and Gabe had held off repeated charges by a horde of NVA so she could escape.

When she got through telling him about that incident, she went on for a while about Fletcher's pet snakes and some of the other things that had made him so well known around Camp Radcliff.

"And when Brody catches up with those snipers," she finished, "they're going to wish they hadn't wasted Fletcher. He and Brody were real tight."

Janson's ears picked up at that one. "Brody is hunting down the snipers?"

Lisa suddenly realized that the mission was probably highly classified and that she had just said something that shouldn't have been said.

"Oh, I just heard someone saying something like that, but you know how rumors are," she laughed, desperately trying to cover up her mistake. "If you believe even half of what you hear around here, the war would already be over."

She grabbed her hat and abruptly stood up. "Well, I have to be going now." She glanced down at her watch. "My shift's almost on."

Janson watched her leave. He didn't even know who she was, and he had not been able to read the faded name tag on her fatigue jacket. He leaned over the bar and motioned for the bartender to come closer.

"Yes, sir?"

"That nurse who was just here," Janson asked, "do you know who she is?"

"Who . . . Lisa? Sure, Lisa Maddox. She works at the hospital."

"Thanks. How about another beer?"

"Coming up."

Janson didn't know if he had a big story, but he sure as hell had a lead that was worth following up. And if he was right, it was a much bigger story than the one about the artillery short round. It also fit right in with that little visit that Brody had paid him the other evening. He could believe that Brody was out there somewhere on a private misson of vengeance. If there was an operation going on to hunt the snipers down, that was worth more than just a few lines.

The bartender brought him his beer and he sipped it slowly. He had heard people talking about an increase in sniping incidents lately, very accurate sniping that had taken several lives. He had seen the mad scramble for flak vests going on down on the flight line. He had seen Fletcher's body brought in and had had the confrontation with Brody about the photos.

In anyone's court, he had enough information to declare that there was an emergency in the First Cav area of operations, an emergency that no one was officially talking about. It smelled to him like a classic military cover-up.

And on top of that, he had just learned about a vengeance mission aimed at those same snipers.

He drained the last of his beer and left his change on the bar as he stood up to go. In the morning, he would ask the PIO about all this, knowing full well that all he would get would be double talk. Then he would go down to Echo Company, First of the 7th, to do a little snooping around on his own.

Missions of vengeance were definitely news.

CHAPTER 25

Camp Radcliff, An Khe

"Colonel," Muller greeted the battalion commander the first thing the next morning. "Captain Gaines did not come back from a mission last night."

"What!"

"Yes, sir," Muller continued. "One of his pilots got sick and he flew as his replacement on a People Sniffer mission."

"Why wasn't I informed of this at the time?"

"I didn't know, sir. I just found out about it myself."

Jordan lit up another smoke. This was just what he needed, what with everything else that was going on. "What's being done to find him?"

"They've got people up looking for him now, sir."

"Where he'd go down?"

"No one is quite sure, but it's somewhere in the Song Re Valley."

"Oh shit!" Jordan said softly. "Keep me informed."

"Yes, sir."

Jordan went on into his office and sat down at his desk. He stabbed his cigarette out in the empty ashtray. What a way to start the day. He looked at his in-box, filled to overflowing again. Life had been simpler back in the good old days in the Delta. Back then all he really had to worry about was getting killed. He fervently hoped that the battalion got a big mission real soon, something that would get him out in the field for a couple of weeks. He reached for the paper on the top of the stack.

"Good morning, Captain Gaines."

Rat opened his eyes to see a tall, blond man in a brown-green-and-gray camouflage suit standing over him. Gaines's hands were tied tightly in front of him, and his head ached.

"Allow me to introduce myself. I am Major Gregor Zerinski of the Soviet KGB, and you are my prisoner."

Gaines swallowed. For a moment he didn't know what to say. Now he had really fucked up.

"Roger S. J. Gaines," he recited. "Captain, United States Army. OF one-zero-two-seven-three-one." It was his name, rank, and service number, as required.

"I know all of that, Captain, it is on your identification card." Zerinski held his hand out with the card in it. "What does the S.J. mean?"

"Stonewall Jackson."

Zerinski's face lit up. "You are from the American South then, the old Confederacy. I have studied your War of Rebellion, a very interesting struggle."

Gaines didn't answer.

"Now," the Russian continued, "you are with the First Air Cavalry Division, is that not correct?"

"Roger Gaines, Captain, United States . . ." Gaines repeated again. It was the only information that a prisoner was required to give under the rules of the Geneva Convention regarding prisoners of war.

"Spare me this endless recitation of your name and rank, Captain, it is foolish. I know you are of the Air Cavalry Division, you wear their insignia." He pointed to the Horse Blanket patch on the shoulder of Gaines's flight suit.

"Also, I see that you fly with a unit called Python Flight." Rat also wore a big full-colored Python patch with the motto 'You call, we maul' under a picture of a coiled python with a saber in its mouth.

"What's a Russian KGB man doing here?" Rat asked, trying to divert attention away from himself. He didn't want this guy to make a connection between him and the Russian pilot he had encountered last month in Cambodia.

"We have been observing you Americans and the way that you make war." Zerinski smiled like a wolf. "It has been very informative."

"I'll bet it is." Gaines noticed the strange rifle one of the Russians was carrying, a long, scoped rifle with a cut-away stock. These had to be the guys who had been shooting down all the choppers in the Song Re and they did have a new weapon. If only he could capture one of those rifles and make it back to An Khe with it. It was all he needed to do to be a hero instead of a dumb shit who had run out of gas in the air.

But Gaines didn't feel too much like the James Bond type this morning. Right now, he felt more like two pounds of shit in a one-pound bag.

"Are you able to walk?" the Russian asked. "We have to leave soon and continue back to our base."

"And if I can't?"

Zerinski smiled again. "Then we will carry you. But I can assure you, it will be far easier on you if you walk on your own."

Gaines saw his point. He didn't really feel like being carried, trussed upside down, on a bamboo pole like a dead animal. "Okay, I'll walk. Where are we going anyway?"

"Oh, Captain, I am afraid that is a military secret."

Gaines knew that, but he had just wanted to see if he could get anything out of this guy. Obviously not. "What's for breakfast?" he asked.

"You are hungry? Good. We will share our rations with you. You will need your strength for the march." Zerinski said something in Russian, and one of the troops untied Gaines's hands. He was given an opened can of sausage and a chunk of bread.

"Don't I get a knife and fork?"

Zerinski laughed. "Captain, I am so looking forward to talking to you when we get back to our camp. I do like a man with a sense of humor."

Gaines ate the greasy canned sausages. When he was finished, he casually tossed the empty can into the underbrush.

One of the Russians saw him do it, shot him a dirty look, and went to retrieve it. "No more childish stunts like that, Captain," Zerinski warned. "Or you will get nothing more to eat."

"How 'bout a little water?"

"Certainly." Zerinski unclipped his own canteen from his field belt and handed it over to the pilot.

Gaines drank deeply and handed it back. One thing was certain. Whoever these guys were, they were pros. Almost as good as the Special Forces people he knew.

"Why did your machine crash last night?"

"You're not going to believe this, Major, but I ran out of gas."

Zerinski studied him for a moment. "For some reason, I do believe you, but I do not understand how a thing like that could have happened."

"Stupidity."

"Ah, I also like a man who can admit to his mistakes. I have a feeling that we will get along very well."

After the Russians sanitized their rest-break area of every last thing they might have dropped, they formed up and moved out. After cautioning him against the futility of trying to run away, Zerinski tied Gaines's hands behind his back and had him walk in the center of their patrol beside him.

They did not talk on the march and kept up a brutal

pace through the jungle. With his hands tied behind his back, Gaines had a difficult time keeping up with them but he did his best. To fall out meant that they would put him on a pole and carry him, and he didn't want that. Even with his hands tied, as long as he was on his own two feet, there was a chance he might be able to make a break. A slim chance, considering the looks of the Russian troops, but still a chance.

"Colonel!" Muller shouted, bursting into Jordan's office. "They found him, they found Captian Gaines." He paused as a confused look passed over his face. "Or at least they found where he was."

"Was?"

"Yes, sir. The found the crash site and picked up the other two men who had been on the chopper, but Captain Gaines wasn't with them."

"Where is he?"

"Well, no one seems to know, sir," Muller frowned. "But the search is continuing," he added as if that made up for his lack of information.

"When those other two men get back here, have them report to me ASAP."

Less than an hour later, Muller was back in his office. "They're here, sir, the other two people who were with Captain Gaines, Warrant Officers Brown and Warner."

"Send 'em in."

The two men in dirty flight suits marched into the office and snapped to attention in front of Jordan's desk. They looked like they had spent a night out in the brush. The colonel returned their salutes and had them take a seat. "Okay," Jordan began. "What happened out there last night?"

Since he had been the copilot, Brown started. Jordan let him go on until he reached the part about Gaines walking off into the night.

"Why in the hell did he do something stupid like that?"

"Uh, I don't know, sir." Brownie could not meet the battalion commander's eyes.

"And how long was it before you noticed that he was missing?"

"Not too long," the bedbug operator broke in for the first time. "Fifteen, twenty minutes maybe."

"Why did it take that long before you knew he was gone?"

"I thought that he was scouting out the area, trying to figure out where we were, sir."

Jordan had to admit that while it was dumb, it made a certain kind of sense.

"What happened to the chopper, anyway? Why did it go down?"

Brown wouldn't meet the colonel's eye. "Fuel problems, sir."

Jordan decided that he would look into this one a little further and check over the crash report. "Okay, men, go get cleaned up and report back to your units. If you think of anything else, let me know."

"Yes, sir," both men said in unison, anxious to be gone from the colonel's office.

When Lieutenant Mike Alexander finally learned that his CO was missing, he immediately went down to the battalion commander's office.

"Sir, I just learned that Captain Gaines is still missing. Is there anything I can do to help with the search?"

Jordan liked the hard-charging young lieutenant. He reminded him of his own younger years. "Well, for the time being, you're in acting command of the company, so why don't you go down to the TOC and see what the S-three's got going."

"Yes, sir." The lieutenant saluted and left.

In the Battalion Tactical Operations Center, the S-3 major was already coordinating the air search for Gaines. Two ships were up flying circles around the crash site, looking for him. There was little Alexander could do to help at this time so he returned to the orderly room.

The first thing he did was to alert Sergeant Zack to have the Blues standing by in case they were needed when the captain was found. The next thing he did was to call over to the 45th Mobile Surgical Hospital and ask to talk to Lisa Maddox. He knew that Rat had been seeing her lately and he wanted to let the nurse know that he was missing.

"Lieutenant Maddox, this is Mike Alexander down at Echo Company. Look, Captain Gaines crashed last night," he said hurriedly. He wanted to get all the bad news over with as soon as he could. "At this time, he is still missing."

There was silence on the other end of the line.

"Now we do know where he went down," he hastily added. "And we've got search planes up looking for him right now."

"Thank you for letting me know," Lisa finally said softly, a slight catch in her voice.

"No problem. I'll call you the minute we hear anything more."

"Thank you."

Alexander put the phone back down. That was one of the biggest reasons why he was still single and fully intended to stay that way as long as there was a war going on in Vietnam. He didn't want anyone to ever have to call his wife or girl friend with that kind of news.

He grabbed his hat and headed out of the orderly room. "I'll be down at operations," he told the first sergeant as he passed his desk.

"Right, sir."

The ready room at Python Operations resembled a morgue instead of the barely controlled riot that it usually was. The *Playboy* centerfolds pinned up on the walls next to captured VC flags, the battered lawn furniture, the overflowing butt cans, and the ancient pool table were all the same. But for the first time in living memory, the pool table was not being used, and the *Playboy* magazines were laying in piles unread.

The off-duty pilots and crew hanging around the room were wearing their customary unique items of clothing and head gear, but they were quiet. No one was laughing and joking or singing bar songs off key.

"You heard anything, sir?" a pilot wearing a VC helmet with a bullet hole in the forehead and a Hawaiian shirt over his flight suit asked as soon as Alexander walked in the door.

"Nothing yet." The lieutenant went past him into the radio room. "I'll let you know as soon as I hear anything."

CHAPTER 26

The Song Re Valley

"Where did you learn your English?" Gaines asked Zerinski as they continued on their way through the dim jungle under the towering triple canopy of the trees. "It's very good."

"My father started teaching it to me when I was a child." The KGB man looked over at the prisoner. "He was in the NKVD and had been assigned to the London mission during the war. Then later, when I joined the KGB, I went to school for further study to prepare me for field assignments. I speak German and French as well," he added with unconcealed pride. "Along with Vietnamese, of course."

"Where are you taking me?"

"To my headquarters, where we can talk." Zerinski smiled. "It's not safe out here in the jungle. There are too many Americans wandering around."

Gaines had been trying to get information out of him all morning, but he was getting nowhere fast and he was starting to become worried. Zerinski was being extremely careful about how he answered Gaines's questions, and he was giving nothing away. The Russian was also being very careful to make sure that Gaines did not escape. Not only were his hands tied, but one of the Russians kept his AK trained on him at all times.

"How much farther is it to this place?"

"Not too far now."

They had been moving at a steady pace all morning, not too fast, but steady, and Gaines was about on his last legs already. Zerinski only called a short halt every two hours, and Gaines wasn't used to this kind of exertion. He was a pilot, not a grunt. Also, the terrain in this part of Vietnam was a real killer. The jungle was as thick as any he had ever seen, and the ground was all either uphill or down.

"How 'bout water?" Gaines asked. "I'm getting a little parched."

"Parched?" The Russian officer looked puzzled. "That must be a southern expression, I have never heard that before. It means that you are thirsty, correct?"

"That's right."

"We will stop soon, Captain, then you can drink."

Gaines continued walking in silence. So far it did not look too good. By now, someone should have spotted the wreckage of the People Sniffer bird and picked up Brownie and the other man if they had not run into another enemy force and were still alive. After they reported that he had wandered off last night, a search would be mounted to find him. But since he was nowhere in the area, and the Russians had covered their tracks so well, there was no way that they could figure out where he had gone. If he got out of this one alive, he was going to have to do it all on his own.

And that was not going to be easy. These Russians were as good in the jungle as any grunts he had ever seen, and they didn't miss a trick. Maybe when they got to this camp, he could figure out some way to escape. In the meantime, though, all he could do was to keep his eyes and ears open and keep on trucking.

"Isn't it dangerous for you Russians to be in Vietnam, Major?" Gaines asked. "Aren't you afraid that someone will learn that you are here?"

"We are careful and take precautions to remain unseen. And our mission here is almost over. We will be gone without a trace long before anyone ever learns that we were here."

"And what exactly is it that you are doing here?"

Zerinski laughed. "Captain, it is so amusing to talk with you. You try to learn secrets from me. You have no need for subterfuge, however. I will tell you what we are doing here. And I will tell you because you will never get back to alert anyone to our presence."

The certainty in the Russian's voice chilled Gaines. Maybe his luck had finally run out.

"Did you see the rifles that two of my men are carrying? The long rifles with the telescopes mounted on them?"

"Yes, I did," he admitted. "I've never seen them before, what are they?"

"Those are the pride of the Red Army, the new Dragunov sniper rifle. We brought them here so that we could test them under field conditions."

"And who are the men with you, KGB?"

"Oh no, Captain, these are the cream of the Soviet Army. These man are Spetsnaz, 'Special Forces,' as you would say. Men like your Green Berets."

Gaines looked at the Russian next to him with new respect. That was why they were so good in the woods, so careful. He realized that he was in much deeper shit than he had first thought.

"I didn't know the Russians had a special forces."

"We have always had Spetsnaz units, ever since the days of the Great War. They are one of our best-kept secrets. That is why so few Americans have ever heard of them."

Gaines lapsed into silence again. He was beginning to think that this was definitely one of those days when the bear gets you. He cursed the guy who came up with the idea of putting bedbugs on choppers.

"Muller," Colonel Jordan barked, sticking his head out of his office. "You got any word on Gaines yet?"

The adjutant jumped to his feet. "No, sir!" he snapped out. "Also, sir, there is a man here to see you, a reporter, he says."

This was just what he fucking needed today, to waste his time with the press. Jordan saw an older, long-haired man in civilian clothes standing next to the screened, open window of the tropical hut that served as his headquarters building. The man turned around and walked forward. "David Janson," he said, extending his hand.

Jordan ignored his hand and slowly looked him up and down. "What can I do for you?"

Janson reminded himself for the tenth time today that he was going to have to stop automatically offering his hand to these people. They were not his friends, and most of them were not glad to meet him. "I'd like a minute of your time, if I may?"

Jordan glanced down at his watch. "Okay, a minute. Come on in."

In the office, Janson took an offered chair and got right to the point. "I understand that you've got a mission underway looking for some snipers."

Jordan butted his smoke in the overflowing ashtray on his desk and lit another one with a practiced snap of his engraved Zippo lighter. He sucked in a lungful of smoke and examined the engraving for a moment. *To Mack the Knife*, it read, *From Advisory Team 59. Sat Cong.* Things had been so much simpler back then. All he had to do was kill Charlie.

"Mr. Janson," Jordan finally said. "You look like you've been in Vietnam for quite a while. I'm sure that you are fully aware that I cannot, and will not, divulge any details about any operations that my battalion may be engaged in at this moment.''

''Well, Colonel, that may be, but this mission seems to be fairly common knowledge around Camp Radcliff, and I just wanted to confirm it.''

Jordan stared at the reporter for a long moment and then picked up the phone on his desk. He dialed a number and waited while it rang through.

''This is Colonel Jordan over at the First of the Seventh,'' he said. ''Let me speak to the PIO . . . Jerry, this is Mack. Look, I've got a guy in my office who's asking questions about my battalion's operations. He says his name's David Janson. . . . Yes.'' Jordan looked at the reporter. ''That's him. Will you tell him to get his ass out of my office before I throw him out?''

Jordan extended the phone in Janson's direction. ''The PIO wants to talk to you.''

The reporter stood up. He knew when it was time to cut his losses and run. ''No need,'' he said. ''I was just leaving.''

''You're also leaving my battalion area completely,'' Jordan added. ''I don't want to see you around here under any circumstances unless you are escorted by someone from the PIO's office. Is that clear, Mister?''

''Perfectly, Colonel. Good day.''

Outside the building, Janson squinted his eyes against the sun as he looked around. Obviously, there was something going on and it was hot. Otherwise Jordan would not have reacted the way he had. Either that or he was just another one of the growing numbers of media-hating army officers he had been running into lately.

The reporter got into the Jeep he had borrowed from the PIO's motor pool and backed out of the graveled parking lot. If the First of the 7th's battalion area was off limits to him, he would try his luck down on the flight line. Someone had to know something about what was going on.

* * *

Two-Step crouched down low and watched the ten-man North Vietnamese patrol heading for them. The black and green stripes of his tiger suit and the green and tan splotches on his face paint made him almost invisible against the leaves. He was well hidden, but it wasn't going to help this time. He had fucked up.

Because of the tangled thickness of the jungle they were passing through, he hadn't spotted the NVA patrol until it was almost too late and now they were going to have to fight their way out of it. There was too great a chance that the gooks would hear or see them if they tried to cut and run for it.

The other men were spread out on either side of him in a classic L-shaped ambush, their fingers poised on their triggers and their grenades close at hand. They were outnumbered two to one, so their only chance of getting out in one piece was to achieve complete surprise.

At the Indian's side, Gambini focused the scope of his sniper's rifle on the last man in line. The grunts would take care of the point man while he knocked off the men in the rear of the formation. His first shot would be the signal for the rest of the men to open up on them.

The sniper set the sight marks in his day scope on the man's head and where he thought that his boots were. He then raised his aiming point slightly, going for a high chest shot. He took in a deep breath and tightened his finger around the trigger. The silenced rifle spat, and the Vietnamese went over onto his back.

The jungle erupted with gunfire as everyone opened up at almost the same time. Three of the enemy went down in the first burst, but the other gooks dove for cover and returned fire immediately.

Two-Step's sawed-off shotgun roared again and again as he whipped the slide back and forth. The steel balls shredded the foliage and tore into the men hiding behind the underbrush. He dropped back down under cover and frantically stuffed shotgun shells into the tubular magazine under the barrel. Racking the slide back to chamber a round, he popped back up and emptied it into them again.

From the short end of the L, Gardner fired his grenade launcher almost point blank into the brush in front of him, hoping that the rounds would travel far enough to arm themselves. With the forest's canopy hanging over them, he could not arch his deadly little 40mm grenades up into the air as he usually did because they would hit the tree branches.

The first round exploded, but the second one didn't. He didn't even try it a third time. Dropping the seventy-nine, he reached behind his back and swung his sixteen around. He triggered off a quick burst right as a gook stuck his head up to throw a Chi-Com stick grenade. The 5.56 rounds caught the Vietnamese in the chest just as the grenade left his hand.

"Grenade!" Gardner yelled, throwing himself to the ground.

Under the adrenaline rush, Gardner's personal time went into slow motion. It seemed to take forever for the Chinese grenade to land. In his mind's eye he could see it tumbling over and over in the air, looking like a soup can stuck on the end of a short piece of broomstick. The black powder fuse was sputtering, and he could almost see the faint trail of smoke it left in the air. He hid his head.

With a dull crump, the Chi-Com stick bomb exploded. A heavy piece of frag slammed into his back, stunning him. He rolled off to the side and came up with his sixteen blazing.

At the other end of the long arm of the L, Chief took his time and placed well-aimed shots into anything he saw moving. Arms, heads, legs, it didn't matter. If it moved, he put a bullet in it. The range was a little too close for accurate shooting with a sniper rifle, but it was all that he had.

After emptying his sixteen in the initial burst of automatic fire, Brody dropped back behind his tree trunk to reload. He dropped the empty magazine out of the bottom of his rifle, slapped a loaded magazine into place, and pulled back on the charging handle to chamber a round.

An AK bullet slapped into the tree by his head, throwing wood splinters into his face. He snatched a grenade from his ammo pouch and pulled the pin, tossing the hand frag out in front of him.

The instant that it exploded, he jumped out and sprayed a full load of 5.56mm into the killing zone. When the bolt locked to the rear on an empty magazine, he dropped back down again. AK fire followed him. It was beginning to look like they had bitten off a little more than they could chew. The gooks were getting serious! The hollow crump of a Chi-Com grenade followed by two more spurred him into action.

He pulled another grenade from his pouch, pulled the pin, and, holding it in his left hand, stuck the muzzle of his rifle around the edge of the tree. He triggered off half a magazine, tossed the grenade, and ripped off another burst.

The explosion was followed by a high-pitched scream. That was a little more like it.

He dropped the empty magazine and reloaded. He crawled off to the side, to take up a new position behind a fallen log. He peered around the end of it and saw a man's leg through a break in the dense foliage. A leg wearing NVA khaki. He flipped the selector switch back down to semi-auto and, taking careful aim, he put an M-16 bullet in the leg.

The gook screamed when the 5.56mm round shattered his thigh. He rolled over, twisting around to bring his AK to bear. Brody calmly put a short three-round burst in his chest. The NVA flopped back down.

The firing slackened a bit, and over the clamor, Brody heard the coughing roar of Two-Step's sawed-off shotgun again. It sounded like he might have a little more business than he could handle.

Keeping low, he dodged through the brush toward the sound of the Indian's gun. He parted the leaves in front of him and almost ran into an NVA soldier trying to make his way around Two-Step's flank. The gook spun around and saw him at the same time. It was a race to see who could pull down on the other first.

Brody won.

His burst tore into the middle of the NVA. Some of the rounds hit the AK, knocking it out of his hands. The man gave a short grunt and went down to his knees, his belly shot open. Brody put another one in his head.

Suddenly all was quiet.

CHAPTER 27

The Song Re Valley

Shots rang out, echoing through the jungle. The Spetsnaz point man in Major Yuravitch's sniper team dove for cover behind a tree. It sounded like the firefight was far away, but sound can play tricks in the jungle. Yuravitch listened to the battle for a moment and recognized the sound of American M-16 rifles above the distinctive reports of AK-47s.

He motioned for the point man to move out toward the fighting and alerted the two snipers for action. It didn't sound like the battle was too far out of their way and, if the Yankees were involved, it was much too good of an opportunity to pass up. Since his long-distance shot the other day, Yuravitch had rediscovered his old love for killing people. He wanted to make up for lost time.

The firing ahead stopped abruptly. The Russians dropped down into cover again. Yuravitch waved the snipers forward, and the two men with the Dragunovs faded into the thick underbrush. The point man cautiously moved forward again, the lighter browns and grays of his camouflage suit somewhat conspicuous against the darker colors of the jungle foliage. The other Spetsnaz security man dropped back to accompany Yuravitch.

Yuravitch pulled the 9mm semi-automatic Makarov pistol from the brown leather holster on his field belt and flicked the safety off. He would have much rather been carrying an AK since he was first and last a rifleman, but traditionally and by regulation, a Russian officer was always armed with a pistol.

Brody and his men cautiously stepped out from their ambush positions, their weapons ready, their fingers on the triggers. There was no movement on the trail. Their ambush had been totally sucessful.

Brody waved them forward to check the kill zone. They went from one dead North Vietnamese to the next, making sure they were dead, and searching the bodies for documents.

"Brody," Gardner called out softly, kneeling on the ground beside one of the NVA. "Over here. This one's still alive."

Brody looked over and saw a young North Vietnamese soldier laying on his back. Both of his legs had been shattered. He looked well fed and, like the rest of them, his uniform was fairly new. He was regular NVA, not VC. There was fear in the man's dark eyes, and he held his hands clasped out in front of him in a plea for mercy.

"Kill 'im," Brody said bluntly. There was no way that they were going to take prisoners now. They couldn't stop and call for a Dustoff to evacuate him. They had to push on.

Gardner pulled his K-Bar knife from the upside-down sheath taped to his assault harness. He looked at the Vietnamese and hesitated. He had never killed a man with a knife before. The wounded man saw the knife and struggled to sit up, babbling hoarsely in rapid-fire Vietnamese, begging for his life.

From across the trail, Chief looked up and saw what was

happening. The Indian raised his silenced rifle and triggered off a quick shot. All Gardner heard was the sound of the round hitting the man in the head, a hollow plop. The Vietnamese fell back down, his fearful eyes still open.

Gardner got to his feet and sheathed the knife. "Thanks," he said, picking up his rifle again.

Metcack looked at Gardner without condemnation for his momentary hesitation. "No sweat, man," he said understandingly. "It's hard to do."

Gambini had taken up the drag position at their rear while the other men policed up the ambush site, scanning the area around them with the scope on his sniper rifle. With as much noise as they had made, if anyone else had been within hearing of the brief firefight, they would undoubtedly come to investigate.

He carefully scoped out the sides of the ambush site and then turned to check along their back trail. He caught a glimpse of movement and froze. It was just a flash of something lighter than the surrounding foliage. But that was enough.

"Brody!" he hissed, waving them to cover. "We got company."

The grunts instantly hit the dirt and fanned out to meet this new threat. Chief slid in beside the other sniper and brought his rifle up, too. "Where?"

"Low," Gambini pointed. "One finger to the right of that big tree."

Metcack focused his scope.

"Treat," he whispered. "It's the Russians!"

The five-man Russian team moved cautiously. Since the firing had stopped, it was difficult to tell exactly where it had originated. Also, the overhanging tree branches of the triple canopy let very little light down onto the thick underbrush, making it even more difficult to see.

One of the Spetsnaz security men was well out to the front on point, slowly crawling closer to the ambush site.

He sniffed the air. He could smell the cordite from the grenade explosions and the rifle rounds. He had to be getting close. He slowly got up on one knee and carefully parted the leaves in front of him to take a better look.

Chief's 7.62mm round took him in the hollow of the throat. He pitched facedown on the ground.

The soft pop of the silenced rifle was again the signal for the rest of Brody's men to open up with everything they had. The jungle erupted with a hail of small-arms fire.

If an ambush worked once, it could work again.

The Russians were stunned by the sudden barrage of automatic fire. They tried to answer the ambush, but the best they could do was to keep their heads down. A grenade sailed through the air and landed in the brush in front of Yuravitch. He saw it coming and ducked for cover behind a log, but the explosion was too close for comfort. He heard the deadly little pieces of frag singing through the air above him.

Whatever it was that they had stumbled into, it was much more than they could handle. "Pull back!" he yelled over the roar of the small-arms fire.

He didn't even give a thought to the dead Spetsnaz they were leaving behind. His only concern was to break contact fast and get out while they could. Staying there and trying to fight it out with an unseen enemy force of unknown size was sheer suicide.

"Cease fire!" Brody called out when he suddenly realized that no one was shooting back at them anymore. "Cease fire!"

He slowly got up to his feet. "Cover me," he told Gardner.

"Got it."

Brody was very careful when he approached the enemy position, but it had been abandoned. The only things they had left behind were a couple of empty AK magazines and the body of a blond man in a camouflage uniform, face-down in the brush. A folding-stock, paratroop model of the AK-47 assault rifle lay on the ground beside him.

Holding the muzzle of his M-16 on him, Brody rolled the body over with his boot. He was dead. The bullet had hit him low in the throat, severing his spinal column. His head lolled limply on his neck. Brody reached down and closed the Russian's staring blue eyes. He had been an enemy, but it was the least he could do for the dead.

He waved the others forward. Kneeling down beside the body, he started going through the Russian's uniform pockets and pack. He found little there except for standard military gear and ammunition, some of it Russian, the rest Red Chinese. It was fairly typical of what he usually found on the bodies of NVA regular troops.

In the breast pocket of the Russian's jacket, however, was some kind of identification card with the man's photograph. The writing was in the Russian alphabet, and he didn't have the slightest idea what it said. He also wore metal identification tags on a chain around his neck. Brody pulled one of them off as well.

Chief looked down at the body. "I told you they were fucking Russians."

"They sure as hell are." Brody handed the ID card up to the sniper. "Take a look at this."

The Indian glanced at it quickly and handed it back. "I wonder what it says."

"Probably about the same bullshit ours does—name, rank, and serial number."

"Ivan sure came a long way to die."

"He isn't the last Russian who's going to die before we get through with these motherfuckers," Brody promised. "They've got no fucking business being here in Nam. This ain't their fucking war." He got to his feet. "I'm going to call this one in to the battalion. I want the colonel to know what we've run into out here."

The men all came to stare at the body. This was the first Russian any of them had ever seen except on television. He didn't look all that different from a blond American. If he had had a bushy Air Cav mustache and was wearing issue jungle fatigues, they couldn't have distinguished him from a dozen other guys in their own battalion.

Brody got on the radio and called back to the Battalion TOC at Camp Radcliff. The signal was very weak. He had to shout to be heard and could barely make out what they said. They were just about at the end of the range for their Prick-25 radio.

"They don't fucking believe us," Brody said, giving the radio handset back to JJ when he was done. "They think that we're either drunk or stoned."

"I guess that they're just going to have to see this," Gardner said, holding up the dead man's ID card.

"We should call for a Dustoff and put this fucker on it." Gambini said, prodding the Russian's body with the barrel of his rifle. "Then they'd believe you."

"I'd love to," Brody said. "But we don't dare. They know we're here now, so we've got to get the fuck outta here ASAP." He turned to Two-Step. "Strip off that guy's jacket, stuff it in your pack, and let's move out."

CHAPTER 28

The Song Re Valley

"How could you have been such a fool?" Zerinski raged. "You never leave one of our own behind! Never! If that American unit finds him, they will have proof that we are operating against them."

Yuravitch's broad face was blotchy red as he strained to control his urge to strike out at the KGB man. Zerinski couldn't talk to Mikhail Yuravitch this way, a decorated hero of the Great War and a major in the glorious Red Army.

"I had no choice, comrade," the major said coldly. "The Yankees were close behind us and we were outnumbered. Also, I think they had a sniper with them."

Zerinski looked at him with a slight smirk on his face. "And just how many of these fearsome Yankee jungle fighters did you actually see?"

The old sniper paused for a moment. "I saw none of them," he finally admitted.

"I rather thought not," Zerinski sneered. "In the jungle, you seldom see your enemies. Were you more experienced with this way of fighting, you would have known that."

The KGB man looked out at the NVA camp hidden under

the towering trees of the jungle. "You have compromised our entire mission here, Major Yuravitch. A complete report of this will be made to the station chief in Hanoi and it will be up to him to assess the damage you have done." Zerinski waved his hand in dismissal. "You can go now."

Yuravitch bristled at being treated as if he was an errant private soldier. It was not the time to make an issue of it with the KGB officer, however. Later, the old sniper vowed, he would teach Zerinski better manners.

Zerinski watched the army major leave the room and smiled inwardly. He was not sorry at all that this incident had happened. It gave him a good excuse to terminate the operation and go back up north. The best thing about it was that any blame for the failure would fall on Yuravitch, not him.

He put his uniform cap on and walked around to the end of the building where his captured American pilot was being held in a bamboo tiger cage. It was time they had a conversation.

"Captain Gaines," Zerinski greeted him with a smile as he walked up. "Now that we are safe, we can have a nice, long talk."

He swept his arm around to encompass the hidden NVA camp. "No one will bother us here, and we can get to know one another a little better. Let me see, where shall we start?"

"You can start," Gaines offered, "by letting me out of this cage."

Zerinski studied the American for a moment. "Of course. How thoughtless of me."

He turned and called out in Russian. One of the Spetsnaz troops ran up to him and saluted. Zerinski spoke briefly.

"I am ordering this man to accompany you wherever you go," Zerinski explained. "He also has orders to kill you instantly should you try to escape."

Gaines looked at the young Russian soldier. He had a very serious look on his broad Slavic face. Gaines believed that he would kill him.

Zerinski untied the door to the cage. "Come on inside

out of the sun," he offered. "We will have a cool drink and discuss the war."

Gaines had no idea what this guy was up to, but he knew that it was greatly to his advantage to cooperate as long as he could. At least as long as the Russian was interested in him, he wouldn't be handed over to the gooks.

The poker-faced Russian grunt, his paratroop stock AK held at port arms, escorted him into the long, low building and stood in the corner of the room.

"Please, have a seat," Zerinski gestured.

"Thank you." Gaines sat down. *Aren't we being fucking polite,* he thought. *When do we get down to the thumb-screws?*

"Now, would you like a drink and something to eat maybe? Are you 'parched,' as you say?"

Gaines had trouble keeping a straight face. "Ah, yes, I would. Thank you."

"You are surprised, Captain," Zerinski laughed. "I can tell. Did you expect me to start beating you or pulling your fingernails out?"

Gaines didn't need to answer that question. It was written all over his face.

The Russian said something, and the guard went out of the room.

"He has gone to get your food," Zerinski explained, leaning back against the small wooden field desk behind him. "You are a victim of your own propaganda, Captain," he continued. "I am an officer in the Soviet KGB, not the German Gestapo. I come from a long line of men who have served the security of Mother Russia. My father was in the NKVD, and my grandfather served in the old Cheka under Lenin."

He pointed out the window to the NVA troops going about their daily tasks. "I am under the impression that you would rather talk to me than you would to those people. Am I not right?"

Gaines nodded.

"Good. I, too, would rather not have to turn you over to

my Vietnamese counterpart out there, Major Van. To be perfectly honest with you, Van is a psychopath and he lives to inflict pain on helpless men. It is not pleasant to see or hear him at his work.'' Zerinski reached into the desk drawer and pulled out a pack of American cigarettes. Salems. ''Would you care for a cigarette?''

Gaines knew that Zerinski was going to start playing hardball with him real soon, but it didn't hurt to have a last smoke.

''Sure,'' he said, feigning a casual attitude that he did not feel. ''I could use a butt.''

The Russian lit it for him, and though he detested menthol cigarettes, Gaines dragged the smoke deep into his lungs.

''Now then,'' Zerinski said. ''Why don't you tell me what you were doing flying around at night so far from your home base?''

Gaines thought for a moment. Why not tell him? But he would tell Zerinski only what Rat wanted him to know. ''We were looking for you.''

The Russian looked startled for a moment.

''Yes,'' Gaines continued. ''We have a massive operation under way right now to find your snipers.''

''They have been effective then.'' It was a statement, not a question.

''Somewhat,'' Gaines admitted. ''But more of a nuisance than anything else. Except, of course, when they kill one of my men.''

''What do you mean?''

''One of your guys killed a door gunner in my unit.''

''Oh, yes,'' Zerinski remembered. ''That was Yuravitch's shot. You know, he was very proud of that one.''

''He won't be so fucking proud if I ever get my hands on him,'' Gaines growled.

''Captain, I am really surprised at you. You are a soldier, you know that men are killed in war.''

''That is true, but this man was killed on a medevac flight.''

''I do not think Major Yuravitch knew that,'' Zerinski admitted. ''But I do not think that it would have mattered had he known. Yuravitch is a true soldier. He lives to kill his enemies. He enjoys it."

"But our countries are not at war."

"Not formally," Zerinski answered. "That is true. But we have been fighting for some time now, using others to die for us. This is just one of the few times that we have met face to face."

"Holy shit! Will you look at that fucking place!" Brody said in amazement as he gazed down on the North Vietnamese camp tucked away on the hillside in front of them.

Brody and Two-Step lay hidden in the brush along the top of a ridgeline overlooking a narrow valley and the next ridge beyond it. From their vantage point, they could plainly see the sprawling collection of small buildings, huts, weapons emplacements, and supply dumps hidden under camouflage netting and the towering trees of the triple-canopy jungle.

It was early afternoon and they had finally reached the objective they had been seeking ever since they had started tracking the Russians.

"It sure looks like Luke the Gook is planning to stay there for a while. That's at least a regimental basecamp." Two-Step focused his field glasses in on it. "And it's far too fucking big for us to tangle with. Now what the fuck are we going to do?"

"I don't know," Brody shrugged his shoulders. "I do know that if we try to just walk in there, they're going to have our young asses for lunch."

"That's most affirm."

Brody brought his glasses down and thought for a moment. "But you know," he said, turning to the Indian, "we might just be able to cut those guys down to something we can handle a litle better."

"What do you have in mind?"

"Well . . ." Brody looked thoughtful. "We can't just go waltzing in there and ask to see their Russian snipers. We need to flush those guys out into the open so we can deal with them, right?''

''Right.''

''Okay, why don't we call an air strike right on top of their asses,'' he said with a wicked grin. ''That'll ruin their whole fucking day. Then, when they run, we can sort them out.''

''That's not a bad idea,'' Two-Step agreed. ''But what if the planes kill all the snipers?''

''That's a chance we'll just have to take.'' Brody shrugged. ''But this is too fucking good to pass up, my man. I want to get a piece of these guys.''

''Sounds good to me. Let's do it.''

Brody made a notation on his map, marking the location of the camp. ''You keep an eye on 'em from here while I duck back and try to get through to somebody who can help us with this.''

The Indian settled down for a long wait. Getting an air strike together could take quite a while. As he sat, Two-Step surveyed the enemy camp, looking for their patrols and trying to pick out their defenses. He also looked for any sign of white men. If they were all wearing those fancy camouflage uniforms, they would be real easy to spot when they tried to make a run for it. All he had seen so far though, was olive-and-khaki-uniformed NVA.

''JJ,'' Brody called softly when he got back to the hidden location where the rest of the team was waiting. ''I need the radio.''

Gardner left his concealed position, crawled up to him, and gave him the handset.

Brody keyed the mike. ''Crazy Bull, Crazy Bull, this is Blue Two, Blue Two, over.'' He waited, listening to the hiss of the carrier wave coming in over the handset. He had been afraid of that. They were too far away from Camp Radcliff and he would have to go through the retrans station at the Special Forces FOB-2 at Kontum. Their powerful antennas would pick up his broadcast and retransmit it to An Khe.

He pulled out his SOI, found the frequency and call sign

for the Special Forces Forward Operations Base, and dialed it into the Prick-25 radio.

"Black Slider, Black Slider, this is Blue Two on your push, over."

"This is Black Slider," came the reply from the powerful radio station in Kontum. "Send your traffic, over."

"This is Blue Two, I need retrans to Crazy Bull, over."

"This is Slider. Roger, wait one, over."

"Blue Two, this is Black Slider," came the call a few moments later. "Your retrans is ready, send it, over."

A retransmission was really very simple. One radio picked up Brody's call, amplified it, and sent it out again on another more powerful radio. Once the call was set up, the system was automatic and you just made a normal radio call.

"Crazy Bull, Crazy Bull, this is Blue Two, Blue Two, over."

"Blue Two, this is Crazy Bull," answered the radio operator at the Battalion TOC back in An Khe. "Go ahead."

"This is Blue Two, I'm on a retrans through Black Slider. Let me talk to Bull Three, over."

"Two, this is Bull Three," answered the battalion operations officer. "Go ahead."

"This is Two, we have followed the Russians to a large basecamp in the mountains north of the Song Re at two-four-seven six-five-three. It looks big enough to be a regimental base. Can you get an air strike in on it today? Over."

"This is Three, copy regimental basecamp at two-four-seven six-five-three. I'll have to see what the Blue Suiters have going today and get back to you on that. Over."

"This is Blue Two, Roger, we'll be waiting, out." Brody had a big grin on his face when he handed the handset back to Gardner. Now they would see some action.

It took a little time to put the air strike together, but the results were well worth it. A little over an hour later, a familiar voice came in over the radio. "Blue Two, Blue Two, this is Mac the Fac, the bluebird of happiness, on your push, over."

Brody looked into the sky, but he could not see the small,

gray Cessna O-2 Push Pull spotter plane of the Air Force forward air controller. He must have been keeping station well out of sight so as not to give the NVA any warning of what was coming their way.

"Mac, this is Two," Brody radioed back. "I hear you loud and clear. How me, over."

"This is Mac, I've got you Ham and Limas. Look, I've got a lot of thirsty birds up here just loitering around in the sky, burning gas, so where's my target? Over."

"This is Two, Roger. Your target is a basecamp complex hidden under camouflage nets and trees. The center mass is at two-four-seven six-five-three. The camp runs north and south along the side of a ridge. Make your runs along that axis and you can't miss 'em. We have seen the usual small-caliber antiaircraft stuff, but nothing major, over."

"This is Mac, Roger, we'll be on the lookout for it. Like the man in the song says, get ready 'cause here it comes. Seven-fifties, nape, rockets, and the whole nine yards, so keep your heads down, over."

"Roger, we're well clear of the target area, but we have it under observation and can direct the strike. Get it going, over."

"Bluebird FAC, Roger. Out."

Brody hurried back up to rejoin Two-Step so he could watch the show. From where they were hiding on the ridgeline, they had a ringside seat for one of the greatest free shows in all of Vietnam, an Air Force tactical air strike.

CHAPTER 29

The Song Re Valley

In the hidden NVA encampment, Gregor Zerinski was the first one to hear the sounds of the diving aircraft. He caught the faint whine of their engines and glanced up. Through the camouflage net overhead, he saw four black bat-like shapes swooping down out of the sky. They were headed straight for him.

The Russian didn't even try to run for one of the many bomb shelters that the North Vietnamese had dug in between the buildings. It was far too late for that now. He just hit the dirt right where he was standing and put his arms up over his head.

It sounded like the world was coming apart when the seven-hundred-fifty-pound iron bombs left the rotary bomb bays of the diving B-57 Night Intruder Canberras and came crashing down in the middle of the NVA camp.

The thundering blasts of high explosive ripped the buildings to splinters, dug deep, smoking craters in the ground, and flung men into the air like broken, bleeding dolls.

Pulling out of their steep dives, the four jet attack

bombers from the famed Doom Pussy Squadron, the 8th Bombing Squadron stationed in Da Nang, made a graceful banking turn high in the sky at the end of the valley and bore down on their target.

Normally, the twin-jet B-57 Canberra bombers stalked the night skies over North Vietnam and the border regions, interdicting the supply traffic moving along the Ho Chi Minh Trail. But today Mac the Fac had been able to get six of them to come down south and play in the Song Re Valley for a little change of scenery.

Stunned by the sudden attack, the North Vietnamese quickly recovered and ran for the many antiaircraft gun emplacements dug in around the camp's perimeter. Whipping the camouflage nets away from the guns, they frantically tried to train their weapons on the diving jets.

A couple of the guns, the deadly twin-mount 37mm automatic cannon, got off a few hurriedly aimed shots. But the glowing orange tracers of the shells sped harmlessly past the speeding Canberras. Most of the gun crews only reached their guns just in time to receive the full force of the second attack.

Each Canberra bomber carried four 20mm cannons mounted in the wings, and the hard points on their outer wings had been loaded down with five-inch high-velocity rockets. The cannon barrels belched flame, and the rockets ignited with puffs of dirty white smoke and lanced down from under the Canberra's broad wings.

The twenty mike-mike HE cannon shells and the heavy rockets slammed into the gun emplacements, throwing shredded bodies and pieces of blasted antiaircraft guns high in the air.

The few enemy gunners who survived that onslaught were burned to cinders when the second wave of the attack, a pair of Canberras playing follow the leader, delivered their five-hundred-pound napalm canisters right on top of the antiaircraft gun emplacements. Now the stench of napalm and burned bodies mingled with the sharp, metallic smell of the explosives.

With the enemy antiaircraft threat blown to smoking pieces, the B-57s were free to continue runs at their leisure. The first flight of four jets made several more low bomb runs, dropping a pair of seven-hundred-fifty-pounders on each run. The other two jets circled the camp and attacked targets of opportunity—anything that moved. It was a massacre.

Lying flat on the bottom of his bamboo prison, Rat Gaines watched the Canberras work the camp over from one end to the other. He usually enjoyed watching an air strike, but from a distance, preferably, from the cockpit of his Cobra orbiting out of range while the Blue Suiters did their thing.

This was the first time that he had ever been caught right in the middle of an air strike. On the ground it was not fun at all but he had to admit it was impressive. It was unbelievable what could be done with seven hundred fifty pounds of C-3 explosive. He saw a smoking gun emplacement, sandbags and all, thrown a hundred meters through the air and land upside down.

The Canberras made another run, laying a stick of bombs less than a hundred meters in front of his cage. He was lifted up off of the ground and slammed back down by the concussion. Though his hands were covering his ears, it felt like his head was being squeezed in a vise, and he was blinded by the dust and dirt thrown up in the explosion.

Gaines was resigned to being blown to bits on the next pass but he consoled himself. If he died in the air attack, at least the North Vietnamese wouldn't get their hands on him.

From their hiding place on the opposite ridgeline, Brody and his men watched as the six B-57s turned the NVA camp into smoking rubble. It looked to them like the attack was right on target, but it was difficult to see much because of the clouds of smoke and dust thrown up by the bomb and rocket explosions.

Fuck! Brody thought, as he scanned with his field-glasses from one end of the camp to the other, trying to see past the towering columns of thick black smoke.

"Blue Two, this is Mac," came the voice on Gardner's radio. "How're we doing down there, over?"

Brody took the handset. "This is Two," he answered. "It looks good to me so far, but the smoke is obscuring the target."

He suddenly had an idea. "Say, can you do some spotting from the air for me, over?"

"Roger, whaddaya need? Over."

"I'm looking for a group of men in camouflaged uniforms." As he spoke, Brody saw the Canberras sweep down low over the camp again, the 20mm cannons in their wings blazing flame. "If you spot them, do not, I say again, do not take them under fire. Just tell me which way they're going. Over."

"This is Mac, Roger. I'll keep an eye out for 'em. Out."

Across the narrow valley, the Canberras made one final pass over the enemy camp. They dumped all of their remaining ordnance and rose back into the sky, heading north. Their job was over and there was cold beer waiting for them back at the bar of the Doom Pussy Club in Da Nang.

A man could work up a real thirst on a bombing run.

Once the bombers had passed over on their last firing run, Zerinski painfully got to his feet. He was covered with dirt, his ears were ringing from the explosions, and his eyes smarted from the smoke. He was amazed to find that he was still all in one piece.

The first thing he had to do was to see how many of his men had survived the air attack and get them out of there as fast as he could. Now that the Americans knew the location of the camp, they would probably follow up the jets with a helicopter air assault to clean up anything that might be left. If that happened, he and his men needed to be somewhere else.

Running through the choking smoke and dust of the ruins of the North Vietnamese camp, he shouted for Yuravitch. He couldn't find the major, but two of the other Spetsnaz staggered out of the smoke. He yelled at them to grab their gear and run for the safety of the woods to the north.

The camp was ablaze from one end to the other, sending even more choking smoke into the air. Everywhere he stepped there were bodies or pieces of bodies. He had not realized just how effective a well-executed bombing raid could be. He made a mental note to never put himself in a position where he could be attacked from the air again.

The bamboo headquarters building they had been using for their quarters had taken a direct hit from one of the seven-hundred-fifty-pound bombs. There was hardly even rubble left. It had been completely ground into nothingness. There was no use for him to try to look for any of his personal gear or the team's radios. They would have to go with what they had until they reached safety across the border in Laos.

He did have his Makarov pistol on his field belt, however. He stopped by the body of one of the Vietnamese dead and stripped off the man's canteen. The NVA's body had been blown apart by one of the cannon shells. He wouldn't be needing it anymore.

Zerinski looked around but didn't see anything else he needed. Stored ammunition was starting to cook off in the fires now, adding new danger. Zerinski decided that he wasn't going to risk looking for Yuravitch anymore. He shouted out in Russian several times to assemble north of the camp along the trail. He then turned and ran for the jungle outside of the limits of the destruction.

One by one the Russians staggered out of the camp. Yuravitch made it out with the last man, hanging on his arm. Zerinski quickly counted heads and discovered only five of the seven remaining Spetsnaz. He waited a while longer, but they didn't show. They had probably been blown to bits. Zerinski hoped so, he didn't want to leave any more evidence behind.

The surviving Spetsnaz had managed to grab their weapons and ammunition, including the sniper rifles. A couple of them had their packs and bits of their field gear. They, too, looked like they had enjoyed just about enough of the war in Vietnam and were ready to move out.

Now that the camp had been discovered, it would be suicide for them to try to remain anywhere in the area. In fact, Zerinski felt that it was time that the test was terminated and they all went back up north. They had proven that the rifles worked well and nothing more could be gained exposing them further. The Song Re Valley was becoming a rather dangerous place for his team to be. First there had been Yuravitch's contact with the American recon team, or whatever they had been, and now this bombing raid. It was time they left before any more Russians were killed.

Zerinski's orders had been to test a new weapon, not to get the men killed. Or himself for that matter.

There was still the very real problem with the one body that Yuravitch had left behind. If it had been captured by the Americans, and Zerinski had to assume that it had been, their secret would be out. The Americans would send forces back into the area to look for the rest of them.

Part of his instructions from Hanoi had been that under no circumstances were the Americans to be allowed to capture one of the rifles or any of the Spetsnaz personnel, dead or alive. But the loss of that body had been Yuravitch's doing. Since Zerinski had not been there at the time, there was nothing that he could have done to prevent it. He intended to let Yuravitch take the full blame for it.

He looked over at the army major. Yuravitch looked like he was in shock.

Anticipating his superiors' response to the loss of the

Russian body, Zerinski had a sudden idea, a way that might make his actions look even better in their eyes. He decided that he would go back into the camp, get the American flyer Gaines out of his cage, and take him back up north with them. An officer captive might pacify them.

"Yuravitch," he ordered, "keep the men here while I go back in to bring out the Yankee prisoner. Get them ready to move out immediately, because as soon as I am back, we leave for Hanoi at once."

Yuravitch stared at him, his face blank. He looked as if he hadn't heard a word that had been said. The old sniper was deep in shock.

"Comrade!" the KGB man barked. "Did you hear me!"

Yuravitch nodded his head slowly, his eyes glazed and unfocused.

Zerinski realized that Yuravitch didn't really need to go back to Hanoi at all. In fact, it might be very much to his advantage if he did not return. All he had to do was to see that the major had a fatal accident before they got to the North Vietnamese camp across the Laotian border.

The KGB officer got back to the camp just in time. Two armed Vietnamese were dragging Gaines out of his cage.

"What do you think you are doing?" the Russian shouted in Vietnamese. "That man is my prisoner."

One of the NVA raised his AK. He was bleeding from a cut on the head and had a wild, crazed look in his eyes. Zerinski drew his pistol and shot him dead.

Swinging the Makarov over to cover the other Vietnamese man, Zerinski repeated, "That man is my prisoner, he is going with me!"

The Vietnamese soldier shrugged and let go of the American's arm.

"Thanks," Gaines said, dusting off his flight suit. "Now what?"

The KGB officer covered the pilot with his pistol. "You will come with me now, Captain."

"Where are we going?"

''Hanoi.''

''And if I don't want to go?''

''I kill you here and now.'' Zerinski's eyes were steady, and the muzzle of the Makarov didn't waver a millimeter.

The KGB man looked like he was not too tightly wrapped, and Gaines realized that this was probably not a good time to make him more nervous than he already was. He shrugged his shoulders. ''Why not,'' he said calmly, ''I've never seen that part of Vietnam.''

CHAPTER 30

Camp Radcliff, An Khe

''Come on, Corky,'' Farmer pleaded. ''You'll like her a lot, I know you will. She's from California and I think she's a Mexican, too.''

Corky looked up from his bunk with a peculiar look in his eye.

''I mean,'' Farmer backtracked as fast as he could, ''her parents came from Mexico. Dammit, Corky, you know what I mean.''

''Okay,'' the machine gunner finally said, swinging his legs over the side of his bunk. ''I'll go over there with you.''

''Great.'' Farmer had been trying all afternoon to get Corky to go to the Red Cross club with him. He had just met a farm girl from Utah there whom he was trying to put the hustle on, and she had a Chicano girl friend from California.

Corky had been in a terrible mood ever since Brody had cut him from the sniper mission. Farmer thought that if Corky had something else to think about, he wouldn't be so down. Corky was not fun to be around when he was depressed.

Since they were on a fifteen-minute standby alert, the two grunts stopped by the orderly room and checked out with the first sergeant before they left the company area and walked over to the club.

David Janson sat in the driver's seat of his borrowed Jeep and stared out over the Golf Course watching the choppers coming and going. The dusty strip of PSP was the world's largest helicopter landing field. Every helicopter he had ever seen or even heard of seemed to be there, everything from the new Hughes OH-1 Loach to the giant Skycranes. It was impressive.

He was at a complete dead end again with his investigations into the snipers. Apparently the word had gotten around, and no one was talking to him about anything. He had suddenly become completely *persona non grata*.

The Cav could tell people not to talk to him, but they could not force him to leave An Khe. They knew better than that. The press could go just about anywhere they wanted to in Vietnam, and on the government's tab at that. A commander who tried to keep reporters away from his unit had to be prepared to tell Saigon why he had done it. Concern about military security was not a good enough reason to keep the press at bay, either. The American public had the right to know what was going on.

He decided to head over to the Red Cross club to get in out of the heat and go over his notes again. Maybe he could make better sense out of what information he did have if he went over it carefully one more time. His reporter's instinct told him that he was just about to get the break he needed for the story. He felt that he almost had his finger on it. Maybe if he tried to shuffle the pieces around, they would come together better.

The Air Cav Red Cross club was typical, kind of a combination small-town library and a junior-high-school party. Paperback books and magazines were available for the GIs to read—no *Playboy*—and there were card tables.

There was always lots of cold Kool Aid and cookies along with hot coffee.

The Red Cross girls, "doughnut dollies" as they were called, were all fresh-faced, young American virgins in crisp light blue dresses. They all had nice tans, short hair, and great smiles. They were there to talk to the guys and remind them of what they were supposed to be fighting for, the American way of life.

The Red Cross clubs had made sense in World War II, but they struck Janson as being a bit bizarre in Vietnam. Maybe he was too old and too cynical, but playing bingo games wasn't what most off-duty grunts wanted to be doing with their spare time. They wanted to head down to the bars of Sin City, get drunk, and catch the clap. Anyway, the club was the one place that he could go in Camp Radcliff and not be hassled. Also, he figured he could use a glass of Kool Aid.

The reporter grabbed his cherry Kool Aid and headed for a couch facing out the window looking onto the Golf Course. He took his pad out of his pocket and started looking over his notes again.

"I'm really sorry that she's not on duty, Corky," came the voice behind him. Janson knew that voice. He glanced around and saw one of the soldiers who had been with Brody at the LZ on the day of the artillery short-round incident, the skinny redheaded kid who looked like he should have been a freshman in high school.

"No sweat," his buddy answered. Janson recognized him, too, a Chicano who was doing his best to look like a Mexican bandit in a grade-B western movie.

"I wonder how Brody's doing?" Farmer asked, trying to get a conversation going.

"Beats the shit outta me. Zack should have never let him go out there with only four guys." Corky still sounded pissed.

Janson froze. They were talking about the sniper mission! He lowered his head and tried to look busy, hoping that they wouldn't notice him sitting there behind them.

''Yeah, five guys isn't a lot if anything goes wrong,'' Farmer continued. ''You think they'll get 'em?''

''Brody's real pissed about the Snakeman, and I think that he'll stay out there until he kills them or they kill him. But fuck it anyway.'' Corky sounded bitter. ''He's on his own this time.''

''What do you think happened to the captain?'' Farmer changed the subject. He was determined that he was going to bring his friend out of his bad mood.

''Fucked if I know. Maybe the snipers got him.''

This was news to Janson. Maybe this part of the puzzle was the lead he needed. He guessed accurately that they were talking about one of their company officers, probably their company commander.

''Boy, I sure hope not, I'd hate to lose Captain Gaines.''

''Yeah, Rat's okay for an officer.''

That was the last piece of information Janson needed, his name.

''Hey, Corky!'' Farmer said suddenly, standing up. ''There she is!''

''Farmer, my man,'' Corky slapped his back. ''You have outdone yourself this time. She's a doll. Come on, introduce me.''

The two grunts got up and sauntered over to the desk where a dark-haired girl was seated. They started talking to her. Janson put his notebook back in his pocket and unobtrusively slipped out the door. Farmer and Corky did not see him leave.

Outside, Janson quickly started his Jeep and backed out of the parking lot. Brody was in Echo Company, First of the 7th Cav, and Echo Company was an Air Cav company. That meant that they had a flight-operations building somewhere down by the Golf Course. That was as good a place as anywhere to start.

At the end of the airfield, he stopped the first man he saw, got directions to Python Operations, and headed over to the building.

* * *

First Lieutenant Mike Alexander was busier than a one-legged man in an ass-kicking contest. He hadn't realized just how much work was involved in playing company commander. Since he was the only other officer in the unit, when Gaines turned up missing, it had all fallen on his shoulders. The first sergeant, Top Richardson, was handling a lot of the routine administrative paper work, but there was still a never-ending flow of the stuff coming into Gaines's office.

And as always, everyone wanted their requests seen to first. Everything was priority, even the routine VD reports. He had moved his part of the orderly room down to the operations shack so he could be right by the radios in case something was reported about Gaines. He had the Blues on fifteen-minute standby along with two slicks and a heavy-gun team. The minute the company commander was found, the turbines would start cranking.

All they had to do now was to find him.

In the meantime, the battle of the paper work went on. Alexander signed the requisition in front of him, put it in the out-box, and grabbed the next one on the top of the stack. He was beginning to wonder if it might not be more fun to remain a platoon leader for the rest of his army career. He was not all that sure that he ever wanted to command a company of his own. He had joined the army to fight, not to put his autograph on an endless stream of bullshit paper work.

"Sir?" the operations sergeant said, sticking his head around the door. "There's a man here to see you."

"Who is it?"

"He says that he's a reporter."

"Tell him I'm busy."

"He was asking for Captain Gaines."

Alexander paused. On second thought, maybe he had better talk to the guy after all, and find out what he wanted.

* * *

''Blue Two, Blue Two,'' came the call over the Prick-25. ''This is Mac, over.''

''This is Two,'' Brody answered. ''Go.''

''This is Mac. I think I found the guys that you're looking for. I've got about six or eight men in camies headed away from the camp at two-five-two six-nine-eight. Looks to me like they're running for the Laotian border. Over.''

Brody made a quick check of his map. Those coordinates were at the end of the small valley just below them. It could only be the Russians. ''This is Two, thanks a lot, Mac. Thanks for everything. Over.''

High in the sky, Brody saw the small gray spotter plane rock its wings back and forth in a farewell gesture. ''No sweat, GI, see you around. Mac the Fac, out.''

''Okay, guys,'' Brody said to the four men gathered around him. ''Mac says that he spotted them here.'' He pointed to the map. ''He says it looks like they're running for cover across the border. If we swing around here, I think that we can catch up and get in behind 'em.'' He looked around. ''Whaddaya say?''

Two-Step studied the map. ''That's going to be a real rough hump, Treat. They've got at least a two- or three-klick head start on us.''

The Indian looked up at Brody. ''Also, don't forget that the woods are going to be crawling with gooks right about now, and we're going to have to dodge them. They've got to have figured out that somebody close by called that air strike in on them, and they're going to be looking for our asses.''

''Are you saying that we ought to just hang it up and go home?''

''No, I'm not.'' the Indian shook his head vigorously. ''I'm just saying that we've got to be real careful, man. I want those bastards just as much as you do, Treat. But I don't want all of us to get killed doing it.''

Brody looked around, his jaw clenched. ''How 'bout the rest of you guys?''

''You're the boss,'' Gardner said, looking down at the

pall of smoke covering the valley. "Let's finish this shit up."

"We're just along for the ride." Chief spoke for both himself and Gambini. "You just find us a target to shoot at and we're happy."

"Okay then." Brody handed his map to Two-Step. "Let's get it. Chance, you take point and set the pace. I want to intercept those bastards before they get back across the border."

"You got it."

Zerinski wasn't in a talkative mood this time as Gaines marched along the jungle trail beside him, his hands tightly tied behind his back. In fact, none of the Russians seemed to be too happy, including Yuravitch, whom Gaines had not seen before. He was the one who had killed Fletcher. Gaines studied him, memorizing his face so he would recognize him later.

Gaines noticed that the KGB man wasn't setting a very rapid pace. Instead, he had his point man moving cautiously as if they were expecting trouble. Gaines didn't know what the Russian was looking for, though. It seemed to him that they had just left all their troubles behind them in the blasted NVA camp.

Then it struck him. How had the Air Force learned about that camp? It had been well concealed under the trees and heavily camouflaged on top of that. He could have flown over it himself and not seen a trace of it. Maybe it had been picked up by the sensors on some of the new surveillance aircraft they were using now, but that would have been a fluke. More than likely, it had been spotted by a ground recon team. Maybe the Blues had tracked the snipers to their base.

That was a wild idea, he had to admit, but it made sense in a weird way. If Brody and his men spotted the camp, there would have been no way that they could have known that their company commander was being held prisoner there, so Brody wouldn't have hesitated to call for the fly-boys to blast it out of existence.

There was also a slim chance that a spotter plane was still in contact with Brody and had told him where the Russians were going. Now all Gaines had to do was to figure out how to get away and link up with Brody.

He didn't think Zerinski was going to be a gentleman about this and just let him walk away peacefully. Gaines knew, however, that he was going to make a run for it the first chance that he had. Getting shot in the back trying to escape was a better way to die than being slowly beaten to death in a North Vietnamese prison camp.

CHAPTER 31

The Song Re Valley

The Russians were setting a vigorous pace, and, with his hands tied behind him, Gaines was having a little trouble keeping up with them. At least they had finally gotten onto a well-defined trail, though, and he didn't have to fight his way through the brush anymore.

"Hey, when do we get to take a break?" he panted to Zerinski, who was marching in front of him.

The Russian turned around and shot him a serious look. "When we get to Laos, Captain. Then you can rest. Until then, you march."

That didn't sound too fucking good at all. Laos meant the Ho Chi Minh Trail and hundreds of gooks swarming all over. It was no place for a round-eye to look inconspicuous while he was beating feet. If Gaines was going to make his move, he had to do it before they got there.

The narrow trail left the valley floor and headed up another steep hillside to a ridgeline. Even Zerinski slowed his pace a little for the climb.

Gaines held back as far as he could until only one of the Russians was behind him, the drag man in the formation.

Halfway up to the ridge, he saw that the brush on the down side of the hill looked reasonably passable for a man with his hands tied. A hundred meters down at the bottom there were lots of big trees and good cover. If he could make it that far, he'd be in fat city.

Covertly, Gaines glanced around. No one was watching him closely. The drag man was checking the back trail, and everyone else was concentrating on lugging their heavy packs up the hill.

Suddenly he darted off the trail. Diving through a clump of bushes, he rolled down the side of the hill, bruising himself when his body hit the hard ground. Staggering to his feet, Gaines took off at a dead run, his head down and his shoulders hunched up, waiting for the inevitable sound of a shot.

Someone yelled. It sounded like Zerinski. He heard the crack of the AKs and the sound of rounds passing close to his head. He didn't even break stride. He continued down the hill, crashing through the underbrush. He had to keep going and reach good cover before the Russians could get those sniper rifles looking for him. If they got their scopes on him, he was cold meat.

The trail was so fresh now that Brody had taken over point for Two-Step to give the Indian a break. From what he saw, the Russians couldn't be too far ahead of them, a klick and a half or less. He couldn't tell how quickly they were covering ground, but the Russians were keeping a steady pace. There was no sign that they had stopped since they had left the camp well over two hours earlier.

The trail entered a little valley and farther ahead it turned uphill again, heading east for the Laotian border. Unless they wanted to risk running into heavy enemy movement coming down the Ho Chi Minh Trail, they had to catch up with the Russians before they got into Laos.

He had just turned around to make the "hurry up" hand signal when he heard the sharp crack of AK fire from the ridgeline in front of them. Instantly, he dropped to the ground. After several rounds, the shooting stopped. It had not been close. Whoever it was had been shooting at someone else, not them.

He motioned Two-Step forward toward the sound. It had to be the Russians. They were closing in on them. Chief and Gambini moved out on the flanks to use their day scopes to check out the area.

"Treat!" Two-Step hissed as he dropped for cover along the track. "Someone's coming."

The five men instantly fanned out in an ambush formation and trained their weapons in the direction the Indian indicated. Brody motioned for the snipers to check it out. Chief and Gambini moved forward to scan the side of the hill with their sniper scopes.

"I got something," Gambini whispered, ranging in his Redfield scope. "Right front."

Chief shifted his rifle to cover that area, too. There was someone coming!

It was Gambini's shot, but Metcack zeroed in on the target, too. He caught a glimpse of a figure in an olive-colored uniform breaking through the jungle, moving toward them. He focused the scope and aimed for a head shot.

"Wait!" he cried, suddenly slapping the muzzle of Gambini's rifle down. "It's an American!"

"Jesus!" Gambini said softly, pulling his head back from the scope. "I was just about to shoot."

The men got up and watched the figure lurch out onto the open trail fifty meters in front of them.

"It's Gaines!" Brody yelled. "Cover me!" He took off down the trail at a run.

Fifty meters away, Gaines looked up to see a man running toward him. He dove off the trail to hide.

"Captain!" Brody called out. "It's me, Treat Brody!"

Brody ran up and helped him to his feet. "Jesus, Captain Gaines, what're you doing here?" Brody whipped out his K-Bar knife and sawed through the ropes around Gaines's wrists.

"I crashed the other night and got captured by a bunch of Russians," he explained, looking at Brody. "They're the guys you're looking for. The snipers."

"I know. We killed one of them yesterday."

"So that's why they were a little spooked. Now I understand what's wrong with Zerinski."

"Who?"

"Never mind, it's a long story. By the way, the son of a bitch who killed Fletcher is a guy named Yuravitch, or something like that. He's some kind of hotshot shooter in the Russian army, and I think he's an officer. He's in his late forties, gray hair, and stocky. You can't miss him. The other officer with them is a KGB man named Zerinski. He's tall, thin, and ugly. A typical KGB type."

Brody led Gaines back to the others, and they had barely arrived when a single shot rang out from the hillside. The round grazed Brody's field belt and slammed into his right-side ammo pouch, spinning him around.

"Sniper!" he shouted, pulling Gaines down into cover beside him.

Chief and Gambini scrambled to find some cover that would still gave them a good field of fire up the hill. The rest of the men kept their heads down. Their weapons wouldn't reach that far anyway, and if they poked their heads up, they were asking to catch a bullet. This was going to be a classic sniper-against-sniper battle.

"How many of them are there?" Brody asked, peering through a break in the leaves.

"Seven, including the two officers. And they've got three sniper rifles."

"Chief!" Brody called out. "Three of them's got sniper rifles."

The Indian sniper nodded his head. That made this a little more difficult. With three snipers, the Russians could easily split their forces and come at them from two sides. That meant he had to send Gambini off on his own to counter that threat, and he didn't like that at all. Chief usually worked snipers in pairs. That way the two marksmen could spot for each other. Now their only advantage was that their XM-21s were silenced and the Russian weapons weren't.

"Chance," Metcack called out softly. "Go with Gambini. Cover him."

Two-Step nodded and moved out to the left flank with the Italian-American sniper just inches behind him. Chief pointed to Gardner, indicating that he was to cover for him. The big man nodded and swung his sixteen around in front of him. The thumper wasn't much use for that assignment. He shrugged out of his pack and the radio, leaving them with Brody.

Brody and Gaines stayed in the brush at the side of the trail. They had good cover and the only thing they would accomplish if they tried to move would be to draw more fire. Chief and JJ crawled to the right, moving slowly and keeping well concealed. If the Russian weapons were anything at all like the American rifles, they were well within range. All it would take would be a momentary glimpse and the Russians would have them.

Another shot rang out from the hillside. The Russians were still there.

They continued crawling until they reached the edge of the valley and could see up the side of the hill. Chief found a good position behind a log. It was situated well back in the shadows and would be hard to spot from the hill. He laid the barrel of the rifle on top of the log and focused in on the hillside. He was a little more exposed than he really liked to be, but he counted on the shadows to protect them.

"I think I got something," Chief whispered. He focused the scope on a patch of what looked like camouflage uniform material. His finger tightened around the trigger. The silence rifle spat.

Chief was concentrating so hard on watching the target through his scope that he didn't notice that the muzzle of his rifle was right over a small patch of almost bare ground. When he fired, the muzzle blast threw up a small puff of dust.

Two shots rang out from the hill. The first round hit the

log, throwing slivers of rotten wood in Gardner's face. The second round knocked Chief's rifle out of his hands.

"Chief's hit!" Gardner shouted. "Cover me!"

Brody, Two-Step, and Gambini opened up on the hillside. Even through it was well out of the effective range of the M-16s, the rounds would still travel that far. It took a very disciplined man to poke his head up when someone was shooting at him.

Ripping off a burst himself, Gardner grabbed the sniper rifle. Taking Chief by his assault harness, he dragged him back further into the jungle. Once he had gotten Metcack back far enough into the deep woods, he stopped and leaned him against the back side of a big tree.

"Thanks," Chief said through gritted teeth. His bloody left arm hung limply at his side.

JJ took the field dressing from the sniper's first-aid pouch and tore the wrapper off. "Wait till I've finished patching you up before you thank me," he said. "I'm not too good at this shit."

The Indian sniper stoically didn't say a word as Gardner clumsily bandaged his wound and splinted the break with a small branch. JJ knew that it had to be painful. The bullet had broken the bone in the sniper's upper arm and smashed the muscle tissue. Fortunately, it had missed the vein on the inside of the arm so it wasn't bleeding too badly. If they got him back to An Khe in time, the arm could be saved.

When he was finished, he helped the wounded man to his feet and they faded into the brush until they reached Brody and the Captain.

"Treat, we got to get him outta here," Gardner panted.

"Captain," Brody said, turning to Gaines. "When that Dustoff comes in for Chief, I think it'd be a real good idea if you got on it, too."

"I'll stay," Gaines replied, "if there's anything that you think I can help you with here."

"No, sir, I think we can handle this end of it, but there is something you can do for us back at An Khe. I want you to take the stuff we got from the Russian we killed yesterday back with you and tell Division about these guys. In case we don't make it back, I want someone to know what's going on here.''

''How you going to get us out?''

''Well, sir, that's the problem.'' Brody thought for a moment. ''I don't want to stop tracking those guys, so I thought that after I call for the extract, we'll leave you and Chief here while we go on after the Russians. There's a little clearing about half a klick back at the other end of this valley that will make a good LZ.'' He pointed it out on his map. ''And you can hide back there until they come. I'll also leave the radio with you so you can guide the choppers in when they show up.''

''If you do that, you won't have any commo,'' Gaines protested. ''You'll be completely cut off.''

''It's okay, sir, we don't really need it,'' Brody reassured him. ''When this is all over, we can just walk out.''

''But what if someone else gets hit?'' Gaines pointed out the obvious drawback to that plan.

Brody shrugged. ''Then I guess they'll die.''

''Look, Brody, you don't have to do it this way. We can get some gunships in on those guys.''

''Sir, that'll take too long.'' Brody's jaw was set. ''By the time the choppers get here, those motherfuckers'll be klicks away and I can't let that happen. I'm too close to them now and I'm not done with this shit yet.''

Gaines recognized the stubborn look on Brody's face and realized that there was little he could do to change his mind. ''Okay,'' he said. ''But you're making it real hard on your people.''

''I know,'' Brody answered quietly.

He motioned for Gardner to bring the radio. ''I'd better get on the horn and see about your Dustoff.''

''Right.''

Brody had to go through the Black Slider retransmission station again to get through to An Khe, but the message was received, and he was told that the birds would be airborne in less than ten minutes. Their flight time to the LZ would be more like forty-five.

"Sir, they're on the way, but it's going to be about an hour," Brody told Gaines. "Here, you're going to need this." He took a bandolier of loaded M-16 magazines from around his neck and handed them over, along with his rifle.

Gaines took the weapon and ammunition. "What are you going to use?"

Brody reached down and picked up Chief's sniper rifle. "I'm going to use this."

Gardner had finished putting Chief's arm in a sling, and the Indian got to his feet. "You'd better get going, Treat," he said.

"Yeah, I know. But we got to get your gear squared away first."

Gardner helped Gaines slip into the radio harness and slung the bandolier of M-16 magazines around his neck. He clipped two smoke grenades to the radio harness. "There you go, sir," he said when he was finished.

Brody dumped Chief's ruck, transferred the XM-21's night scope and ammunition to his own pack, and threw all of the rest of his gear into the brush. The wounded sniper still wore his field belt with his canteen, poncho and grenades. Chief also took the pistol from his shoulder holster and stuck it in his belt, where he could reach it with his good hand.

"I guess we're ready then," Gaines said.

"Good luck, sir." Brody nodded his head.

"You just get those guys," said Chief.

"You can count on that."

The four grunts watched Gaines and Chief head back down the trail.

"Okay." Brody cradled the sniper rifle in his arms. "It's time to get serious. First I want you to dump all your extra gear. All the radio batteries and anything else we don't need. We've got to travel light if we're going to catch up with those bastards."

CHAPTER 32

Camp Radcliff, An Khe

"Sir! Sir!," the radio operator shouted excitedly, racing into the CO's office in Python Operations where Alexander was talking to Janson. "They found him! Brody found Gaines, and he's alive!"

"Outfuckingstanding!" Alexander yelled and jumped to his feet. "Get 'em cranked up," he ordered.

"Yes, sir!"

"And if you'll excuse me, Mr. Janson," Alexander said, dismissing the reporter. "I've got to get back to work."

Janson didn't have to ask who had been found. He knew. He also knew that he wasn't going to learn anything more from Alexander. He hadn't gotten very much information out of him anyway, so he got up and walked out into the pilot ready room. Through the window, he saw men racing for the choppers and the big rotor blades turning over as the pilots cranked up their birds. The smell of kerosene burning in the hot air carried all the way into the building.

He could hear Alexander talking on the phone in the other room, but couldn't make out what he was saying. A second later, the lieutenant came running out, his rucksack, helmet, and rifle in his hand. The officer crashed through the door and raced for one of the slicks.

The reporter also heard the radio traffic from the loudspeakers in the radio room at the other end of the building. He decided to stick around and eavesdrop. After all, a source was a source. He picked up a six-month-old copy of *Playboy* magazine from a battered coffee table and pretended to be reading it. If anyone asked him what he was doing there, he could always say that the lieutenant had told him to wait.

On the flight line, Gabe had *Pegasus* fired up, and he was ready to go. He keyed his throat mike. "Python Niner Seven, this is Five Eight," he called to Lance "Lawless" Warlokk. Warlokk was leading the heavy-gun team and acting as the Python flight leader.

"I'm ready to roll, Lawless. Where the hell are those grunts? Over."

"Five Eight, this is Python Lead," Warlokk radioed back. "Keep it in your pants, Gunslinger, they're coming. Out."

"Tell 'em to get their fucking asses in gear," Gabe muttered to himself.

A three-quarter-ton truck screeched to a halt on the PSP right outside the radius of the slick's spinning rotors. The grunts in the back jumped out of the truck before it had even come to a complete stop and scrambled on board the two waiting slicks. A Jeep brought the last four men just as Alexander stormed out the door of the operations shack at a dead run.

"Get it, get it!" Gabe shouted to the Blues over the whine of his turbine.

Within seconds, everyone was inside.

"Python Lead, this is Five Eight, we're go," Gabe radioed.

"Roger."

From the left-hand seat of his Huey Hog, Warlokk switched his radio over to the control-tower frequency.

''Golf Course Control, this is Python Lead, request permission to take off, over.''

''This is Control, wait one, Python, the field is not clear.''

''This is Python, that's a fucking negative, Tower,'' Warlokk snapped, his scarred face set. ''We have an emergency and we are taking off now.''

''Python, you cannot take off,'' came the panicked voice from the tower. ''You are not clear!''

''Just watch me, asshole,'' Warlokk snarled. ''Python Flight, this is Lead, follow me.''

With Warlokk's Huey gunship, *Sat Cong*, taking the lead, the four other gunbirds and two Huey slicks full of the Blues revved their turbines and taxied onto the PSP runway.

''Python, Python, this is the tower,'' the voice on the radio was frantic. ''Hold your position. You are not cleared for takeoff!''

''Roger,'' Warlokk called back cheerfully. ''Thank you, Tower. Python Flight taking off now.''

The pilot nudged the cyclic forward and gave it a little collective, tilting the rotor mast and bringing the blades into the air. When Lance Lawless Warlokk wanted to take off, he took off.

One right after the other, the six choppers raised their tails and started down the runway in a perfect gunship takeoff. Once they had built up enough airspeed, they pulled more pitch on their rotor blades and were airborne, lifting up into the clear blue sky. As soon as they had cleared the An Khe flight pattern, the seven chopper pilots twisted their throttles all the way over against the stops. With the wicks turned up all the way, they streaked for the Song Re Valley as fast as they could fly.

Rat Gaincs glanced down at his watch. From what Brody had told him they still had another fifteen or twenty minutes to wait.

Gaines and the wounded sniper were hiding in a clump of bushes at the edge of the small clearing that Brody had directed them to, waiting for the Python ships to get them the hell out of this mess. The only problem was that the woods were swarming with gooks and they were probably going to be dead by the time their rescuers got to them.

It was beginning to look like this part of the woods was the place that NVA survivors of the air raid on the camp had picked for a new campsite. Gaines could hear them calling to one another and moving around in the brush nearby. His luck hadn't been worth a shit for quite some time now, and it didn't look like it was getting any better.

He switched the radio over to the Python Flight frequency and hoped that someone back in An Khe had had enough brains to bring a couple of gunships along with the pickup slick. If they hadn't, he and Chief might as well just stick their heads between their legs right now and kiss their young asses good-bye. The woods around the clearing were crawling with pissed-off NVA, and there was no way that a lone slick was going to make it down and pick them up.

He keyed the handset and quietly spoke into the microphone. "Python, Python." He paused and released the push-to-talk switch on the side of the handset. What in the hell was his call sign anyway? On the ground he didn't have one and, according to the radio security people, you were never supposed to use your name on the radio. *Fuck them,* he thought, *what were they going to do, send him to Vietnam*?

"Python, Python," he repeated. "This is Rat Gaines, over."

"Rat, this is Lawless," came Warlokk's welcome voice. "I am ten minutes out, send your status, over"

"This is Rat. We are up to our asses in alligators here, but they still don't know that the Rat is in the swamp. We are going to need gunship cover. Also, I have one Whiskey India Alpha with me, routine priority. Over."

"This is Lawless, Roger copy. I think we can lend a

hand. I've got a heavy team with me and the Blues. Can you vector us in, over."

"This is Rat, that's a negative, I don't have a map. Fly to the grid coordinates you were given, and I'll listen for you. I do have smoke and will pop one when I spot you. Over."

"Lawless, Roger, copy. My Echo Tango Alpha is eight minutes. Anything further, over."

"Negative, out."

In the air, Warlokk looked over his shoulder at the four Huey Hogs flying on one side of him and the two slicks full of the Blues on the other. If the Old Man were up there with them today, he'd be real proud of how his people looked. Warlokk knew that he sure was.

Warlokk also knew that the main reason that the Python pilots flew so well and looked so good today was because of the man they were speeding to rescue. In the few short months that Rat Gaines had commanded Echo Company, he had changed them from being a bunch of drunken assholes into a crack outfit, both in the air and on the ground. Gaines demanded, and received, the very best from all of his people.

Warlokk almost hated to admit it, but Rat Gaines was one of the best pilots and officers that he had ever known. In the beginning he hadn't felt that way. In fact, Gaines had had to use his quick fists to hammer Lawless Warlokk into the ground to get him to see the error of his ways.

Lance Lawless Warlokk was a hard-drinking, hard-living warrant officer-chopper pilot of the old school. His scarred face reflected the life he had led. Most of the scars had come from drunken brawls. His reputation as a bad ass had been well known, and people had wisely given him a wide berth. Everyone, that is, until he ran into Rat Gaines. The soft-talking southerner didn't move out of the way for anyone.

Gaines had not been impressed with Warlokk's attitude, not in the least. He had also not been impressed with Warlokk's reputation as a bad ass. As the saying went,

Gaines feared no evil, because he was the meanest motherfucker in the valley. And he had proven that fact to Warlokk. Twice.

Now, however, Rat Gaines had no stauncher a supporter than Lance Lawless Warlokk. When a professional bad ass discovered someone who could whip his ass ten times out of ten, he quickly made friends. It was a law of the jungle.

Now Warlokk was racing to save the man who had said that he would kill him the next time he stepped out of line.

In Warlokk's left-hand seat, manning the weapons, was Joe Schmuchatelli, Gaines's copilot-gunner. Better known around the flight line as Alphabet because of his impossible last name, Schmuchatelli was worried. He never liked Gaines to fly without him, and now he was down on the ground with all the gooks in the world swarming all over him. If those motherfuckers killed his AC, there was going to be hell to pay.

The young warrant officer-gunner tightened the fingers of his nomex gloves for the second time and checked over his firing controls for the third. He was impatient to kick somebody's ass.

In the lead slick, Lieutenant Mike Alexander and the men of the Blues waited for their orders. The young platoon leader studied his map, trying to get a feel for the terrain they would be dropping into. The map was not all that informative. All it showed was dense jungle and steep ridgelines, not a very hospitable place at all. The worst thing was that he did not know exactly where his company commander was hiding out. They would have to find him first and then jump in to save him.

He realized that this could get a little hairy and he was glad that he had a full heavy-gun team backing them up today. When they hit that hot LZ it was going to be nice to have Warlokk's people working overhead.

With Brody and the guys out on that sniper mission, Corky, Farmer, and Bunny were all that were left of his 2d Squad, and they were flying with Sergeant Zack in the second slick. The battle-hardened black platoon sergeant was as calm about this mission as he was about any of them. It all counted toward his twenty years' retirement, and he had only a year and a half left to go before he hung up his war suit for good. He could do another year and a half standing on his shaved head.

One more desperate firefight in the jungle against an enemy that he couldn't see was no big deal to Leo the Lionhearted. He had been through so much of that shit, first in Korea and then Vietnam, that it just didn't even matter to him anymore. He knew that they would get on the ground, kick some gooks in the ass, load the bodies back into the birds, and fly back to Radcliff. No sweat.

The most they could do to him was kill him. And that was no big deal, either.

He looked over at the men from Brody's squad. Cordova still had a real case of the red ass because Treat hadn't taken him on that sniper hunt. Well, he'd better get his head out of his ass today or Zack would put his boot in it. They were shorthanded and Zack was going to need everyone's best work down there.

"Cordova!" Zack yelled.

Corky turned in the open door and looked at him.

"You're acting squad leader today."

The machine gunner nodded and turned back.

Zack made a mental note to himself to keep a close eye on what was left of 2d Squad when they hit the LZ.

Farmer sat in the open door next to Corky and looked down at the jungle rushing by below him. It looked like a real motherfucker. For the first time, he would be going into battle without Brody and Gardner fighting beside him. It bothered him a little.

Even though Brody was on his case a lot about nickel-and-dime shit, Farmer looked up to the more experienced man. Brody was only two years older, but most of those two years had been spent in the Nam and it showed. He always seemed to know what to do even in the worst of circumstances, and Farmer depended on Brody to keep him out of trouble.

The young grunt also missed having Gardner with him. To Farmer, the big man had almost become an older brother. As long as Jungle Jim was fighting beside him, Farmer felt invincible. This time, he was going to be more or less on his own.

Sure, Corky was going to be there with him, but he didn't feel as close to the Chicano machine gunner as he did to Brody and Gardner.

Suddenly the dark jungle below him looked even more sinister. He shivered.

CHAPTER 33

The Song Re Valley

In the woods right outside the clearing, Rat Gaines's luck had just run out. They had gone too far back into the brush, and an NVA soldier looking for a private place to take a crap stumbled into the clump of bushes they were hiding in.

Gaines heard the man approach and crouched as low to the ground as he could, his finger around the trigger of the M-16. Chief reached over and laid his hand across his mouth. Motioning for Gaines not to shoot, the Indian sniper pulled the K-Bar knife from the sheath tied to his boot top with his good hand and made a slashing motion across his own throat.

Gaines nodded. He laid the rifle down and got ready.

When the Vietnamese came close enough, Gaines sprang up. Clamping his hand over his mouth, he jerked the smaller man off of his feet and spun him around. Chief slammed the knife into his lower back, burying it to the hilt.

A muffled scream escaped past Rat's hand as the Vietnamese struggled.

"Vinh!" They heard another NVA voice call out from a few meters away. *"Chuyen gi vay?"*

Gaines kept his hand clamped tightly over the dying man's mouth. Chief stabbed him again. "Oh, fuck!" he muttered under his breath. Their gook had a buddy.

Once the NVA went completely limp, Gaines quietly let him to the ground and pulled him into the bushes with them. He picked up his sixteen again and slowly brought it up, moving as quietly as he could. Beside him, Chief shoved the bloody knife back into its sheath and pulled the .45-caliber pistol from under his belt. He quietly clicked the safety off and thumbed the hammer back.

"Vinh?" the voice called out again. They heard the Vietnamese coming closer. He stopped in front of their hiding place. When the barrel of an AK parted the branches in front of him, Gaines fired.

"Get it!" he shouted, pulling Chief to his feet. The two men jumped up and fought their way through the underbrush, running as fast as they could for the clearing. They would be more exposed out there in the open, but if they stayed in the woods they wouldn't be able to signal the choppers.

AK rounds sang past their heads, but all that did was make them run even faster. At the edge of the clearing, Gaines spun around and triggered off a full magazine of 5.56mm into the jungle behind him. He heard someone scream.

Pushing Chief ahead of him, Gaines plunged into the elephant grass that covered the clearing, reloading the sixteen as he ran. Usually the sharp-edged, tough grass was asshole deep to a tall water buffalo, but at this altitude in the mountains, it only reached up to their waists. More shots rang out and they dove for the ground.

Gaines rolled into a firing position and grabbed the radio handset. "Python, Python," he shouted. "This is Rat, over."

"This is Python," came Warlokk's calm voice. "Go."

"This is Rat, you'd better get your asses down here on the double. They found us. Over."

"Roger," he answered. "We're almost there, be prepared to pop smoke, over."

"Smoke out, over." Gaines snatched a smoke grenade off of the radio harness and pulled the pin. He tossed it out to the side, far away from them so it wouldn't draw fire. The thick green smoke billowed into the air.

"Rat, this is Python. I have lime and I am one mike out. Just hang on, over."

A new storm of AK fire snapped through the grass close by their heads. The NVA knew what the smoke grenade in the clearing meant. They had to get the Americans before the choppers showed up.

"Roger, green. Don't waste any fucking time getting down here, man." Gaines thought he saw movement in the grass in front of them and ripped off a quick burst. The movement stopped.

Suddenly, Gaines heard the distinctive wop-wopping sound of Huey rotors and glanced up. A single Huey Hog was bearing down on the wood line in front of him. It was the most beautiful sight he had ever seen, and it had to be Lance Warlokk at the controls. The rest of the gun team was still half a klick behind him.

The front of the gunship suddenly looked like it had burst into flame, but it was just Alphabet triggering off everything that he had all at once. The thumper in the turret spit 40mm grenades, the side-mounted miniguns blazed fire at 4,000 rounds a minute, and he volleyed 2.75-inch HE rockets from the pylon-mounted pods, one right after another. The recoil from all the weapons firing at once was almost enough to stop the diving chopper dead in its tracks.

The tree line in front of him exploded, and Gaines ducked his head. He couldn't see who was on the guns, but it had to be Alphabet. No one else was crazy enough to make a banzai firing run like that.

The gunship flashed past them, chased by green tracer fire from the AKs. The NVA were pissed.

Warlokk pulled the nose of his ship up sharply, banked her over on her side, and savagely kicked the tail around. The heavily laden gunship staggered in the sky, hanging right on the edge of a stall, her rotors unloading and losing lift. He was far too low and flying much too slowly to try that kind of maneuver, but right at the last moment, Warlokk got her under control. Snapping his ship back upright, he bore down on the jungle again, his guns blazing.

By this time, the rest of the gun team had arrived and they paired off to start their runs, coming in from the opposite direction. For a short time, the gunships had it all their own way, whiplashing the hidden enemy from both directions. Then it got serious.

With the gunships doing their best to keep the gooks' heads down, Gabe and the other slick driver swooped down low to the ground and flared out to land in the clearing. As soon as the troop ships were committed and couldn't pull away, from the other side of the clearing a storm of AK fire slammed into them.

Before the skids had even touched the ground, Zack jumped out the open side door. "Go! Go! Go!" he yelled, waving the men forward.

The Blues followed their platoon sergeant, screaming their war cries as they leaped from the slicks into a storm of fire.

The weight of the ruck on his back drove Farmer to his knees when he jumped from the gunship. AK tracer rounds flashed over his head. He ducked and rolled out of the line of fire. To his left, Corky was up on one knee hosing down the wood line with long bursts from his Pig. The barrel of the M-60 was already smoking. Farmer crawled over to his side and added the fire from his rifle to that of the machine gun.

Lieutenant Alexander was lying on the ground next to his radio operator, yelling into the handset, trying to get the gunships turned around to work on the gooks who had his platoon pinned down.

Zack looked around the LZ. The grunts were stopped cold. In just a few seconds, when the gooks got zeroed in on them, they would start taking casualties. It was time to get the boys off their asses and onto their feet. If they were going to die in this stinking little LZ, at least they could die like men.

He pulled an M-26 hand grenade from his ammo pouch and got to his knees. "Grenades!" he bellowed over the storm of rifle and machine-gun fire, throwing the hand frag as far out in front of him as he could. "Give 'em grenades!"

The M-79 grenadiers came to their senses. From their prone position, they started sending a barrage of deadly 40mm grenades toward the tree line. The sharp cracks of their explosions could be heard above the roar of small-arms fire. Not wanting to be left out of all the fun, the riflemen started throwing grenades, too.

It wasn't the same as mortar-fire support but it sounded similar, making the NVA think they had brought a light-weight 60mm mortar. The AK fire slackened just as the first of the gunships flashed overhead. Dirty white smoke blew back from the rocketpods as 2.75-inch missiles lanced out from the side of the ship in pairs. Now they had some real down-home fire support.

The ripping chainsaw sound of the miniguns firing 4,000 rounds a minute filled the grunts' ears. The solid stream of fire tore into the underbrush. Nothing could live through it, and the gooks were no exception.

"Let's get it!" Zack screamed, jumping to his feet and triggering off a full magazine at the wood line. A handful of men stood up with him.

"Come on!" The black NCO swept his arm up over his head in a classic Fort Benning Infantry School "follow me" gesture. It never ceased to amaze him, but it always seemed to work. The day Zack stood up and no one followed would be the day that he died in battle. But that was not going to be this day or this firefight.

Yelling like maniacs, the Blues charged the wood line, their weapons blazing.

Farmer ran beside his platoon daddy, emptying one magazine after another into the jungle, reloading as he ran. Another gunship swept low over their heads, the downblast of its rotors buffeting his face. Hot, empty cartridge cases from the roaring miniguns rained down on him. This was war, with the smell of the powder, the feel of the rifle bucking in his hands, his ears filled with the roar of battle. Farmer threw back his head and screamed, "Eat shit and die, motherfucker!"

The bolt of his M-16 locked back. He was out of ammunition. Farmer dropped the empty magazine out of the bottom of the rifle and jammed a loaded one into place. He hit the bolt release, chambering a round, and laid down on the trigger once more. "Motherfucker!" he screamed again.

An AK round slammed into him, spinning him around and driving him down to his knees. Panting with adrenaline he patted his chest, feeling for a wound. But he wasn't bleeding. His flak vest and assault harness had stopped the bullet. He would be black and blue in the morning, but right now he didn't feel it at all.

Zack's big hand reached down. Grabbing him by the ruck, the burly sergeant jerked Farmer to his feet. The young grunt ripped off a short burst and took off running. "Motherfucker!"

By this time, Zack's charge had taken the Blues to the edge of the tree line. The men plunged into the brush only to find that the gooks had vacated the premises for quieter surroundings.

Zack gave the men a minute to catch their breath, then wheeled them to the right and kept on going. There was still work to be done.

With First Squad moving out on point, they started

clearing the wood line all the way around to the other side of the LZ.

Overhead, the gunships circled like vultures, waiting for a target to appear through the open spaces in the tangled jungle canopy. With his RTO walking beside him, Alexander vectored the choppers in to anything the grunts ran across. If they even thought that a couple of gooks were hiding behind a bush, he had the gunships blast them out of existence. There was no point in taking chances. They weren't out there to get themselves killed.

As Lieutenant Alexander's hero, General George S. Patton, had once said, "No son of a bitch ever won a war by dying for his country. He won it by making some other poor son of a bitch die for his."

CHAPTER 34

Deep in the Jungle

From the top of the ridgeline, Zerinski watched the American gunships in the valley below.

Smoke rose from the sites of the helicopters' rocket strikes. He saw the deadly black-and-red flowers of flame bloom into brief existence and then wink out as new rockets hit their targets and exploded. Each fiery flower meant that men were dying.

He had an uncomfortable feeling that the Americans would soon be following him. He wouldn't be safe until he had gotten all the way across the border and linked up with the major NVA units based in Laos.

"Move out," he commanded. His men jumped.

Down in the valley, Brody and his remaining three men headed west to Laos.

On the ground, Zack and the Blues were mopping up the last of the North Vietnamese. Still stunned by the Canberras' earlier air attack, most of the NVA were in no frame of mind to stick around and fight it out with the

Python gunships. They had had more than enough death from the sky for one day.

Lieutenant Mike Alexander walked up to where Gaines waited in the center of the clearing. "Captain, I think we can get Gabe in here now without him getting shot full of holes again."

The young platoon leader's face was flushed, and he mopped the sweat off with the back of his hand. The battle had gone far better than he had imagined it would. The Blues had only taken two casualties and neither man was badly wounded.

Gaines looked around the LZ. "Yeah, I think I've seen just about enough of this place. Let's get the fuck outta here."

While four of the gunships circled protectively overhead, Gabe and the other slick pilot dropped their birds down and flared out for a landing. One of the gunships also swooped down beside them. Warlokk stuck his head out of the pilot's side window and yelled over to the small command group. "Hey, Rat! Get in!"

Gaines ran over to the gunship and climbed into the back. A grinning Alphabet turned around in his armored seat and handed Gaines a flight helmet. He found a seat in between the ammo cans for the side-mount miniguns and quickly plugged the cord into the chopper's intercom system.

"Nice to see you boys, now let's get the fuck outta here," he growled.

"You got that shit right, sir," Warlokk called back as he hauled up on the collective. "We're gone."

The Huey Hog gunship rose into the air, and, as Warlokk made a gentle banking turn off to the southeast, Gaines felt himself start to relax for the first time since the People Sniffer bird had run out of gas. He still had to have his little talk with Brownie about that massive fuck-up. Warrant officer or no warrant officer, that guy was going to be in charge of the shit-burning detail for a month.

"We'll have you on the Dustoff pad in a little over half an hour," Warlokk informed him.

"Skip the hospital," Gaines clicked in. "I'm okay. Just take me back to the company."

"Roger."

On the trip back to An Khe, Gaines didn't say much. He was deep in thought. It had been a close one. What shook him up the most was not that he had almost been killed, but that he had been captured and had almost spent the rest of the war in a cage. He shuddered. Dying he could deal with, but not in a prison camp.

Warlokk taxied up in front of the Python Flight operations shack and shut the rotor down. Gaines had never thought the battered, old tropical hut could look so good to him. Most of the pilots and crew in the company were on hand to greet him when he stepped down to the ground.

"Hey, Captain Rat," someone yelled. "What took you so long? You run outta gas?"

A gale of laughter swept through the men, and Gaines grinned in spite of himself. He knew that he would spend the rest of his army career trying to live that one down.

He shrugged his shoulders, "Y'all know how it is." His southern accent deepened. "You just can't get good help nowadays."

The men crowded around him to shake his hand and pound him on the back. They were glad to have him back and let him know it. After making his way through the crowd, he went into his office and sat down in his chair. He rubbed his hand across the stubble on his face. The first thing he wanted to do was to grab a hot shower and a shave. He could smell himself and he didn't smell so good. But before he did any of that, he had to call Lisa and Jordan. She would be worried sick about him. And he had to tell Jordan about the Russians.

He rummaged in his desk drawer until he found a pack of his thin cigars. He fired one up and sucked the smoke deep into his lungs. Christ, it was good to be back. He reached for the phone.

Gaines was sorry that he made the call to Jordan first. As soon as the colonel heard he was back, he ordered the pilot to report to him immediately. Rat grabbed a new brush hat from his locker and ran for his Jeep. He'd call Lisa after he found out what this was all about.

In the battalion headquarters, Muller jumped to his feet when Gaines came tearing down the hall. ''Glad to have you back, sir!'' he sang out.

Rat swept right on past him without saying a word and went into Jordan's office. Jordan looked up from his desk. ''Rat, come on in,'' he said.

Gaines flopped down in the chair right next to the desk. ''I sure hope this is real important, sir, I'm bushed.''

Jordan butted his smoke. ''It is, Rat, believe me. Brody started a real shit storm on high with his claim that he ran into Russians out there. Did he say anything to you about that?''

''He didn't have to,'' Gaines explained. ''I was captured by a Russian sniper unit.''

''You're shitting me!''

''No, sir, not one millimeter.'' Gaines reached into his breast pocket and pulled out the Russian ID card and dog tag Brody had given him to bring back.

''Here's some of their calling cards,'' he said, handing them over the the colonel.

Jordan stared at them for a moment, turning the card over and over in his hand. ''They're Russian all right. Where'd you get these?''

''Brody's people had a run-in with those guys and wasted one of them.''

''When was that?''

''Yesterday, I think.''

''Jesus Christ! That's when he called in. The G-two's going to shit himself,'' Jordan said halfway to himself. ''Everyone around here thought that he had been smoking dope or something. Who else knows about this?''

Rat shrugged. "I don't know, sir. Brody and his bunch, me, of course. Oh yeah, that Ranger sniper over at the hospital, Metcack."

"I'd advise you not to tell anyone else for the time being."

"Sure, sir. But why the secrecy?"

"I don't know. but I do know that everyone's real jumpy about it."

Jordan stared at the Russian ID card for a moment before reaching for the phone. "There's some people here from Saigon who are going to want to see this stuff and talk to you about it ASAP."

"Can it wait till I get cleaned up first, sir? I'm just a little grungy."

"Sorry, Rat," Jordan answered. "I wish I could, but this is a hot one."

"You say that he called himself Zerinski?" The G-2 major asked Gaines.

"Yes, sir," Rat answered wearily. This intelligence debriefing had been going on for over two hours. He was bone tired, and it was starting to piss him off. "Major Gregor Zerinski of the Russian KGB."

Gaines was beginning to get real tired of repeating himself to these people. For some reason, they were having a difficult time accepting what had happened to him at face value.

"And he spoke fluent English?" his other interrogator asked. He was some kind of spook in civilian clothes who had not bothered to introduce himself. From the way he acted, he had to be from the State Department. Even the CIA wasn't that stupid.

"That's what I said," Gaines told him one more time. "He told me that he'd learned it in a KGB school in Russia."

"Weren't you surprised that he said these things to you?"

"Why not?" Gaines shrugged. "He didn't think that I was going anywhere except back to Hanoi with him."

"Then why do you think that he let you escape?" the interrogation-team leader asked sarcastically.

That question was the last straw. Rat leaned forward in his chair.

"Major, I have enjoyed just about all of this shit that I can stand today. I have spent a pretty rough couple of days and I am dead on my feet. I have told you how I escaped several times. Zerinski had no intention of letting me go, and if it had not been for Sergeant Brody's men, I would have been killed or recaptured."

He got to his feet. "Now, sir, if you are not going to charge me with some crime under the UCMJ because I was captured by the enemy, in this case Russians, then I suggest that you let me go back to my quarters, take a hot shower, and get caught up on my sleep. Sir!"

The intelligence officer was taken aback. "But I didn't say that I was going to charge you with anything, Captain."

"Then why the third degree?" Gaines snapped. "You have my report and I stand by every fucking word of it."

The major stood up. "That will be all for now, Gaines, thank you."

Gaines spun on his heels and marched out of the room.

CHAPTER 35

Camp Radcliff, An Khe

"Rat, I was scared shitless," Lisa said, gripping him tightly. Gaines held her and stroked her hair. He understood exactly how she felt.

"So was I," he admitted.

"How could you have done something like that?" she asked, referring to his having run out of gas in the air.

"Well," he quipped, "I guess I just had my head up my ass and my mind in neutral again."

That got a small chuckle out of her. Gaines could always brush her fears away and make her laugh.

"Don't you ever scare me that way again."

"I'll try not to, love."

Lisa looked up at him through tear-stained eyes and smiled. That was the first time he had ever called her by a pet name. She liked how it sounded. It made her feel secure.

"Now what are we going to do?" she asked in a quiet voice.

Gaines knew what she meant by that question and the answer that he saw forming in his mind scared him a little. He had always prided himself on his independence, telling himself that he was the carefree, professional bachelor type who was never going to settle down. He pictured himself as a daring aviator who lived only to fly and who made his home wherever he hung his flight helmet for the evening.

For years now he had gone from one army BOQ room on some army airfield to the next, telling himself that he would always live that way. But he had not then met Lisa Maddox. This was not just a wartime shack job, and that frightened him a lot. If things kept going the way they were, he'd be living in married officers' quarters as soon as his tour was over.

"Hey," he said, brightly changing the subject. "I'm hungry. Put your face back on and we'll go out for a steak."

"You got a deal," she laughed, wiping her eyes. "Just give me a moment."

As always, the steak at Division headquarters mess was thick and juicy, the salad had real iceberg lettuce in it, and the rolls were hot. Rat and Lisa were drinking their coffee when the nurse looked up and noticed Janson taking a seat at the bar.

"Oh, Rat," she said quietly, "there's something I forgot to tell you. Something that I think's important."

"Oh? What's that?"

"See that guy at the end of the bar?" she nodded in his direction.

Gaines looked over. "Yeah, why?"

"He's a reporter and he was talking to me the other night about those snipers. He was trying to get information about what's going on."

"But that's classified." Gaines was stunned.

"I know," she answered softly. "And I think that I really fucked up. I let it slip that Brody was out hunting them."

"Oh, shit."

"I didn't mean to. He got me talking about Snakeman Fletcher, and it slipped out."

"Not your fault." Gaines looked grim. "Those guys have a way of doing that, getting you to tell them what they want to know."

Janson spotted Lisa, too, and raised his glass. When she looked away, he got up from his barstool and walked over to them. "Mind if I join you?"

Gaines locked eyes with him and smiled with only his mouth. "Sure, have a seat."

Janson stuck his hand out. "I don't believe we've met, I'm David Janson."

Rat ignored his hand. "You're right, we haven't met. But I understand that you've been pumping Lieutenant Maddox here for information. Classified operational information."

Janson instantly realized that he had probably just bitten off a little more than he could chew. "Wait a minute, Captain. . . ."

"Gaines, Rat Gaines."

"Captain Gaines, I can explain."

Rat rocked back in his chair, his eyes locked on the reporter like the twin minigun barrels in his Cobra's gun turret.

"This had better be fucking good, mister." Gaines's voice was cool. " 'Cause you're about to find your ass in deep *kim chee*."

"Well, the other evening I was talking to the lieutenant here and . . ."

"That's what I understand." Gaines's voice was silky smooth but sharp, rather like the blade of a Japanese Samurai sword.

Janson instantly saw his mistake. Gaines was obviously the beautiful nurse's lover. It was time for him to tread softly. Otherwise he was going to have his head handed to him on a plate.

"Look, Captain, Lieutenant," Janson began, spreading his hands in a disarming gesture. "This isn't coming out right. Please let me try to explain."

"Please do," Rat said laconically.

"I'm not trying to get anyone in trouble. This started out when I heard the rumors floating around the camp about these sniping incidents. I thought that there was a story in it, so I started looking into the situation and talking to people. So far, I've seen men on the flight line fighting over flak vests, and I saw the body of a young door gunner brought in."

"Snakeman Fletcher," Gaines interrupted him. "He was one of my men."

Janson didn't know if he should try to continue his explanation or just get up and run for his life. Everywhere he turned, he ran into people who had known the dead man. Suddenly it clicked in his mind. Now he knew who Gaines was. Not only was he the Echo Company commander, he was also the guy who had been captured and rescued by the men who were out hunting the snipers. The man he had heard about while he was trying to talk to Alexander.

The reporter started from square one. "Captain Gaines, I would like to invite both you and Lieutenant Maddox to my quarters for a drink." He held up his hand before Gaines could answer.

"Now, before you tell me to get lost," he hurriedly continued, "please let me explain. What I'm seeing here is a tremendous story about a small group of men who are trying to eliminate a threat and, at the same time, avenge the death of a friend. Apparently a very popular and well-loved friend." He paused.

"And for some reason, the PIO's office is being a little less than candid with me about all of this. They claim that they know nothing at all about the operation. I'm not trying to learn military secrets, I simply want to tell the story of some men who felt that they could do what the Air Cav couldn't, namely to eliminate those snipers."

Gaines's held his eyes steadily on Janson. There was just a faint possibility that this guy was for real and not just another asshole reporter.

"I'll tell you what," he said, standing up. "You tell me what you know and then I'll decide if you need to know any more."

"That's fair enough."

"Rat!" Lisa's concern was plain on her face. Even she knew that talking to reporters about operational matters was a one-way ticket to trouble. "Is that safe?"

''Trust me.''

In Janson's room in the VIP quarters, the reporter tried to make his guests comfortable. ''Can I get you something to drink? I can offer you a good bourbon, a decent brandy or beer. What'll you have?''

They both had brandy.

''Okay,'' Janson said after they had their drinks in their hands. ''Here's what I've picked up so far.'' He launched into his side of it. ''And,'' he finished, ''I understand that you were rescued from the jungle by these same men earlier today.''

''Just how did you come across that little tidbit?'' Gaines's eyes were narrow slits.

''I overheard some radio operators talking about it.'' Janson did not add that it had been Gaines's own people whom he had overheard. He didn't think that it would be wise to let him know that at this time.

Gaines sipped his brandy. ''There's two things that I can do about this: One, I can trust you and tell you the rest of the story. Or I can turn you over to the G-two and have him investigate what you're doing under the espionage regulations.''

He held his glass out for a refill. ''Oh, I realize that all the G-two could do is to get you thrown out of the country since you guys don't seem to be subject to the law. But, it would be an inconvenience. So to prevent that, how about telling me why I should trust you.''

''Well,'' Janson said, looking him straight in the eye, ''you should trust me because I think I have finally figured out what this war is all about. You can help me tell a story about a handful of American GIs who are out there all by themselves taking on a mission of extreme danger. Those guys are putting their lives on the line because their friends were being killed and no one seemed to be able to do anything about it.''

For a minute, the reporter looked as if he didn't know how to continue. Gaines glanced at Lisa. She was looking at

Janson with a puzzled, yet sympathetic expression on her face.

"I went out with Brody and his men on a mission the other day and, as you know, we got shot down." Janson sounded grim. "Things got pretty hairy out there for a while, and I was scared shitless. Also, I was pissed at how the men treated me. Brody in particular acted like it was somehow all my fault that they were in danger. And perhaps in a way it was. I was after Brody's ass. I'd had a run-in with him earlier, and I let my pride overcome my ability to see clearly what was going on."

He paused and took a drink. "Now I've had time to think about what happened out there. Even though those men didn't like me, they did their jobs and saved my life in the process. The thing that impressed me out there was the courage and dedication that those grunts exhibited. It goes way beyond the call of duty. They are doing things out there that the average Joe Blow back home only fantasizes about in his wet dreams.

"Then a couple of days later I took that picture of Fletcher's body on the Dustoff pad after he had been killed by the sniper. The only thing on my mind then was what a sensational shot it would make for my next article. It wasn't even a dead body to me. It was just an opportunity to make something for myself. Shortly after that, Brody paid me a visit. Basically, he said that if I published that picture, he was going to kill me.

"He was so calm about it and so sure of himself that I stopped and took another look at what I was doing. And maybe for the first time, I was able to see past the 'story' to the actual people involved in it. Now, it seems like everywhere I go I meet someone who was one of the dead man's best friends. Last night it finally hit me like a shot in the head."

The reporter took a deep breath. "Two days ago, Fletcher was a living, breathing, walking man. A man who had friends, family, maybe a lover, I don't know. But he was alive and he was fighting a war. Like most of these kids,

Fletcher probably had little or no idea of the bigger picture of what's at stake here. He was just doing a job and doing it the best he could. Now his friends are out there trying to finish it up for him."

Janson stared out the darkened window for a moment. Lisa started forward as if to comfort him, but Gaines waved her back.

After a moment, Janson looked back at them. "I guess that all I'm trying to say is that having spent time with your people, I have finally come to realize that you guys are real. You're not just names in a story, or statistics in the fucking 'Five O'Clock Follies' at MACV in Saigon. You're real. You bleed like everyone else. And you die like everyone else. Somehow, in trying to find the 'big story,' I managed to forget that.

"You guys are fighting for your lives out there in a foreign country, and it seems as if everyone in the press corps is shitting on you for doing it. I want to make up for that if I can. I realize that my efforts may not come to very much, but it's the least I can do for you." He took a long drink from his glass. "There. That's it." Janson leaned back in his chair. "All of it. Will you help me?" he finished solemnly.

Gaines studied the man for a moment.

"Okay," Gaines finally answered. "I'll tell you what you need to know to understand what's going on. And there's a lot more to it than you have any idea about. One hell of a lot more."

CHAPTER 36

The Song Re Valley

As the sun sank slowly behind the ridgeline in front of them, Brody's men were still following the Russians' trail. With the sun gone, darkness came swiftly to the jungle. This was the most dangerous time of the day for them. It was not dark enough to use the Starlight scopes, but too dark to see well without them. A good time for an ambush.

Brody halted. The trail was still fresh, perhaps too fresh. He tried to guess what the Russians were thinking. Did they want to slip away in the night or were they going to turn and fight, now that the darkness gave them an advantage?

"Whaddaya think?" he asked Two-Step.

The Indian looked around in the gathering twilight. "I don't know, man. But I do know that we'd better go real easy for a while until it gets dark enough for the Starlight to work."

The sky was clear overhead. As soon as it got completely dark, the stars would be out in their full tropical brilliance. The Starlight scope would amplify this faint light over 50,000 times and turn the night into a glowing green day.

"You got any idea if Ivan has any Starlights?" the Indian asked.

"Beats the shit outta me," Brody replied, shrugging his shoulders. "But they've got to have some kind of night scope. Maybe infrared."

The light-intensifying Starlight scope was new to Nam, an example of what American technology could do to solve the age-old battlefield problem of how to see the enemy in the dark. Before Starlight there had been infrared telescopes that picked up heat radiation. The infrared scopes couldn't penetrate as far as the Starlight, nor was the sight picture as clear. They also picked up heat signatures from animals. But they had worked well enough to kill in World War II and Korea. With the Starlight, though, killing at night had become much easier. Almost as routine as killing by day.

"We'd better get something to eat now," Brody decided. "And give it a little time to get dark. I don't want to walk into anything with my pants down."

"Sounds good to me."

Two-Step went back and told the other two men to take a break. When he got back to where Brody was watching the trail, he found him mounting the big TVS-2 Starlight scope on the sniper rifle. "You know how to work that thing?"

"Nothing to it. You just focus it like you do the day scope and shoot."

"Sounds easy enough."

"The only thing that you have to be careful about is aiming it at visible light. White light can burn out the optics inside."

"There shouldn't be too much danger of that out here." Two-Step looked out at the swiftly darkening jungle on both sides of the trail.

"That's a big rodg."

Gardner sat with Gambini in the drag position, keeping

watch on their back trail as he wolfed down a package of LRRP-ration beef and rice. He had been carrying the plastic bag inside his fatigue jacket for the last hour and the rehydrated freeze-dried meal was more than warm. The fact that it carried a faint aroma of his armpits didn't bother him at all.

He followed the Lurp with a long drink of warm, stale water from his last two-quart canteen. He shook the plastic container. It was almost empty. Time to refill with local water as soon as they hit a stream or a village well. He would have killed for a cold beer. He took the bottle of bug juice from his pocket and applied it to his exposed skin. Army-issue insect repellent didn't help much against Vietnam's different bugs, and he didn't have any of the potent Vietnamese *nuoc-nam* fermented fish sauce that some grunts used to keep the mosquitoes away.

He rolled his sleeves back down. It was almost time to go back to the war. The nice thing about this mission was that it had totally taken his mind away from his problems with Sandra. He hadn't even thought about her for the last couple of days. Maybe if he just stayed in the brush long enough, she would go away.

He had thought about Mai, though, remembering the evening he had spent with her before they had lifted out. That had been one of the most erotic nights of his young life. Now he knew for himself why some of the guys went completely ape shit over Vietnamese women. Guys like Brody, for example.

He had not known that a woman could be so sexual, that she could just plain enjoy fucking the way Mai did. He felt a stirring in his groin as he remembered the way her long black hair flowed down her back as she rode him from one shuddering climax right into another. Sandra had never been like that, even in the good old days before she had gotten pregnant.

Ruthlessly he shut those thoughts out of his mind. He was not here to dream about pussy, he was out in the woods to kill someone. He got to his feet and picked up his weapons. "I'm going up to talk to Brody," he told Gambini.

"Ask him when we're moving out again," the sniper said. "I'm getting cold."

The talk with the reporter had taken Rat longer than he had expected, causing him and Lisa to be late for his crash party. But even though he was supposed to be the guest of honor, no one seemed to have minded. In fact, as far as he could tell when he walked in the door, no one had even noticed that they weren't there. The party was moving along quite nicely without them. It was just as well. Rat just wanted to stumble off to bed somewhere, preferably with Lisa, and sleep for a week.

But along with its privileges, command also had its responsibilities, and one of those responsibilities was putting in an appearance at the club. He had been the one who started the tradition of having a company party every time someone went down. He could always sleep in late in the morning.

A cheer broke out when someone noticed that they had finally arrived. "What's the matter, Rat," someone else yelled out. "Run out of gas again?"

The club erupted with howls of laughter. Gaines winced. It was quickly becoming a very old joke. He shot the guy a one-finger salute and guided Lisa over to the bar. One short drink, maybe two, and he'd call it quits. "What're you having?" he asked.

Lisa looked exhausted. It had been a hard day for her as well. Because of the hurried intelligence debriefing, Rat had not been able to contact her for several hours after he had gotten back. She had first learned that he was safe when she talked to Chief. And when she had heard the story of the firefight and the rescue, she had really gotten upset.

She looked up at him. "Just a Coke, please. Another drink will put me out like a light." Lisa looked around the small club. She didn't feel like partying, either, and the usual antics of the pilots and their guests were not amusing tonight. In fact, she thought that the whole thing was rather stupid. Grown men, supposedly professionals, acting like they were college freshmen at a fraternity party.

Suddenly it hit her all at once—her worry about Rat when he had been missing and the fear that he had been killed, the knowledge that as long as he was in Nam, he could be killed at any time. She thought of the endless stream of broken, bloody young bodies she had cared for in the hospital. The next one could very easily have Rat's face. She remembered talking to Janson about the uselessness of Fletcher's death, dead children, the impossible, stressful job of patching up young men who should have not been injured in the first place, doing her best to be strong all the time and trying to feel like a woman while living in primitive conditions.

The war. The damned war. It was more than she could take at that moment. She shuddered and put her head down in her arms. She fought to keep the tears from coming, absolutely determined not to cry in front of the laughing, shouting, drunken idiots.

Gaines didn't seem to notice her distress. He was busy playing the heroic company commander again. As much as she loved him, sometimes she felt like taking the smooth-talking southerner by the neck and banging his head against the wall. He was always so calm and poised in a crowd, and she didn't understand where he got that from. Didn't he ever feel like just screaming at the world to shut up and go away?

She watched him joking with someone about crashing and being captured. He was as calm about it as if it had been a lark, a Sunday walk in the park. Suddenly, she hated him. She hated the way he seemed to thrive on the war, the way that danger and death stimulated him. Every day she had to fight to be strong, to keep the war from overwhelming her, but he just sailed on through it all, doing what he had to do and making a big joke out of it.

She reached across the bar and grabbed a bottle of brandy off the shelf. "Put it on my tab," she told the startled bartender as she stuffed it in the side pocket of her fatigue pants. He nodded and wrote the bottle down on Rat's bar bill.

"Rat," she said softly. "I'd like to go home now."

Gaines, who was talking animatedly to the battalion operations officer, nodded. "Just a second." He didn't even turn his head to look at her.

She stepped down from the barstool and headed out the door. When he did turn around, she was gone.

A shot rang out in the darkness. Brody dropped to the ground along the trail and crawled over to a log. The Russians were waiting for them. He swung the heavy sniper rifle around and started scanning the terrain in front of him. They had to be somewhere fairly close. The shot had sounded like it was no more than three or four hundred meters away.

Two-Step wiggled up beside him. "Did you see 'em?" he whispered.

"No," Brody growled softly. "But that fucker's got to be out there somewhere. Get Gambini up here. I need some help with this."

The Indian quickly came back with the other sniper. Gambini lay down beside Brody and brought his rifle up to his shoulder. "Okay," he said. "You take the left side and I'll take the right. We're looking for body shapes and outlines. Those camies they're wearing are going to make it a little tougher, but look for anything that doesn't match the background."

Brody brought his eye up to the sight reticle and turned the Starlight scope on. Through the lens, the velvety blackness around them suddenly glowed green. He could plainly see the same patches of light and shadow in the jungle that he would have seen during the day.

He scoped out the immediate area first and then turned

the scope to check out the ridgeline in front of them. It was a good four hundred meters away, almost at the limit of the Starlight.

It was also almost at the limit of the night scopes that the Russians had mounted on their Dragunovs. The Russian PSO-1 sniper scope was designed for both daytime and night use. At night, a small light illuminated the sight reticle, and a built-in infrared metascope, a heat-radiation detector, came into play. It allowed the scope to operate in the passive IR mode. In that mode, the scope detected natural infrared heat sources and any IR night-vision devices such as tank searchlights.

The scope could also be used in what was called an active IR mode by mounting an IR source to illuminate the target with invisible infrared light. That was what the Russians were doing tonight, trying to pick out Brody's men with the IR lights. All four snipers were on the ridgeline overlooking the jungle trail below, slowly sweeping their scopes from side to side, hunting for them. The Starlight scopes couldn't pick up the Russian IR emissions, however, and had to depend upon the enemy snipers exposing themselves by coming into the open.

It was a battle of differing technologies.

Brody thought that he saw something move. He focused in tighter on it. It could have been a man's arm or leg. He wet a finger and held it up to test the wind. There was none.

Running Chief's instructions through his mind, he centered his target in the sight reticle and took a deep breath, his finger tightening on the trigger. The silenced rifle spat.

Through the scope, he saw that the target was gone. He didn't know if he had hit it or not.

"What ya got?" Gambini whispered from his position beside him.

"Fucked if I know, but it's gone."

The long silencer fitted on the end of the barrel not only silenced the round, it also hid the muzzle flash. It could not, however, hide the heat signature of the round.

For a few seconds, the end of the silencer was warmer than the surrounding air. That heat source was visible to the Russian IR scopes.

Zeroing in on that small speck of light, the Russian Dragunovs spoke. Brody and Gambini huddled behind their log as a dozen bullets whined over their heads and smacked into the other side of the log.

Gambini crawled over to the end of the log and stuck the barrel of his rifle around the corner. While the Russian scopes could pick up the heat of their rifles firing, the Starlight could pick up the Russian's muzzle flashes. The Dragunov rifles only had muzzle brakes and flash hiders on the end of their barrels, not silencers. From the front, the muzzle flash was visible.

"I got 'em," Gambini shouted triumphantly. He started firing at the points of brighter, light green he saw through his scope. The Russian fire faded as quickly as it had started.

"Time to move," Gambini said. "They've got us zeroed in." He cautiously got to his feet and dashed off. A single shot followed him.

"You okay?" Brody asked.

"Yeah," came the voice from the darkness. "The fucker missed me."

Brody crawled backward into the brush himself. "How're they spotting us?" he asked the sniper.

"I don't know, maybe IR or something like that. We'd better stay in the brush. It'll hide us better."

Brody was used to fighting at night. Unlike many Americans, he did not view the night as an enemy, but as an ally. It could hide him as well as it hid Charlie. Tonight, however, it was not a shield as it had been before. This time the enemy could see him, so it was back to daylight tactics.

He crawled behind a big tree and slowly eased his rifle around the side. "Hey, Gambini," he called out. "Shoot at 'em, draw their fire."

The other sniper fired three quick shots and ducked

back under cover. As Brody had hoped, one of the Russian's answered and he saw the brief muzzle flash in his Starlight. It was to the right of a large solid light mass, maybe a rock. He slowly took aim, fired two quick shots, and ducked back behind the tree.

He tried that same trick again, but the Russians had caught on and didn't want to play anymore. Finally, Brody had the men make a cold camp for the night.

CHAPTER 37

The Song Re Valley

Gardner watched the sun rise suddenly behind the ridgeline. Its rays were scattered by the morning mist hanging low in the valley, giving a very familiar look to the landscape. Were it not for the M-16 in his hands instead of his old .30-30 Winchester deer rifle, he would have thought he was back home in the mountains during deer season. But he was not hunting harmless little four-legged animals. His prey was of the two-legged variety, and they could shoot back.

He realized that if he did make it through his tour and finally got home, he would never hunt deer again unless he was starving. In fact, maybe he would take his old lever-action rifle into the hills during hunting season and give the deer a little covering fire. He chuckled to himself, thinking of the expressions on the faces of the big, bad hunters when the deer starting shooting back at them.

It was almost light enough to get going again. He pulled his poncho liner tightly around him and walked over to where Brody was sleeping. He leaned down and softly called his name. Brody awoke instantly.

"It's time," Gardner said.

"Jesus!" Brody sat up and looked around. "I was dreaming that we were back at Radcliff and Fletcher was still there. Shit."

Gardner didn't want to talk about dreams of dead men. "I'll get Two-Step and Gambini going."

"Yeah, do that. I want to move out again as soon as we can."

"You think they got away during the night?"

"No," Brody shook his head. "I doubt it. I'm getting the feeling that those fuckers want us about as much as we want them."

"Why?"

"Beats the fuck outta me and I can't say why I think that. It's just a feeling I have." He got up and stretched. "Whoever's in charge of that bunch of bastards is going to do his best to kill us."

Gardner looked up to the ridgeline. "Then I guess we're just going to have to kill them first."

"You got that shit right."

Brody didn't even want to take time to have breakfast. They could eat on the go. He was on the trail of the Russians again in ten minutes.

"You are mad!" Zerinski shouted at Yuravitch. "I should kill you right now." He drew his Makarov pistol from the holster on his field belt.

"Go ahead then, if you do not have the stomach for it," the old sniper sneered, boldly standing his ground. "Run for safety if you like. But I will remain here. I have Yankees to kill."

The KGB officer hesitated for a moment. Short of killing the stubborn old bastard, there was no way that he was going to force Yuravitch to give it up. He was acting like a man possessed. He could not live knowing that he had run from a fight. Zerinski lowered his pistol. On second thought, he could let the old sniper stay there and die.

"All right, Yuravitch. You stay, but I will not wait for you. As soon as I reach the North Vietnamese camp across the border, I am going back to Hanoi. Good hunting." Zerinski turned to go.

"My men stay with me."

The KGB man turned back sharply.

"They came here to use their rifles to kill Yankees," Yuravitch continued. "Not to turn and run as soon as it becomes difficult. They are Spetsnaz, the finest of the Red Army. Not KGB cowards."

Zerinski did not react to the insult.

"We did not come here to test their courage, comrade. We came here to test the Dragunov," Zerinski pointed out. "And that is completed."

"Oh, no, it is not. The Yankees are pursuing us and the rifles will get one last test by killing them."

Zerinski knew that if he left now, he would have a difficult time explaining why he had left Yuravitch and the snipers behind, not to mention the weapons themselves. Additionally, he did not relish the thought of traveling unescorted to the Laotian border. He realized that the best solution at this time was just to give in to the reactionary old bastard. "All right, we will try it your way for a while. How do you want to do this?"

For a moment Yuravitch looked stunned. Zerinski's sudden acquiescence made him suspicious. He pushed the thought from his mind, though, now that he was finally having things his way.

"In the Great Patriotic War my snipers always worked alone, not in teams as we have done here so far. Since we do not know who is following us, or why, and have no idea of the size of their unit, I propose to send the snipers out alone, back along the trail to hold them up and to learn more about them."

"How long do you think this will take?"

"As long as it takes." Now that his plan had been adopted, Yuravitch was condescending again. "Patience is the first weapon of a sniper."

"All right," Zerinski acknowledged. "I will give you the day to accomplish this. But tomorrow, I leave for Laos."

"If the Yankees will cooperate, that should be sufficient."

"That is a big 'if,' comrade."

"Oh, I think that they will," Yuravitch smiled. "I can feel it. They are out there."

The army major finished his coffee and put the cup back into his pack. "I will issue the orders to the men."

Even piled high with paper work, Gaines was glad to see his desk in the operations shack again. Crashing around in the woods with his hands tied behind his back was not his idea of a fun-filled vacation. In fact, he was going to try real hard never to get shot down again. He refilled his coffee cup from the pot in the radio room and sat back down at his desk to get to work.

Before he tackled that, however, he wanted to check in on Lisa. He had been surprised when he had discovered that she had slipped out of the club last night. He couldn't think of anything that he had said to make her mad at him. Maybe it was just that time of the month for her. He picked up the phone and rang through to the hospital.

The nurse who answered the phone said that Lisa was on the ward and that she would tell her that he had called. He hung up with the definite impression that he had been lied to. He mentally shrugged and reached for the top piece of paper in his in-box. He didn't have time to worry about that right now.

The first thing that he looked at was a supply requisition for replacement Prick-25 radios. Suddenly, he remembered that Brody was out there with no commo. He had given Gaines his radio so they could call in the choppers. In all the excitement he had completely forgotten about that.

Gaines got up and stuck his head into the operation

sergeant's office. "See if you can find Warlokk for me," he said. "I need to talk to him."

"Yes, sir."

Ten minutes and several pieces of paper later, the warrant officer-pilot stuck his scarred face around the door of Gaines's office. "You wanted to see me, sir?"

"Yeah, Lance, come on in."

Gaines lit up one of his thin cigars and leaned back in his chair. "How can I get a radio out to Brody when I can't talk to him and don't have the slightest idea where in the hell he is?"

Warlokk had a puzzled look on his face. "Sir?"

Gaines laughed and went on to explain. "Brody gave me his radio yesterday so I could talk to you guys. He's out there somewhere now with no commo. Can you think of anything we can do about that?"

"We could air-drop one to him. If we could find him."

"Okay, how do we find him?"

"Beats the fuck outta me, sir."

"Let's think about this, there has to be a way." Gaines leaned back in his chair. At least he knew the general area that Brody was working in. It wasn't like Gaines was going to have to chase all over II Corps to find him. In fact, he could go back to yesterday's LZ and try to fly up the trail that the Russians had taken.

"Got an idea." Gaines blew out a perfect smoke ring. "Where can we borrow a Bullshit Bomber?"

"A what?"

"A Bullshit Bomber, you know. A Psyops bird with the loudspeaker setup that they use to make propaganda broadcasts. We don't need the chopper, though, just the sound set."

"What are we going to do with it?"

"Well," Rat grinned, "I was thinking that we could mount it in your gunship and then fly over that part of the Song Re and try to talk to him. We can tell him to come out into the open so we can drop him a radio."

"That's one of the craziest ideas I've ever heard, sir."

"Isn't it just?" Rat grinned.

Warlokk shrugged. "Why not? It makes about as much fucking sense as him going out there in the first place."

Lisa had been standing by the phone in the nurses' office when Rat's call came through. She had already given instructions to the nurse on duty that she wasn't available if he called. She didn't want to talk to him. In fact, she didn't want to talk to anyone in An Khe, or Vietnam for that matter. Suddenly, she was tired of the whole thing. She wanted a rest from it all.

She needed a break, a chance to wind down a little. She thought of taking a little vacation, going to Vung Tau or Nha Trang and lying on the beach for a while. She knew that she was very tired, as tired as she had ever been. She also knew that she was confused about her feelings for Rat Gaines.

Ever since she had finally gone to bed with him, she was terrified that something would happen to him, that she would go out to meet a Dustoff, look down at the body, and it would be him. If that happened, she didn't think she could deal with it. It would put her in a VA hospital psycho ward for the rest of her life.

Lisa was scared that she might be falling in love with the pilot, and that was the last thing she needed. Her job was distressing enough, and she doubted whether she was in any shape to deal with the inevitable ups and downs of a full-fledged love affair. Especially with a pilot, a man who ran a daily risk of getting himself killed.

Tears welled in the corners of her eyes just from thinking about him being killed. She turned away from the other nurse abruptly. She didn't want anyone to know that she was coming apart at the seams. It was okay for her to realize that she didn't quite have it all together at the moment, but it wouldn't do for anyone else to know.

"I'm going down to the colonel's office," she told her supervisor.

"Are you okay?" the duty nurse asked.

"Yeah. I'm fine, just fine."

Colonel Hardell, the hospital commander, was an old friend of Lisa's father and he had known her since she was a young girl. He took one look at the nurse and immediately gave her time off. To make it official, he had her hand-carry a requisition for medical equipment to Nha Trang. He also told her not to come back for at least a week.

An hour later, she was on the morning ash-and-trash run, the daily chopper to IFFV Headquarters. Next stop, the sun-drenched beaches of Nha Trang.

CHAPTER 38

Camp Radcliff, An Khe

As it turned out, finding a Huey Bullshit Bomber was fairly easy. The 8th Psychological Operations Battalion always had a couple of them stationed at An Khe. Talking the Psyops boys out of one of their sound systems proved to be a little more difficult than locating them, but mounting the bulky loudspeakers on one side of Warlokk's Huey Hog was the real problem.

''Captain,'' the maintenance warrant said, wiping a greasy hand across his sweaty face. ''The only fucking way that I am going to get these fucking things mounted on Warlokk's bird is if I take the guns off one side. But then she's going to be off balance and I can't guarantee you how good she's going to fly.''

''Chief,'' Gaines said, laying a hand on the man's broad shoulders. ''You just figure out how to put those suckers on and hook 'em up. Warlokk and I will worry about flying it.''

''Yes, sir.'' He walked off, shaking his head and muttering to himself. He was convinced that Gaines had really lost his mind this time. What in hell was he going to do with those goddamned speakers, play rock-and-roll music up there and kill dinks by scaring them to death?

Just as the chief walked off, Warlokk drove up to the maintenance hangar in Rat's Jeep, coming to a screeching halt inches from where Gaines was standing. He had a big white Styrofoam box on the passenger seat. "I think I've got the radio situation figured out," he said, pointing to the box. "It's packed in there."

The Styrofoam container had originally arrived in Vietnam loaded with 2.75-inch rocket warheads. The boxes were a highly prized salvage item used for beer coolers.

"I cut up a couple more of them," he explained, "and used the pieces to pad out the inside around the radio. I also fitted a couple of extra batteries in there like you asked."

Gaines went around the side of the Jeep and lifted the package out. It didn't feel all that much heavier than the radio pack by itself.

He grinned at Warlokk. "This oughta do it. But what're you going to use for a parachute?"

"Well, seeing as how it doesn't weigh all that much, I thought I'd tie some flare chutes onto it and try that out."

Gaines raised his eyebrows. "And just how're you going to do that?"

"Oh, I'll just take it up a thousand feet and drop it over the side," he said casually, making a falling-parachute motion with his hand. "If it doesn't work, we can always get us another radio."

"I can just see myself explaining that one on a report of survey," Gaines laughed. " 'The AN/PRC-25 radio was destroyed while testing its air-drop capabilities.' Sure, why not, they're cheap."

Warlokk quickly secured three of the small parachutes to the straps around the Styrofoam box and carried the whole thing over to his chopper, placing it on the copilot's seat. The small chutes were ordinarily used to drop artillery flares at night. Grinning at his own cleverness at finding a new way to use the chutes, he called over to the control tower. After heatedly arguing with the control-tower operators for a couple of minutes, he finally got permission to make a five-hundred-foot hover over the field and drop the box.

Leaning his head out of the pilot's window, Warlokk gave Gaines a thumbs-up signal as he cranked the turbine over. He ran the rotors up to speed and was airborne in seconds.

Gaines stayed on the ground and watched Warlokk's bird slowly ascend. When the pilot reached the prearranged altitude, one of the crew chiefs threw the package out of the open door. The chutes deployed and gently lowered the radio to the ground. In fact, the little chutes worked so well that Gaines had to chase after the box as the wind caught them and blew the radio halfway across the landing field.

"I think we're about ready," Gaines said when Warlokk landed. "As soon as they get the bitch boxes hooked up we'll take off. One thing, though, I want to put some ammo and water on board, too. They might need it by now."

"I'll get right on it."

"Also, I want you to fly as the AC on this one. I'll take the guns. If we run into those guys that Brody's chasing, I want to get a shot at those bastards myself."

Warlokk looked at Gaines, highly surprised. Rat never let anyone else fly him around. He had to be really pissed off at the Russians. Warlokk wisely decided not to say a word.

The sun was directly overhead, blazing down through the thin mountain air. Brody blinked the sweat out of his eyes and focused the scope of the XM-21 on the valley floor in front of him. Heat waves shimmered above the thick vegetation. If he was a Russian sniper, he asked himself, would he be somewhere down there in the jungle or would he be hiding up on the next ridgeline, waiting for the grunts to start down the hillside?

He opted for their being on the ridgeline. They had undoubtedly booby-trapped the trail through the valley as well as covering it from the hillside.

He turned around and waved Gambini forward to join him. The camouflaged face of the other sniper poked through the leaves. All of the men had taken the time to refresh the black and green camouflage grease paint on their hands and faces that morning. With the Russian sniper scopes looking for them, they needed all the help they could get to stay hidden.

"I think they're on the next hill," Brody whispered. "That's where I'd be."

Gambini carefully scoped out the area himself. "I can't see nothin'," he said, taking the rifle down from his shoulder. "But you're probably right. What d'you want to do now?"

Brody paused for a moment, scanning the valley floor again. He wanted to be absolutely certain. Finally he turned to the sniper. "I'm going to go down into the valley to see if we can come up on the other side at the end of that ridge and flush 'em out."

Gambini nodded. "Sounds good to me. I'll keep watch from here and cover you."

Brody signaled Gardner and Two-Step. "I want to get up on the end of that ridge," he told them, pointing to the ridgeline, "and work back to the left. Chance, you take point, but stay off that trail down there."

The Indian nodded and started down the hillside into the valley. A few meters down, the brush got thicker, offering better cover but making it far more difficult to travel through. Gambini stayed where he was at the top of their ridge, scoping out their path. He would move out after them as soon as they got down to the valley floor.

* * *

Yuravitch had broken his forces up as well. Two of his snipers were on the ridgeline just as Brody had feared, but the third man was positioned down on the valley floor, with the two remaining security men stalking the jungle.

The sniper didn't think that the Americans would be foolish enough to boldly walk down the trail. After scouting the terrain, he had positioned himself at the far edge of the valley where he could cover any movement through the brush. He sent his security men into the jungle to scout for him.

The Russian Spetsnaz trooper was the best of three remaining snipers, a true student of Yuravitch's teachings. He had been under the man's tutelage for almost five years now. He, too, craved the kill and, like his mentor, he was patient. At their last stop, he had mixed red mud and painted it over the lighter colors of his camouflage suit to make it a better match to the colors of the jungle. He had also used the mud to cover his face, hands, and blond hair.

Focusing his eye through the scope of the Dragunov, he patiently scanned the valley floor, waiting for his prey to show.

Once they had all moved into the thick jungle in the valley, Two-Step halted to let Brody catch up with him. "I think we'd better move out of line here," he said. "That's the only way we can sweep this area."

"Yeah, you're right," Brody said, looking around. It was so thick in there that if they went in a file, their flanks would be vulnerable.

Two-Step moved off to his right fifty meters and Brody waved Gardner over to his left. On line, the three grunts started breaking brush again.

It was the worst kind of stalking. Each man was basically on his own, the others too far away to be able to support him if he ran into trouble. The brush was so thick that even if they had been closer, they wouldn't have been able to see each other.

Brody moved slowly, scoping out the jungle ahead of him before he moved forward to the next covered position. It was slow, but it was safe. The Russian sniper scopes were just as good as his, and he had no intention of presenting them with a target if he could help it.

He remembered to take time to scope out the trunks of the trees as well as their low-hanging branches. In this kind of jungle, a man hiding up in a tree would have a real good shot.

Suddenly, Brody caught a faint movement ahead of him and dove for cover behind the trunk of a big tree. Cautiously, he eased his head around the side to take another look. There it was again! A quick glimpse of a lighter color where no color other than the green of the foliage should have been.

He eased the barrel of his rifle around the side of the massive tree trunk and focused in on the clump of bushes a hundred meters in front of him. Through the leaves, he could see the light gray and brown colors of the Russian camouflage uniforms. He quickly ranged the scope in on it and triggered off three quick shots.

There was no return fire or movement. He must have been right on target.

Brody waited a few seconds, keeping the scope on his target, before slowly stepping out into the open. He kept the sniper rifle aimed at the Russian as he worked his way through the brush. For the first time since this mission had started, he wished that he had his sixteen with him instead of the longer, more awkward XM-21. The sniper rifle was a real pig in the brush.

The Russian still hadn't moved. Brody kept him covered, though, as he slowly moved toward the man. There was no point in taking chances. When he finally got up to the clump of brush and parted the leaves to see his kill, his heart jolted in his chest.

What he had thought was a sniper was a decoy, a Russian camouflage jacket draped over a bush. It had several of Brody's 7.62mm bullet holes in it. A cord had been tied to a limb of the bush so that the slightest tug would make it move, simulating a man hiding behind it.

He'd been had!

He was just straightening up when he heard a noise in the brush behind him.

Brody spun around, frantically trying to bring the long-barreled sniper rifle around to bear. It was too late. The sonofabitch had him cold!

''They've got to be somewhere around here,'' Gaines said, looking at the large map spread out on his lap. ''This is the trail the Russians were on, and it heads directly for Laos.''

He reached back and got the microphone for the loud-speakers. He turned on the amplifier and keyed the mike. ''Brody,'' he said. ''This is Captain Gaines. If you can hear me, pop smoke.''

In the right-hand seat, Warlokk flew the gunship while Gaines repeated his message. He hadn't wanted to mention it, but as far as he was concerned, Gaines was completely out of his rabbit-assed mind. They were never going to find Brody. Those guys could be anywhere, dead or alive.

CHAPTER 39

Deep in the jungle

The booming roar of Two-Step's sawed-off sounded close to his left flank, once, twice, three times. Brody dropped to the ground and rolled under cover. There was silence. He parted the leaves in front of him and saw the Indian crouched over, snaking through the brush with the dead security man's folding-stock AK-47 in his hand.

Brody carefully stepped out into the open and signaled his buddy. "Thanks, man," he said when Two-Step dropped down beside him. The Indian quickly stuffed twelve-gauge shells into the magazine of his shotgun to replace those he had used to kill the Russian.

"*De nada,*" he answered curtly.

"That fucker had me completely faked out. He put up a decoy." Brody seemed surprised.

"I know," Two-Step snapped the shotgun slide forward with a sharp click. "Look, man, we've got to get serious here. We're fucking up by the numbers trying to do it this way. These guys aren't a bunch of local-force VC, they're real pros. The one I wasted had to have been a security man for a sniper, and now he knows that we're here." He looked around at the jungle.

"Why don't we get Gardner and Gambini back here, Treat, take this thing a little slower, and cover each other like we're supposed to."

"You're right." Brody nodded his head. "It's slower that way, but we're in no fucking hurry. We've got the rest of the month."

"I sure the fuck hope not." The Indian sounded weary. "This shit's getting a little weak." He got to his feet. "You hold tight here and I'll go get 'em."

"Right."

Two-Step was back in fifteen minutes with the other two men and Brody filled them in.

"Okay, here's the new game plan. Chance thinks that the guy he killed was a flanker for a sniper, so he's got to know that we're here now. Gardner, I want you and Two-Step to go out front while Gambini and I hang back with the sniper scopes. But don't get so far ahead that we can't see you. And take it slow. Real slow."

Gardner checked the magazine in his M-16 and flicked the selector switch down to the rock-and-roll position. "Okay," he said, getting to his feet. "Let's get this fucking show on the road."

Side by side, the two grunts faded into the brush, the colors of their camouflage suits blending in perfectly with the leaves.

From his concealed hiding place, the Spetsnaz sniper heard Two-Step's shotgun blasts. He also noted that there had been no return AK fire. Either the Yankees had been shooting at shadows, which was very unlikely, or they had just taken out one of his security men.

The shots had come from his left and sounded two hundred meters or so away. He scoped out the area to his left flank and saw that farther out, the light was too dim under the trees to get a good sight picture. He turned on the sight reticle light in his sniper's scope. That helped a little.

The faintly glowing orange cross hairs in the scope gave him a better aiming point in the shadows.

Halfway up the trunk of a tree, the sniper had cut branches, carving out a concealed position in the foliage. That high up, he had good fields of fire for well over a hundred meters in all direction.

Gardner and Two-Step were twenty meters apart, moving in bounds to cover one another. The Indian was out front while Gardner guarded his rear. The big man wiped the sweat out of his eyes and retied the bandanna around his forehead. Not much sun was making its way through the dense canopy overhead, but it was still hot and muggy.

Two-Step turned around and waved him forward. Gardner got up from behind his clump of bushes and slipped up beside him. The Indian pointed to the right where a clump of underbrush provided good cover. Gardner nodded and dropped down. Cradling his M-16 in his arms, he crawled low through the thick grass while the Indian covered him.

Every few feet, he stopped for a minute to look around and listen. He saw nothing, and the only thing he heard was the buzzing of gnats. He started forward again, crawling through thick grass, when the muzzle of his rifle caught on something. He looked down and saw that it was a trip wire.

He froze for just a second and then tried to back away, but the front sight of the rifle was hung up. He reached out to free the sight when he saw the barrel of an AK-47 poke through the brush and center on his head. A grinning, mud-covered Russian face was behind the AK stock.

Gardner let go of his sixteen and frantically tried to roll out of the way. He was too late. He saw the Russian security man smile as he brought the AK up to shoot him in the head.

From his left side, the roar of Two-Step's sawed-off pump gun sounded through the jungle. The Russian gave a yelp and dove back into the bushes. The shotgun roared again, and the deadly steel balls sang over Gardner's head.

The Russian was crashing through the brush, frantically trying to get away.

Shaking all over, Gardner freed his rifle, got up to one knee, and sent a full magazine of 5.56mm after him. He looked over his shoulder and saw Two-Step rising from the grass. The Indian had gotten worried when Gardner took so long to cross to the next position and had started out after him.

JJ made a motion of wiping his brow in relief. The Indian grinned back and moved out again in the direction the Russian had gone. He, for one, would be very glad to get the fuck out of the jungle and go back home. The cat-and-mouse game was wearing him down. They had gotten their revenge on the Russians for Fletcher, but if they weren't careful someone was going to have to seek vengeance for them.

Gardner carefully traced the trip wire, but he found that it was not connected to a booby trap. The Russian had put it out just to slow up anyone coming that way in order to ambush them. It was a slick trick and it had almost worked on one PFC Jim Gardner.

Brody came up from behind and stopped for a moment. "That's two of 'em," he said, examining the blood trail the Russian had left.

"That was fucking near one of us, too."

Gardner was still shaking from the overload of adrenaline and he desperately wanted a cigarette. That was as close as he had ever come to buying the farm, and he didn't like the feeling at all. Even taking that rocket frag hit in the side last month hadn't scared him that much. Getting hit in a firefight was one thing. You were so charged up from blazing away that if you took a round, it wasn't a surprise. But crawling right up on a shot in the head was something else. He shuddered.

"Look," Brody said. "You drop back and work with Gambini. He's about twenty meters behind you. I'll go ahead and cover the Indian."

"Okay." Gardner had no qualms about taking the trail right now.

Brody hurried up to slip in behind Two-Step. When Brody had him in sight again, he slid in behind a tree and rested the silenced muzzle of his rifle in the fork of two branches, covering Two-Step as he inched his way through the brush. It was nerve-racking to move that slowly, but necessary.

Two-Step halted beside a fallen tree. The next fifty meters were deeply shadowed by massive overhead foliage and offered very little cover. He turned around to signal Brody that he was going to skirt the open area, when a shot rang out.

The Indian went facedown in the dirt behind the log. Brody held his breath, but Two-Step scrambled up tightly against the back side of the log and signaled that he was not hurt. Frantically, Brody swept the scope across the jungle in front of him, scanning the trees and underbrush.

Another shot rang out, slamming into the fallen tree trunk. It hit high on the log, and Brody suddenly realized that it had been fired from above him. The bastard was in a tree!

Brody brought the barrel around the side of the trunk and quickly checked the trees on the other side of the open area in front of them. The sniper had to be in one of them, but where? He extended his search to cover the trees a little farther out.

He saw what looked like a big clump of leaves in the "Y" of a big tree eighty meters away. A clump of leaves where no branches should have been.

"Two-Step!" he yelled out. "Stay down!"

The Indian went flat on his face and Brody fired. The round went into the tree trunk next to the leaves. The leaves fell out of the way, and Brody saw the camouflaged figure hiding behind them swing his rifle around. He was bringing it to bear when Brody fired again.

Through the scope, he saw the bullet tear into the sniper's upper chest, the puff of dust when the round hit, and the spurt of red that followed.

The sniper pitched forward, his rifle falling from his slack hand. He tumbled out of the tree and landed at the base with a heavy thud. He was dead, but Brody put two more rounds into him. Just in case.

Under the watchful sights of Brody's rifle, Two-Step picked himself up off the jungle floor and cautiously approached the body. The Russian's light blue eyes stared blindly from his mud-camouflaged face. The Indian waved Brody forward.

"You okay?" Brody asked.

Two-Step's face was almost white, and his breath was coming in gasps. He turned around and showed Brody where the Russian's round had ripped sideways through his pack, less than half an inch from his spine.

"Jesus!"

Two-Step didn't say a word.

Brody knelt down beside the body of the Russian sniper. He looked just like the other Russian he had seen—young, blond, and fit. He pulled the ID card from the dead man's pocket and ripped the dog tags from his neck. One more of those motherfuckers was dead, but was he the last?

Brody had no way of knowing how many there were. All he knew was that he still hadn't seen the older man who Gaines had said shot Fletcher. If he had been an officer, as Gaines had thought, maybe he had ordered these guys to hold them up while he got away.

Gardner and Gambini had joined the two men. Brody picked the Dragunov rifle up off the ground and handed it to Gardner. "Hang on to this thing."

JJ slung the Russian rifle over his shoulder with his thumper. "You think that's the last of 'em?"

"I don't know, JJ," Brody replied. "One sniper and two security men could have been the whole team. But we're real close to the Laos border. The rest of 'em might have beat feet already."

He got to his feet. "Let's at least check out that next ridgeline."

"It is time to go, I tell you!" Zerinski screamed. "It is over, you are beaten. They have killed two of your men already and wounded a third. You only have three men left, and one of them cannot fight. We are almost to the border. The Americans will not follow after us."

"None of that matters," Yuravitch said stubbornly. "I will not leave Vietnam until every last one of them are dead."

"Who, the rest of your men?" Zerinski pointed to the two remaining Russian troops who were bandaging their wounded comrade.

The old sniper glared at him. "No, you fool, the Yankees. I will stay here and kill them myself if I must, but they will die."

Zerinski briefly contemplated drawing his pistol and finally settling the issue, but the Dragunov casually laying across Yuravitch's lap was pointed right in his direction. If he went for his weapon, the reactionary old bastard would kill him.

As the American CIA liked to say, Yuravitch was beyond salvage. It was time for Zerinski to leave, and any of the Spetsnaz who wanted to go with him were welcome to come along.

"All right," the KGB man said. "Stay and continue this senseless, childish game of yours. I am going back to Hanoi."

Just then, one of the Spetsnaz pointed up at a distant black speck in the sky. "Look," he shouted. "The helicopters are here!"

From across the valley, the Russians heard the loudspeakers on Gaines's ship booming. "Brody, Sergeant Brody. This is Captain Gaines. Pop smoke and I'll drop you a radio."

Yuravitch looked up at the chopper with a savage smile

on his face. Zerinski didn't bother saying another word. If the American helicopters were coming, he was leaving. He had had more than enough of this madman and his insane passion to kill Yankees. The KGB man turned and started down the trail leading off the ridge as fast as he could, heading east for the Laotian border. It was a little less than a kilometer away.

One of the Spetsnaz helped the wounded man get up to his feet, and the two of them started after Zerinski. They said not a word to their major. A moment later, the third soldier shouldered his pack and followed them, fearfully looking over his shoulder at the chopper.

Only Yuravitch remained sitting on the ridgeline, a broad smile on his face as he watched the helicopter draw closer. He picked up his Dragunov rifle and moved into a well-covered position in the rocks halfway down the side of the hill.

The day was not quite over yet.

CHAPTER 40

Deep in the jungle

Brody heard the booming voice call his name over the loudspeakers.

"Brody, this is Gaines," the message was repeated. "If you can hear me, come out into the open and pop smoke, I've got a radio for you."

Brody pulled back into the clump of bushes, turned, and whispered over to Gardner. "Go back to the trail and pop a smoke. We'll cover for you."

Gardner backed away into the brush and fought his way to the trail along the valley floor. The path was not quite wide enough for a pickup zone, a PZ, but it was the closest open ground. The next suitable area was the ridgeline which the Russians were on. When he reached the trail, he didn't step into the open. There was still too much of a chance that the Russians had the trail zeroed in. Taking a smoke grenade from his assault harness, he pulled the pin and tossed it out into the open. The dull red smoke billowed into the air.

"This is Gaines," came the amplified voice from the chopper overhead. "I have spotted your strawberry. I will make one fly-by, come back, and drop the radio. Watch for the chutes.''

Warlokk dipped *Sat Cong*'s nose and made a low pass over the densely wooded valley. Gaines sat tensed at the gunship's firing controls on the left side, ready to open up on anything he saw. But all was quiet.

''Okay,'' he said, unbuckling his harness. ''I'll go back and kick it out.''

Gaines got out of his armored seat, climbed back into the cargo compartment, and plugged his helmet cord into the intercom. ''Okay, I'm ready. But take it slow, I don't have a lifeline.''

Warlokk throttled back almost to flight idle as he aimed the gunship down the narrow trail. He didn't like to be flying that low and that slow, but he wanted the radio to land on the trail where the men could get to it. If it got hung up in one of the trees, they wouldn't have a chance in hell of finding it.

Gaines looked down to judge their forward speed and watched the red smoke to calculate the wind drift. At what he prayed was the right moment, he stepped out onto the skid and tossed the radio over the side.

The three small parachutes deployed instantly, and the radio floated slowly to earth. It came to a gentle landing at the edge of the trail.

Gardner scrambled out of the brush. Grabbing the box by the chutes, he dragged it back under cover with him. It took but a minute for him to cut the box open with his K-Bar and retrieve the Prick-25. It was already set to the Python frequency. He keyed the handset. ''Python Lead,'' he called. ''This is Blue Two Tango. How do you hear me? Over.''

''This is Python Lead,'' came Gaines's voice. ''I have you loud and clear. What's your situation down there? Over.''

''This is Two Tango, we have killed two more Russians so far today. Two is at the east edge of this valley. He is getting ready to move on up to the ridgeline in front of us. Over."

"This is Python, Roger. Go back to his location, tell him that I want to talk to him, over."

"This is Two Tango. Roger, out."

Gardner slipped into the radio's pack straps and raced back to the edge of the woods. "The captain wants to talk to you," he said when he reached Brody's side, handing him the microphone.

"Python Lead, this is Blue Two, over."

"This is Python," came Gaines's voice in the handset. "You are only a klick or so from the border, I think you ought to call this off now. How copy? Over."

Brody didn't answer for a moment.

"Two, this is Python, did you roger my last transmission? Over?"

"This is Two, I copied. Over."

"Two, this is Python. Give it up now, son, it's over. You've taken it as far as you can go. I'm calling for your extract."

Maybe Gaines was right, maybe it had gone about as far as it could. The remaining Russians had to be running as fast as they could for the safety of Laos. If he tried to follow them his men would go with him, but he'd just wind up getting everyone killed.

Reluctantly, Brody keyed the mike again. "Python, this is Two. Roger, I'll move up to where the trail breaks and heads up the hill in front of us. I think a slick can get in there. Over."

"This is Python, Roger. I'll stay on station here till he shows up. Out."

On the eastern ridgeline, Yuravitch lay behind his boulders and watched the lone Huey circle just out of range. If the machine came just a little closer, he would try to add it to his collection of kills. He turned his scope back to the tree line facing him. The Yankees had to be somewhere in there. He had not understood what the loudspeakers had said, but he had caught the English word for radio. That meant that the men on the ground were in communication with the helicopter and they had to be calling for reinforcements. That left him with very little time to make a last kill.

A darkly camouflaged figure broke out of the tree line in front of him. Yuravitch brought the cross hairs of the PSO-1 scope to bear and triggered off a shot. The figure jumped back into the brush. Yuravitch cursed himself. In his rush to kill, he had jerked the shot. He settled down into a better position. Patience, he reminded himself.

From his position in the air, Gaines saw Two-Step dive back into the brush. "Blue Two," he called down to the grunts. "This is Python, what's your situation down there, Over."

"This is Two," came Brody's voice over the head phones in his helmet. "We have found our sniper. He's on that ridgeline in front of us. Over."

"This is Python. You want me to make a pass and smoke him out for you?"

"Negative!" Brody shouted over the radio. "I say again, do not take him under fire. He's mine. Do you roger, Python?"

In the gunship, Rat Gaines watched the grunts deploy into the edge of the trees. It made no military sense. The gunship would make short work of that last Russian. But since Brody and his people had tracked him for so long, it was only fitting that they should be the ones to take him out.

He keyed the mike. "Two, this is Python. Go get him. I'll stand by. Out."

Brody put the handset down. "Gambini. Keep him busy here, I'm going to work my way around to the left and see if I can come up on his flank."

"You want me to come with you?" Two-Step asked.

Brody's face was set. "No. I've got to do this myself."

The Indian looked at him for a long moment. "Okay,"

he finally said. "But keep your fucking head down. That guy's got us cold."

"Give me five minutes." Brody unhooked his field belt and let it fall. He took an extra magazine for the sniper rifle and stuck it in his side pants pocket. "After five, start shooting at him. Try to draw his fire and get him to shift his position."

"You got it."

Brody moved into the brush and took off to the left. A hundred meters down, he carefully crawled to the edge of the tree line. Parting the leaves in front of him, he peered out. He looked down at his watch. It was almost time.

A few seconds later, Gambini opened fire in the rock pile with several carefully aimed shots. Brody saw the puffs of dust thrown up as each bullet hit. That should keep the Russian busy. He got to his feet and sprinted up the hill, dropping back down into cover behind a rock fifty meters up. He looked around the edge of the boulder. He wasn't up high enough yet to have a good view of the Russian's flank.

He looked over to where Gambini and the rest were hiding and made the arm-pumping signal to pick up the fire. In the next flurry of shots, he scrambled up the hill again. This time, he thought he had it. He brought the muzzle of his rifle up.

Below him, Two-Step suddenly broke out of the brush, offering himself as a target. It worked.

The Russian snapped off two quick shots. Gambini's answering fire splattered around the rocks. Through the scope, Brody saw movement in the sniper's position, just a flash of his mottled camouflage uniform. More fire splattered around the rocks as Two-Step took him under fire as well.

Gardner crept up beside the Indian. Taking the thumper from his shoulder, he flipped open the breech and stuffed a short, fat 40mm round into it. The sniper was right at the maximum range for the M-79, but it might reach. He slid the bar on the sight all the way up, squinted through it, and triggered it off. He could see the slow-moving round as it sailed through the air and landed in front of the rock pile. The puff of dust and black smoke briefly obscured the target.

With a practiced flick of the wrist, he snapped open the breech, ejected the empty cartridge and stuffed in a new one. This round landed a little farther up. He tried again.

This time it worked! The Russian moved to get a better position to fire back at Two-Step and Gardner. Through the Redfield scope, Brody saw him come into view. He had a clear shot at him now. Quickly he focused the scope on him, estimating the range to be just a little over five hundred meters. He saw his target's face for the first time.

The sniper was an older man with short-cropped, graying hair. From Gaines's description, he knew that this was the man who had killed the Snakeman. He lowered his sights for a moment when he felt his heart pounding in his chest. Slowly he raised the rifle again as the adrenaline shot through his body.

Running Chief's instructions through his mind, he took a deep breath and held it. Letting it out slowly, he tightened his finger on the trigger, all the time keeping Yuravitch lined up in the cross hairs of the scope.

The rifle spat. Brody saw a look of astonishment come over the Russian's face when the bullet took him in the chest. A bright red stain appeared on the front of his uniform. He staggered back and fell to his knees among the rocks.

"I got him!" Brody cried out triumphantly. "I got the motherfucker! Cover me!" He lurched to his feet and started running for the top of the ridgeline.

"Brody, wait!" Gardner shouted back, scrambling to his feet. "I'm coming with you."

Two-Step grabbed him by the arm and held him back. "No," he said quietly. "Let him do this by himself. He needs to face it."

"Face what?" Gardner didn't understand.

"He needs to learn that it didn't work."

"You're not making any sense, man."

"Fletcher's still dead," the Indian tried to explain. "And killing the Russian didn't change that. Deep down inside Treat knows that, but he has to see it for himself. He has to learn it all over again."

Gardner stood silently and watched Brody scramble up the side of the hill. There were still quite a few things about war that he just didn't understand. He probably wouldn't until he had been in the brush as long as Two-Step had. He glanced over at the Indian, wondering if he would ever last that long.

Brody slowly approached the Russian, the muzzle of the sniper rifle trained on him, his finger resting on the trigger.

Yuravitch lay back against the rock, his Dragunov on the ground beside him. He was still alive, but just barely. Bright red blood seeped from the wound in his chest, staining his camouflage uniform, and the corners of his mouth. Brody carefully reached down and picked up the rifle.

"Who are you?" Yuravitch croaked in heavily accented English.

"Brody. Treat Brody."

"Why you do this?" Yuravitch weakly gestured with his hand, a movement that took in not only his own wound, but the long-running sniper battle in the jungle.

"You killed a friend of mine," Brody said evenly. "The man in the helicopter."

"But men die in war." Yuravitch sounded surprised that there was a reason for this to have happened.

"Yes," Brody agreed. "But this is not your war. You killed him for no reason."

"But," the Russian protested, "I am a sniper, a good sniper."

"No, you are a bad sniper." Brody smiled tightly. "You lost."

He raised the muzzle of his rifle. "This is for the Snakeman."

He pulled the trigger.

The 7.62mm round caught Yuravitch right between the eyes and slammed his head back against the rock. A look of disbelief remained on his face. Brody slung the Russian weapon over his shoulder and knelt briefly by the body to retrieve Yuravitch's documents. He left the Russian where he lay and slowly started back to the others. It was over now and they could all go back to An Khe.

"Treat," Gardner said when he walked up. "The captain's on the horn again. He says he's got a slick on the way for us."

Brody just nodded his head. Suddenly he was tired, more tired than he had been in a long time. He found a seat on a boulder and stared back up at the ridgeline, Chief's rifle cradled in his lap. His mission of vengeance had been accomplished. The Russian sniper who had killed Fletcher was dead, along with several of his comrades.

And so was the Snakeman. No matter what Brody did, that was something that would never change. Tears formed in the corners of his eyes, but they felt good. He let them flow. Fletcher would have understood.

"Treat," Two-Step said quietly. "Gabe's here to take us home."

Brody looked up and saw the familiar Huey slick approaching. He had not even heard the rotors drawing closer. "Okay."

He got to his feet and handed Chief's XM-21 to Gambini. "Here," he said. "You'd better take this back to your company."

"That was a great shot," Gambini said. "Have you ever thought of becoming a sniper?"

Brody hesitated for a moment. "No," he said softly. "I think that I've had about enough of snipers."

CHAPTER 41

Camp Radcliff, An Khe

On the chopper flight back to Camp Radcliff, Brody sat silently in the back of the slick. He stared out the open door at the jungle racing by below. The other men sitting beside him were also quiet. Everyone was exhausted, and there was none of the post-mission grab-ass to wind down. They were all more than ready to have it all behind them.

As Brody watched the sun sink lower on the horizon, his hands resting on the two Russian sniper rifles he had captured, he hoped that something good would come out of it. At the least, he knew that the bunch of Ivans wouldn't be killing any more American grunts. And if the Russians were smart, they would stay out of Vietnam from now on.

There was a small crowd waiting for them at the edge of the chopper pad when Gabe flared *Pegasus* out for a landing in front of the Python operations shack. He saw Sergeant Zack with Lieutenant Alexander and Captain Gaines, the three of them standing with two other officers, both majors. As soon as the chopper's skids touched down, Brody jumped to the ground and walked over to Zack and Alexander.

"It's over," he said simply.

"I know," Zack replied, laying a hand on his shoulder. "There's a bunch of officers here waiting to talk to you and the men."

Brody looked over at them. "I guess we'd better get that over with first."

"They've scheduled a debriefing for you over in the brigade headquarters," Alexander said. "Tell your people to get in the Jeep, and I'll drive you over."

"Yes, sir."

"You can drop your gear with me," Zack said. "I'll take it all back."

No one said much on the short ride over to Brigade headquarters, but Brody was glad to be back. The sandbag palaces and tropical huts of Camp Radcliff had never looked better. He didn't even mind the red dust thrown up by the Jeep's wheels. This was home.

In the briefing room Brody saw several more officers, most of them wearing the shoulder patch of the MACV headquarters in Saigon.

"Come on up here, men." A full colonel from MACV motioned them to the front of the room when he saw the grunts walk in. "We'll get started on this right away."

Brody and the men found seats in the first row of folding metal chairs and sat silently, looking around the room at each other.

"Okay," the colonel began. "Let's get going. My name's Colonel Sanderson, and my assistants are Major Robins and Major Brindly. "We're from the MACV G-two's office."

He pointed at the Dragunovs in Brody's hands. "Those must be the rifles that everyone's talking about."

"Yes, sir, they are." Brody handed them over to him.

A dark-haired major took one of the weapons and left the room immediately. Someone was in a real hurry to get a closer look at it.

"Okay, Sergeant," the colonel continued. "Let's have your report."

First Brody took the rest of his Russian souvenirs out of his pockets. "I think you'll want these, too, sir," he said, holding them up.

The other major whisked those items away as well.

Brody still had one set of Russian ID that he hadn't handed over. He had wanted to keep something to remind him of the operation.

"Well, sir," he began. "We first picked up their trail at . . ."

The debriefing lasted well over an hour. All of the men were given a chance to tell what they had seen and they were all questioned at length about what seemed to them to be nit-picking little details. The colonel wanted to know everything, from what the Russians had been wearing to how well they had fought.

"Okay, I guess that's about all for now," the colonel said, looking at his two staff officers. "I'm sure that you men want to get cleaned up. But one last thing," he said seriously. "I want to caution you people to remember that your mission has been classified as top secret. You are not to say anything to anyone about this incident or about the Russians. You are not even to talk among yourselves about it."

"Why not, sir?" Brody was confused and a little pissed. "Isn't it going to be made known that Russians were here in Vietnam?"

"No, Sergeant, I'm afraid it isn't," the colonel stated flatly. "Washington has ordered a complete silence on this matter."

Brody was stunned.

"Is that fully understood?" the colonel from Saigon asked.

"Yes, sir."

"You men are dismissed."

They stood up and filed out of the briefing room. Outside the building, Brody stopped for a cigarette. He couldn't fucking believe what he had just heard. They had just killed several Russians who had been killing American grunts, and no one was ever going to learn about it. He shook his head.

"Sergeant Brody."

He looked up and saw Captain Gaines standing there. "Let's go for a walk," the officer said.

"Yes, sir." He fell in beside Gaines.

Rat took a thin cigar out of the breast pocket of his flight suit and stuck it in his mouth. Flicking open his Zippo with a practiced snap of his fingers, he fired it up and touched the flame to the end of the cigar.

"Ahh," he signed. "There's nothing like a good smoke after listening to something like that. It helps take the taste out of your mouth."

Brody didn't answer. Obviously Gaines had something on his mind.

"Now," Gaines continued, "there are several things that you can do with the information that you have. You can run your mouth off about it and find your ass in a heap of trouble." He paused. "Or, more wisely, you could quietly talk to the right person and see that what you know is made known to everyone."

The cigar glowed as Gaines took another drag on it. "Now, I happen to know that there is a reporter here in the camp right now. I think you know him, a man named David Janson. Well, it seems that he is working on a story about those snipers. And I am sure that he would love to hear what you have to say."

Gaines turned to face him, a big smile on his face. "But as your commanding officer, I feel that I should caution you against saying anything to Janson about the mission. I realize that he could protect his source of information under the first amendment of the Constitution and that no one would ever know who had given him the information. But I also know that you have a good sense of what is right, so I am counting on you to do what is right."

Brody studied his face for a moment. There was nothing that he could read in Gaines's eyes, but he knew what he was really telling him. He, too, was outraged at Washington's orders. At the same time, he had to keep his hands clean.

"Yes, sir, I think I do know what needs to be done."

"Good man. I thought that you would. Here, have a cigar."

"Thanks, sir."

"No sweat. We southerners have to stick together. Even southern Californians."

Brody laughed. "You got that shit right, sir."

Rather than going back to the company area right away, Brody decided to stop off at the hospital and check in on Metcack. He knew that the Indian sniper hadn't been wounded that badly, but he wanted to pay him a short visit and fill him in on how everything had turned out.

He found Chief in the recovery ward, his left arm in a cast. "Hey, Brody!" the sniper said when he walked in. "Glad to see you back."

"How you doing?" Brody said, looking at the cast.

Metcack waved his cast around in the air. "Not too bad. I can't pick my nose with this hand for a couple of weeks, but other than that, I'm okay."

Brody locked eyes with the Indian sniper. "We got 'em," he stated.

Chief looked around the ward to see if anyone could overhear them. "I've been told to keep my mouth shut about that," he said very quietly. "Everybody from Division brass to a bunch of REMFs from Saigon have been in here talking to me."

Brody chuckled. "I've been given the same treatment. I just got out of a briefing with a bunch of fucking brass from Saigon."

"What did they say?"

"Not much actually. I did all the talking. But they did tell us that we couldn't even talk about this among ourselves. Something about the White House getting in on the act.''

''So it was all for nothing.''

''No, not really,'' Brody shook his head. ''We nailed them and they're gone.''

''For now at least.'' Chief was not convinced that it was all over. ''What're you going to do now?''

Brody smiled and looked around the ward. ''Be a good little troop, just like they told me to, and keep my mouth shut.'' He winked at Chief.

''That's a bitch.''

''You got that shit right. Is there anything I can get for you?'' Brody asked, changing the subject. He didn't want anyone getting any ideas about him not playing the game. Not even the other guys.

''No, thanks. The guys from my company have been keeping me pretty well stocked up.'' He pointed to a pile of *Playboys* and lurid paperbacks on the steel nightstand beside his bed.

''Maybe I'll try to sneak you in a beer tomorrow,'' Brody laughed.

Chief reached down under the sheet and brought out a can of Budweiser. A church key had been taped to the side of the can. ''They've taken care of that, too.''

''Well . . .'' Brody stuck his hand out. ''If there's nothing else I can do for you, then I'll head on back and get cleaned up.''

Chief took his hand. ''Thanks for stopping by.''

''No sweat.'' Brody turned to go and stopped. ''Thanks, man, thanks for everything.''

''Hey, I'm glad you asked me to go along. This is going to make a great story for my grandkids someday.''

''Take care.''

''You, too.''

Outside the hospital, Brody lit up another smoke and headed on over to the company area. There was one last thing that he had to take care of before he finally got cleaned up. Corky Cordova.

He found the Chicano machine gunner flaked out in his bunk. "Cork," he said walking up, "let's have a talk."

"You got it, *amigo.*" Corky sat up and swung his legs over the side of the bunk. "Where do you want to go?"

"How 'bout the ammo bunker?"

"Sounds good to me."

The two grunts didn't say a word to each other on the way to the usual site for unofficially settling differences. When they arrived, they faced off.

"You still think you want to kick my fucking ass?" Brody asked bluntly.

Corky looked him up and down in the faint illumination from the perimeter lights. "Yeah, I really think that I should, man. I don't have no choice. That was a real shitty thing you did to me."

"Yeah, I guess it was," Brody admitted. "I'm sorry, man. I coulda used your Pig out there after all."

"Then why the fuck d'you tell me to stay back?"

"I guess I wasn't thinking too good, man. I don't know," Brody brushed his hand across his hair. "Let's get this over with, Cork." His voice sounded weary. "I've got to get cleaned up."

"That's all you got to say to me, Treat?" Corky's voice rose. " 'Let's get this shit over with'? What the fuck's wrong with you, man? You been out in the fucking sun too long?"

"What do you want me to say?"

"How 'bout saying something like 'I'm sorry, Corky, old buddy, I had my fucking head so far up my fucking ass they had to pipe sunlight in to me.' How 'bout something like 'I'm sorry, man, I'll never treat you like a piece of dog shit again.' Brody, what the fuck is wrong with you, man?"

"I'm just tired tonight, that's all. Look, I'm sorry, I did fuck up." He let his arms hang harmlessly at his sides. "So if you want to kick my ass for it, go ahead, I won't stop you."

"Man, you can be one of the stupidest motherfuckers

I've ever seen sometimes. We've been tight for years now. What the fuck are you talking about, man. All I want is that you don't ever go out there again without the old Cork and his fucking Pig with you, *comprende*?''

''Comprende.''

''Okay.'' Corky laid a hand on his shoulder. ''Tell you what. As soon as you grab a shower, let's go get a couple brews.''

''Not tonight, man. I'm beat.''

The machine gunner backed off again. ''Then I'm going to have to kick your fucking ass after all.''

''Fuck you, Corky.''

''It'll be the best piece of ass you ever had.''

Brody laughed.

CHAPTER 42

Hanoi, North Vietnam

Gregor Zerinski lay naked on top of his bed. He was in the downtown Hanoi hotel that had been reserved exclusively for the Russian military mission to North Vietnam and their military advisors. The girl kneeling above him was young and beautiful in a petite, small-breasted, Oriental way. She was also very enthusiastic and energetic, a real sexual athlete.

This was the only thing that he was going to miss about Southeast Asia. Skillfully she brought him to another climax. His third for the day.

The KGB officer was scheduled to leave Hanoi on the morning flight back to Moscow, so he had planned his last day in Asia to be something that he would remember for quite some time. He chuckled to himself as he watched the girl modestly get back into her *ao dai*, her play of wantonness all gone now. He lit an American cigarette, savoring its mild flavor.

He was "short" as the American soldiers said when they were going home. The KGB officer had every reason in the world to be pleased. He had finally gotten transferred out of the godforsaken country. The only thing that he was going to miss was its women. He paid the girl much more money than he usually did, but he could afford to be generous.

His interview with the Hanoi KGB station chief the day before had gone much better than he had ever dreamed that it would. The man had bought Zerinski's story completely. As he got up from the bed and went to shower off the sweat of his exertions, he realized that there were many advantages to having had a father and grandfather in the service of the Russian secret police. The least of them was that the station chief had served with his father back in the days of the old NKVD.

No matter what the two surviving Spetsnaz troopers said now, their stories would not be taken seriously. The third one, the man who had been wounded, had not made it out. He had not been able to keep up with them. The word was out now that Yuravitch had lost his mind out in the field, that the old sniper had simply broken under the strain of trying to fight a young man's war in the jungle.

The station chief had already sent a cable to the Red Army command reprimanding them for having sent an old reserve officer to Vietnam for such a dangerous assignment in the first place. Modern jungle warfare was for young men, fit men who did not have their minds cluttered up with dreams of glorious days back in the Great Patriotic War.

Zerinski's report of the Dragunov rifle test, however, had been well received by the military advisory staff. It had performed much better than they had expected. They had already forwarded a recommendation that the weapon be put into immediate full-scale production. His personal insights on the tactics they had used to kill the helicopter with the rifles had been so valuable that he had even been able to gloss over the loss of two of the rifles to the Americans.

The chief of the military mission to Hanoi, an army colonel, had almost had a heart attack when he had learned of their loss, but Zerinski had covered himself quite well on that point.

"After all," he had explained calmly, "the Dragunovs were under the personal command of the late Major Yuravitch. And, as I have explained, the man was simply not in his right mind."

That fiction had gone down only because the army did not like to acknowledge that the KGB was in control of their covert operations in Asia. Once again, the friction between the two Russian services had been very helpful to him.

Zerinski whistled an old Russian folk tune to himself as he stood under the cold shower. He would get dressed now and go out for an early dinner at his favorite restaurant. After that, he would get a bottle of good vodka from the KGB stores and come back to the hotel for the rest of the evening's entertainment, a pair of twins not yet seventeen years old. He had been guaranteed that they were both virgins.

Knowing what he did about the women of Vietnam, Zerinski couldn't possibly see how that could be true. But he had been promised that it was true and no one would knowingly lie to an officer of the KGB. For a moment, he wished that the American pilot Gaines had not gotten away. He had admired the man's courage, and would have been quite willing to share the girls with him as a gesture of soldierly comradery before turning him over to the Vietnamese prison camps. It would have been the civilized thing to do.

And Gregor Zerinski considered himself to be a civilized man.

Two weeks later in Saigon, Janson knocked on the door of the air-conditioned office of his editor at the Independent News Service. On the strength of his story about the Russian snipers, the reporter had been taken on by the news agency as one of their full-time reporters. So far however, his big story had not been sent out over the wire services, and he had been put to work covering routine stories that any recent graduate from a journalism school could have handled.

"You wanted to see me, Mr. Hemmings?"

"Yeah, come on in, Janson. Sit down. I need to talk to you about your sniper story."

He took a seat in the overstuffed chair. Though the editor had raved about the story initially, for some unknown reason, it was still sitting there on his desk.

"Is there something wrong with it?" Janson eyed the man critically.

"No, not really, your story's a solid piece of work, real great. But I've decided that we won't be running it after all."

"What do you mean you won't print it!" Janson exploded. "You have to!"

The editor leaned back in his chair, a smug smirk on his face. "I don't have to do a fucking thing, Janson. And if you're going to continue drawing your paycheck here, you'd better get used to that."

Janson shut his mouth and tried to calm himself. He didn't want to blow this job, too. "Why won't you run it?"

"Why? I'll tell you why. But first, I don't think that you really understand the role of the press in this war, Janson, so I'm going to explain it to you. The sole job of people like you and me in Vietnam is to bring this war to an end as quickly as possible."

The reporter couldn't believe what he was hearing. "What in the hell are you talking about?"

"It's real easy." The editor's voice assumed a regal tone. "The American people are not behind this war at all, and it is not in our national interests. Therefore, as the voice of the American people, it is up to us, the members of the press corps, to get this mess stopped as soon as we can. One way or the other, the war has to end, and our troops have to be sent home."

Janson cut in. "You're going to end the war by misinforming the public and withholding the truth about important matters like Russian involvement?"

The editor snorted. "We do it all the time and you know it. We," he patted his chest proudly, "are the ones who decide what is and isn't important in this country, not our elected officials. National policy is what the press says it is, not the secretary of state. Or the president, either, for that matter."

"But this is important," Janson argued. "Proof of Russian military involvement in the ground war in Southeast Asia. They've been killing American troops, for Christ's sake, and we can prove it!"

"Proof? You don't have proof," Hemmings sneered. "All you have is the word of some stupid fucking grunts who've been out in the brush too long. You don't have any real proof. Where's your Russian prisoner? You know, for a man who's been around this business as long as you have, Janson, sometimes you can be a real dumb shit."

Janson slowly got up out of his chair and walked over to the editor's desk. For the first time in a long time, he felt good about what he was going to do next.

He reached down, grabbed Hemmings by the front of his clean, freshly starched, white shirt and jerked him to his feet.

"You sorry cocksucker," he snarled in the startled man's face. "You wouldn't know the fucking truth if it came up and bit you on the ass. You're not going to print the story because it would upset your ass-kissing friends back in Washington. American kids are dying out there trying to keep the Communists out of this country and you don't even give a shit. All this war means to you is a chance to further your own career."

"Janson," the editor's voice rose shrilly, "you're fired! And you're never going to get another word of yours published anywhere in Southeast Asia, I can guarantee you that, you sonofabitch."

Janson laughed. "See if I really give a shit, asshole.

But before I go, there's something I've been wanting to do to somebody for a long, long time. This is for the Snake-man."

With a big grin on his face, the reporter drew his fist back and hammered it into the editor's face as hard as he could, once, twice, three times.

Hemmings screamed, "You've broken my nose!"

The reporter opened his hand and let the man fall back into his swivel chair.

"No shit." Janson turned on his heel and walked out the door. "And just what are you going to do about it, Hemmings? Send me to Vietnam?"

The editor could hear Janson's laughter ringing all the way down the hall.

GLOSSARY

ALPHA The military phonetic for *A*
AA Antiaircraft weapons
AC Aircraft commander, the pilot
Acting jack Acting NCO
Affirm Short for affirmative, yes
AFVN Armed Forces Vietnam Network
Agency, the The CIA
AIT Advanced individual training
AJ Acting jack
AK-47 The Russian 7.62mm Kalashnikov assault rifle
AO Area of operation
Ao dai Traditional Vietnamese female dress
APH-5 Helicopter crewman's flight helmet
APO Army post office
ARA Aerial rocket artillery, armed helicopters
Arc light B-52 bomb strike
ARCOM Army Commendation Medal
ARP Aero Rifle Platoon, the Blue Team
Article 15 Disciplinary action
ARVN Army of the Republic of Vietnam, also a South Vietnamese soldier

ASAP As soon as possible
Ash and trash Clerks, jerks, and other REMFs
A-Team The basic Special Forces unit, ten men
AWOL Absent without leave

BRAVO The military phonetic for *B*
B-40 Chinese version of the RPG antitank weapon
Bac si Vietnamese for "doctor"
Bad Paper Dishonorable discharge
Ba-muoi-ba Beer "33," the local brew
Banana clip A thirty-round magazine for the M-1 carbine
Bao Chi Vietnamese for "press" or "news media"
Basic Boot camp
BCT Basic Combat Training, boot camp
BDA Bomb damage assessment
Be Nice Universal expression of the war
Biet (Bic) Vietnamese for "Do you understand?"
Bird An aircraft, usually a helicopter
Bloods Black soldiers
Blooper The M-79 40mm grenade launcher
Blues, the An aero rifle platoon
Body count Number of enemy killed
Bookoo Vietnamese slang for "many," from French *beaucoup*
Bought the farm Killed
Brown bar A second lieutenant
Brass Monkey Interagency radio call for help
Brew Usually beer, sometimes coffee
Bring smoke To cause trouble for someone, to shoot
Broken down Disassembled or nonfunctional
Bubble top The bell OH-13 observation helicopter
Buddha Zone Heaven
Bush The jungle
'Bush Short for ambush
Butter bar A second lieutenant

CHARLIE The military phonetic for *C*
C-4 Plastic explosive
C-rats C rations
CA A combat assault by helicopter
Cam ong Vietnamese for "thank you"
C&C Command and control helicopter
Chao (Chow) Vietnamese greeting
Charlie Short for Victor Charlie, the enemy
Charlie tango Control tower
Cherry A new man in your unit
Cherry boy A virgin
Chickenplate Helicopter crewman's armored vest
Chi-Com Chinese Communist
Chieu hoi A program where VC/NVA could surrender and become scouts for the Army
Choi oi Vietnamese exclamation
CIB The Combat Infantryman's Badge
CID Criminal Investigation Unit
Clip Ammo magazine
CMOH Congressional Medal of Honor
CO Commanding officer
Cobra The AH-1 attack helicopter
Cockbang Bangkok, Thailand
Conex A metal shipping container
Coz Short for Cosmoline, a preservative
CP Command post
CSM Command sergeant major
Cunt Cap The narrow green cap worn with the class A uniform

DELTA The military phonetic for *D*
Dash 13 The helicopter maintenance report
Dau Vietnamese for "pain"
Deadlined Down for repairs
Dep Vietnamese for "beautiful"
DEROS Date of estimated return from overseas service
Deuce and a half Military two-and-a-half-ton truck

DFC Distinguished Flying Cross
DI Drill instructor
Di di Vietnamese for "Go!"
Di di mau Vietnamese for "Go fast!"
Dink Short for *dinky-dau*, derogatory slang term for Vietnamese
Dinky-dau Vietnamese for "crazy!"
Disneyland East The Pentagon
Disneyland Far East The MACV or USARV headquarters
DMZ Demilitarized zone separating North and South Vietnam
Dog tags Stainless steel tags listing a man's name, serial number, blood type and religious preference
Donut Dolly A Red Cross girl
Doom-pussy Danang officers' open mess
Door gunner A soldier who mans a door gun
Drag The last man in a patrol
Dung lai Vietnamese for "Halt!"
Dustoff A medevac helicopter

ECHO The military phonetic for *E*. Also, radio code for east
Eagle flight A heliborne assault
Early out An unscheduled ETS
Eighty-one The M-29 81mm mortar
Eleven bravo An infantryman's MOS
EM Enlisted man
ER Emergency room (hospital)
ETA Estimated time of arrival
ETS Estimated time of separation from service
Extract To pull out by helicopter

FOXTROT The military phonetic for *F*
FAC Forward air controller
Fart sack sleeping bag

Field phone Hand-generated portable phone used in bunkers
Fifty The U.S. .50 caliber M-2 heavy machine gun
Fifty-one The Chi-Com 12.7mm heavy machine gun
Fini Vietnamese for "ended" or "stopped"
First Louie First lieutenant
First Shirt An Army first sergeant
First Team Motto of the First Air Cavalry Division
Flak jacket Infantry body armor
FNG Fucking new guy
FOB Fly over border mission
Forty-five The U.S. .45 caliber M-1911 automatic pistol
Fox 4 The F-4 Phantom II jet fighter
Foxtrot mike delta Fuck me dead
Foxtrot tosser A flamethrower
Frag A fragmentation grenade
FTA Fuck the army

GOLF The military phonetic for *G*
Gaggle A loose formation of choppers
Get some To fight, kill someone
GI Government issue, an American soldier
Gook A Vietnamese
Grease gun The U.S. .45 caliber M-3 Submachine Gun
Green Berets The U.S. Army's Special Forces
Green Machine The Army
Grunt An infantryman
Gunship Army attack helicopter armed with machine guns and rockets

HOTEL The military phonetic for *H*
Ham and motherfuckers The C ration meal of ham and lima beans
Hard core NVA or VC regulars
Heavy gun team Three gunships working together
Hercky Bird The Air Force C-130 Hercules Transport plane

Ho Chi Minh Trail The NVA supply line
Hog The M-60 machine gun
Horn A radio or telephone
Hot LZ A landing zone under hostile fire
House Cat An REMF
Huey The Bell UH-1 helicopter, the troop-carrying workhorse of the war.

INDIA The military phonetic for *I*
IC Installation commander
IG Inspector general
IHTFP I hate this fucking place
In-country Within Vietnam
Insert Movement into an area by helicopter
Intel Military Intelligence
IP Initial point. The place that a gunship starts its gun run
IR Infrared

JULIET The military phonetic for *J*
Jackoff flare A hand-held flare
JAG Judge advocate general
Jeep In Nam, the Ford M-151 quarter-ton truck
Jelly Donut A fat Red Cross girl
Jesus Nut The nut that holds the rotor assembly of a chopper together
Jet Ranger The Bell OH-58 helicopter
Jody A girlfriend back in the States
Jolly Green Giant The HH-3E Chinook heavy-lift helicopter
Jungle fatigues Lightweight tropical uniform

KILO The military phonetic for *K*
K-fifty The NVA 7.62mm type 50 submachine gun
Khakis The tropical class A uniform
KIA Killed in action
Kimchi Korean pickled vegetables

Klick A kilometer
KP Kitchen Police, mess-hall duty

LIMA The military phonetic for *L*
Lager A camp or to make camp
Lai dai Vietnamese for "come here"
LAW Light antitank weapon. The M-72 66mm rocket launcher
Lay dead To fuck off
Lay dog Lie low in jungle during recon patrol
LBJ The military jail at Long Binh Junction
Leg A nonairborne infantryman
Lifeline The strap securing a doorgunner on a chopper
Lifer A career soldier
Links The metal clips holding machine gun ammo belts together
LLDB *Luc Luong Dac Biet*, the ARVN Special Forces
Loach The small Hughes OH-6 observation helicopter
Long Nose Vietnamese slang for "American"
Long Tom The M-107 175mm long-range artillery gun
LP Listening post
LRRP Long-range recon patrol
LSA Lubrication, small-arms gun oil
Lurp Freeze-dried rations carried on LRRPs
LZ Landing zone

MIKE The military phonetic for *M*
M-14 The U.S. 7.62mm rifle
M-16 The U.S. 5.56mm Colt-Armalite rifle
M-26 Fragmentation grenade
M-60 The U.S. 7.62mm infantry machine gun
M-79 The U.S. 40mm grenade launcher
MACV Military Assistance Command Vietnam
Ma Deuce The M-2 .50 caliber heavy machine gun
Magazine Metal container that feeds bullets into weapons; holds twenty or thirty rounds per unit
Mag pouch A magazine carrier worn on the field belt

Mama San An older Vietnamese woman
MAST Mobile Army Surgical Team
Mech Mechanized infantry
Medevac Medical Evacuation chopper
Mess hall GI dining facility
MF Motherfucker
MG Machine gun
MI Military intelligence units
MIA Missing in action
Mike Radio code for minute
Mike Force Green Beret mobile strike force
Mike-mike Millimeters
Mike papa Military police
Minigun A 7.62mm Gatling gun
Mister Zippo A flamethrower operator
Monkey House Vietnamese slang for "jail"
Monster Twelve to twenty-one claymore antipersonnel mines jury-rigged to detonate simultaneously
Montagnard Hill tribesmen of the Central Highlands
Mop Vietnamese for "fat"
Motengator Motherfucker
MPC Military payment certificate, issued to GIs in RVN in lieu of greenbacks
Muster A quick assemblage of soldiers with little or no warning
My Vietnamese for "American"

NOVEMBER The military phonetic for *N*. Also, radio code for north
NCO Noncommissioned officer
Negative Radio talk for "no"
Net A radio network
Newbie A new GI in-country
Next A GI so short that he is the next to go home
Niner The military pronunciation of the number 9
Ninety The M-67 90mm recoilless rifle
Number One Very good, the best

Number ten Bad
Number ten thousand Very bad, the worst
Nuoc nam A Vietnamese fish sauce
NVA The North Vietnamese Army, also a North Vietnamese soldier

OSCAR The military phonetic for *O*
OCS Officer candidate school
OCS Manual A comic book
OD Olive drab
Old Man, the A commander
One five one The M-151 jeep
One oh five The 105mm howitzer
One twenty-two The Russian 122mm ground-launched rocket
OR Hospital operating room
Out-country Out of Vietnam

PAPA The military phonetic for *P*
P Piaster, Vietnamese currency
P-38 C ration can opener
PA Public address system
Papa San An older Vietnamese man
Papa sierra Platoon sergeant
PAVN Peoples Army of Vietnam, the NVA
PCS Permanent change of station, a transfer
Peter pilot Copilot
PF Popular Forces, Vietnamese militia
PFC Private first class
Piece Any weapon
Pig The M-60 machine gun
Pink Team Observation helicopters teamed up with gunships
Phantom The McDonnell F-4 jet fighter
Phu Vietnamese noodle soup
Point The most dangerous position on patrol. The point

man walks ahead and to the side of the others, acting as a lookout
POL Petroleum, oil, lubricants
Police To clean up
POL point A GI gas station
Pony soldiers The First Air Cav troopers
Pop smoke To set off a smoke grenade
Prang To crash a chopper, or land roughly
Prep Artillery preparation of an LZ
PRG Provisional Revolutionary Government (the Communists)
Prick-25 The AN/PRC-25 tactical radio
Profile A medical exemption from duty
Project Phoenix CIA assassination operations
PSP Perforated steel planking used to make runways
Psy-Ops Psychological Operations
PT Physical training
Puff the Magic Dragon The heavily armed AC-47 fire support aircraft
Purple Heart, the A medal awarded for wounds received in combat
Puzzle Palace Any headquarters
PX Post exchange
PZ Pickup zone

QUEBEC The military phonetic for *Q*
QC *Quan Cahn*, Vietnamese Military Police
Quad fifty Four .50 caliber MG's mounted together

ROMEO The military phonetic for *R*
RA Regular army, a lifer
Railroad Tracks The twin-silver-bar captain's rank insignia
R&R Rest and relaxation
Ranger Specially trained infantry troops
Rat fuck A completely confused situation
Recondo Recon commando

Red Leg An artilleryman
Red Team Armed helicopters
Regular A well-equipped enemy soldier
REMF Rear echelon motherfucker
Re-up Reenlistment
RIF Recon in force
Rikky-tik Quickly or fast
Ring knocker A West Point officer
Road runner Green Beret recon teams
Rock and roll Automatic weapons fire
Roger Radio talk for "yes" or "I understand"
ROK The Republic of Korea or a Korean soldier
Rotor The propellor blades of a helicopter
Round An item of ammunition
Round Eye Vietnamese slang for "Caucasian"
RPD The Russian 7.62mm light machine gun
RPG The Russian 77mm rocket-propelled grenade anti-tank weapon
RTO Radio telephone operator
Ruck Racksack
RVN The Republic of Vietnam, South Vietnam

SIERRA The military phonetic for *S*. Also, radio code for south
Saddle up To move out
Saigon commando A REMF
SAM Surface-to-air missile
Same-same Vietnamese slang for "the same as"
Sapper An NVA demolition/explosives expert
SAR Downed chopper rescue mission
Sau Vietnamese slang for "a lie"
Say again Radio code to repeat the last message
Scramble An alert reaction to call for help, CA, or rescue operation
Scrip *See* MPC
SEALS Navy commandos
7.62 The 7.62 ammunition for the M-14 and the M-60

SF Special Forces
Shithook The CH-47 Chinook helicopter
Short Being almost finished with your tour in Nam
Short timer Someone who is short
Shotgun An armed escort
Sierra Echo Southeast (northwest is November Whiskey, etc)
Sin City Bars and whorehouses
Single-digit midget A short timer with less then ten days left to go in The Nam
Sitrep Situation report
Six Radio code for a commander
Sixteen The M-16 rifle
Skate To fuck off
SKS The Russian 7.62mm carbine
Slack The man behind the point
Slick A Huey
Slicksleeves A private E-1
Slope A Vietnamese
Slug A bullet
Smoke Colored smoke signal grenades
SNAFU Situation normal, all fucked up
Snake The AH-1 Cobra attack chopper
SOL Shit Outta Luck
SOP Standard operating procedure
Sorry 'bout that Universal saying used in Nam
Special Forces The Army's elite counterguerrilla unit
Spiderhole A one-man foxhole
Spooky The AC-67 fire-support aircraft
Stand down A vacation
Starlite A sniper scope
Steel pot The GI steel helmet
Striker A member of a SF strike force
Sub-gunny Substitute doorgunner
Sweat hog A fat REMF

TANGO The military phonetic for *T*
TA-50 A GI's issue field gear

TAC Air Tactical Air Support
TDY Temporary duty assignment
Terr Terrorist
Tet The Vietnamese New Year
"33" Local Vietnamese beer
Thumper The M-79 40mm grenade launcher
Tiger suit A camouflage uniform
Ti ti Vietnamese slang for "little"
TOC Tactical Operations Center
TOP An Army first sergeant
Tour 365 The year-long tour of duty a GI spends in RVN
Tower rat Tower guard
Tracer Ammunition containing a chemical that burns in flight to mark its path
Track Any tracked vehicle
Triage The process in which medics determine which wounded they can best help, and which will die
Trip flare A ground illumination flare
Trooper Soldier
Tube steak Hot dogs
Tunnel rat A soldier who goes into NVA tunnels
Turtle Your replacement
201 File One's personnel records
Two-point-five Gunship rockets
Type 56 Chi-Com version of the AK-47
Type 68 Chi-Com version of the SKS

UNIFORM The military phonetic for *U*
UCMJ The Uniform Code of Military Justice
Unass To get up and move
Uncle Short for Uncle Sam
USARV United States Army Vietnam
Utilities Marine fatigues

VICTOR The military phonetic for *V*
VC The Viet Cong

Victor Charlie Viet Cong
Viet Cong South Vietnamese Communists
Ville Short for village
VNAF The South Vietnamese Air Force
VNP Vietnamese National Police
Void Vicious Final approach to a hot LZ, or the jungle when hostile
Vulcan A 20mm Gatling-gun cannon

WHISKEY The military phonetic for *W*. Also, radio code for west.
Wake-up The last day one expects to be in-country
Warrant officer Pilots
Waste To kill
Wax To kill
Web belt Utility belt GIs use to carry gear, sidearms, etc.
Web gear A GI's field equipment
Whiskey papa White phosphorus weapons
White mice Vietnamese National Police
White team Observation helicopters
WIA Wounded in action
Wilco Radio code for "will comply"
Willie Peter White phosphorus
Wire, the Defensive barbed wire
World, the The United States

X-RAY The military phonetic for *Z*
Xin loi Vietnamese for "sorry 'bout that"
XM-21 Gunship weapon package
XO Executive officer

YANKEE The military phonetic for *Y*
Yarde Short for Montagnard

ZULU The military phonetic for *Z*
Zap To kill
Zilch Less than nothing

Zip A derogatory term for a Vietnamese national
Zippo A flamethrower
Zoomie An Air Force pilot

BROWN WATER HELL!

The men of the First Air Cav encounter heavy enemy forces when they race to save the crew of a riverine patrol boat ambushed on the Song Boung River. Outnumbered but undaunted, Brody and his crew make the waters run red in a brutal . . .

CHOPPER #13: **RIVERINE SLAUGHTER**

ABOUT THE AUTHOR

THE AUTHOR served two tours of duty in Vietnam as an infantry company commander. His combat awards and decorations include the Combat Infantryman's Badge, three Bronze Star Medals, the Air Medal, the Army Commendation Medal, and the Vietnamese Cross of Gallantry. He has written three novels and many magazine articles about the war. He and his wife make their home in Portland, Oregon.